DEATH ON THE FERRY HYGEIA

Printed in Australia

First Printing: March 2022

Shawline Publishing Group Pty Ltd
www.shawlinepublishing.com.au

Paperback ISBN- 9781922594594

Ebook ISBN- 9781922701053

A catalogue record for this
book is available from the
National Library of Australia

Death on the Ferry Hygeia

WILL SPOKES

I have group of people who encourage my writing and provide continued motivation. Chief among these people is my wife Lyn without whom I would be lost.

To the others I offer my sincere thanks.

Author's Note

Thanks first and foremost to my wife Lyn, my first and most genuine critic. I have been blessed by her love and companionship through some very good times and some very hard times and for richer or poorer when I wake up in the morning, she is still by my side. There is only so much a man can do on his own.

Oskar, Willow and Toby. The next generation.

Thank you to Andy Whitebourne for your encouragement.

Thank you to anyone who picks up my book and takes pleasure in the story and its characters.

Special Acknowledgement to:

Down the Bay. T K Fitchett

Bay Steamers and Coastal Ferries Jack Loney

The Age Newspaper archives.

The Herald archives.

The Melbourne Museum

Songs of The Sentimental Bloke C J Dennis

CHAPTER 1

1925

MELBOURNE'S SEASONAL CONFUSION

The spirit of Christmas was in the air, bringing with it a tingle of anticipation and an infectious sense of wellbeing that affected adult and child alike.

Cutting through the azure waters between Queenscliff and Sorrento, Hygeia's powerful twin engines spewed a column of dark grey-brown coal smoke from her twin funnels set back at a slight angle, navy style. The plume overshadowed the pure white foaming wake which contrasted brilliantly with ocean and sky. Her passengers were treated to Hygeia's personal eau-de-cologne, a mix of intoxicating aroma's that the world's best perfumers would struggle to best. Coal smoke, heated engine oil and steam. To her captain and engineer, this was ambrosia.

At the southern reaches of the bay, a huge area of shoals known as Mud Island was rich with sea life. Fat, healthy fur seals, abundant dolphins and many species of diving seabirds that delighted the ships passengers. Migrating whales were frequent visitors along with their potentially dangerous cousins, the orcas. It was also an area populated with a variety of sharks that shared the bounty offered by the bay's shallow waters. Bronze whaler sharks that followed the migrating snapper into the bay had been known to attack swimmers. Deadly white pointers, although scarce, were often perceived as a threat but not all threats were in the sea.

As she progressed, the Hygeia generated a pleasant pulsing beat from her steam engines driving the massive eight-meter paddle wheels that churned the sea to foam with a pleasant rhythmic *swoosh, swoosh, swoosh.*

Those that weren't watching the sea life, were focussed on the dance floor where the ship's band had enticed many happy couples swirling, sometimes a little unsteadily, to the music as the ship met the ocean swells coming through the heads. No one had wanted to miss the season's most wonderful charity event, and despite the stipulation that dress was to be cocktail rather than the formal, the female passengers had left no stone unturned in their quest to dazzle. Gorgeous gowns, and the very latest styles had the hems creeping upward away from the ankles, shocking the more conservative. Magnificent jewellery and one or two lush furs encased the wealthy women of Melbourne who intended to leave a mark on this occasion.

Others aboard were studying the Portsea Quarantine Station or simply engaged in happy chatter, anticipating their wine and hors d'oeuvres to be enjoyed at the seaside park at Sorrento.

A more pleasant setting for a picnic would be hard to imagine, a glorious sunny day, the old township of Sorrento at their backs, and the sparkling waters of the bay spread out before them. The break in the excursion would be a precursor to the five-star meal prepared and presented by one of Melbourne's most sought-after French Chefs, Franco de La Vere as Hygeia turned north towards its destination at Mornington.

The excursionists were enjoying a gorgeous summers day. The sea and sky were a palette sampler of blues, in sharp contrast to the pure white clouds drifting in from the open ocean; yet aboard the Hygeia, a dark malevolence was about to make its presence felt.

Only the ever-present seagulls appeared to notice the well attired body tumble over the stern rail, its expensive shoes momentarily brushing the ship's ensign as it disappeared silently into the churning sea in Hygeia's wake.

Hygeia was moving at a comfortable fifteen plus knots and in five seconds was over a hundred yards away from where the body entered the water. It would have taken the sharpest eyes to note the victim's unfortunate departure from the security of the ship or what circumstance led to the plunge. Was the victim already dead when he hit the water? Was it accident, suicide or murder?

The resultant investigation would fall on the shoulders of an ambitious but flawed young policeman, Senior Sergeant Jim Foley and his uncle, the Deputy Police Commissioner of Victoria Police Francis Foley.

The tidal movements in the southern part of Port Phillip Bay were formidable and the mouth of the bay known as the Rip, notorious. The powerful current was generated by the enormous pressure of the outward running tide as the bay empties into Bass Strait. Often running at six to eight knots, the recently deceased corpse committed unceremoniously to the sea was swiftly scooped up as just another piece of flotsam and jetsam by the ebbing tide, drawn rapidly towards the treacherous Rip where it would be discharged into the deep, open waters of Bass Strait.

CHAPTER 2

DECEMBER 1925

AUSSIES LOVE A BET

Melbourne has always been the centre of culture and sophistication, leading the rest of the nation since the heady days of the gold rush that created massive fortunes and drove the rapid development of the city, creating much angst in a certain city to the north. Unlike other cities, Melbourne had not been treated as a dumping ground for convicts and the dregs of society. The citizens were mainly free settlers came to scoop up the gold nuggets in the rivers and streams or to found businesses to service the population explosion.

One scribe in the daily newspaper had become embroiled in the Melbourne-Sydney rivalry. His retort against his opposite number in the Sydney Morning Herald became much quoted.

'Sydney was founded as a convict settlement and has gone downhill ever since.' He asserted, quite snootily.

As a result of the wealth coming out of the goldfields, Melbourne became the financial centre of Australia and between 1901 and 1927 was actually the official capital of Australia and the second largest city in the British Empire after London. Australia's first stock exchange was established in Melbourne in 1861.

The citizens of this community were generally entrepreneurial, hardworking, free or assisted settlers of British stock.

Early in their history, some previously unrealised kink in their genes caused an almost unnatural interest in sport. With almost unlimited space, favourable weather and general prosperity, sport quickly became a fascination for Melbournians.

Their eager participation and interest in sport of all sorts, such as football, horse racing, athletics, tennis and cricket particularly against the English test teams could become feverish at times. Among the elite, lawn bowls, croquet and even Royal Tennis gained popularity.

Lacking the deadly effects of Spanish Influenza virus, it was the gambling virus that infected the general population, almost universally generating huge flows of black money through the economy. For the poor and unemployed, it was one of the few pleasurable outlets they had. Thoroughbred racehorses attracted strong followings, as did the VFL football teams. In the early years of the twentieth century, betting facilities were only available 'on course' at the race meetings denying access to the poor. This restriction created a huge demand that was quickly and efficiently satisfied by thousands of illegal bookmakers throughout the suburbs accepting small bets from the lower orders. Some of these SP (Starting Price) bookmakers turned over massive amounts by the standards of the day. All from bets of threepence or sixpence. The Melbourne Cup was the big attraction when everyone in town and country had a bet and an opinion. Small communities and work places ran sweeps and even kids were known to run sweeps in the schoolyards.

The infamous John Wren, proprietor of the largest totalisator in Melbourne and possibly Australia was born in Collingwood and left school at the age of twelve, working in a wood yard. He began supplementing his income with gambling activities, eventually earning over twenty thousand pounds a year from his premises in Johnston Street Collingwood.

'Gambling is the child of avarice, the brother of iniquity and the father of mischief,' said George Washington. Hence the driver of crime and misery in Melbourne.

Eugene Wallace Bradfield, had also enjoyed a successful year well above his expectations. He had been Christened Lawrence, but felt it was not theatrical enough. He plucked Eugene out of a book somewhere and went by that thereafter. People close to him called him Gene, which he quite liked. In 1925, he featured in several roles in theatres around Australia and to his delight, was to finish the year in an extended season of his current production followed by a further live three act offering at the Theatre Royal.

Eugene was successful in winning the leading role of a moving picture based on the life of a World War One flying ace; an experimental production that went on to be well received by the critics and audiences alike.

With a predilection for gambling, he would soon come to be very familiar and dependent upon John Wren's totalisator. An owner of racehorses, a pony track, boxing and wrestling promotion and possibly the biggest bookmaker in the country, Wren was a very dangerous man. He was an ardent supporter of the Collingwood Football Club and, in a weird alignment, shared an intricate friendship with the powerful Catholic Archbishop Daniel Mannix. Wren lived opposite Mannix's official residence, Raheen in Kew, and the two were often seen walking to their respective offices together along Studley Park Road.

Eugene's current circumstances allowed him to enjoy a fairly high standard of living, and his celebrity saw him as the popular guest at many society functions. As an inveterate gambler, he naturally gravitated to the racetracks along with the social set during the fashionable spring carnival. Being a celebrated actor, he was used to the spotlight and never failed to create a stir with the wit and charm of a true bon vivant. No woman who fell under his deep and penetrating gaze could resist his smooth patter. Married, single or virginal, they fell for Eugene Wallace Bradfield, master seducer.

On a more personal front, Eugene had never experienced the want of anything in his theatre life. There were always sycophantic stagehands hoping to gain the attention of the stars by offering to fetch and carry the usual range of legitimate goods and services. Some of these hands also seemed to possess an uncanny ability to locate the nearest betting shops or produce an ounce or two of marijuana or the occasional line of cocaine that was coming into fashion of late. For these services, they were usually well rewarded.

Melvin (Skinny) Jackson was a master magician in this area and could often be found slinking around the dressing rooms like an alley cat waiting for the canary's cage door to be left open. His greatest assets were a mind like a steel trap and a prodigious memory, cataloguing all the sins and peccadillos of colleagues and in particular, the cast of whatever play he was involved in.

He was a favourite of Eugene, who treated him with the respect reserved for a valued household servant. Other members of the cast and crew called him a, 'little brown-nosed weasel.'

'Mr Jackson, may I see you in my dressing room please?' Eugene's clear penetrating voice that could be heard clearly in the back stalls of any theatre, rang like a bell in the ears of the responsive Skinny Jackson. A light rap on Eugene's dressing room door within seconds announced the arrival of Skinny Jackson, whom Eugene thought of as 'my man.'

The door was padded in rich damask material, as much for its luxurious texture and appearance, as for its sound deadening qualities. A factor not overlooked by Eugene when he was 'rehearsing' with a member of the younger female ensemble.

'I believe in nurturing young talent whenever I can. It's my way of paying back the gift I have been granted,' he was often heard to say, usually with his nose in a balloon of expensive cognac striking a theatrical pose one leg over the other, cigarette in a tortoiseshell holder held aloft to one side to avoid ash falling on his rich crimson brocade dressing gown. Every inch the glamourous star of the theatre.

'Come in please Mr Jackson.' Skinny not so much entered, as insinuated himself into the dressing room, redolent with Eugene's au de cologne and the rich pomades he used to control his thick lustrous hair. Added to this was the sweet aroma of the joint he was smoking down to a wet stub skewered on a toothpick.

Eugene pointed to a chair just inside the door and with an imperious wave of his well-manicured hand indicated Skinny should sit, and like a well-trained lap dog, Skinny sat.

'Now Mr Jackson, I am in need of two things and I sincerely hope that you will prove useful in your usual manner.' Eugene sucked the last life out of the spliff and dropped it carelessly into the waste bin, onto cotton waste moist with nail polish remover and other dangerous inflammables.

Skinny's eyes widen in expectation of a minor explosion.

'Yessir Mr Bradfield, whatever I can.'

'Well, for a start you can find me some more of this magnificent herb.' he stuffily pronounced it 'erb' with a silent aitch.

'No worries, sir, she'll be right, I'll have it for you by the end of the matinee session this afternoon, sir.' Skinny's head nodded furiously in affirmation.

'The other thing might take a bit of doing, so I need you to listen very carefully.'

Eugene dropped his voice a little. After years of training, he had refined his speech to a firm, penetrating deep-toned voice designed to reach the further corners of any theatre, but not so good for a conspiratorial whisper.

'Mr Jackson, you know where Mr Wren has his place of business in Johnston Street?'

Eugene received a nod of acknowledgement, 'I want you to take this letter around there and give it to Mr Wren.'

The letter contained a 'contract' that Eugene had discussed with

Wren the week before at the track, giving him an account at Wrens Totalisator. Eugene handed Skinny another envelope. 'This must reach him before the mile race at Caulfield this afternoon.'

Eugene was placing a large wager on a horse he fancied at good odds but as they say, 'on the nod.' That was the reason for the 'contract', it was in fact a written guarantee to settle his account on a monthly basis. This was a rare benefit bestowed on very few by the dangerous man, John Wren.

Eugene was granted the 'honour' for the fact that he had starred in several successful plays performed at Wren's theatres.

Joyfully, the bet of one hundred pounds each way on the 12/1 chance came home, giving Eugene a substantial betting pool. Wren had lost nothing; he laid the bet off with two other unhappy bookmakers who had no choice but to accept it.

This set a pattern for Eugene's future betting, but it was not his only gambling outlet.

He dabbled for a little while with a two up school, that he referred to as 'quaint' but found the company beneath him. He was then invited by other members of the Victoria Club to a poker school that was attended by a group of bookmaker pals in a club owned by a notorious individual Matthias Vogel, an immigrant from Austria known as 'The German'.

Chapter 3
May 1924
Eugene Bradfield Sets a Pattern

The life of the great thespian, Eugene Bradfield, could be described as bittersweet. He was granted enough good fortune to keep him interested but sadly he too often bottomed out to circumstances he described as deplorable. If he should stop and take note of how these changes occurred, he would find the answer in the overlaps of the different spheres he was subconsciously drawn to. Those spheres he moved in had significant overlap. His theatrical life merged into his social life, which again crossed paths at the racetrack. His membership of the Victoria Club brought him into contact with some powerful legal figures, including one or two judges, several skilled and high-priced Kings Counsel and top of the town advocates.

Eugene saved his energies for a very active social life. Being on everyone's invitation list, he appeared at every major fashion show in town, sometimes being called on to assess and judge the stylings presented.

Inevitably, his flamboyant lifestyle led him into contact with some of the less desirable elements of society. And so it was that Eugene had enjoyed a pleasant day at the races, winning some, losing some, and generally flirting with the society ladies. Here was a splendid cross section of Melbourne's elite, some minor aristocrats sprinkled among a crowd of high-flying businessmen, old money types from the elite suburbs, all of whom were either horse owners or lovers of the equine sports.

He was drowning his sorrows in the members bar after the last race at Flemington, having finished the day in arrears failing to pick a single winner when he was approached by a member of John Wren's staff who handed him a sheet of paper that was composed like a bank statement.

It detailed all the wagers he had laid on his account with Wren's Totaliser. It was a disappointing read and displayed a total at the bottom, written in red ink.

'Mr Wren would like to see this deficit reduced Mr Bradfield and if I were you sir, I would make some inroads as quick as possible.' Curly Barker leans in and lowers his voice to a whisper, 'Mr Wren ain't known for his philanthropy in such cases as yours.'

'Why thank you for your courtesy, Mr Barker,' Eugene responded sarcastically, 'I can see that it has caused you some pain to deliver it.'

Curly came in chest to chest, pressed Eugene back against the bar, his foul tobacco breath causing Eugene to recoil as a large gnarled finger jabbed him in the ribs.

'I would strongly advise you to avoid bein' a smartarse you fuckin' ponce, or you might find yourself in a world of pain.'

From his uncomfortable position, Eugene nodded, blood draining from his face. No one had ever spoken to him like that and if Curly was attempting to frighten him, he had succeeded.

All this time, a man of small stature had stood quietly by Curley's right elbow and now his right hand came up to cover his mouth as he cleared his throat for attention.

'Ah yeah, sorry cobber,' said Curly, turning to the dapper little gent, 'Mr Bradfield, allow me to introduce a fan of yours and my colleague, Mr Joseph Taylor.'

Bradfield extended a hand to the man whose grip puts Eugene in mind of holding a dead fish.

'Please to meetcha Mr Bradfield, most people call me Squizzy, Squizzy Taylor. Yeah, I loved that movie of yours with all the planes and stuff, very real it was.' He reached into his pocket and for one crazy second Eugene thought he was about to produce a gun but instead he proffered a scruffy autograph book. 'For me girlfriend, if ya don't mind, Mr Bradfield.'

'Aah certainly yes, a pleasure sir.' Eugene's hand shook slightly as he signed the little killer's autograph book.

A new low for the man known as Eugene Bradfield, who was born into a theatrical family in London, England. His great grandfather had been a successful trader and put the family fortune in place with cargoes of the Orients finest teas, spices and china. His ship ran opium into china returning with the fine china plate ware, expensive teas, spices and ornamental artefacts the products of the suffering Chinese artisans. It was a hazardous business with attacks on his ship by Warlords who bitterly resented the effect the drugs were having on the peasantry. Heavily armed with very capable crews, he was able to hold off attacks on three voyages, returning with enough riches to set he and his family up for life. Like other ship owners, he was granted a title despite an unfortunate incident with the wife of an influential Earl setting a trend for his hot-blooded descendants.

Wallace Bradfield was knighted by a grateful sovereign for the wealth and fineries he brought into the country. The efforts of he and other opium runners had helped weaken the Quing Dynasty and Chinese Governments forcing China to open specified treaty ports.

His wealth enabled his son to avoid the odious requirement of working for a living and instead gave him an opportunity to follow his favourite hobby. Laurence Bradfield squandered a good deal of his father's fortune on buying theatres around the country then staging very ordinary productions that invariably lost more of the family fortune. He married one of his leading ladies duped into thinking she came from a wealthy family but was little more than a lacklustre actress, which had another definition in those days. Her greatest performance was perhaps luring Laurance into wedlock.

This narcissistic pair were Eugene's grandparents. By the time he came around, his parents had barely enough money to send him to a minor public school that had an emphasis on the arts. As a border, young Eugene had suffered miserably with Latin, mathematics and sciences but sprang to life when acting in school plays or writing scripts. On leaving school, his mother used what little influence she still had after the untimely death of his father to find him work in the theatres that the family once owned. Acting in juvenile roles won him acclaim, aiding his climb up the ladder of theatrical success.

Unfortunately, the twenty something year old had another passion aside from the theatre and that was gambling. Horses, cards or dice it mattered not, nor with whom. Eugene had accumulated several large losses into one crushing debt. With little hope of ever repaying, he chose to flee the land of hope and glory for the colonies ahead of a creditors agent, a notorious prize fighter who delighted in 'makin' me mark on them deadbeats.'

And mark them he did, with the aid of his brute strength and a pair of knuckle dusters.

The clearly terrified Eugene took the first boat he could find and headed south.

Once in Australia as an urbane thirty-year-old Eugene disregarded Sydney as a gauche and grubby place, and instead found his thirst for entertainment assuaged in Melbourne still swimming in the riches of the goldfields.

The city was fresh and clean, with magnificent architecture and public spaces. There was most importantly a thriving theatre industry and he quickly made a name for himself, earning high praise from the City's theatre critics. He was home.

CHAPTER 4

THE CUCKHOLD

Eugene's introduction to the notorious Squizzy Taylor, who was rumoured to be a killer, had left him shaken. The fact that he was introduced by Curly Barker, John Wrens heavy was the stuff of nightmares. The meeting had served its purpose and was enough to make him more aware than ever of his gambling debt to the terrible Wren. He ordered a double scotch, downing it with a shaking hand spilling a little down his wrist.

The intimidating duo had left and now the members' bar was almost empty. He decided to seek security among friends if he could find some and slid off the padded stool and headed to the stairs.

Back in the general population, Eugene soon found the sort of company he most obviously desired, the feminine variety, of course. The object of his attention in this case was Lucille Yarborough, the wife of a Lucille Yarborough with a hereditary title. She had met her husband Sir Rupert several years before when he visited Australia as a member of a touring sports team. Already wealthy as the heir to his family fortune, he had seen great opportunities to increase his personal wealth in this burgeoning country and when he clapped eyes on the lovely young socialite, his mind was made up. A short whirlwind courtship and his marriage proposal was accepted followed by a honeymoon on the continent. While in Europe, a visit was organised to 'Mater' and 'Pater' in the old family estate in order to introduce his bride and then back to Melbourne to build on his fortune. Mater and Pater were a little askance at the colonial their son had chosen, but none the less welcomed her, if just a touch stiffly. Lucille may have been a colonial but she was equipped with very sensitive social antenna, the in-laws' silent assessment of her didn't go unnoticed. Back home in Australia, the early glow continued to fade as her husband spent more time in business than in the matrimonial bed.

Eugene Bradfield had the unerring eye of a hunting lion, allowing him to identify the weakened target in the herd. He had previously noticed this beauty with the yearning eyes as one likely to succumb to his charms given the right set of circumstances.

'Oh Lord, what a balm for my sore eyes and weary heart?' Eugene stopped and bowed from the waist, taking her hand in his bringing it to his lips.

'My dear Eugene you are a silver-tongued devil.' She's said coquettishly.

'Not to be too forward, darling Lucille, but you have had more than a fleeting experience of my tongue.' Eugene responded with a witty double entendre.

Lucille blushes charmingly as Eugene loops his arm through hers and steers her toward the saloon bar.

Eugene ordered champagne, and after two glasses and some amusing flirtatious conversation, he decided the time was ripe and suggested they have dinner somewhere in the city. There were still plenty of cabs waiting patiently outside the track for tardy patrons and Eugene, playing the gentleman, ushered Lucille into the rear seat and slid alongside her making her blush with the intimate contact.

He leant in and kissed her gently on the lips and then more passionately, exploring her neck and décolletage. By the time they arrived at the restaurant, they had raised the temperature in the cab and caused the driver to lose concentration and nearly leave the road. There was no doubt where this was headed.

Cunning Eugene chose to dine in the restaurant at the Windsor hotel where he has his apartment. The meal was consumed with a soundtrack of Eugene's suggestive conversation eliciting enticing smiles from Lucille, their libidos at record highs. After a swiftly consumed meal, they adjourned hastily to his rooms on the fifth floor. They were welcomed by his valet Chris, who was immediately dismissed for the night. A familiar circumstance for him.

He spends the evening with his lover, a beautiful boy who came as a member of the media to attend an interview session with Eugene conducted by the Age Newspaper's senior theatre critic Madame R G Parmentier after a rehearsal of his new play at His Majesties

Theatre. The relationship was recognised immediately by the young man Johnny (Janos) Kovacs for the opportunity it presented to get the gossip on the great actor Eugene Bradfield, and he got plenty.

At first, he relayed the pillow talk stories to his mentor, the sour faced old fruit bat Rosetta Gloria Parmentier, the ancient journo who was rumoured to have eaten her first two husbands like a mating spider, but nothing was proven. Johnny was peeved to receive no credit for his efforts. He started filing his own theatre gossip with the infamous gossip rag *The Truth* until he was discovered and fired on the spot. But his reputation was made by then and he became another gay theatre critic in the small army of gay theatre and culture critics swarming about the city scamming free tickets and meals dealt out by producers in exchange for good reviews.

Fortunately for Eugene's valet Christoffel Bern or Chris, a Swiss migrant who learnt his trade in the major hotels of Zurich, his hometown, he was unaware of Johnny's duplicity or more correctly, it was fortunate for Johnny. Chris had a volcanic temper and a hair trigger and was more than capable of strangling the treacherous little rat.

Meanwhile, back on the fifth-floor apartment of the master Lothario, the temperate rose as the action moved to the boudoir. Say what you will about the narcissist Eugene Bradfield, he worked hard at pleasing his lady lovers and this night was no different.

Post love making, the couple were still entwined in Eugene's king size bed smoking contentedly and enjoying the sensation of the still naked body of their partner in adultery.

A bedside table holds a new record player, filling the room with sweet popular love songs.

Isham Jones was crooning, *I'll See You in My Dreams,* silencing any conversation.

Eugene was about to say something when their world turned upside down, literally. A shattering explosion of noise as the apartment door burst open announced the arrival of Eugene's worst nightmare. Heavy footsteps rapidly approach the love nest. The bedroom door shattered and in the opening, stood a very large and very angry Sir Rupert Yarborough. Yarborough, who had played tight head prop for Great Britain's Lions rugby team that had toured Australia and New Zealand, was still a powerful athlete who could take his place in that triumphant team again tomorrow. This was not going to end well.

Lucille screamed in a thoroughly clichéd style, 'It's my husband!!' As if lover boy hadn't caught on. Just in case he hadn't, Sir Rupert was about to deliver a lesson about messin' with the wife of an angry man. (Apologies to blues composers everywhere)

Across town, two gay men were similarly nestled down post love making as Johnny was delicately extracting whatever he could about Eugene's latest.

'You don't mean *that* Lucille, surely not? Oh my God, her husband is a mad man and if he finds them out, my dear man, you may be out of a job.'

'Well, he is a gambler and knows the odds. Here light me up.' Chris had been rolling a big fat joint and sucked in a huge lung full, holding it in for maximum impact. 'And gamblers will always play until they lose. One fine day my lord and master will lose irretrievably and find himself in deep do-do.'

As he spoke, an ambulance was rolling away from the Windsor Hotel, heading for the casualty department

of the Alfred Hospital bearing a barely recognisable Eugene Bradfield.

Painfully, his leading role in another proposed movie had flown like the front teeth that had been the centre of his winning smile which Chris found bloodied on the bedroom carpet the following morning.

CHAPTER 5
MAY 1923
POLICE STRIKE; CIVIL UNREST

The city of Melbourne was undergoing a great metamorphosis from the wide open 'anything goes' days of the gold rush era into the flamboyant opulence of the Victorian era of great individual and communal wealth. The city wrestled with societal change as she settled into a rough semblance of Mother England's class structure. Problems came and were surmounted, such as the police strike of 1923 on the eve of the spring racing carnival. Rioting and looting broke out in the city and rolled on until a force of special volunteers was sworn in. Eventually, pay and conditions improved for the aggrieved force. It was into this turmoil that twenty-four year old Jim Foley plunged fired with a burning ambition to be the best cop in the land.

Constable James Hartwell Foley was a disappointment to his uncle the Chief Superintendent. The young recruit Foley had shown great promise, initially excelling in his studies after passing the entrance exam. He was an intelligent, fit man who enjoyed physical training and coupled with his natural leadership rapid advancement was expected until an extraordinary run of unfortunate events had befallen the man. He felt it was not simply stalling his rise in the ranks but acting as lead weights dragging him backwards. Strangely enough he never lost his enthusiasm for policing, always exercising his sharp intellect and observational skills that should have had him at the top of the game. But for that rotten luck of his.

Jim's adoring mother Lillian had given birth to James and then a sister Carmen and finally a golden-haired little angel Marita who was taken by Spanish Flu. Carmen was nine when little Marita was taken as a three-year-old. Jim was heartbroken and swore on her tiny coffin to make his life mean something.

They were sitting by the fire in Uncle Frank's sitting room, sipping a scotch while waiting for Aunt Isabelle to call them into the dining room to carve the roast.

The happy family group consisted of Lillian, Jim's mother, Carmel his sister, Maureen his wife, and the twins George and Harry. Isabelle Foley, Jim's aunt, had failed to produce any children and when Jim's father failed to come home from the War, his uncle who was already a Victoria Police star in his own right, took him under his wing. Trying valiantly to keep him on the straight and narrow path, he was sure would lead his intelligent ward to rise through the ranks, hopefully to bring pride to his family and allow Chief Superintendent Foley to bask in the collateral glory.

'Jim' (always Jim, never James) 'a side effect of the current low crime rate is its limited opportunities for you to exercise your skills, but we still need to be ever alert. Opportunity can spring up without warning and as I have said on many occasions, luck is when preparation meets opportunity.' Foley senior shook his head and scratched his whiskered chin, 'However there is great credit in staying the course and delivering reliable service even if it becomes mundane. Never forget that the community depends on us to maintain order.'

Having delivered this little aphorism, he settled back puffing on his pipe, looking every inch the wise and venerable mentor. Sometimes this superior attitude got on Jim's nerves but he had learned to value his uncle's advice.

The following morning the weather had broken into a fine day, adding to the general atmosphere of cheerfulness across Melbourne. Full employment and low crime rates contributed to the buoyant atmosphere. The War, although never to be forgotten, was well in the past and the deadly Spanish flu had disappeared. This was the 1920s, the era of jazz. Cheap radio gave access to the lively music, news and opinion and magazines published details of the crazy new fashions. Flappers were dancing themselves into the floorboards at every venue around town as the young began to exert their presence.

The Foleys had gathered at the Chief Commissioner's large Edwardian home to celebrate his birthday. Life was fine, but could be a little better for Jim if it weren't for a couple of embarrassing occurrences.

The year before, as a young and eager constable, the police were tipped off to a brothel and bar being conducted by a second string petty criminal Soapy Mullins a member of Squizzy Taylors Burke Street Rats and managed by Mrs McKillip a fearsome old battle-axe. The police planned their operation well, surrounding the premises quietly with a 'picket line' of which Jim Foley held an important position. Their role was to arrest any fleeing patrons while the flying squad smashed their way into the bawdy house.

Everything went according to plan and when a whistle was blown, the action commenced. Foley was poised, waiting at the end of a narrow alleyway leading out to the network of streets with their crowded slums and myriad bolt holes. He didn't have long to wait. As soon as the sound of the whistle faded, he clearly heard running feet coming towards him. In seconds a dark figure charged out of the lane and ran into a full-on hip and shoulder tackle delivered expertly by Foley, knocking the runner unconscious to the cobblestones. Immediately, a press photographer leapt forward. His camera flash lit up the scene and preserved for posterity the unconscious form of the head of the Robbery Squad Detective Sergeant Clarence (Buster) Yarrow. His trousers were clearly (and embarrassingly) still unbuttoned, his braces tangled up under his arm. Yarrow in his defence, would later claim to have been conducting an undercover operation but could not find one witness within the force to corroborate his story.

In the meantime, his face was plastered on the front page of *The Truth* with the headline, 'Caught with His Pants Down: Senior Police officers under the covers work revealed.'

A deliberate play on the phrase 'under cover.' Clever job of sub-editing for which 'The Babe Ruth' in rhyming slang was noted but very damaging to the top cop's reputation. The unpopular cop in question would be facing demotion after the enquiry, plus earning relegation to a small town in the Western District and possibly an extensive suspension. A dreadful comedown for one of the state's most feared coppers. Further to that, he would find himself before the courts on charges coming as a result of his perversions in the bawdy house.

Sadly, this did not bode well for the aspiring Foley who was seen as something of a pariah by the rest of the force despite the facts of the case. His counsel advised him strongly against abstaining from testimony. His uncle agreed and came down hard with a lecture on police corruption having to be weeded out, and it was all for the good of the force. Constable Foley straightened his spine, adjusted his uniform, and tucked his cap under his arm and marched into the hearing to lay down the facts as they occurred. He left nothing out without once referring to the notebook in his hand. All the time under the icy gaze of the accused. A man with fourteen years in the force and an even longer memory who was now unlikely to see a pension at the end of his service.

After the hearing Foley was standing in the outer foyer talking to a tough young copper from the bush, Bluey Farnsworth, who was on a course at the training centre in Melbourne with Jim. They had gone through induction together and hit it off. Bluey was eager to tell Jim that he had been transferred to Melbourne West and they would be working together. As they chatted the accused copper Buster Yarrow swung around the corner searching the crowded foyer.

'Uh-oh here's trouble,' said Bluey out of the corner of his mouth.

Yarrow's eyes immediately locked on Foley and he strode towards him. Instantly recognising the imminent peril, Bluey Farnsworth placed his considerable bulk front of the dodgy copper and Foley, coming face to face with him.

'Mate, if you're not the biggest bloody drongo this side of the black stump, I'll go he for tiggy.' Blueys no nonsense voice failed to weaken Yarrow's resolve, 'This ain't the place to start a Barney.'

Bluey leaned right in the disgraced copper's face. 'And let me give ya a bit more advice for the record. Keep your pecker in yer pants in future, ya tosser.'

'I'll give you some advice right back. Your cobber here is in more shit than a Werribee duck an' he better be watchin' 'is back.'

The crowd had become aware of the fracas and started to gather in for a better look, expecting a blow up, but were disappointed when a senior officer stepped up instead.

But not before a newsman's camera flash captures the tense scene between the two.

'I can see yooz blokes aren't plannin' a game of two-up, so I suggest ya get yer arses out of here.' The Senior's voice was quite firm. 'Foley leave the area. I think your uncle's looking for you outside.'

'Fair dinkum Yarrow can yooz blokes pick your arguments away from headquarters,' the officer advised them, 'or you're all three of yez are gunna wind up getting the push, now piss off and bloody quick.'

'C'mon Jim, let's get a beer,' said Bluey, 'I'm as dry as a kookaburra's bum.' The two PCs headed for the nearest watering hole after receiving comments from Jim's uncle on his courtroom performance. By the time he was finished Jim was desperate for the soothing effects of a cold pot of beer.

It took some time for things to calm down after that, but it wouldn't be long before fate would cause Jim to put his foot in it again. And once again, it would not be through any real fault of his own.

The most common unlawful act in the community was the selling of sly grog, mostly from the workers cottages in poorer areas. Trade was conducted by old women who had no other way of supporting themselves. Another growing category of crime facing Constable Foley and his superiors was the drug trade. It developed in interaction with the sly grog profiteers who could readily purchase opiates from chemists and after refining by the criminals, sold in small packets for two shillings. The young coppers were schooled in how to deal with opium smokers of Little Lonsdale Street while the powders and liquids were ignored, confusing the effects of heroin or 'smack' with the milder familiar effects of opium. For the average copper on the beat these more lethal drugs would have the same effects as the sedative opium giving the user a 'pleasant sleep.'

It became fairly obvious that a lot of money was coming out of this trade and like bees to honey, along came the standover men with their heavy tactics and guns.

The depth of evil surrounding illegal drugs was only just beginning to show.

CHAPTER 6
AUGUST 1924
JIM DEFENDS THE WEATHER AND GAINS A LESSON

Jim Foley loved his city and was a staunch defender of her despite her foibles and fancies, and he never let the 'wits' have their way without a challenge.

'Don't like the weather? Wait five minutes.'

'Melbourne, four seasons in one day.'

'Oh, how very droll,' remarked Jim Foley to a senior policeman who had joined Victoria Police after moving from Sydney. 'That's the first time I've heard those jokes,' he paused, 'today!!'

The resulting sniggering from the other junior constables in the room sent the humourist red faced from the room straight into the commissioner's office to lodge a complaint of insubordination against the impertinent young constable. Apart from being classed as a trifle rude, it went into his file as demonstrating a lack of respect for a superior.

'Melbourne has an undeserved reputation for foul weather which is not surprising as it sits on a latitude just above the roaring forties,' preached Constable Irene Therese McCarthy, Jim Foley's companion.

'I don't really give a damn Constable' snapped Jim still rankled by the bollocking he received from his uncle the Chief Superintendent, 'we have a job to do and this blasted rain is not helping matters.'

Constable McCarthy was a devout Catholic girl, raised with a deeply entrenched sense of duty to her community. Her father had wanted her to join the Loreto Nuns as a teacher. A gifted student from an influential catholic family, she had been guaranteed a position at Loreto Mandeville Hall, a very new school for girls in

Toorak opening in 1924 and the governors set about recruiting the very best teaching staff available. Upon graduation, Irene McCarthy with her father's influence and her own inherent talent, would walk into a teaching position. However, she had other ideas away from the strictures of the church and after a blazing row with her father and the timely intervention of her strong-willed mother, she enlisted in the police force. Her application was one of only four women accepted into the force in 1924.

Now here she was in her second year assigned to subordinate duty alongside Fallible Foley, as he was referred to in some quarters already.

Constables Foley and McCarthy had been assigned to patrol the area around Flinders Street Station, where a gang of pickpockets had been reported to be preying on travellers.

The rain had made their observations very difficult because the sudden proliferation of umbrellas effectively shielded any chance of detecting the subtle sleight-of-hand movements that might indicate something dishonest occurring.

'Now we really need to concentrate and forget the weather Constable.' Jim Foley believed like all men of his day in the natural superiority of the male gender and therefore his offsider would need constant instruction, 'As you have been instructed, pickpockets do not generally work alone but often in teams of three. They employ what was called a distraction method.' Ahem! 'Now then number one 'accidently' bumps the target and removes the wallet or fob watch, number two brushes past number one and receives the item and then number one moves away from the scene of the crime while number two places the goods into the hands of number three who also leaves the scene.' He looks down face to face with the diminutive Constable McCarthy to ensure she was hearing him and importantly, understanding what he said.

'Yes, Constable Foley, I do understand and I'm watching for that tell-tale series of movements, in fact I've just been watching one.'

'You have, where... what, give me something girl and quick about it?'

'Newsboy, two to his left in dark green flat cap is holding the goods, number two is tailing number one who is over under the clocks on the right wearing a full-length mackintosh and light blue scarf.'

'I've got 'em. Keep watching and we'll create an encircling movement, slowly now slowly and when they try it on again, we pounce.' No hint of congratulations for her keen-eyed observation, 'I'll take number one you put the cuffs on number three. Okay, let's move.'

They had been standing in the lee of the famous Young and Jackson's hotel on the corner of Swanston and Flinders Streets, giving them what should have been a perfect view of the pickpocket's hunting ground. This should have been a simple enough task, but it had been complicated by a large crowd bolstered by rowdy tourists who had come to Melbourne for the Spring Racing, fashion industry events, and the general hospitality of restaurants and the buoyant mood of the great city.

Add the current torrential rain and the football crowd from the MCG making their way into the city for refreshment at the many pubs before they closed at the mandatory six o'clock. It was across this hodgepodge of humanity that the two police officers were desperate to observe the strategy of a gang of the slickest operators in the country. No mean feat!

Jim Foley and Irene McCarthy split up. He walked west for fifty metres while she crossed directly across the intersection along with a moving tide of people intent on catching their train home. Jim plotted a safe transit before plunging into the mixture of road traffic that was dominated by motor cars and trucks still with many horse-drawn vehicles threading their precarious way along Flinders Street in both directions. There was an almost deafening cacophony of internal combustion engines, tooting of claxons from the cars, horse's hooves in contact with the macadam roadway and the screaming and shouting of the drivers of the mishmash of vehicles.

Other pedestrians were testing their luck by ducking in and around this stream from both sides of the road, all in a hurry to avoid the rain and get to where they were going. The road surface itself was a treacherous mix of rainwater, mud, animal manure and motor oil leaking from the inefficient old motors presenting a further hazard to Jim Foley's official size ten police boots as he attempted a stealthy approach to his quarry.

His stealth was brought undone by the exceptionally slippery tramlines running in both directions on the crown of Flinders Street. He was making good progress with his eyes locked on the felon who he now recognised as one of Melbourne's most notorious thieves and an associate of Squizzy Taylor. So excited was he that all thought of personal safety went out the window. The result was an unseemly face plant in the Flinders Street muck, drawing the attention of the surging mob and unfortunately Foley's quarry. The fellow took one look and with the canny sixth sense of the criminal element, melted back into the milling crowd within the station precinct. Foley took off in pursuit but Fallible Foley had to return to pick up his truncheon, losing his quarry in the rush-hour crowd before running to the aid of Constable McCarthy who was attempting to place handcuffs on the man holding 'the goods.'

Irene McCarthy was experienced in confronting tough criminals who had no respect for the officers of the law, male or female. Having grown up with five older brothers she was capable of mixing it with almost anyone twice her size. So she was more than ready to take this felon down. The suspect turned out to be a dark-complexioned lad of no more than fourteen or possibly younger, but nevertheless still a dangerous 'stop at nothing' type eager to please his gang mates.

'Constable McCarthy Victoria police, you are under arrest sir.'

Irene's hand on his collar got an instant reaction, with the young thief firing up straight away. He would have been wise to go quietly, had he known that the apparently vulnerable female law officer confronting him had grown up with five hulking brothers and was well used to looking after herself. She was very handy with her fists, but preferred to save them in this instant.

'No flamin sheila's gunna take me in.' The audacious young crook shouted for the world to hear, winding up to throw a punch at the diminutive officer bearing down on him.

Two seconds later he lost his power of speech and independent movement as Constable McCarthy's truncheon made solid contact with his skull through the grubby flat cap favoured by back-alley crims.

When he came to, Blacky Richardson was sitting handcuffed under the watchful eye of the lady law officer as Jim Foley, having lost his quarry in the crowd, finally arrived to assist her. Pushing his way through the gawking crowd, he immediately set about trying to restore his dignity by claiming success in Constable McCarthy's arrest.

'Right, I'll be taking over now Constable. I'll thank you to disperse this crowd so that we can get back to the station.' Jim Foley stood there, hands on hips in what he hoped would be an expression of his leadership with the dreadful Flinders Street muck still dripping down his face and his mackintosh looking like he had been dragged to the scene.

'You might want to wash your face first, Constable Foley,' she responded, trying gamely to cover her amusement at her colleague's misfortune as the crowd erupted in laughter.

The incident in all its mud splattered detail reached the station house at the speed of light, giving the critics of the Chief Superintendents Golden Haired boy another opportunity for some hilarity and spiteful jibes, some of which found their way onto Constable Jim Foleys locker door.

An embarrassed Jim Foley, washed and dressed in a clean uniform, faced his station chief standing at attention with his helmet under his arm to sheepishly explain his less than glorious part in an otherwise well-planned operation.

The conservative upper echelons of the force were cursing that it hadn't been Constable McCarthy who had come a cropper. This would have reinforced their misogynist attitudes, but instead they were faced with the task of placing another commendation in Constable McCarthy's service jacket and another black mark against the unfortunate Foley.

⚜

CHAPTER 7
SEPTEMBER 1924
THE GREAT LOTHARIO BROUGHT DOWN

Eugene, the great seducer had just experienced the substance behind the old Biblical phrase that "the wages of sin is death" . Well, almost.

Occupying a private suite in The Alfred Hospital, the bruised and battered Eugene Wallace Bradfield cut a forlorn figure that, should he be able to replicate it for one of his stage or screen plays, would surely gain critical praise.

Eugene was propped up against his pillows, sucking his lunch through a straw that sat neatly in the space where his front teeth had once shone pearly white. His dislocated jaw was still unable to manage so much as a sandwich with the crusts removed. The nurses were solicitous and fuss about the heartthrob actor squabbling over whose shift covers service to his room. Their attraction to him was as much on reputation as looks. Most women will tut-tut about a player like Eugene, but for some reason they were endlessly fascinated by such tainted characters.

No one told him, but he was no longer the good-looking rooster he once was. His face had been radically altered. He suffered fractures to his cheekbones and the wounds on his face are not of the romantic duelling scar type, though they still lend a certain character to his features and may not be too bad once the stitches were removed. He was nursing an arm in a sling resulting from a broken clavicle. Assorted cuts and contusions rounded out his list of war wounds which when all was said and done, was not too bad for a bloke attacked by a rampaging rhinoceros, reports Chris to Johnny Kovacs.

His butler Chris had been paying regular visits to bring books, scripts and the latest form guide to him on a regular basis. Eugene managed to place his bets despite the crowd of well-wishers and sycophants that filled his room with noise and flowers for the entire available visiting hours. One unthinking fool had brought a box of toffees that was quickly despatched to the nurses' station after an admonition that left the guilty party thoroughly embarrassed and crawling away down the ward with a flea in his ear.

Chris ran messages for him and placed the phone calls for bets on the races for which he had lost no enthusiasm. His betting account was up and down and so long as he didn't go too hard on a horse the Wren Totaliser accepted his bets. Eugene recognised the fragility of the relationship he had with the infamous bookmaker and took the precaution of cultivating a connection with one or two other large bookmakers around town. Just in case.

Barely able to speak, he managed to convey to Chris his appreciation for his service but never offered to pay for his employee's tram fares as he went about on Eugene's own business.

On one auspicious occasion, he was visited by the casting director of the movie he had expected to star in. The gentleman offered his sympathy and assurance that he would not be forgotten when further roles came up.

'After all Eugene, actors of your calibre are few and far between. Get well quickly and we'll see you up and around soon.'

An assistant stepped into the room and deposited a massive bunch of aromatic roses on his bedside table, along with a card signed by various people employed in the movie industry. Eugene began to sniff, heralding the onset of a huge sneeze that rattled his bruised bones.

A disgusting combination of snot and blood erupted to land on the crisp, white sheets, followed by a pained groan.

Eugene was left with the unmistakable impression that he had just had his last contact with the studio judging by the man's repulsed expression when he first laid eyes on him and his sudden need to exit the room, redolent with hospital smells and now this nauseating sight.

Meanwhile, not too far away, Chris and Johnny were sipping a cold glass of Chablis in a little bar in Chapel Street discussing Chris' boss.

The two expatriate Europeans were speaking in French, a language they were both comfortable with.

'*Eh bien au moins vous avez gardé votre employ Dearie il aurait pu être bien pire.*'

(Trans.) 'Well, at least you've kept your employ Dearie. It could have been a lot worse.' Johnny said comfortingly.

'That may be for now, but I need to keep my eyes open for another opportunity. I think my man is headed for a fall.'

'What makes you say that? Surely he has learned a lesson from this awful beating?'

'No, I don't mean his womanising. It's his gambling.' Chris grumbled.

'He keeps making losses and chasing them with bigger and more extravagant bets. And he is betting with some very serious people my dear.' Chris shook his head and frowned deeply, before going on, 'I mean, these people will take your hands off if you fail to make your debts good.'

'How does he look? Is he healing well?' The gossip columnist was always prospecting.

'He looks as you would expect a man to look who has been hit by a prize fighter.'

'I wonder, my dear friend, if you would do me a very big favour for which I would be forever in your debt?'

For some time, Chris had suspected that his lover Johnny was using him to have access to Bradfield, and now he was feeling more than a little unsettled.

'I'm not sure I like the direction this is taking my Johnny boy.' Chris was practicing caution, perhaps a little too late. 'What would that favour be per chance? And please don't assume that our relationship gives you an advantage.'

Johnny's hand finds Chris's under the table and gives it a reassuring squeeze. 'Now don't get upset dear man, it's a nothing really.' Smiling his most disarming smile, 'I merely want to pop into his room, with you of course, and take a little snapshot of the poor dear man in his pitiful state.'

'What? No, are you mad?' Chris attempted to stand, but Johnny still had a firm grip on his hand preventing him from rising.

'Just one quick snap for our readers who are expressing concern for their star.' Now his smile has become an obsequious grin. 'I would hate for you and I to have a spat and have the source of my scoops revealed. That would never do now would it?'

Chris was horrified. If his disloyalty was made public, he would never get another position in Australia. He might as well go home to Switzerland to empty chamber pots in some low-grade rural hotel.

'Oh Christ. Alright, but we'll do it on my terms or not at all and to hell with you and your ridiculous gossip rag.'

Between them they work out a way that Johnny can get by the over-protective matron on the ward outside visiting hours, preferably in the morning before Eugene has had a clean-up visit from his nurse. The staff are used to seeing Chris come and go on Eugene's errands and shouldn't be surprised to see him come in at that hour with some theatrical looking person.

Johnny dons a white coat like the orderly's wear and carries his camera in a duffle bag. The camera was the type predominantly used by the press, a 4' x 5' Graflex Speed Graphics with attached bulb flash. Its state-of-the-art but rather bulky. Johnny lines up his shot and hits the shutter. The resultant flash from the bulb lights up the small room like a lightning bolt, startling Eugene out of his post breakfast nap. Johnny hits the eject button and the flash bulb pops out rattling away under the bed. Quickly inserting a fresh bulb for a second shot, he was grabbed by the scruff of the neck by the burly matron alerted by the camera flash who was now in a state of high dudgeon.

'And who might you be, you miserable little worm and who in God's name allowed you to come into my ward bothering my patient?'

Eugene, trying to express his outrage unsuccessfully around his painful jaw and in his agitation, upset the full urine bottle standing on his overbed table waiting for collection. The product of his night time relief landed on his lap, saturating him and his bed. Johnny took advantage of the matrons' distraction to snap a second shot of the now thoroughly distressed actor and bolted out of the ward like his backside was on fire.

The photos appeared across the front page of The Truth with a lurid description of Bradfield's physical condition and the full background story with a by-line by Johnny.

Chris was left standing in the hospital ward with his mouth flapping up and down as questions are fired at him from Eugene via matron Arbuckle the Indomitable. Chris was discharged from his duties at once and left for Sydney by coastal steamer a week later.

Johnny was arrested for committing an obscene act in a public toilet two weeks later and was convicted in the magistrates' court. For him, his notoriety was his undoing. He had once involved the magistrate's niece in a salacious and unsubstantiated piece, and now it was the judge's opportunity to seek payback. He was sentenced to twelve months' hard labour and held in Ballarat goal. He was found hanged in his cell five months into his sentence.

CHAPTER 8
OCTOBER 1924
REGGIE BECOMES RICHARD

Often misquoted is the expression that money is the root of all evil when, in fact, it is the lust for money, not money itself. Consequently, wherever there are large amounts of money to be found or made, the attraction to the felonious and the unblemished alike is irresistible. So too is the drawing power of thoroughbred horse racing. The gorgeous animals parading around the mounting yard bearing diminutive jockeys in the flashy colours of their mounts stable all work to draw the eye and the money of the sharp-witted and gullible just the same.

The crowd attending are generally a cross section of the city's population, from the shabby to the chic, and the working class in between, all hoping for their favourite horse to cross the line.

Heavily represented was the upwardly mobile and burgeoning middle class displaying their nouveau riche status with fine clothes, throwing large denomination bank notes about in a show of careless arrogance. The ladies take the opportunity to parade in their very finest fashions, showing little interest in the equine activities.

'Oh, look at all the pretty horses.'

'Oh Narelle, aren't the little jockeys so totally cute?'

And at the top of the social food chain are the wealthy. The old money, the wealthy graziers and horse owners and the industrialists who reaped a fortune from the war years. Swarming about them are the sycophants, the celebrities and the would-be types. This demographic was mostly hidden away in the security of the members' only grandstand. They tend only to emerge, shot glass in hand to urge their four-legged investment on when the field turns into the home straight and the cracking of whips can be clearly heard above the roar of the crowd.

Moving smoothly among this upper-class throng was an urbane character who had emerged onto the Melbourne social scene recently. He styled himself as Captain Richard Jenkins, claiming to have served in the Fourth Royal Indian Cavalry Division in the first war.

His demeanour spoke loudly of a military career and the confidence he exuded was that of a man of substance. However, he was in fact a smooth conman working his way around the world searching for the monied and gullible.

Reggie Watford had emigrated from England via the United States, where he had found the opposition from the Italian and Irish gangs far too heavy for his liking. It was when reading an article in the sports section on the popularity of horse racing in Australia when he was struck by the wonderful opportunity it presented. His brief research revealed no record of organised crime in the innocent city of Melbourne that was awash with the wealth of the gold fields. Without a moment to waste, Reggie Watford packed his bags and took a Cunard Liner out of New York to eventually land in Sydney, emerging from his cabin as Francis Willoughby Fifth Baron Middleton of Walloton in the County of Nottinghamshire. Wealthy property investor and miner.

His first mission was to present his credentials and expertly forged letters of credit to a suitably impressed bank manager dazzled by an aristocrat, a Baron no less. Equipped with a cheque book supplied by his new fawning bank manager he succeeded in passing dozens of small cheques all around the city of Sydney before jumping aboard a coastal steamer narrowly avoiding the fraud squad who would inevitably be on his case as the flood of cheques began bouncing all over the city. The steam ship Southern Star arrived in Melbourne in July, giving him time to tap into the local culture which seemed to centre on a strange indigenous game of football. The next favourite pastime was gambling on horses. In time he learnt gambling extended to anything really, including as some said betting on the flies crawling up the wall. This was the perfect environment for a shyster like Reggie Watford.

After he settled in, he started to educate himself on the racing scene and in doing so managed to insinuate himself into the upper circles of this far-flung colony. The spring racing carnival would come around later in the year, by which time he hoped to have developed the network that would become his hunting ground.

Reggie Watford lost no time in ingratiating himself into Melbourne society, first booking a hotel suite in Windsor Hotel and proclaiming himself to be Captain Richard Fairlie Jenkins. Late of His Majesty's 4TH Indian Cavalry Division. The usually jaded bellboys were suitably impressed and jumped to when asked to take the captain's baggage up to his room, a third-floor suite suitable for an officer and a gentleman.

After settling in, he decided to take his leisure with a gin and tonic in the bar in order to check out the denizens of this wonderful old Victorian establishment that must be bursting with the wealthy and naïve.

He was reading an article in the local daily newspaper *The Age*, provided by the management about the Melbourne Cup, noting one trainer by the name of Richard Bradfield who had won the event three times. Now, *there* was an envious record.

The 1924 Melbourne Cup would be won by Backwood, the fourth Cup winner trained by Richard Bradfield. The previous two cups had been trained by a celebrated trainer James Scobie. Richard Bradfield would become an important cross connection for Reggie Watford aka Captain Richard Fairlie Jenkins.

By the time he was up to his second Gin and Tonic, he heard a bit of a fuss at the concierges' desk. The concierge seemed to be trying to appease a sharply dressed individual he refers to as Mr Bradfield. Could it be? What a stroke of luck? Without a moment's hesitation, Reggie Watford transforms into the tall soldierly and sophisticated Captain Jenkins and intercepts Eugene Bradfield at the mid-point of the foyer.

'Good afternoon sir, do I have the honour of addressing Mr Bradfield?'

Eugene, who was used to people thrusting themselves upon him, was usually safe from such tiresome interference in the sanctuary of his hotel. He turns to see who this upstart might be and was confronted by an obviously well-to-do gentleman in a superbly tailored three-piece suit.

'That is correct sir, and who might you be?'

'Forgive me, I am Captain Richard Fairlie Jenkins. Late of His Indian Majesty's 4TH Cavalry Division at your service.' Reggie was suddenly concerned that he might be overdoing it a bit. 'It's an absolute pleasure to meet you, sir. May I be so bold as to offer you a glass of champagne in return for a moment of your time?'

Eugene had already come to the conclusion that this may be an interesting person to become acquainted with and accepted the invitation with a genuine smile.

As they settle down at the table by the window looking out onto Spring Street and the Treasury Gardens. The pale autumn sunshine fell gently through the window washing their faces in gold. They exchange small talk until their waiter has delivered their order for a magnum of Great Western champagne and flutes for two.

'So Captain Jenkins, you are rather young for your rank. Did you serve?'

'Sadly I did sir, our Division suffered a high casualty rate among our officer ranks which I'm sure presented me with an opportunity to gain my status.'

Jenkins claimed to have served in the Fourth Royal Indian Cavalry Division in the first war.

The gallant officer bore the scars of combat while passing himself off as the recipient of a fortune that allowed him to live an extravagant life style. He was adored by the female contingent and lionised by the media. Tall for his time, at a little over six feet with the build of an athlete, his hair was cut short in military style and framed a tanned classically handsome face generally lit up as if by some secret inner amusement.

'Ah, my condolences on the loss of your comrades, it must have been very difficult.'

The champagne arrived and Captain Jenkins, still under the impression that he was addressing the winning trainer of a number of Melbourne Cups proposed a toast.

'May I propose a toast to you sir and your astounding success in winning three Melbourne Cups?'

Eugene was so startled he almost dropped his champagne flute. 'What? No! Oh dear, I'm afraid you have the wrong man, sir.'

The embarrassed captain, was suddenly flustered. 'But aren't you Richard Bradfield the trainer?'

'Indeed sir, my surname is Bradfield, but I am Eugene Wallace Bradfield, thespian,' he responded, a touch haughtily with a slight bow.

'Good Lord, please do forgive me. I was just reading about that trainer's success in the paper as you came in and I heard you announced as Mr Bradfield and immediately jumped to the wrong conclusion. Please accept my apologies.'

'Apology accepted but only because I had bet one hundred pounds on a magnificent animal that crossed the line for me today.'

'You don't say? Oh capital, well done that man.'

The two men who had been strangers only moments before

looked at each other straight faced and simultaneously burst into loud laughter.

By the time they had lowered the level in the second bottle and reserved a table for dinner, they were fast friends and arrangements had been made to attend the races together at the first suitable opportunity.

This was a perfect opportunity for Captain Jenkins to impress himself on the high society in the member's enclosure, who were equally impressed with the gallant cavalry officer. Introducing him as a friend did no harm to Eugene's standing either. By day's end Eugene had more or less broken even thanks to a plunge on the winner of the last at good odds. The gallant captain placed a substantial bet on an imported English horse from His Excellency the Earl of Stradbroke, 'The Night Patrol', an outstanding thoroughbred that possessed remarkable turn of foot that had won more than he had lost.

The bet was placed with some of the cash the good captain had harvested with the aid of rubber cheques in Sydney so now he had a wad of legitimate cash with which to sow more opportunities and he didn't have long to wait for that opportunity to bob up.

Eugene had been basking in the reflected glory of his heroic new friend, making a point of introducing him to all the wealthiest and most influential people in his circle. He was hoping, of course, that one or two might be sufficiently impressed to entertain a proposal to invest in the new show he was planning. And if there was any possibility that Captain Jenkins may become a patron of the theatre, Eugene would be delighted to be his mentor, so to speak. This was the tactic employed by Eugene that he hoped would lead to some heavy investment from the Captain as he inevitably fell in love with the dramatic arts.

This tour de force played right into the fraudulent hands of Captain Jenkins aka Reggie Watford as he worked the crowd oozing charm and bonhomie, managing to extract business cards from one or two and dinner invitations from several smitten dowagers. As he chatted with various groups, the busy press camera men were snapping photos for the social pages and Captain Jenkins featured in several charming group photographs.

Even Reggie himself could not be more impressed with his progress. In a matter of days, he had moved from an unknown to become a sought-after guest in some of Melbourne's finest homes. This was going to be a very lucrative field in which to sow the seeds of his greedy misrepresentation.

CHAPTER 9

SEPTEMBER 1924

HYGEIA CRUISING SEASON; THE CREW

Hygeia was preparing to depart Port Melbourne for her Queenscliff run as her crew awaited orders that would be shouted from the bridge, requiring concentration to hear above the hubbub of the crowd excitedly jostling for space along the rails and onto the decks. The crew were mostly experienced Able-Bodied Seaman or AB's

The entire crew of Hygeia were well trained and experienced in their individual roles working together to ensure the smooth operation of ship and the enjoyment and safety of their guests. At the centre of the crew list were several outstanding characters highlighted by their nicknames that had developed out of their strong friendships.

Able Seaman 'Daisy' O'Connell was taking the passenger count at the top of the gangway, concentrating hard when he was called. Daisy O'Connell earned his nickname after he came aboard one day wearing a straw boater with a flower in the hatband to celebrate the fact that he had just become engaged. He was a popular and conscientious young sailor who shared the same level of responsibility as a crewman with whom he had become great mates. Froggy Dempster was another colourful character who earned his nickname out of misfortune after surviving a week lost in a primeval swamp while on a duck shooting expedition. He was a talented banjo player and kept the other crew members amused when they were all off watch. But he was totally devoid of any sense of direction and was possibly the worst navigator on the Bay. Now he and Daisy shared the responsibility of making an accurate count of passengers coming aboard. It was an important safety factor to count passengers on and off against ticket sales to avoid the loss of some fool with too much grog on board finding himself overboard and lost.

'Mister O'Connell, what's the count?' First Mate Bully Masterson demands.

'We're almost there, Sir, just another half dozen.'

'Right then Daisy my lad, gangplank away on your count.'

Captain Fergus Galbraith cut an imposing figure as he stood on the bridge deck of his vessel, the bay excursion paddle steamer Hygeia. Both hands thrust firmly into the pockets of his navy style double-breasted jacket bearing the four gold bars on his sleeves and the gold braid on his peaked cap signifying his rank as captain. His feet were planted firmly apart to steady him against the slight roll of the ship. As was the fashion among seagoing captains, he wore a neatly trimmed full beard that reached down over his collar, obscuring the top of his tie. He was a traditional sea captain and a strict disciplinarian. He saw his role as not only captain of a ship but also protector of his many passengers, who relied on him for their safe passage across a sometimes-turbulent Port Phillip Bay. This was not the navy but Captain Galbraith ran his ship on navy disciplines.

The Hygeia's deck crew served in different roles and were rotated to keep them sharp. Manning the sponsons (outer edge of the paddle box) forward and aft, forward capstan, aft capstan and taking a turn at the wheel.

The crew were also expected to control the decks, ensuring the safety of the passengers.

But they weren't the only crew; the restaurant, barber shop and bars were all operated by people trained and efficient in their roles. Often when the day was hot and the beer had been flowing, a disagreement or two would break out amongst over refreshed young bulls who fancied themselves. The crew were more than able to handle the situation, threatening to give any stubborn types the deep six or the old, 'walk the plank.' In reality, the worst they ever had to do was to employ the old belaying pin as a billy club. As a last resort, the ship had the capacity to confine a problem passenger in a strong room below that the crew referred to as 'the brig' that in reality had very rarely been used for that purpose. The population explode to bursting point as the Bourke Street Rats were packed in for safe keeping, howling and swearing, threatening retribution.

Hygeia carried the usual compliment of 1ST 2ND and 3RD Mates, who were strict and expected their orders to be obeyed with skill and haste. Each of them were career officers and were careful to carry out their duties efficiently lest they be overlooked for promotion.

The first Mate Bully Masterson was still a very young man built like a 'brick outhouse' as Froggy described him to a new crew member. He shared his nickname with many other 'mates' in the trade as a traditional moniker. Having completed his apprenticeship on clipper ships sailing in the grain race out of Adelaide to The Lizard Point in Cornwall England

He had a powerful voice that could reach the ears of his crew over the loudest storm.

A ship's officer on a windjammer or square-rigged clipper ship needed to be heard from the poop deck to the upper yards in clear or stormy weather.

'Mister Masterson make ready to lower the anchor with all possible haste.' Captain Galbraith's own stentorian voice boomed out. The Hygeia's great engines had shuddered to a stop her huge paddle wheels coming to a stop. She had just broken a rudder chain while off Mornington and was forced to anchor while repairs were undertaken. At that time, the crew had a nice little sideline collecting the empty beer bottles from the bar which were later recycled for a refund. The anchor was never used, so its storage space in the forepeak became the obvious place to store their haul.

The captain's order caused panic among the crew who could see their prize haul being reduced to splinters as the anchor chain was let go. Daisy and Sparra were the first to react and swiftly organised a team to move their collection out of harm's way. Sparra Dempsey was a diminutive man who darted about the ship like his namesake and was the perfect fit for the urgent job at hand and swiftly went to work.

Bully Masterson stood by the hatch, calling back to the bridge. 'Right Sir, anchor aweigh. A slight delay sir.'

And in a harsh whisper to the crew, 'For God's sake boys, hurry up.'

Disaster averted, the bottle collection saved and Hygeia rode safely at anchor allowing the crew to make repairs and continue its voyage.

Altogether, the crew from deckhands to caterers to AB's and the Mates were a well matched and cheerful lot pleased to be employed in a pleasant trade that paid a good wage. Most blue water sailors, as international and coastal sailors were called, could be away from home for months on end, whereas the ferry crews mostly slept in their own beds at home each night and seldom had to deal with life-threatening storms at sea.

Captain Galbraith was in the habit of delivering a briefing to his officers before the season began and met with them individually at the conclusion of each of their excursions to receive reports of any maintenance requirements or complaints. The most important report in his engineer's mind was that of the ship's engineer. The engineer was often accused of being short-tempered as he had no tolerance for people who could not appreciate the wondrous workings of a steam engine.

'I want to find and make good any faults before we throw off our lines.' Engineer Gabby McInerny stated firmly, more than once.

'I am in total agreement with our engineer,' asserted Captain Galbraith, 'attention to detail prevents us finding ourselves without power at sea in the middle of a gale.'

Galbraith's conscientious approach was engrained by one or two personal experiences at sea when laxity had resulted in accidents that had claimed at least one life, injured several and caused damage to the ship and shore facilities.

On another occasion, again under the command of an earlier captain, Hygeia had run afoul of a sandbar north-east of Sorrento jetty, becoming well and truly stuck. While attempting to turn around away from the pier, Hygeia was caught by a south-westerly squall that drove her onto the sandbank on a falling tide. Her passengers were taken off and she was re-floated the next day with the assistance of the company's new powerful tug Nyora. The whole rescue mission provided hours of entertainment for the locals, who were totally engrossed in the proceedings and crowded the clifftops not wanting to miss a thing.

Captain Fergus Galbraith was determined he would run his ship incident free and was largely successful.

The demand for the excursion boats came from the many trades picnics similar to the famous Butchers Picnic. The various trades were requested not to sell more than fifteen hundred tickets, but greed often got in the way. So as to avoid overcrowding, an Able Seaman was stationed at the top of the gangway keeping a count, when it reached the maximum legal number the gangplank would come up, leaving some people stranded on the dock howling complaints at the departing ship. Sometimes family members were separated, creating great panic.

The ship's master occasionally mixed with the passengers, enjoying friendly banter and answering the many questions put to him by the landsmen and women to whom sea life was a mystery. Not all passengers were of the carefree picnicking kind. Wherever there were crowds the artful would gather like sharks circling a school of mullet. The Hygeia was not always free of such parasites and occasionally applied for police assistance in order to protect the law abiding and innocent passengers.

CHAPTER 10
MID-NOVEMBER
JIM IS BRIEFED BY HIS SUPERIOR FOR UNDERCOVER WORK

Senior Sergeant George Manifold had called Jim Foley into his office. The air was thick with tobacco smoke forming into a small stratus loitering above the Seniors balding head. The smoke was produced in a pipe that was a permanent fixture in the sergeant's mouth and such was its potency that his choice of tobacco was the subject of much speculation among his subordinates. On one rare occasion, Senior Sergeant Manifold had been called away urgently, leaving his beloved pipe in the ashtray on his desk. A very cheeky young constable decided to sabotage it in his absence. Carefully removing the plug of tobacco, he inserted a good pinch of pencil shavings and fluff, then just as carefully he replaced the wad of tobacco. To no-one's surprise, the returning Senior Sergeant promptly relit his adored smoking apparatus and without flinching puffed away contentedly while he concentrated on his reports.

Usually there was very little air movement in the room to disturb the smoke cloud or the fly that hovered in lazy, monotonous circles just below it. It was a musty, airless room at the back of the Russell Street police station lit by one hanging bulb, its small light's feeble luminosity almost negated by fly dirt. To aid the sergeant's strained eyesight, an old brass desk lamp glowed heroically on the right-hand side of the heavily scarred and battered desk. On the left-hand side of the desk, a framed picture of a frumpy-looking woman in a hat that appeared to have been hammered into place grimaced at the camera rather than smiled. Possibly taken at a funeral, thought Jim who now had been elevated to the rank Senior Constable due largely to his work in bringing a crooked copper before the courts.

A small dirty window high up on the wall opposite the door shed little additional light into the dusty room that was like the inside of an old suitcase. Faded posters and information leaflets hung from drawing pins in a corkboard behind the sergeant's head, adding to the general air of dejection.

The Senior Sergeant himself was a thin-faced joyless man wearing a cloak of continuous disappointment. His wife took shelter from the world under a similar shield friendless and rarely smiling. She would go to her grave believing some forgotten sin had caused her to remain a barren failure to her husband. f asked he would struggle to recall the last time he and his wife had found anything to laugh about.

Jim Foley stood rigidly at attention before his superior, expecting to receive another bollocking for some forgotten slight but quietly thanking the fates that he didn't have to work in an environment like this.

Senior Sergeant Manifold cleared his throat and began in the formal, clichéd style beloved by speakers unaccustomed to making speeches, giving evidence before the courts.

'Ah yes now, young Foley. I suppose you're wonderin' why I've called you 'ere.' Foley wisely remains silent. 'Well, it's no secret that you've 'ad something of a rough trot since starting out. I know your uncle,' he paused with a wiggle of his walrus moustache for effect, 'a good man,' another similar pause and wiggle, 'and a good copper who has been a little embarrassed by some of the things you've got yourself into.' Here he looks up and makes eye contact for the first time flexing a mirthless smile that reveals a set of teeth in sore need of a dentist below a bushy moustache stained with the smoke from the pipe that may well have grown out of his mouth like the tusk of an old boar.

'I've a job you should find a challenge and give you an opportunity to prove yourself as the capable newly appointed Senior Conny we know you are… or ah, *can* be that is,' he stutters. More moustache gyrations, this time with a loud wet sniff. 'We 'ave 'ad complaints from operators of the excursion vessels plying their trade on the bay.' He stops to ensure that Foley was paying attention, waggling his upper lip this time pushing it out with his bottom lip the way moustachioed men the world over do.

'It seems some of the crafty types are plying their trade on board these picnic ships as well, croolin' peoples leshertime.' The stem of his pipe destroying the clarity of his speech.

Jim had the fleeting thought that if you took away the Seniors pipe and moustache, he might lose the power of speech.

Removing the pipe from his mouth to give full weight to his words, he went on. 'It will come as no surprise Senior Constable Foley that these miscreants do not have an official picnic day, ah-la the Butchers Picnic, the Retail and Greengrocers Picnic or the Tinsmiths Picnic.' Manifold seems pleased with his bon mot illustrated by a strange throaty rumbling that passes for laughter. 'But that has not prevented them from minglin' in with the citizenry to commit mischief. So I am assigning you and Constable Irene McCarthy to patrol the vessel, aah,' here he pauses again and consults a sheet of paper as if the name of the vessel in question was too complicated to recall. 'Ahem, yes here it is, the Hygeia, and clap the 'and cuffs on a few of these gutter snipes.'

Jim Foley had stood patiently as his sergeant prattled on. It would certainly be a change from patrolling the filthy backstreets of Fitzroy and Carlton but should he see it as an opportunity or another admonishment stealthily applied. Plus, he'd have the company of the female who showed him up recently. He can't help but think he's truly cursed to be lumbered with this woman who had, despite his preconceptions, proved to be capable. His resentment came from two sources. One: He had found himself distracted for her safety, neglecting his own. Two: Her lack of stature. He would feel more secure with a hefty ruckman at his back than a five foot six female. And three: He was a typical male who resented being shown up by a female and noticed the comments around the squad room about her being Jim's caddy. A snide reference to a golfing caddy who carried the players balls. However, he took his orders stoically and assured Manifold of his commitment to carry them out.

'Remember Foley, you need to restore your uncles' faith in you so do your best. Oh, and by the way, this is an undercover role, so dress in mufti to mingle with the hoi polloi. You and Constable McCarthy should appear as a couple, that is, as in fellow travellers. Understood?' Moustache wiggle wiggle.

'Understood Senior Sergeant, thank you Senior Sergeant I won't disappoint you.'

The next Sunday morning found Jim Foley and Irene McCarthy waiting on the dock at Port Melbourne in the midst of a large crowd waiting to board the impressive paddle steamer belching dark smoke from her twin stacks into the early morning air.

A light rain had settled on the waiting crowd. Heavier seasonal downpours had flushed gutters earlier of their foul stench and left the roadways glistening. It wasn't until the grime was gone that Jim realised how badly his city could smell at times. There was no denying the Yarra River was nothing but an open sewer due to the proliferation of tanneries and other noxious industries dumping their wastes into the long-suffering waterway. Should anyone fall into it the threat was less about drowning and more about dying from typhoid.

Standing in the close crowd Jim became aware of another aroma usually more prevalent in winter. It was the peculiar smell of wet woollen clothing. As he looked about, he could see steam rising from the shoulders of the patiently waiting passengers their damp clothing heated from within. The rain was unexpected according to forecasts but in spring anything could be expected.

'This will be the first time I've been aboard one of these ships constable.' He received a nudge in the ribs from his partner to remind him that they were undercover. 'Oh, sorry const.. ah..Irene. I must say she's a lot larger than I expected.'

'I can't help but feel a little excited, as if we were part of the picnic.'

'Understandable, but we're here to do a job, so sharp eyes now. See if you can spot any of the known pickpockets in the crowd. We did well at Flinders Street Station, let's see if we can repeat the exercise.'

Irene McCarthy makes mental note of the 'we.'

She wasn't out to bring further embarrassment to her partner, but she wanted to be acknowledged for her part in any arrests. Given the attitudes of the day, she wondered if it was worth raising the matter but decided to keep it for a more appropriate time.

The crowd began to shuffle forward to the boarding gangplank. This is the Boot and Shoe Trades Picnic and Jim has been passed an appropriate ticket to get them aboard. He noted the sailor at the head of the gangway keeping a count of passengers but not really demanding to see any tickets. That was a laxity that would allow the scoundrels free and easy access to the ship. Jim makes a mental note that will eventually go into his report.

'I think we should make our way to the back of the boat.' He was interrupted by McCarthy, who corrects him.

'It's called the stern Jim.'

A little snippily he thanks her and goes on, 'as I was saying we should make our way to the *stern* and work our way forward to the... ah the front of the boat putting an eye on as many of the passengers as possible.'

Constable McCarthy had been on the verge of explaining that the *front* of the boat, the pointy end as it were, was referred to as the bows. But it was more correctly known as the stem or prow. Wisely, she buttoned her lip as she had felt a little resentment coming her way from Senior Constable Foley since the situation at Flinders Street. She thought he was starting to look more like an average copper on the beat than the potential world beater the upper echelons of the force had held hopes for. Nevertheless she would do her duty and set off on her first patrol of the ship.

Under her feet the decks began to throb as the ships big steam engines power up and drive the enormous paddle wheels that clawed at the sea, hauling them to their destination.

Jim took a different route and soon had a suspect in his sights. Jonathon Showbag Rutledge, leading member of the street gang known as the 'Burke Street Rats,' leant casually on the bar in the ship's saloon, casing the crowd for an easy mark. When Jim spotted him, the policeman immediately pulled his flat cap over his eyes and crouched slightly to conceal his true height. He found a position behind a large potted plant where he was partially concealed but still had a clear view of the felon.

As he watches his quarry, another member of the pickpocket gang casually walked past Rutledge. It was the gangs' middleman Roger the Razor Wood who avoids making eye contact with his confederate or tip his hat. Jim's excitement was rising and his heart rate was up. He determined to find McCarthy before she stumbled into the gang members and was recognised. As he attempted to slide away from his concealment, his coat caught in the potted plant which topples crazily back and forth, spilling soil on the deck before Jim manages to bring it under control and kicks the soil out of sight. One small curious boy looks on wonderingly.

'Watcha doin' mister? You'll get in trouble if ya make a mess. Why ya hidin' in that plant for anyway?' Looking around for clues to Jim's game he asks, 'are you some sort of perve?' The kid ramps up the fuss in a loud voice. 'Mum there's a pervy bloke behind the bushes, Muum.'

Oh my God, that's all I need, another embarrassing stuff up, Jim berates himself. 'Nick off youngster, just lost me balance is all. Go on, piss off before I give you a boot in the backside.'

The lad scuttles away to a safe distance before giving Jim a rude gesture with a lusty, 'Get stuffed'.

Senior Constable Foley shook his head in dismay and manages to evade further interrogation from the cheeky nine-year-old without creating too much of a scene. As discreetly as he can manage, he scuttles away along the starboard side of the ship searching for his partner. He finds her chatting amicably to a young mother with a push pram admiring the young mum's baby. Jim realises she has invented a perfect cover, allowing her to maintain a lookout while looking like another happy picnicker. He walked past and caught her eye, raising an eyebrow and cocking his head to signify he was onto something. McCarthy was quick to pick up on his body language and broke off her conversation to join him.

Jim was still feeling awkward using his partner's name and stuttered a bit but got his message across about Showbag and Razor Wood.

'I'm sure I saw that little grub the Plover but he would still be in custody, surely?' she said.

'I spent some time in the records department last night.' Jim replies, 'Plover Richardson is from a large family in the Fitzroy slum area. His father died from liver disease and his half native mother has had six kids on her hands from a series of fathers since he passed. Plover is the third in line and he most assuredly, is still behind bars. They may have recruited his older brother Martin, known as Ferret, he'd be a pretty good look alike I would think.' Jim looked around, scanning the crowd. Satisfied they were safe to do so, suggested they take the air on the upper promenade deck, an area a lot smaller than the lower deck that wouldn't take long to survey.

'There, there over by the rail on the other side. See him? In the check coat and trilby hat, that's Ferret Richardson I'll wager. So the whole gangs here.' Jim's excitement has peaked now.

'Do you have a theory on what they intend to do, James?'

'Only my mother calls me James.' Jim responded with a smile, not wanting to incite any further friction between them. 'If I were in their shoes, and thank God I'm not, I would be worried about operating in such a confined space. There might be rich pickings on board, but if they are detected, they have nowhere to run, so I'm guessing they might just blend in looking for an easy mark or two and then strike towards the end of the voyage.' McCarthy nodded in agreement.

'Makes sense. Once we're back alongside the pier they can jump ashore and disappear back into their city ratholes with their spoils.'

'Well, we're going to make sure that they not only leave empty-handed but in handcuffs. Make sure you keep yours handy.' Under his breath he said somewhat apologetically, 'I'll try not to mess things up again.'

Constable Irene McCarthy wordlessly accepts Jim's vague apology with a smile.

The rest of the voyage was sailed in perfect weather, relatively flat seas and a fresh breeze from the south-west kicking up white horses on the cobalt sea. Overhead, a single line of uniformly white clouds drifted along in stately procession like an exotic caravan in the skies.

The constables have continued to patrol keeping an eye on the dodgy trio. Alongside Mornington Pier, they become concerned that the crooks might disembark and make their play while on shore and return to Melbourne by train.

'But that would surely take hours,' reasoned McCarthy, 'and besides, they would need to know something of the train timetables.'

'Yes I think you're right Irene, these blokes would get lost this far from home. Well, let's see if they go ashore first and we'll take it from there.'

Hygeia tied up and lowered her gangway and before too long, the passengers were streaming up the steep hill to the park overlooking the bay where a game of cricket was planned, while the ladies select their picnic spot spreading a blanket on the grass under the huge cedar trees.

Jim and Irene watch the local kids fishing for mullet and squid along the pier, the dark ink stains left by the cephalopods on the wooden planking indicating success. The thought of eating the slimy squid made her stomach turn.

To err on the side of caution, they positioned themselves where they had a view of the gangway without being too obvious. But they shouldn't have worried as the trio of rogues took advantage of the bar being almost devoid of customers and were happily downing pints of cold beer and scoffing the free pickles, boiled eggs and nuts.

The undercover constables took a table in the restaurant, trying to stay out of sight of the wary young crooks and ordered a simple lunch of beef and bacon pie with vegetables, sure and certain that their quarry was settling in for a good old booze up in the bar.

'They won't want to take on too much of that grog or they'll be less than able when the time comes.'

'True. But it might make them less aware and easier to handle when we collar them.'

They both share a bit of a chuckle at the thought. 'Drink up lads, that'll be the last grog you have for a long while if we're lucky.' And as an afterthought he added, 'I must speak to the Captain about serving alcohol to minors.'

This time, oh glory be, Jim's luck was in and he and Irene nabbed the miscreants dead to rights. The pockets of their fence Razor

Wood were bulging with their ill-gotten loot, reassuring Jim that he wouldn't escape by jumping overboard for fear of sinking to the bottom under the weight.

They had watched fascinated as the gang systematically worked their way around the ship targeting preselected targets coming at them from different angles in different guises. The stolen goods passed off to Razor Woods who stood close to where the passengers will disembark ready to make a quick getaway. All of this had happened with military precision within the last half hour of the cruise as Hygiea approached Port Melbourne.

With immense satisfaction, Jim slapped the cuffs on Razor before he could blink.

'You've been a very naughty boy, young Master Woods, but I can assure you, you will no longer be a boy by the time you've done your porridge.'

Jim left him unable to move, handcuffed to the rail while he went and rounded up the rest of the gang.

'Irene, you bloody beauty.' He found her cuffing Ferret and Showbag to the back of a bench seat.

Daisy O'Connell and Sparra Dempsey have assisted her by providing a bit of muscle for which Irene was most grateful. She pointed at the men's toilet.

'Good work yourself,' she said triumphantly, 'you'll find that little rat Tweaky Thompson in there with one of the crew holding him down.'

'What?' Jim's flabbergasted, 'did we miss him?'

'He was apparently in reserve and my goodness, they needed extra hands to hold all their loot. Go get him Senior Constable.'

Jim got him alright slapping the cuffs on just a tad tight.

'If this doesn't make old Leather Lungs happy, then he's beyond help.'

'Do you think so?' said Irene, 'I think he was behind the door when they handed out the sense of humour.

CHAPTER 11

OCTOBER 1924

ONE THREAT DEPARTS, FOR NOW

Eugene was on a roll with his gambling recently. He had made a remarkable recovery from the brutal bashing he had received from the cuckolded husband of the beautiful Lucille Yarborough. One lesson learned the hard way. However, another lesson was yet to be learned and would prove even more damaging; never chase your losses.

Sir Rupert Yarborough had been so furious and massively humiliated by his wife's infidelity that he had stepped back from the various boards he served upon, leaving his business affairs in the hands of his most trusted colleagues. He retained his directorships and power of veto while continuing to make the important decisions affecting his enterprises by telephone or telegram. He felt the need for a break as he had taken on an enormous workload since arriving in Melbourne and a break would recharge his batteries and also side-step some of the embarrassing comments he had overheard here and there around town.

Needless to say, Eugene Bradfield breathed a sigh of relief when Yarborough's ship pulled away from the dock. He was not so gauche as to actually wave him off with streamers and a farewell banner but for peace of mind, confirmed Sir Rupert's departure with the newspapers shipping news and a discreet phone call to the shipping line.

So now with the memory of that violent clash fading quicker than his scars, he was back in the fray cutting out an attractive young lady from the herd now and again regardless of their attachments. He had found that his facial disfigurements had come with some distinct advantages, one of which was the sympathy showered on him by the opposite sex, although there were not too many males who would shed a tear of sympathy for the cad.

Eugene's stage appearances had dried up due to his lack of confidence. His make-up artist had guaranteed he would look as good as ever, but he rejected the offer as he sat dejected in front of the mirror, gazing wretchedly at his reflection.

'Dear God Letitia, I have enough powder, paint and foundation to cover a house. The very weight of it is intolerable.' Tearing the protective sheet away from his neck, he balled it up and hurled it at his reflection. 'No! It will never do. I'll just have to continue with the skin preparations you've been giving me and hope time will see an improvement.'

Saturdays found him at the track more often, enjoying the social atmosphere and the thrill of the racing. He had grafted himself onto a couple of the leading stables, opening up a rich vein of information that enabled him to land one or two very good betting triumphs.

It was at one race meeting that he bumped into a little group that included his theatrical agent Rhoda Day, who was accompanied by Hugo Marcovitz, the producer of the movie that Eugene had hoped for, and Elvira Rochester.

'Rhoda darling, how utterly delightful,' Eugene, at his charming best, graces her hand with a kiss, 'Elvira my dear how are you?' Elvira Rochester receives the same greeting. 'Well, I never, if it's not my old friend Hugo Marcovitz? Are you keeping these delightful ladies out of trouble on this beautiful afternoon?' Turning to Marcovitz, with a humble bow from the waist and a handshake proffered. 'Hugo my dear, dear man. May I call you Hugo? I am delighted to see you. Do we have your company for the afternoon?'

'Thank you Gene. May I call you Gene?'

'You may call me anything, so long as you don't call me late for an audition.' Everyone laughs politely at Eugene's droll little witticism.

In seconds, Eugene has organised a table and champagne to entertain the ladies answering their innocent questions about the various horses, jockeys and trainers. Hugo Marcovitz spends time reading the form guide which he confesses may as well be in Latin for all the sense it made to him. Now and then, the group was interrupted by a strange little man Skinny Jackson who rans up and whispered in Eugene's ear and received either a shake of the head or a slip of paper.

'Eugene darling, I am so dreadfully sorry that you were unavailable for my movie,' Elvira stated sincerely, using a beautiful silk and ivory fan to cool her over-made-up face. 'But I'm sure you understand the pressures under which we labour in the business darling. Our backers, impatient swine that they are, cannot tolerate any delay in getting their dividends back into the bank, so despite you being perfect for the role we had to forge bravely ahead.'

Eugene feigns sympathy, 'Such is life my dear, perfectly understandable, but one lives in hope that another opportunity may pass my way.'

'I am going to say something now Gene and I want you to understand that it's meant in the kindest possible way.' Elvira lays a hand on Eugene's forearm, fan still pumping as she casts a quick glance toward Hugo, possibly for approval or to make sure he was listening.

'Your face.' Here she pauses and looks deep into his eyes, trying to convey sincerity. 'Your recent, aah, shall we say *experience* has changed your appearance and here I'm being quite sincere. It has added an air of mystery, of worldliness, am I being too dramatic to say a veneer of mystique.'

Eugen had coloured and appeared a little at odds with her words, which she had carefully framed to bolster the insecure actor's confidence.

Rhoda, wishing to add her two-pence worth, while anticipating a mild blow-up jumped in quickly. 'Now Gene darling please listen to El.'

Eugene was staring at El open-mouthed, looking shocked but absorbing her every word.

'Gene, here it is. I believe the change in your appearance will lead you into more and better opportunities and I already have a script I would like you to read.'

'Why Rhoda, I would be delighted and very thankful for the opportunity.'

'Rhoda is perfectly correct, Gene. Your face now has a depth of character that will be brought out on the big screen.' And in an almost apologetic tone Hugo Marcovitz adds, 'some of our most successful actors have similar aah shall we say *distinguishing* features.'

Eugene nods as though agreeing with every word while trying to picture those highly successful types, without much luck. He's not so clumsy as to ask just which ones specifically.

Rhoda was about to chime in again when the odd little man scuttles in and taps Eugene's shoulder.

'Yes, Mr Jackson, how did we go?'

Skinny Jackson shook his head, 'A very heavy track sir.' and Eugene cursed. He took out a notebook, scribbled in it and handed the torn-out sheet to Jackson and muttered 'A hundred the win.' Jackson dashes out again. 'And find a hairbrush, you scruffy individual.' Eugene shouted after him.

'Who is that odd little man Gene? He looks familiar,' queried Rhoda.

'He's my man from the theatre darling, I bring him along to the track to run my bets for me, so as I have more time to attend to you gorgeous ladies.'

'Oh Gene,' she responded with a laugh, 'you are so full of shit you sweet man.'

Skinny Jackson was kept busy by Eugene over the last three races sans hairbrush. Ordinarily, Martin, as he prefers, was well groomed, but he had been in a scuffle defending his employer. A push of young coves who were obviously readers of the Babe Ruth (*The Truth* Newspaper) recognised Skinny and mouthed off about Eugene. Skinny responded as a man should and decked the kingpin with a beautifully timed left hook.

But in light of his bosses' negative comments about his looks, he might take a different tack next time. Eugene and Rhoda arranged a reading of Elvira's script at her office the following week.

Hugo surprisingly asked if he could be there for the read and was, of course, included.

The conversation then returned to industry gossip, but Eugene hardly hears a word.

He was trying to supress his excitement about movies; the silver screen, the new exciting medium, oh Dear God, who knew where that might take him?

Eugene was still bubbling about the opportunity given to him. Especially when he was at such a low personal ebb depressed by the damage to his major asset, that was, his looks. His handsome visage had graced many billboards across the country, large format images that sent a thrill up his spine each time he saw them. Eugene had always appeared almost as a twin to screen idol John Barrymore but now felt he looked more like Lon Chaney star of horror movies. Tragically, fate would see Gene's life imitate John Barrymore's; mourned for the loss of his grace and wit at the track or card table as much as for his brilliance at the height of his acting career. He had doubted that the face he now possessed would ever hold pride of place on another poster. At best, he might share the background with the other less important cast members except that now he has received this unsolicited compliment that may just open another door on his career.

In the meantime, he had committed one of the cardinal sins of punting. First, he failed to concentrate and second, he had begun to chase losses. After the ninth race, Skinny returned and stood at the top of the stairs in Eugene's line of sight and when eye contact was made, he indicated that his boss should join him there.

Eugene excuses himself and crosses the floor, suddenly realising he may have been a tad rash with his most recent bets.

'Sir, Mr Plowright has asked for you to speak with him. I think he might want you to settle up sir.'

'Mr Jackson, thank you for your service today. Here is your fee.' He passed over the appropriate bills, and rested his hand on Mr Jackson's upper arm. Leaning close he hissed, 'Mr Jackson, I will settle up in my own time. in the mean-while I don't care what you think.' He held a threatening finger in Jackson's face, 'I still have a solid relationship with Gordon Plowright so keep that big trap of yours firmly shut, do ya hear?'

There was no way on God's earth that Jackson was going to keep mum on this choice bit of gossip and before Eugene had even cleared the racetrack, word had got around. Out of luck, Eugene would find avenues to credit tightening up across town.

When Eugene returned to his hotel, he found Plowright wasn't the only one looking to balance the books. Curly Barker was waiting for him with a message from John Wren.

'Where money's concerned, Mr Bradfield, friendship only goes so far and you 'ave passed that point some time ago. Now Mr Wren is asking when he can expect you to settle sir.'

'Mr Wren need not lose any sleep over me, old boy.' Eugene tried hard to remain calm, 'Please pass my regards to Mr Wren and assure him my obligations will be met.' Striking a confident posture he brashly inserted his cigarette holder into his mouth and arched his left eyebrow in best dramatic fashion.

Curly loomed, almost chesting Eugene, his foul breath once again causing him to blanch, as he swipes the cigarette holder out of Eugene's mouth with a large rough hand.

'Mr Wren don't lose no sleep over the likes o' you Bradfield. Just see ya do or yez know what to expect,' his spittle spraying Eugene's face liberally.

Good God, does this man ever clean his teeth? thought Eugene, *his breath could peel the paint off a barn door.*

The now thoroughly anxious actor trudged wearily through the foyer, heading for the bar when he hears his name called. It's his new friend Captain Jenkins.

'What ho Bradfield,' Jenkins doing his best PG Wodehouse, 'you look like a man who has just lost his best friend.' Jenkins greets Eugene with a pat on the back. 'Come on old chap, it can't be all that bad. Join me in a scotch and tell the captain all about it.'

Eugene has a light bulb moment. He needed money and Jenkins had it.

Inversely, Captain Jenkins was on the lookout for vulnerable marks and he believed he'd just found another one.

They adjourned to the saloon bar and occupied a snug booth that gives them privacy. Both men had an agenda and they were mentally rehearsing their lines, hoping to pull it off.

'Don't tell me Gene, you've had a bad day at the races.'

'I'm afraid I have, I'm afraid I have.' He drops his head into his hands in the dramatic style he has practised his whole adult life. 'Oh God, what a fool I am. What have I done?'

'Ah look, here's our drinks.' The waiter carefully put down two coasters and a crystal tumbler of scotch on each. 'Come on Gene, take a dram. I'm sure you'll feel better.'

'I would have felt better if that blasted twenty to one chaff bandit hadn't gotten across the line half a head in front of my selection. Blast and damn, where do they get these damned nags?'

'Please Eugene, excuse my saying so, but do I take it sir you may have bottomed out?'

Cagey Eugene doesn't want to appear destitute, which he technically was, as it may cruel his next move which was to relieve his military friend of a sum of money sufficient to get that accursed criminal element off his back. 'Oh, if *only* I could get through life without coming into contact with the lower orders,' he mumbles.

'What's that Gene, I didn't quite catch you?'

Reggie Watford, aka Captain Jenkins was waiting for the desperate punter to call for the lifeline which he will cast with some feigned reluctance. He must wait patiently for the right moment, nursing Bradfield along while metaphorically laying the trail of breadcrumbs all the way into his trap.

'No, my dear captain, I am a long way from bottomed out as you put it. Just a temporary ebbing in the tidal flow of my finances. But I am jiggered until a fresh transfer from my London bankers arrives on Thursday week.'

Aah, there's the hand waving above the waves, thinks Jenkins, his patience rewarded.

There the hook is baited, now to wait for the fish to tug on the line, Eugene thought.

There can only be one winner from this verbal fencing. Each dualist believes he has the better of the other, but a keen observer would surely have the captain ahead on points. He has control as he has the gold and it's true that he who has the gold…

'If this is only a short-term problem surely your bank will see you right Gene?'

'Oh dear, you are an innocent dear boy, banks don't like gamblers full stop and they view a losing gambler like a leper in a bathhouse.' Eugene decided to share a little common knowledge with this innocent. 'Besides, a gentleman doesn't tell his banker anything about his sporting life, heavens we'd all be wound up if that were the case, despite the fact that some of the biggest gamblers I know are bank managers.'

'I am concerned for you.' Jenkins' voice dripped with sympathy, 'Please let me help you with a loan. No one needs to know about it, it will be simply one gentleman helping another and when your London bank comes through, we can square things up again.' He opens his hands in a gesture of trust and sincerity. 'What do you say?'

Eugene projects the anxiety and confusion of a man torn. He has the life ring firmly in his grasp but does not wish the life saver to know how glad he was of it.

'Look this is terribly embarrassing, but the fact is my money won't come through quickly enough to satisfy the thugs I owe it to. Oh, my dear Captain, what have I done to put myself in the hands of these usurious thugs?'

'Never mind all that old chap, how much do you need?'

Eugene does a great job playing the man whose morality has been deeply assaulted while he tosses around in his mind several differing sums. The real amount he was owing, or a lesser amount that would be more palatable to the captain, or perhaps a far larger amount from a man to whom money was a mere bagatelle. He decided on the latter, to give himself some breathing space.

'Captain, it pains me to tell you and I won't think badly of you if you refuse. You are a gentleman and an officer and I respect you greatly but…' Here he was loath to reveal the extent of his liability. He takes a deep breath and holds it.

'Come on man, you've made it clear that we would have an obligation here based on friendship and trust.'

'Oh, very well then, fifteen hundred pounds, that's it. I need fifteen hundred.'

Eugene slaps the table in emphasise, and sits back in his chair looking the captain firmly in the eye.

'Phew! That's quite a sum Gene.' The captain need not feign shock. 'I can see now why you've been so downhearted. But look, I made an offer and I will see it through, so now relax and finish your scotch while I get a fresh one in.' He signalled the waiter who had been hovering in the background, having correctly identified drinkers who would demand more than one round.

'Obviously Eugene, I don't carry quite that amount of cash on my person,' he said with sardonic chuckle, 'and I'll be required to pay a visit to my bank in the morning to acquire the cash. I assume you'll want cash in dealing with these types. Am I wrong?'

'No sir you are not, I don't believe they favour promissory notes.' Relieved, Eugene feels he can breathe again. Their attentive waiter arrived with their second scotch and Eugene and Jenkins salute each other and sip their whiskeys.

The next morning, the two met for lunch in the hotel restaurant and Captain Jenkins made quite a show of brandishing a shiny leather valise that he placed on the vacant chair beside him. Eugene couldn't take his eyes off it.

Instead of handing over the wads of currency, Jenkins removes a file and places it on the table. He takes out his fountain pen and deliberately and showily removes the cap from it. Next he opens the file taking a single sheet of paper from it covered with closely typed copy and with a flourish signs the bottom of it. All the while, Eugene's eyes follow his performance.

'Now Gene, I have taken my money from the bank and have it here for you, but as anyone in business will tell you, never hand over large sums of money without some form of security 'eh?

At the risk of embarrassing you, may I ask you to simply sign the document there and here?' The complete irony of this advice was lost on the shyster.

'Oh aah, one moment, may I read it first Captain?'

'But of course, sir. What man would sign a binding agreement without perusing it?'

Eugene was so eager, so desperate for the cash from that satchel that his ego would not allow him to admit to suffering short sightedness and the writing appeared as a blur. The consummate actor made a good show of scanning the handwritten document in detail, even making appropriate noises as he did so.

'Well, that appears to be fair and reasonable Captain, I am happy and most grateful for your assistance. Pen? If I may.'

Barely able to contain the smirk that was creeping across his face, Captain Jenkins passes his pen to the foolish man across the table. He has this actor wrapped up in the silken strands of personal obligation.

The deal was done, Jenkins pocketed the carefully folded document and Eugene's shaking hand grasps the valise with its precious contents to his heart as their meals are placed before them.

Eugene raises his glass and proposes a toast.

'A toast to a good friend, from a friend in need. God bless you sir, my everlasting thanks.'

'What are friends for? Here's to your future prosperity sir.'

We'll see how thankful you are if you fail to repay that loan, thought the captain.

Now I have a chance to get back in the game and recover my losses, thinks Eugene.

Both men knew that the money would be gone in a flash and the prospect of it being repaid was nil, each smiling like a Cheshire Cat. Captain Jenkins would not be the loser. He would own the snobbish little fool and would bleed him, and bleed him, to the last drop.

Eugene strongly suspected that the man styling himself as Captain Jenkins was a fraud, but his money was still good and when the pressure was applied to repay the loan, then Eugene would do what any good citizen should do and report him to the fraud squad.

Word of the day: *duplicity*.?

CHAPTER 12

MID OCTOBER 1924

IT'S A JUNGLE REALLY

The lad was no more than twelve but looked much older, as all these backstreet ruffians did. He appeared from a dark alley as the two gentlemen walked down the centre of the sideroad on their way to their regular poker game carrying more cash than was wise. They had exited a taxi cab at the end of the street and were chatting about whom they could expect to meet and their chances of taking the pot that night.

The untidy wafer-thin youth had emerged from the shadows and stood in their path. The urchin knew well where these two silver-tails were headed and that they were likely to be carrying plenty of cash on them. He calculated that they might be persuaded to spare a shilling or two if he was lucky. He knew he was taking a great risk, the casino owner Matthias Vogel, known as The German was very protective of his patrons. The scallywag's gnawing hunger made the risk worthwhile. He hadn't eaten for two days and that had been some dried-out cheese and a crust of bread so hard he had to soak it in a horse trough to soften it.

"Ullo gents' lovely night fer a stroll 'eh? Don't s'pose yez could spare a deener or two for a bloke ta git a feed could yez?' From his trouser pocket he allowed a glimpse of a wicked looking blade and as his demand sinks in, he checks his surrounds to ensure his escape route was clear should this go wrong.

Knowing the area like the back of his hand gave the little assailant confidence with all its myriad laneways, backyards, empty warehouses and gutted buildings all offering a bolthole where he knew they would never catch him if he runs.

The two startled gents know it's far better to give the blasted rogue what he wants than to risk being slashed by that knife. They each respond to the request with a florin each and a curse to go with it flung at the feet of the rapscallion who snatches up the coins and scampers away like a rat into the dark recesses of a laneway.

'God blast that little swine!' said the first gent, 'The city's overrun with rats and thieves and they should all be dealt with in the same manner mark my words.'

'I thought The German had put the frighteners on those scum and provided protection around here. I'll have a word with him in no uncertain terms.'

Another few paces and they find sanctuary behind a large red industrial doorway. The door, surprisingly, was ajar and reveals a stairway that takes them up to the first floor where there was another heavy-duty door. But this next one was firmly bolted and guarded by a large hard looking scoundrel who demands to know 'oo sentcha?'

'Never mind who sent us you blockhead,' said the first gent. 'Why aren't you looking after your patrons on the street? We were just accosted by a ne'er-do-well with a knife.'

The disappointing response to their complaint was an unintelligible grunt as the big thug opened the door for them, ushering them into a smoke-filled room with a number of tables spread around the space. Thankfully, the bar at their right was open and inviting after their experience. Some of the tables were still empty at this time of night, waiting for the theatre crowd perhaps, and others were given over to Blackjack or roulette. In the far corner was the high stakes table the two recent arrivals were heading for.

They were greeted warmly by their host, a notorious illegal bookmaker, standover man and pawn shop owner. 'Mine host' Matthias Vogel stood to one side of the group watching the cards fall. He was built rangy and long-legged, standing six foot two inches, dressed in a perfectly cut three-piece pinstripe suit set off by gold cufflinks and bracelet that caught the light and the eye of the two arrivals. Vogel was well-groomed with a black neatly trimmed military moustache that highlighted his glistening white teeth as he smiled and shook their hands.

Matthias had arrived in Melbourne in first class passage as a European emigrant from war torn Austria. He had occupied a first-class cabin on the journey out, always appearing for meals in the ship's saloon well-dressed and displaying respect and courtesy to his fellow passengers.

On the third night of the voyage, he had noticed an interest in cards from several of the gentlemen passengers who were already displaying symptoms of boredom. The suggestion of a game of cards was leapt upon and so began a nightly routine of cards and whisky after the women had dined and departed to their cabins, most of whom were grateful to be out of sight while they gave themselves over to mal de mare.

Playing cautiously over the course of the voyage, Vogel accumulated sufficient winnings to cover the cost of his travel without making enemies of his fellow travellers.

Matthias had equipped himself with the very finest travel luggage, amongst which was one nondescript strong box. A firm believer in the power of cash in the major currency's the box contained the hard-won results of his not so gentlemanly activities in his homeland and the gains made in London. Most of which was ill-gotten.

The box contained jewellery, gold coins and some fine art rolled up tight and sealed in waterproof cloth. It also contained a large amount of English currency, which he was assured would be accepted here in this English colony by the unsophisticated peasants that inhabited the land.

When he stood and stretched his back, he was seen to be as lean as a garden stake. That lack of muscle had fooled one or two who thought he was a weakling who could be taken easily; he was not.

They paid for their poor judgement painfully and once fatally. Matthias never even looked back as his assailant bled out on the cobblestones of his old hometown of Graz near the border of Slovenia. With a price on his head, he had gathered his worldly (stolen) goods and slipped across the border into Slovenia and made his way across country, finding his way to Trieste. Here, the owner of a large fishing boat took him across the Adriatic to San Marino for a handsome fee where he met with some corrupt officials who were easily bribed into providing passage on a ship to England.

While trying to convert his stolen jewellery into cash, he ran into trouble once again and was forced to defend himself with extreme violence.

Fortunately, he had traded enough to give him the cash to equip himself as a European gentleman and book passage to Australia where he intended to make his life anew.

Once in Australia, it didn't take him long to use his cash and gold to establish himself in the business of pawnbroking. He realised quickly that he had landed in a nation of gamblers as every second customer in his shop wanting short-term loans were pawning goods to cover their gambling losses. He decided to cut out the middle-man (himself) and open up his own casino. He was smart enough to keep the lucrative pawn broking business operating that guaranteed a cash flow supporting the high stakes gambling club until it was in profit.

The site for Matthias' club was a property he purchased from a wool trader who moved on to larger premises. The property was perfect for the purpose in the industrial area south of the city just across Princes Bridge.

He converted part of the office area into a neat little apartment with a one-way glass panel that enabled him to keep an eye on the floor. The building had several exits that could be utilised if raided, including one in the small office that was cleverly concealed by a bookcase. Once again, wise in the world of criminality, he had ensured his security with a hefty bribe paid to the local senior cop to keep him off his back and protect him from other criminals with take-over lust in their eyes. Well paid and trusted henchmen protected Matthias in the event of attempted robbery.

The wealthy devotees of poker, some of whom travelled down Toorak Road from their fine homes, would arrive by cab alighting discreetly several doors away from their destination in a minor side street running off City Road.

The jackals of society, attracted to the area by the scent of money, planned to rob successful gamblers as they left the premises to head home. This required a pair of eyes on the inside watching the tables to see who won and who lost. No point pulling a stick up on a loser for obvious reasons. The target would be shadowed out of the door so that the watching thieves would be called into action by a simple hand signal.

After this had occurred once or twice, The German had to take action to protect his patrons and his casino and he did so in a manner that was never forgotten by street gangs south of the Yarra River. He had his eye on a particular little prat who was always present in the casino, but never put so much as a shilling on the tables.

Then he noticed that sly sawn-off rat was always there when a robbery had been staged. Putting two and two together, he prepared his men for a job they would do well and relish.

The German noticed a big winner leaving the club and that he was tailed out the door by the artful one, who followed at a discreet distance down the stairs to street level.

Vogel, convinced this was going to be a robbery, sprang his trap. The two hold up men were nabbed dead to rights and the devious spotter was held as well. Vogel had them stripped naked and whipped their naked hides. They were then dragged down the street to be hurled screaming into the toxic waters of the Yarra River to sink or swim. Vogel couldn't care less one way or the other if they could swim and as it happened, only one made it back to the bank. Word spread quickly and anyone wanting to test The Germans resolve after that did so at their own risk.

As a result, armed robbery in the area was at almost non-existent levels, a circumstance the police commissioner claimed credit for. If only the public knew the truth.

A personal favourite of The German was the mercurial actor Eugene Bradfield who graced his casino on a regular basis and almost always accompanied by a number of acolytes who shed money like autumn leaves. Vogel was more than happy to provide this star of the theatre a line of credit that was usually called on by Bradfield when he had a bad run, but happily he was a better card player than he was a judge of equine flesh. His preferred game was poker and he was always warmly welcomed to the high rollers table. Minimum bet ten pounds and the maximum was agreed by general consensus. When the cards were running hot for Eugene, he would routinely bet a hundred on one turn of the cards. He had been known to have laid two hundred pounds worth of chips on the table and bluff the opposition out of a pot worth over eight hundred pounds with a pair of deuces in hand.

Predictably, as a compulsive gambler, Eugene Bradfield on the very same evening as he had been handed salvation by Captain Jenkins, walked through the door of the Germans casino. With his valise bulging with the huge wad of borrowed notes and a level of optimism out of all proportion found himself warmly welcomed by Vogel himself.

'Mr Bradfield sir, alvays an honour, please allow us to take your hat and coat,' Bradfield kept a firm grip on his valise as he hands hat and coat to a steward, 'Villiam take care of zese for Mr Bradfield.'

Eugene was shown to the high stakes poker game, as though he needed guidance, his feet would find their way in his sleep. He did appreciate the courtesy, however.

The air over the table was thick with cigar and pipe smoke, the ashtrays already overflowing. A variety of glasses empty and otherwise crowd the players' elbows and Vogel barked an order to the staff to clean up and take fresh drinks.

Eugene took his place and was issued with a stack of chips to the value of a thousand pounds. Before he can pick up his hand, a glass of scotch was placed before him along with a large, quality Cuban cigar. The table demanded a ten-pound ante on the first card. The first hand was uninspiring and he folds. The second hand was a little better but still too weak, but it gives him a chance to throw out some false 'tells' that will lead the other players up the wrong path later. Twenty down and he hasn't played a hand yet. It goes like this for a few more hands until he was dealt two aces and a queen. He picks up another ace and a queen for a full house and carefully raises by twenty. They take the bait and the pool grows by fifties, and then hundreds. Eugene sits patiently watching and calls with a hundred of his own. The players show their cards and are a little dismayed to see Eugene's hand. No one beats a full house, so he scoops the pool and he's back to even.

All a man could do was watch the fall of the cards and hope the Gods of poker grant him a win or two. Eugene continued to play conservatively and has those wins, enjoying himself and getting a feel for the cards.

A couple of mediocre hands win him just over a hundred pounds. The rest of the table were falling for his fake tells, but that won't last long. His ante goes out to join the other chips in the pot and the cards are dealt. He has several superstitions like most players and one dictates that he never looks at his cards until the deal was complete. Eugene scooped up his cards fanning them out, and eyeballed them, hoping for some substance. It's not too bad. Four red cards, hearts and diamonds giving him a reasonable chance for a flush. He drops the odd card and receives its replacement, another heart. He has a flush, a strong hand in poker. This was where he might accidentally show a 'tell,' an indication that he's holding a strong hand. Now he has to be very calm and deliberately dropped his head slightly to indicate disappointment. The move was picked up all around the table as shoulders straighten and hands involuntarily flicker toward the players' stack as a tactic forms in their minds. Question is, go heavy and put Eugene out? Or play it slow and see what develops?

Eugene's turn comes around, he eases out fifty, which throws everyone off. What the dickens? Was he holding two pair and hoping for a full house again or was he bluffing?

His involuntary body language earlier said he was bluffing. Chips are pushed forward, lifting the pot higher, Eugene drops another fifty on the table and two players lose their nerve and drop out.

One player was watching Eugene with a steely gaze and he was certain that if he wasn't bluffing, he wouldn't have a very strong hand. Laurence was a successful businessman and dedicated gambler who had seen Eugene in action at the racetrack and knew he was inclined to reckless betting. He was always looking for the big score riding the high and lows of fortune and always on the edge. Brown decides he's bluffing and he'll take him on.

'Sir, I will see your fifty and raise you a hundred.' It was said with no emotion as he adjusted the cigar in the corner of his mouth and took a puff.

There was a flutter of cards and a slap as hands are thrown in or slammed down in disgust around the table, leaving just the two antagonists.

Eugene felt an icy finger on his heart but was committed to his ploy. He could throw his hand in or take Brown on. To hell with it, Brown has only won one or two small pots, he must be bluffing. He took a long pull on his cigar and exhales the rich tobacco smoke, endeavouring to look calm and collected.

'And my hundred said you need to pay more Mr Brown if you wish to see my cards.'

'Gladly, Mr Bradfield gladly, let's make it another hundred, shall we?'

Eugene's blood rose and its pressure drives all common sense out of his head, replacing it with adrenaline. A smart play at this stage would be to add the hundred to the pot and take a look at Brown's hand, after all, a flush was a pretty strong hand ranking as the fifth highest but not unbeatable by any means. Doing the sensible thing was far from being Eugene's strong suit when it comes to betting. Instead of forcing a showdown, he decides to increase his bet hoping to force Brown to drop. He sips his scotch and considers the cards in his hand, looking at them as if he hadn't seen them before and then, with what he hopes was an inscrutable smile, pushes out a stack of five hundred pounds in chips.

'Mr Brown, I have raised you five hundred, your move sir.'

'Well sir, now we are going to a place I feel most comfortable. I'll see your five hundred and raise you another five hundred.'

Eugene attracts the dealer's attention. 'I need more chips if you would be so kind.' He removes the large leather wallet from his inside coat pocket and counts out a thousand pounds, for which he receives that amount in chips delivered across the table.

'You know dealer, I have a strong feeling I might be in for a long battle here, please may I have another thousand?' This was another shot at destabilising his opponent mentally.

Eyebrows are raised around the table that has suddenly become crowded with spectators drawn to the table by the hubbub and electricity in the air. 'Mr Brown, it seems that you are determined to continue so let's see what you're made of, shall we?' Eugene scoops up the first stack of chips passed across from the dealer and with great deliberation places them in the pot wearing his inscrutable smile again. Unfortunately, rising nervous bile defeats his facial expression turning it into more of a grimace.

'Mr Bradfield, I must, as I have done many times when you were on the stage, applaud a magnificent performance. But now it's time for the curtain to come down and take our bows. I'll see your thousand.'

Eugene was sure he'd either drop out (most unlikely) or continue to raise the betting, so he was a little flummoxed now being expected to lay down his cards.

The whole room holds its collective breath as Eugene's cards are revealed. A chorus of voices announced it. 'A flush!'

All eyes turn to Brown, who sits there enigmatically, his cards still face down before him. Now it's his turn to act deadpan and cool. He puffs on the last inch and a half of his Cuban and locks eyes on Eugene through the exhaled smoke. Without looking down, he flips his cards over and announces, 'Full house, eights over two's.'

A cheer goes up and Brown stands and bows to his audience, laughing and calling for a fresh scotch and one for Eugene who, at that moment looked like he had been punched in the midriff as the blood drained from his face.

Eugene's eyes followed the multi coloured pile of chips as they are raked in by the winner, taking his hopes of redemption with them. He watched in disgust as Brown slowly and ostentatiously counts his winnings, a breach of etiquette and one of Eugene's primary superstitions. Eugene could drive a knife into the bastard's ribs at this point. He had run his line of credit with Vogel down to zero and lost half the cash he borrowed from the captain. What should he do? He was in a very precarious situation. He was still into the gangsters for a pile and Jenkins for fifteen hundred pounds,

All he has to his name are the remnants of Jenkins' loan in his pocket. Common sense would dictate that he should get up from the table and leave immediately, but common sense and Eugene were never close allies. What he really should be doing was leaving the country, and fast. Word of this will get around like greased lightning. Before that regrettable leak he had one more chance at survival. He was still holding a thousand pounds. That was more than he needed, more than any gambler needed, to get into the game. It is a well-known theory that a compulsive gambler gambles to lose and will not stop until he reaches that inevitable point. *But I'm not a compulsive gambler*, he thought, reassuring himself, *I'm a card player and I'm still in the game.*

There was still a bit of fuss going on over Brown's big score and Eugene waited until it settles down and invites players back to the table.

'Gentlemen, are we still playing?'

Two hours later, Eugene leaves the club and enters a cab that Vogel has called for him. His wallet is a little lighter than when he arrived, despite making a gallant comeback playing a shrewd game and not allowing himself to be drawn into a head-butting contest that almost took everything he had. Before he boarded the cab, he vomited quietly into the gutter and hands shaking and stomach churning he goes on his way. He would retire to his apartment and calm his nerves with a cognac and another cigar before sleeping.

CHAPTER 13
SEPTEMBER 1924
THE COLD IS NOT THE REAL DANGER BEWARE, A BLUE EYED CHILD

'Strike me lucky Bobby boy, this bloody kids got a bit of cheek to take us on?'

The police pair had confronted the skinny runt in relation to a series of shoplifting incidents along the Smith Street shopping strip in Collingwood.

The police in question were Bob Barrows and Bluey Farnsworth, who had recently been patrolling in the dark heart of the Fitzroy slums. An impoverished area of shanty shacks, outside toilets and laundries in corrugated iron sheds adorning the fringes of the industrial zone. All manner of manufacturing was conducted in this area providing employment for hundreds, but there were always those that could not or would not work.

The kid in question had come to the attention of the police on more than one occasion. His criminal career kicked off even before the recent turbulent Great Police strike of 1923. With the streets wide open, he had joined in the blatant looting of some local stores enjoying temporary free rein. He had already been earmarked by the local patrol as a potential troublemaker training as a pickpocket with one of the gangs.

If they had known the background of this cheeky kid, they may have been a bit more circumspect in handling him. He appeared as a bright eyed, pleasant looking yet grubby underfed young lad, but he was more akin to a scorpion with a lethal sting in his tail. His sting took the shape of a straight razor fitted into the waistband of his shabby trousers. Constable Barrows stepped forward, swiftly grasping the youth by the left arm. A split second later he staggered back, arterial blood spurting from a gash under his upper arm as his assailant disappears into the maze of alleyways.

'Oh Christ, I think he's done for me.' The shocked young policeman cried as Constable Farnsworth struggles to stem the blood flow from his colleagues' potentially fatal injury. The Constable whips off his belt and applies it as a tourniquet to his colleagues' arm and with the blood flow staunched temporarily assists Barrows to the main road of Brunswick Street hopefully to flag down a motor vehicle to assist him to the nearest hospital emergency at Saint Vincent's on Victoria Street.

Constable Barrows can't expect too much sympathy or support from his employer, who places him in harm's way. No medals, no commendations, no compensation. Just harden up and get on with it. He counts himself lucky to have his medical bills paid. Such were the career benefits of a serving constable in Victoria Police in the mid nineteen twenties

There was, however, another side to the coin that was in its infancy.

The government had introduced six o'clock closing in 1916 that closed two thousand hotels. While this was a success in reducing public drunkenness, it created an insatiable demand that was met by illicit liquor stores and back street establishments selling alcoholic beverages of a wide variety to a still thirsty public. The determined drinkers were drowning their sorrows with some highly toxic brews that left them either blind or dead.

The real threat to society was not crime, but crushing poverty; the mother of desperation. There were three distinct classes in metropolitan Melbourne. As always, at the top of the tree were the wealthy elite who enjoyed a princely lifestyle and influence. Their lifestyles underwritten by generous tax concessions, a class that had never experienced hunger or cold.

The wage earners were still an amorphous middle-class group, enjoying reasonably comfortable housing with access to good food and fashions. Many owned and drove motor cars and took regular holidays to the beach in summer or the ski-fields in Winter. The working class subsisted on low wages, barely surviving one week to the next.

The poor and unemployed lived in shocking conditions in dark shanties in narrow laneways, suffering malnutrition and all the diseases that swept through slum precincts the world over. There was no such thing as liveable welfare, so if the breadwinner lost his job or his life, there was no safety net for the family left behind. They simply had to scrape a living by any means. An age pension had been introduced in 1900 for those over 65. A disability pension and a maternity allowance was introduced a couple of years later, but neither was adequate.

The result of this paucity of government support was a substantial level of poverty across Australia in which women and their families were inexorably trapped. Even the widows of Australia's gallant war dead were basically ignored. The pension for widows of private soldiers was set at one pound per week.

Desperate mothers were known to boil weeds or whatever they could find, such as discarded cabbage stalks scrounged from garbage bins along with other 'trash' to provide some sustenance for their children.

These were conditions that should have bred an epidemic of lawlessness and disease, and it was a minor miracle that it hadn't. Senior Constable Jim Foley was well educated and well-read, and being well aware of these social shortcomings that caused so much pain to the poor tended to go a bit softly on any miscreants from this demographic. This in turn, led to him bumping heads with his superiors who held to an unswerving hard-line approach.

'If they done the crime, an' they get caught, they can expect a hard boot up the arse,' Sergeant Leather Lungs Manifold bellowed, 'it's how the game is played. If ya want respect' ya gotta earn it.'

Constable Jim Foley was unlike most coppers, especially those on the beat. He was a man who read the finance columns and studied politics. He was not a philosopher or economist, but he was a fairly competent student of human nature, society and criminality. Discussing the situation with his uncle, the Chief Superintendent gave him no further insight. His uncle was an old time hard headed copper with a firm belief in the deterrent value of rap over the head with his lead weighted truncheon and capital punishment.

And 'anyway if you hang 'em there's one thing for sure, they won't by God offend again.' This cold-hearted sentiment was always followed by a great guffaw of laughter, as though it was the first time he'd said it.

Jim confided in a friend that his uncle thought that hanging was almost being soft on crime.

'Are you serious Jim? That was his preference?'

'Probably the old medieval thing, you know, 'Hung, drawn and quartered." Jim laughs ironically.

'Mind you, there is no reason on earth to keep some of these murderers alive, but there's always a chance we get the wrong man and there's no going back from a death sentence.'

Despite his egalitarian attitudes, Jim continued to pursue a career, studying hard and passing his exams at each level. Sadly for the young eager crime fighters, there was very little *organised* crime in their city at that time. Nor was there a rash of serial killings or seemingly unsolvable murders or conspiracies upon which to put their new-found skills to work. But there was no shortage of petty criminals and ruffians of all stripes creating a never-ending stream of street crime.

Certainly there was no Chicago style organised crime, which was not to say there wasn't a criminal subculture. There were certainly plenty of criminals and dangerous ones at that to tangle with. If only he could get a chance.

There was one word from the wise worth its salt. Follow the money. If you followed the money, inevitably you would find someone from the wrong side of life hanging about looking for the main chance and one of Melbourne's biggest chancers, was a sawn-off runt by the name of Joseph Taylor known colloquially as Squizzy Taylor. Squizzy was a pint-sized bully who could pull off a bank robbery or run a two-up school on the same day but was mostly a licentious crook with his hand in as many criminal enterprises as could be imagined.

A reputation for extreme violence preceded Squizzy where ever he went, giving him an immediate edge over his victims.

Thoroughbred horse racing, greyhounds, pigeon races, two up and illicit card games were all grist to Squizzy's mill. And God help them that came between Squizzy and his target. He had been implicated in several murders and bank robberies, avoiding conviction on technicalities, but would not avoid his own murder in a shootout with another low life criminal John 'Snowy' Cutmore, who also died in the same gunfight from a bullet wound to the chest.

Squizzy Taylor was a notorious underworld figure, but not the only criminal willing to exercise violence to make a point. There were plenty of others who would chance their hand against the law.

The money trail led to the races at the key metropolitan tracks Caulfield, Mooney Valley and Flemington, where all of the Major races were held during the year and privately owned courses such as Epsom to the south of the city. Finally, there was greyhound racing at several venues around town for the truly desperate punters. There was no convenient official betting service in the suburbs requiring the punter to attend the track if he wanted to place a bet. By 1930 betting was permitted at racecourses with licensed bookmakers and the totalisator This restriction was the root cause of the growth in off course betting, Starting Price bookmakers flourished in every pub and neighbourhood. From little backyard SP's taking sixpenny each way bets from mums and dads in the blue-collar neighbourhoods and even in the dark alleyways of the slums. Young boys were employed as runners, collecting bets and delivering the winnings to the lucky few.

The big end of town, always had access to bookmakers through private men's clubs in the CBD where they could wager hundreds of pounds 'on the nod' and not a worry in the world. But that's the way of the world again, the rich enjoy what the poor can't access.

So it was, that the concentration of police powers focussed inevitably on the sixpenny punter at the bottom of the food chain while up there in the elite white churches such as

St Pauls and Scots Church the congregation were pure as the driven snow as far as the enforcement of the law went. God might bless them, but dark shadows moved amongst them.

Jim Foley had now after several years on the job patrolling the dangerous back street slums at night gained sufficient experience to be considered for promotion. His coup aboard The Hygeia with Constable Irene McCarthy the previous spring was a notable success that earned a letter in his file and lifted his personal profile within the force.

Senior Constable Foley was an introspective man who went about his job and did it to the best of his ability and where opportunity allowed he would use that opportunity to go one step further. Somehow, lately when he had taken one of those steps, he had managed to figuratively step into dog droppings.

But since then, it had been nothing but mundane, petty law breaking such as jay-walking as well as social crimes of spitting on the pavement. He was itching to have real success with a good 'collar' or two again.

It was Sunday afternoon at the end of a tiring week dealing with the low life types that were beginning to creep out of the foul back alleyways drawn out into the sunlight by the milder weather and the rich pickings presented by the many visitors to Melbourne for the spring racing carnival.

Apart from the 'professional' crimes of picking pockets and petty fraud there was another handful of minor offences such as a shoplifting charge that concerned a young mother snatching another woman's string bag of shopping and running off. Unluckily, she ran right past Constable Foley, who was alerted by the victim's cries. A fairly petty matter by some standards but frowned on by the judiciary who in all likelihood would sentence the female offender to confinement in one of the city's prisons. Jim Foley had been able to track the woman to the hovel where she lived, unable to shake off her pursuer even with her intimate knowledge of the back lanes and byways of the slum area.

The dark sodden alleyway that the offender called home stank of poverty and the putrid water running down the gutter formed by the cobblestones that lined the laneway. The drain was blocked with all manner of garbage, creating stagnant pools where mosquitos bred and children splashed about barefoot and careless.

Overflowing garbage cans spewing their contents into the mix were a rich source of scraps for the teeming hordes of rats that lived on what even the most destitute human couldn't.

Choking down his nausea, he had little difficulty locating the tumble-down hovel where he was sure the woman had disappeared. He had just glimpsed her as he rounded the corner into the laneway. He couldn't expect too much co-operation from the neighbours, so eventually by guess and by guile he located the right hovel and was shocked by the conditions he found. The woman dressed in filthy rags was shielding four equally impoverished children, all under the age of eight. All of them, mother and children, were suffering illness of one sort or another. Rickets was evident in the eldest, sallow starved complexions under the dirt caked faces. The shack was constructed from repurposed timber and sheets of rusty corrugated iron. Hessian potato sacks covered the spaces that served as windows and doors while the floors were bare earth with an open fire in an old oil drum in the corner that provided heating and some light.

She had lost no time in getting a battered frying pan on the fire in hopeful anticipation that her stolen bag might contain a sausage or a chop for her famished offspring. She must have been watching her victim filling her shopping list and grabbed the bag from her when she knew it contained protein for her kids. The children all appeared to be drooling in anticipation of what was probably their first and only meal in days and when Jim's big frame filled the doorway and his ominous shadow fell over the little tribe, they all recoiled, the eldest child grasping the youngest protectively and the mother letting out a startled cry.

Jim found himself uttering the clichéd words. 'Now then. what have we here?'

The mother dropped the pan into the fire and moved to protect her children. She sat beside a makeshift bed nursing her youngest daughter to her chest begging Jim not to arrest her as her husband was dead and she was all the kids had.

Jim had become inured to the poverty and deprivation of the poor from over exposure. Coming from an upper middle-class family who enjoyed privileges these people could not even dream of, he had met with unimaginable sights, sounds and smells on his patrols that he could not describe when pressed for details by his mother. Above all else was the stench of the slums, an assault on the senses that no words could possibly describe. As far back as the 1850s slums existed in inner Melbourne. Most often lacking basic plumbing or sewerage. Slum dwellers lived a squalid existence in ramshackle housing with leaky roofs and holes in the walls, their waste running into the lanes.

Jim was no longer moved by the sights that caused him to recoil from those horrors, having hardened as he conducted his duties. Prosperity had spread across the nation as the First War and Spanish influenza diminished in the populations' psyche. Quite clearly, it had not yet penetrated the crushing destitution that still lay like a grim black cloak over Melbourne's slum neighbourhoods.

Jim was not exactly insensitive, particularly where it came to children, but the sight that greeted him in this hovel caused him to gasp in shock. One child looked to be at death's door, lying on the pile of threadbare blankets and old hessian bags over layers of old newspapers used as extra insulation.

The sight of this social failure, his society's' negligence caused him step back in shock.

'Dear God, calm down madam, for the children's sake stay calm.' Jim held his hands palms out. 'What's your name?' he asked gently.

Reluctantly she stuttered, 'Miriam, sir. Please don't take me away, me son has the flu and will surely die if left on their ownsome.' Now on her knees hands clasped together, she begged Jim with all her heart and soul.

'Look you've been caught committing a blatant crime on the high street for which you could be gaoled and then where would your children be?' He can't help falling into lecture mode but realises how silly his words are feeling heat rising up his neck and cheeks with embarrassment. 'You need help and your young one needs a doctor. I cannot overlook the matter of the theft but I can get you some assistance.' He turns to leave, intending to find help. 'I'll be back very soon.'

Jim gets back to the high street and finds a telephone. After organising a doctor and a Salvation Army officer he knew, he returns to the hovel to give Miriam the little mother some good news. The hovel was empty, the bird had flown. The little mother and her brood are long gone and unlikely to be found.

Back at the station, Jim was asked to explain his decisions in the matter and found he was in hot water again.

'You are a Senior Constable,' roars his sergeant, his pipe held between his teeth spewing clouds of smoke and ash like a mini volcano, 'you are not employed as a welfare officer. If you wish to pursue such a career, perhaps you should report to Major Dalton of the Salvation Army around the bloody corner.' The Senior Sergeant leaps to his feet and leans across and thumps his desk to further express his anger, his thick black eyebrows almost meeting in the middle with his indignation. 'In the meantime, I have an outraged citizen on my doorstep wanting to know why that creature is not behind bars.' His voice finished at a volume that rattled the windows of his office and echoed around the building.

'What the hell?' queried a constable at the far end of the corridor.

'It's just Old Leather Lungs Manifold de-briefing Fumble Fingers Foley.'

Constable Jim Foley is required to complete a study sheet on community relations and police responsibilities before resuming his duties.

The family Sunday dinner was once again a tense affair despite the efforts of Isabelle Foley, Jim's mother, ordering the men to calm down and leave professional matters outside the door. Jim's uncle and aunt reside in a large rambling Victorian home inherited from Jim's forebears, whose wealth came from a rich vein of good luck in the Ballarat goldfields. The family's finances were solidly invested and carefully guarded to guarantee them all a comfortable and stable life.

The dinner was called by Isabelle to celebrate the elevation of Jim's uncle from Chief Superintendent to Deputy Police Commissioner Francis Foley by the Chief Commissioner Alexander Nicholson. The tone of the evening was set as soon as Jim stepped through the front door. The newly appointed DPC waited for him in his library, looking grim faced and angry.

'The very day I receive confirmation of my promotion and here you at the centre of a stuff up again. Explain yourself sir.'

'Uncle, I have no idea why these things occur only that when I am motivated to do something good, I find a way to foul things up and I assure you sir, that it's not done to embarrass you.' Francis Foley looked unconvinced and sought further explanation on the grocery thief.

'Uncle if you could've seen what I saw when I confronted that poor woman in the most abject poverty imaginable, sheltering four small children under the age of eight. If you could have experienced the smell and the cold of that pathetic hovel, I would challenge you as a Christian not to want to render them some assistance.' Jim shook his head while wringing his hands in his frustration. 'I cannot understand why, in a country with so much wealth simply dug up....'

Francis Foley remained unmoved, interrupting the younger man, angrily emphasising every word. 'For God's sake Jim, you are a copper! She is a thief. That's all you need to know.'

And that, thought Jim, *is what is wrong with the whole bloody police force.* But rather than voice that bit of insurrection he remembered his manners.

'Sincere congratulations on your promotion sir, I'm sure your vast experience will bring great benefit to the community we have vowed to protect.'

The newly appointed Deputy Police Commissioner was left wondering if that was a genuine sentiment or a thinly disguised bit of sarcasm.

Chapter 14

1924

Melbourne's Love of Theatre

Melbourne citizens can always tell when a summer thunderstorm is on its way. It gives notice with stifling humidity as the sky closes in with distant lightning flashes and muted rolling thunder before it strikes with full unrestrained fury. Wind speed and rain reach peak intensity as the front passes over, followed by a big drop in temperature.

In a similar a manner, social rumblings were an early warning of a scandal about to be unleashed, creating suspicion, shattered reputations and injured pride that would last for years. Sadly, no one recognised the early signs of the coming Maelstrom.

Madame Rosetta Gloria Parmentier, Age Newspaper's senior theatre critic, and Captain Richard Jenkins were chatting at a charming little soirée at the home of one of Melbourne's most important philanthropists. The large, richly decorated salon of the sprawling Gothic revival home was crowded with the city's elite eager to be seen as supporters of the Arts. In this case the principal theatre in Melbourne, His Majesty's Theatre in Exhibition Street. In the first decades of the new century, many changes had been made to the building increasing the foyer capacity and the construction of a three-story building to house sets; props and wardrobes and other backstage items. Now, more money was required for further renovations. In 1909, Dame Nellie Melba had declared the acoustics 'dead' following a private sound test. Now she had performed again years later in a largely refurbished theatre to great acclaim.

John and Nevin Tait theatre managers and concert promoters had merged with J C Williamson Ltd. Prospective shareholders were expectant of great returns and by investing in the company also curry favour by 'rubbing shoulders' with influential community leaders. The current thing in society circles was to be seen and to be seen supporting the arts. There was a strong rumour that Anna Pavlova the Russian Prima Ballerina who would soon perform on the stage of the recently gender reassigned venue from *Her Majesty's,* to *His Majesty's,* in honour of King George V. If correct this would be a sensation and no stone was left unturned in efforts to attract the first lady of Russian and indeed the worlds ballet with her company to His Majesty's Theatre and all the glitterati would sell their children into slavery. They were so eager, in fact, that many of them threw fiscal caution to the winds and right there was where Captain Jenkins set his nets.

Captain Jenkins had worked diligently to inveigle himself into the upper echelon of society, where he planned to unearth the rich pickings to be had at those lofty heights. Nothing so crude as mere cash, although his hard and fast rule went: if someone offers you cash, take it. No, the real prize to be had here was the inferred integrity he gained by being accepted into this select company.

The genuinely privileged 'old money' have an inborn sense that allows them to detect unerringly the presence of fakery, the thin veneer of civility and affectation designed to cover the origins of the low born social climbers and snake oil salesmen. But the one thing they could not resist was celebrity and the utterly charming and decorated Captain Richard Fairlie Jenkins, Officer in His Majesty's 4th Indian Cavalry Division DSM Veteran of Flanders, France. He was eagerly sought as a guest at any social gathering either in the grand homes of the cream of society or at the thoroughbred races where Captain Jenkins could be seen martini glass held delicately in a manicured hand with a beautiful woman on the other.

At the same time, he had built on his core business of loan sharking short-term loans to losing card players and punters burdened with debts to the hard bookmakers. These bookies operated in the level below the leading bagmen of the racetrack. Famous bookies such as Sol Green and Mannie Lyons would have none of them on credit. These giants of bookmaking were too shrewd to be caught with bad debts and would direct those suspect gamblers and their poor credit standing off to the lesser bookies who were not averse to violence in pursuit of settling debts. Standing ready to assist was Captain

Jenkins, who played usurer at rates to make a shylock blush without the recipients realising they were stepping out of the frying pan into a very hot fire.

Captain Jenkins struck savage interest rates on loans to the desperate, repayments collected by a small well rewarded bunch of merciless thugs well practised in the delicate art of leg breaking.

It was during card games that Jenkins began to build his list of 'investors.' One by one and with great caution he expertly cut out gullible but wealthy business people who believed strongly that they were living in the age of opportunity and that it was they out of all their kind for whom miracles were wrought and were entitled to everything that the earth could give them. Many of them were the descendants of 'struck it rich' miners and inheritors of the gold mining companies that had since morphed into corporations in a multitude of directions. The common denominator was their wealth and blind greed for more.

Although there were many examples of law breaking in Melbourne business circles, many business people were still lacking in awareness, leaving them ripe for fraud, embezzlement, copyright breaches and all manner of direct theft of product. It was a naivety born of inexperience and following the instincts of a true parasite, Captain Jenkins homed in on the blood scent.

It was after a particularly exciting and high stakes game of poker in his apartment that had Captain Jenkins and several survivors of the cut and thrust of the poker table were relaxing with a fine cognac and cigars when one of the chaps put a question to him. One or two thought it a little indelicate, but were equally curious themselves.

The enquirer was Gordon Plowright, leading Melbourne bookmaker, who pointed his cigar at Jenkins as he asked the question.

'Captain, you must have seen some sights while you were serving in India, such a fascinating and exotic place. May I beg of you to entertain us with a tale or two?'

Now this may have been a massive stumbling block for any ordinary conman and indeed it caused Captain Jenkins' heart to flutter slightly, not with anxiety but with excitement as he looked about at his companions and saw the excitement and expectation in their eyes.

Just as a gold miner would scan the face of his mine shaft looking for that golden glint, Jenkins instantly saw another rich vein before him. Instead of blurting out all manner of romantic nonsense that would be barely believable and perhaps impair any fruitful chances, he demurred.

'Indeed, gentlemen, India is a country rich in many ways and my experiences there could quite literally fill a book.' Here, he expertly faked a yawn and shook his head. 'I would be delighted to share some amazing stories of Rajahs and Tiger hunts but right now I hear my bed calling.'

Captain Jenkins took this idea to bed with him and spent the night tossing and turning as his fevered imagination whipped up a fantastic tale that he would use to lever even more money out of the gullible and greedy public. By the time he swung his legs out of bed in the morning, he had the bones of an extraordinary tale that would stimulate imagination and foster intrigue. Jenkins continued to work on the yarn as he savoured his morning coffee, polishing to perfection a stirring tale of high adventure, treachery, death and fabulous riches. He thought it was so good that he dropped all thought of a Ponzi type scheme altogether to concentrate on his new scheme.

As a fictitious cavalry officer of the Royal Indian 4th Division the 'decorated' Captain Jenkins was naturally accepted indisputably as an expert on the politics and history of the Raj and all that went before it back to the days of the Maghul Emperor Shah Jahan (Shahab-ud-din Muhammad Khurram) the builder of the fabulous Taj Mahal in memory of his deceased wife.

During the reign of the Maghul Empire, great wealth was accumulated from which the Taj Mahal was an example. Much of which came from trading the silks, gold and precious gems, artefacts, religious icons, ivory products, spices and products of India and broader Asia that were transported to the world along the Silk Road, the great trading artery of ancient Asia. The Silk Road entered Indian Territory at several points. All of this was true. Captain Jenkins took these facts and added a 'little' embellishment.

Captain Jenkins' story of daring would feature well in any 'Boys Own' publication and unabashedly presented to his captivated audience had them in enthralled. With the demise of the Mughal Empire and the advancement of British interests' rumours abounded of a hidden hoard that would make Ali Baba's cave of the Forty Thieves look like the local pawn shop. Hundreds of years of trading and pillaging, hoarding all the glories of Asia secreted away in a location known only to a few. It was thought that at the end of the Maghul Emperor's rule, those with the knowledge had died out and those that weren't dead soon were to protect the vast fortune that someday might finance a new army. As the decades passed, all knowledge and lingering memory of those rumours faded and were forgotten.

The East India Company continued to create enormous wealth and virtually ruled India as the Mughals descended into disorder. The British, under Robert Clive, established firm rule from 1740 with India and Indians adopting many of the British laws, customs and culture.

After an exhausting game of cards for high stakes and seemingly a little under the weather, Jenkins would curse his luck and 'accidently' blurt out a desire to return to India where he knew of a King's Ransom.

The bait was thus set and the first bite would come within seconds. Jenkins would be invited to dinner or drinks obviously 'without any special agenda merely for friendship's sake.' After a discreet interval, the first tentative references are made to the 'slip of the tongue.'

Jenkins would be embarrassed into explaining himself and reluctantly relate the story that would have his audience on the edge of their seats and their cheque books appearing as if by magic.

CHAPTER 15
JUNE 1924
JULY CAPTAIN JENKINS SPINS A TALE

Captain Jenkins' tale had it that he and his unit were patrolling in the area known as the Northern Frontier. When they made camp for the night, a small frightened boy crept into their encampment carrying a small bundle. A sentry brought the young shepherd to Captain Jenkins' tent.

'I found this sly little bugger creepin' 'round the picket line sir, I don't know what he wants but 'e's the type would steal the pennies off a dead man's eyes 'e would sir.' The corporal thrust the boy forward into the light where he stood trembling in terror.

'Alright Corporal, leave him with me.'

The young lad stood nervously before Captain Jenkins, clutching a bundle about the size of a house brick to his chest. Apart from being dirty and dusty, the boy smelt highly from his daily contact with his flock and against his first instincts to throw him out of his tent, there was something about the little shepherd that intrigued Jenkins. Speaking in Hindi the language dominant in the North Indian Ganges plains he asked the boy why he was there and what did he want.

'Sir, I am tending my father's flock of sheep and I have been expecting him to come with food for me, but he appears to have abandoned me. I am starving.' Holding his bundle out towards Jenkins he pleads, 'Please sir, will you trade with me for food?'

Jenkins took the bundle and laid it on his campaign desk. Carefully, with the end of his small riding crop, he peeled back the filthy covering to reveal an astonishing sight. Beneath a thick layer of grime and dust was an intricately carved piece of jade. Jenkins picked it up and feels the weight of the object. The carving was Chinese and the quality of the jade was top grade. He was no expert but he believed this piece alone would be worth a great deal in any currency.

Keeping the object covered, he called for his aide to bring a meal for the boy and watches him patiently while he eats. Finally satiated, the lad sat back and looked at the captain dreamily, who began to gently interrogate him hoping to get some answers before the exhausted lad dropped off. The boy agreed to show him the area where he discovered the precious object the next day and almost instantly fell into a deep sleep.

Leaving a subaltern in charge of the patrol with orders to continue back to their headquarters if he failed to return in two days, Captain Jenkins left with the boy upon a donkey, guiding the way. After many hours riding in the harsh arid landscape they came upon the boys' flock grazing amongst the rocky hills. The boy must have walked for days to reach Jenkins' encampment. The boy who had introduced himself as Pillai, one of the names of the Lord Ganesha which to Jenkins was wholly appropriate as the Elephant God of new beginnings, remover of obstacles, the patron of arts and sciences and the deva of wisdom. Pillai seemed to be regaining his bearings as he had slept on and off as they travelled and each time they stopped to rest and water the horse.

'Well Pillai, where to from here my young friend?'

His friend may have been young, but he was born of a tribe of great traders and he knew that the carved jade he had presented to the soldier was worth a lot more than one meal.

'Sahib, we must talk. I can show you where I found this sacred item, but what will be my reward?'

Jenkins was then forced to make a deal with the crafty young shepherd whereby he would put the item into auction and pay an agreed share to Pillai and his father, first ensuring they were sworn to secrecy about their transactions. Jenkins was not in the business of financing the lifestyles of a bunch of goat herders, and had already decided he would need to deal with these peasants.

Pillai guided Jenkins to a rocky outcrop where he had searched for strays an area deeply fissured with gullies and riddled with caverns of all sizes. It was a unique piece of geological abnormality. This was where Pillai discovered the jade, in a deep dried out creek bed washed up with the flotsam and jetsam of recent floods.

Jenkins spent several days exploring the area and was convinced that the great treasure of the Mughal Empire was at hand, discovering some intriguing rock carvings that seemed to be very old and perhaps providing a guide to the ultimate prize. If only he had more time he was sure he could locate it in this maze of caverns and blind gullies. But he had to get back to his patrol or be declared AWOL. After making some careful sketches and a detailed map of the area he eventually made his way back to his command.

On arrival, he received the news that they were shipping out for France and the war in Europe.

At this point of his exciting tale, his audience was on the edge of their seats with their tongues literally hanging out. Captain Jenkins would give a huge sigh of frustration that would be the perceived as the full stop in the fascinating anecdote.

'Jenkins please go on.' pleaded Godfrey Beckmann, a very successful property developer and possibly the greediest bastard Jenkins had ever encountered.

This is going perfectly to script. The next step would follow automatically. Build the interest, tease him with the possibilities, put it out there take it back. Jenkins exaggerated the effects of alcohol, swaying slightly and looking a little unsteady.

'I have one or two who have expressed very keen interest in financing an expedition back to India who are at this very moment (burp!) pardon, raising the finance to lock a partnership away.' Jenkins belched thunderously. 'Dear God, that's better. Where's that bottle?' fumbling about, he almost dropped the scotch.

Jenkins was expertly driving the 'mark' insane, his greed and lust for easy riches almost causing his head to explode. And now annoyingly, Jenkins appeared to forget the whole thing by falling asleep under the influence of alcohol, leaving the mark to go crazy. He finally emerges from his haze and announces that yes, he would accept the bloke as a partner as he seems like the right type and on the condition that he provide a minimum twenty thousand pounds surety to finance the expedition and he just happens to need one more partner to achieve a solid team. Preferably in cash, of course.

Jenkins was cunning enough to have created solid reason for cash. 'We are certainly not working with people who have regular banking facility's and would more than likely light their pipes with your promissory notes.' Generally, the saps can't get to their banks quickly enough and Godfrey Beckmann is a perfect example. Captain Jenkins just happened to have a pre-prepared partnership document at his elbow and whipped it out now to seal the deal. All the greedy mark can see are the mountains of gold and precious jewels described in great detail by the captain and eagerly splashes his signature across the bottom of the document as he willingly hands over a wallet full of cash that Jenkins just as swiftly deposits in his pre-arranged offshore bank account. Caveat emptor.

CHAPTER 16

MAY–JUNE 1924

BRADFIELD'S NEGOTIATIONS WITH HOTEL MANAGEMENT

Eugene Wallace Bradfield was becoming a bit of a nuisance, having worn out his welcome in several gambling establishments and with one or two bookmakers. There was a strong undercurrent of dissatisfaction with the elegant thespian who had not only reneged on his gambling debts but additionally was mounting a huge unpaid hotel bill that had management very nervous. Gene himself was becoming very nervous indeed.

An enquiring letter from the family bank in London asked him to provide details of his current income, as very little had come back to reduce his overdraft. Then, oh bedamned, the blasted bankers had cut off all access to the money held in trust by them and refused to allow access to it until he could provide reason.

His biggest concern would have been with his debt for hospitality. He couldn't face being evicted and to have to beg friends for shelter. In order to circumvent that possibility, he came up with a scheme that just might save his neck. But first he needed to get approval from his manager and the management company of His Majesty's Theatre to allow him to carry out his plan. He was currently presenting a rather weary version of Shylock (ironically) in the Merchant of Venice. After explaining what he wanted to do and giving guarantees it would be a definite one-off they consented, although a little reluctantly.

He took his proposal to the management of the Windsor Hotel, where he was presently ensconced paying nothing for his rooms or his bar and restaurant tabs. It was becoming extremely embarrassing for Eugene and management alike as he slipped further and further into arrears.

Many visiting actors from the United States came as a result of growing interest in the cinema industry in Australia and chose to stay at the Windsor based recommendations from Eugene. His PR value as a noted Shakespearean actor was wearing a bit thin, so he decided to go on the front foot with a scheme that came to him after a sleepless night pacing the carpet.

In a nervous meeting with the hotel manager, advertising and media manager and accounts department, Eugene haltingly laid out his plans for redemption.

Simply put, he would present a special one-off performance in the hotel of a popular play by William Shakespeare, The Comedy of Errors. 'Lots of comedy and slapstick, it would be a lot of fun.'

The play would be presented by Eugene and a small cast. Furthermore, he suggested that the hotel restaurant present a special fixed menu that would be served to the play's patrons included in the fee. The evening would be promoted as the season's most glamorous and desirable event held in the Windsor Hotel, and probably Melbourne, since the gold rush days. Eugene swore he could attract such luminaries as Dame Nellie Melba to attend along with the city's elite.

With the heat in state politics in the lower house, every party leader would turn up. The be-whiskered Labour Leader George Prendergast, Sir Alexander Peacock of the Nationalists and John Allen of the Country Party who would lead the Coalition to victory. Leading Industrialists and fashionistas and a who's-who of the city society. The hotel's Grand Ballroom would provide seating for a minimum of one hundred and fifty and at an average ticket price of fifty pounds, the evening could produce a staggering six thousand pounds. Eugene would present the production at no cost to the management and all revenues would be against his outstanding debt. Even allowing for overheads such as the fare in the restaurant and extra wages for staff, it would more than wipe out Eugene's debt and leave him with enough credit to cover his future bills for quite some time.

Wisely, Eugene would never see the takings. They would remain in the hands of management, relieving them of any risk of a delinquent account.

While not exactly bowled over by Eugene's presentation, his concept struck a note of cautious approval with the four executives as each one looked at his colleagues and heads began to nod very slightly at first. Eugene, a man well practised in reading body language, detected a positive reaction early. Besides, what other choice did they have?

Eugene was thanked for his presentation and assured that it would receive serious consideration. The manager stood and shook his hand, guiding him to the door.

'Well, gentlemen, that was an interesting proposal by our prize lodger. What do we think?'

The three other decision makers are almost falling over each other to express an opinion all of which indicate that Eugene will get his opportunity.

'This could be sensational,' Mr Asprey Advertising and Media Relations said, 'wonderful publicity for us, yes, yes I think we should do it.'

The manager was looked down at the boardroom tabletop, frowning as he absorbed Eugene's concept. 'You know I agree with you Asprey and if this is a success there is no reason that it could not become an annual event.'

Mr Pinchback, the appropriately named company accountant, as expected presents a contrary opinion of course, his total repugnance for entrepreneurial risk-taking the very cornerstone of his trade.

Having won his reprieve, Eugene whooped with joy when he received a request from hotel management to present his play as discussed. The request was put to him in a manner that would seem to be as a result of their ingenuity as hospitality experts in order to win acclaim from shareholders and the public alike.

The event when run was indeed the social highlight of the year, with all of Melbourne's finest and many of Sydney's elite who arrived in Melbourne to attend. A huge social, financial and advertising triumph. In fact, the revenue that came as a result guaranteed Eugene's accommodation for a couple of years. Eugene financially stable once more, exited stage left to continue exactly as he was accustomed to doing.

But Eugene, being Eugene, was off and running rampant around the bookmakers and card games, winning small fortunes and losing larger ones with equanimity. He continued to win acclaim for his brilliant acting and censure for the 'mentorship' he unstintingly offered to younger members of his cast. It was true that he was an inveterate gambler lacking completely in moral responsibility for his debts, however, very few of the general public were aware of his punting peccadillos. As far as the general public were concerned,

Eugene Wallace Bradfield was a consummate thespian well above the lower orders and mundane problems of the world. His was a face seen most regularly on theatrical posters in theatre reviews and social columns of the daily newspapers. Eugene moved in two worlds. One was the genteel world of theatre and the arts and the other was the semi-legitimate world of gambling where a darker demographic lurked in the shadows.

Melbourne's version of the underworld was a collective consisting of card sharps, race fixers, conmen, drug dealers, pickpockets, pimps, wife beaters and substance abusers of every stripe that traipsed around the gambling dens and racetracks of the city desperately searching for the big hit, the impossible fall of the cards or longest price galloper, harness racer, or greyhound to cross the line.

CHAPTER 17

1920–1930

MELBOURNE BLOOMS AS THE LARGEST CITY IN THE EMPIRE AFTER LONDON

Melbourne still had yet to form anything like a sophisticated criminal organisation. The underworld swirled and morphed into various agreements and pacts similar to the never repeated patterns of the crystals in a kaleidoscope.

Only a fool would try it on with these guys, genuine hard men but somehow attractive to certain types who enjoyed the thrill of being in the presence of danger and notoriety seeing their photo in the society columns flirting with dangerous men who in turn garnered a kind of integrity from their legitimate company. It was a kind of symbiotic relationship similar to a shark and its consort of remora fish. Several of the bad boys were enjoying the write-ups they received in the daily papers and the much-loved *Truth,* the weekly scandal rag that was a popular read with the proletariat.

Racing news and racy news all grist for the mill, some of it bordering on factual depending on how gullible you were and replete with the mandatory page three girl all boobs and no visible sign of intelligence. In their interview published alongside their head and boob shot, they professed to be studying a variety of scientific disciplines or artistic endeavours along with hobbies such as horse riding or walking in the rain.

At times there was some serious friction between the various criminal alliances causing wild brawls in pubs or backstreets and the odd shot that ruined windows and woodwork but seldom found their intended mark. These ructions erupted over territories or the spoils of their handiwork and more than once over the charms of a particularly alluring woman.

On occasion, a criminal might identify an opportunity and require the skills of a safe cracker or forger to complete a job. One of those skills that found constant employment involved the laying on of hands. Not in the biblical sense, but with fists clenched and pain dispensed in a dosage appropriate to the degree of the indiscretion.

Get-away drivers were becoming vogue as the vehicles of the day were cantankerous and generally required a skilled operator. It would never do to be in a stalled vehicle outside the bank you had just robbed or the house you had sprayed with bullets.

It was an era of opportunity for an honest hardworking criminal.

Pickpockets were drawn to public events like flies to practise their adroit skills on the happy and prosperous crowds. Horse racing was a consistent draw and public celebrations such as Empire Day, Boxing Day, New Year's Eve and Royal Show Days when crowds gathered in numbers and all their finery, where alcohol could be depended upon to dull the senses.

A recidivist pickpocket team, all of whom had run afoul of Senior Constable Jim Foley and Constable Irene McCarthy were hard at work around the football crowds lifting wallets and fob watches from the incautious attendees. Here they were again. 'Showbag' Rutledge, all show and Marlon 'The Plover' Richardson skinny legs led by Roger 'Razor' Wood (Sharp as) were doing okay, but looking forward to the richer pickings of the spring racing carnival.

'Tweeky' Thompson was a recent recruit to back-up Showbag who had been unwise enough to try and lift a fat wallet from the inside pocket of a jacket belonging to a member in Curly Barker's gang.

Showbag could and should have chosen a softer target. The result was that Showbag's hands would take six months to heal to the point where he could use a knife and fork again. Curley no slouch himself at the delicate art of picking pockets (usually with his gun jammed into the victim's ribs) had taken exception to one of his mob being robbed by 'this little bastard' and put Showbag's hands in a workshop vice and screwed it up hard until the audience to this brutality could clearly hear the bones in Showbag's hands cracking even above his screams of agony.

'What the bloody 'ell was you thinkin' you bloody drongo? Now that's lost revenoo to our company wif yooz outta action, revenoo what we'll never see… no wait, what you'll never see.' Razor Wood admonished his dim-witted companion Showbag Rutledge, 'I'll keep yooz on but yooz'll need to work it off some 'ow.'

Razor ran his mob like a small business that had to meet predictable profit margins or go independent. Working together ensured success and safety in numbers.

Right at that moment they were on a Red Rattler, the nickname for Melbourne's Tait trains, on their way to Flemington Race course for a minor Saturday meeting at which they were expected to meet with a leading bookmaker Gordon Plowright and his colleague, the colourfully named Harry the Hatchet Sidell. The crowds at these autumn meetings were fairly sparse as many of the horses in the early races were inexperienced two-year olds learning their trade. With the majority of races offering small prize money insufficient to attract quality entrants, only the dedicated or fanatical racing fans would come out in the cold blustery weather.

Razor continues to lecture his team about his expectations for them.

'An' if yooz numbskulls stuff up this job or try anyfink on that man 'arry 'you'll find out why they call 'im 'arry the 'atchet.'

On the same train was a regular police patrol of Constables Dottie Green and Bluey Farnsworth, who changed carriages at each stop along the Flemington line, eyeing off the crowd in each carriage looking for the usual suspects and surprise, surprise there they were. Some of Melbourne's finest.

'Well, hello lads, what a treat to meet you like this. Now don't tell me, let me guess, you're on your way to a church picnic, right?'

'Ha ha, very droll if I don't say Mr Farnsworth sir.' The ever ready with a quip Showbag ventures. 'So are ya takin' ya girlfriend to the races are ya Constable Farnsworth sir?' said Showbag with just the right mix of humour and a touch of respect to avoid a baton over his skull. Both his hands were still bound by the filthy remains of what were once plaster casts.

'Constable Green is more than capable of taking care of a grub like you and I expect you'll be seein' more of her in your immediate future, you cheeky little shit.'

Bluey notes Showbag's hands and fires a wise crack back at him. 'Workplace injuries are they Rutledge?' Indicating the grubby bindings with the baton, he uses it to direct the gang to stand up and show respect to his colleague. 'Allow me to introduce you to a collection of Melbourne's finest scumbags Constable Green,' and putting a restraining arm out, 'and I would advise you not to get too close to this lot or ya might lose your valuables.'

Showbag couldn't help showing off his wit with another wisecrack.

'Ha ha well don't worry, her virginity's safe then.' The carriage echoes to the sound of Bluey's baton cracking on Showbag's skull.

The train pulls into the Flemington station, discharging its passengers directly into the racecourse. A few people notice the three youngish blokes half carrying, half dragging their mate with the roughly bandaged hands along the platform.

'Look at that. So drunk he can hardly stand and at this time of day! Why don't those constables do something about it? What a disgrace!' exclaims a concerned citizen.

The 'disgraceful trio' are watched in amusement by the two constables who were applauded by the fellow riders in the carriage where Showbag felt the weight of Bluey's baton.

Showbag was parked on a bench until he regained his full (by his standard) senses, then they moved off to their meeting in the public bar under the public stand where Gordon Plowright and Harry the Hatchet waited patiently for them to outline the mysterious mission Plowright had for them.

Apparently, the plan involved the adroit skills of a seasoned pickpocket planting something on someone rather than relieving them of their wallet or watch. Why that was so important was beyond the cognizance of the pickpocket gang, but for a good reward they were happy to oblige.

It was one of the early days of spring with an odorous blanket of smog laying over the city from the burning of late falling autumn leaves, which was a passionate pastime of Melbourne homeowners. Added to the smoke from thousands of household fires, it made for a fine old smog. Homes depended on wood fires for heating and in a lot of homes wood fired stoves were used for cooking. It lent a sombreness to the days that would not be relieved until the regular breezes and rains of spring kicked in across the country and the home fires were extinguished. In the meantime, life went on as the citizenry saw no reason to put away the winter woollies overcoats or the brollies.

Rather than make their craft of pickpocketing more difficult, the heavy clothing was actually easier to access as the targeted victim tended to carry their wallets in the outer pockets of their overcoats rather than fumble under overcoat and jacket to retrieve it.

Gordon Plowright and Harry the Hatchet watch amused as the bunch of street punks staggered through the light crowd, bumping people intentionally or not. It's hard to say for sure, but no doubt some of the patrons would be going away with lighter pockets.

Plowright was in no mood for nonsense. 'You cannot help yourselves, can you? For Christ's sake stay out of trouble until ya get this little job done for us.' Plowright stopped talking and looked around, studying the crowd intently before continuing.

'Right you blokes, I want yez to get to know the Irish 'orse trainer O'Farrell who's having a bit of success at the moment with the horse he's training, Tidal Wave.' He made eye contact with them one by one and can't help noticing that the one called Showbag looked like his eye balls were rotating in their sockets.

'Yeah, well, here's what I want from you. On Sat'dy, I want yez to get back here and find O'Farrell and keep an eye on him until just before the main race. That's race seven at 4.15, got it? Well before he heads back to his stable to collect his horse, I want you to drop this little paper into his pocket.' He handed the paper to Razor, who pretended to read it while slipping it into his own pocket.

'Now pay attention, or do ya want me to write this down? When ya get here on Sat'dy, ya look up the race book and you'll find the stable number of O'Farrell's horse here,' Plowright displayed a current race book and pointed to the relevant information. 'It won't be Tidal Wave it'll be another one of his called Ginger Biscuit or The Anteater. Ginger Biscuit is expected to perform well after being rested for a minor injury.'

The one called Showbag looked like he was dropping off. 'Shit, is he alright? Are you taking this in stupid? I can't have some dopey bugger messin' things up.'

'Stupid' snapped upright, his head lolling about, eyes blinking at the light looking like a wombat disturbed from sleep. Bluey Farnsworth's baton has obviously found the sweet spot.

'Yes, Sir Mr Plowright no worries, good as gold me.' Poor old Showbag showed signs of concussion and was having problems focussing, occasionally holding his hand out at full stretch to study his fingers, as if he'd only just noticed them.

'Right, well, this is important. You know where the stables are don't ya?' They all nodded their affirmation. 'Okay, when you locate O'Farrell's stable, I want you to hide this at the back of it. Don't hide it too well and don't make it too bloody obvious either. Have you got it?'

'What is this shit, Mr Plowright?' Queried Razor Wood.

'Nothin' you need to know about boy but remember this, if yooz fuck up you'll answer to me, got it?' said Harry the Hatchet, displaying his most repellent grin and pointing to himself with a sausage sized finger.

'Okay thanks Harry.' Plowright tempered the threat, 'Do this right and it will be a good payday for you,' said Gordon Plowright, all solicitous and concern, 'I'll pay you half now and the other half when the jobs done. I think you know I'm a man of me word so rely on it. But remember Harry will be your contact from now and I will ignore you if you approach me. I know you won't want upset Harry, now will ya?'

'If yez do a fair dinkum job on this, there just might be some more work for ya. Okay?'

'Thank you Mr Harry, we'll get it done, thank you Mr Plowright.'

'Right now, piss off and if anyone asks, you never been here, right?'

Gordon Plowright as a major bookmaker, or rails bookie as he was known, was holding several huge bets on Blaine O'Farrell's horse in the upcoming Melbourne Cup. Ego got in the way of common sense when accepting the bets from Vogel. The gambler and the bookmaker had been duelling in the betting arena for several seasons, and some of their contests were reported in the papers. The average punter could retire in comfort without a worry in the world on the amount of money risked in just one bet from these 'Titans of the Turf' as the press dubbed them.

Tidal Wave was the current equal favourite and a magnificent stayer over from New Zealand after winning the Wellington and a follow up win in the Adelaide Cup last year. Matthias Vogel had a majority share in the magnificent stayer and he has placed two very large bets with Plowright. With its breeding and performance to date, it looked like a dead cert. If it ran and won, Plowright would be close to bankruptcy. What made him accept the bets in the first place was the equal five to one favourite Contraband that Plowright thought had the goods to beat Tidal Wave but in the interim it had torn a Suspensory Ligament in its hind leg. The tear was so severe that the vet predicted a six to twelve-month recovery and perhaps an end to its racing career. This left Tidal Wave as outright favourite. The two bets totalled ten thousand pounds and at five to one Vogel stood to collect fifty thousand pounds, an enormous sum.

There were one or two other mounts showing talent and expected to win a spot in the big race, but at this point nothing stood out like Tidal Wave.

If Blaine O'Farrell was found guilty on a serious breach of the rules of racing his stable would be disqualified from the sport and that would mean Tidal Wave was a non-starter. Plowright's problem would be solved by planting a vial of a banned substance in

O'Farrell's stable and a handwritten instruction on its administration in his pocket. He had no trouble finding the banned substance; he only had to look in his own garden shed for that. Upon discovery O'Farrell the Irishman would be dropped like a hot rock. It would only take an anonymous phone call to put the Stewards on to him and let things take their course. It would be the biggest scandal in Australian racing circles in decades. Plowright knew that he was risking more than money in this scam.

If his scam were uncovered, he would lose his only means of making a living with a cancelled bookmaker's licence leading to a total loss of the assets he had spent a lifetime accumulating and last but not least, the strong possibility of a long gaol sentence. On top of that, by scamming Vogel's horse Tidal Wave, he was literally flirting with death. The man was known to have a vicious temper and was suspected to have been involved when a couple of street kids who had upset him were rumoured to have been drowned.

Christ, what would he do if he found out that Plowright was at the bottom of his horses' disqualification? Sure, his bets would be refunded, but the massive prestige that came with being the owner of The Melbourne Cup winner would be snatched away from him.

It would be unlikely to happen a second time. Drowning might be a good outcome if he was caught out by Vogel. This was a serious criminal conspiracy, not to mention a morally bankrupt act.

Constable Bluey Farnsworth and Constable Dottie Green had been patrolling quietly around the public area of the vast Flemington Race Course, observing the crowd on the lookout for any unsociable behaviour. It was a quiet day due partly to the sombre weather and the chill that had come with a fine rain that seemed to be setting in early.

'You would need to be a pretty keen racing fan to be out here on a day like this don't you think Roger, er sorry, I mean Constable Farnsworth?' Said Dottie fixing the collar of her overcoat against the rain and chill.

'Yeah, I for one would rather be at home with my feet up in front of a nice warm fire with a good book. And between you and me, we don't need all that formality. Everyone calls me Bluey and I invite you to do the same unless we're in company, okay?'

'Okay. Thanks Bluey, she laughed yeah, the idea of a nice warm fire and a cup of tea sounds very attractive right now. Oh, by the way, how is constable Richardson doing after his assault?'

'Yeah poor bugger. It was a close one, but we managed to get him to the hospital before he bled to death. It was frightening but they patched him up good as new.' They continued walking and talking as they headed for the public bar.

'But it shook 'im up a treat and he's gone and snatched it. He can't wait to back 'ome an check on the fences an' stuff. Gone back to his parent's farm up in New South.' Bluey shakes his head sadly, 'He reckons controlling jumbucks is easier'n controlling the street push.'

'Yeah that's a shame, he was always a fair go as a copper, but who could blame him. An' now what about that cuppa you promised a girl?' She said as she bounced lightly on her toes, spinning around as though she were on her way to a birthday party.

'Well look at you, enjoying yourself are ya? The cup of tea is easy, we can get a decent cup in the public bar where they have a facility for duty cops like us.' Now he puts on a fake stern face, 'provided you won't sing or dance.'

The cheerful pair assumed the posture of coppers the world over with their hands clasped behind their backs as they wandered casually over to the public bar looking forward to the restorative powers of a cuppa. It was still relatively early in the day, but the pair had been on duty since early morning and a hot cup of tea and maybe a biscuit would be very welcome. Their eyes were still everywhere, checking out the activity of the sparse crowd. In the next few weeks, crowds would swell in this area until they were shoulder to shoulder as more and more horses were brought in from all around Australia and New Zealand to contest the major races over spring.

Entering the bar area, Bluey Farnsworth spots the pathetic gang of pick pockets apparently in deep conversation with Gordon Plowright and a tough-looking thug he knows as Harry the Hatchet.

'Dottie, try not to be too obvious, but do you see our larrikin push over there at the back of the bar area?'

Bluey was looking in the opposite direction, trying for a bit of subtlety, 'See the two blokes they're talking to, that's Gordon Plowright the leading rails bookmaker and the rough nut with him is a charming character known as Harry the Hatchet, wanna know why?'

'I could probably imagine but I'd like to be able to sleep tonight.'

'Yeah, he's that bad. But I'd give a few quid to know what they're talking about? Some 'ow I don't think they're swappin' tips.'

CHAPTER 18
AUGUST 1924
MELBOURNE CUP CANDIDATES STRUT THEIR STUFF

Matthias Vogel had placed two huge bets with the bookmaker, Gordon Plowright. This followed a mountain of research into the horse he had purchased through an agent. He studied its breeding, chosen its trainer for his background and subsequent proven skills and had his agent attend the early morning jump outs or barrier trials at its home track in Taranaki Street Wellington. When the horse arrived in Melbourne, Mathias naturally attended Epsom and Caulfield training sessions. He was like a smitten teenager spending as much time as he could with the beautiful animal. Matthias had put a lot of time into this horse and believed explicitly in its talents. As a majority shareholder, he had been there to see it streak home to take out the Wellington Cup in its fourth year of racing and win the prestigious Adelaide Cup in a canter. Now she was set for the Melbourne Cup and Gordon Plowright was apparently happy to set the horse Contraband against Tidal Wave.

At this time of year, it was common for high-flying punters to come to town to take on the books. The general public lapped up the reports in the papers of the incredible amounts of money being wagered on a horse race. The massive bets were several times the price of a decent house in a good suburb and the average working man who might risk a ten-shilling bet if he was a bit flush would have a heart attack laying out this sort of dough. The general public were infatuated by the colourful international playboys who came to town with all the glamour and scandal of Hollywood. The press gave them exciting nicknames like 'The Fireman' who never seemed to run out of money and 'Hollywood George', who would always appear with a bevy of beautiful woman and flash cars. Asian and Middle Eastern Royalty were colourful visitors to the racing carnival.

Racing aficionados around the country were watching the rivalry keenly as the Tidal Wave camp and the Contraband team shadowed boxed each other in preparation for the spring. Racing commentators were evenly split on each horse's chances and at this early stage they were posted as five to one equal favourites. Vogel's two bets of five thousand pounds each would bring winnings of fifty thousand pounds if Tidal Wave crossed the line with its nose in front.

Plowright was now cursing Vogel's and his own out of control ego in equal measure.

Matthias Vogel's trainer Blaine O'Farrell had arrived in Australia after a successful career as part of a very successful racing stable in Ireland and the UK where success didn't necessarily translate into a lot of money. He was a younger member of a world-famous racing dynasty and the reputation of his personal achievements had spread around the world with theirs, eventually reaching Australia via newspaper and trade publications. His name was mentioned often enough and his family were so well known that eventually a sponsor made him an offer he couldn't refuse, so before you could say giddy-up he was on a boat to the great southland. He quickly created a reputation as an expert horseman and a charming raconteur, the lilt of his Irish accent charming all and sundry. Owners of superior thoroughbreds sought him out for his training skills and his company at their soirées, where hopeful mothers tried in vain to pair him off with unmarried daughters. Although a little naïve or perhaps immature, he had his sights set and would not be diverted.

Vogel had entered into a contract with O'Farrell and guaranteed him a very lucrative bonus if he can get Tidal Wave into the field for the Cup and he would double it if the horse won. This was the sort of opportunity Blaine O'Farrell had travelled across the globe to find and he would give it everything to achieve his employers' ambitions. Achieving those goals would enable him to send for the beautiful fiancé he had left behind in County Kildare or alternatively, return home in triumph.

O'Farrell came from a long line of notable horse trainers. His father, grandfather and great grandfather had been members of the Turf Club and had many successes on their home track The Curragh over several decades.

While he was recognised as a talented member of this distinguished racing dynasty, he had to compete with three brothers and two sisters who all stood between him and individual renown. He decided he needed to create his own dynasty. With his father's blessing, he had accepted Vogel's offer making a promise to his fiancée that he would succeed and call for her to join him or return in two years to take her hand in marriage. After a lively send-off party and a tearful farewell to his sweetheart, he set off to Australia with a grand dream in his heart.

At his training establishment at Epsom Racecourse on the southern fringe of Melbourne in the suburb of Mentone, Blaine O'Farrell set about his daily routine totally unaware that he was about to find himself at the centre of the greatest scandal in Australia's racing history and what several daily newspapers would refer to as the crime of the century.

CHAPTER 19
JUNE–AUGUST 1924
WINTER: COLD BITTER WINDS AND TREACHERY

While Blaine O'Farrell exercised his horses on Mentone beach, Matthias Vogel was engaged in a matter not quite as salubrious at his gambling den in South Melbourne. The previous night had been a very busy one with an influx of internationals arriving to gamble and party landing on his doorstep. They were players and supporters of the National Welsh Rugby Union Club touring the 'colonies' playing exhibition games before paying crowds of expatriate Welshmen and British who had left the game at home and were hungry to enjoy the barely controlled mayhem on the field. The local teams that went up against the Welsh were in the words of one unimpressed sports writer, 'cannon fodder.' But no matter, it was the game they played in Heaven and that was all they cared about.

The Rugby players weren't some underfed street urchins that could be thrown into the Yarra River if they played up. These boyos were big, well fed and fully trained athletes who could 'drop kick a sack of spuds across' that self-same Yarra River. Add to that a prodigious thirst and a very high tolerance for pain, and you have a lethal mix.

The big lads were most welcome at first, their money being as good as anybody's and they settled into the tables like they were born to it.

Matthias had to send an urgent message to his liquor supplier at one stage to keep up his stocks that were disappearing down the throats of his new guests like rain down a storm-water pipe.

Then the inevitable trouble started. One of Vogel's most trusted dealers was accused of dealing from the bottom of the deck. An unheard-of accusation hotly denied by the management and then by Matthias himself.

'Zis establishment has alvays maintained za highest levels of integrity,' he protested in his version of English to an alcohol deafened pair of ears.

'Zo take your money off my table undt apologise to my dealer, you numbskull.' The player mumbles something and moves off. It could've been an apology in Welsh, who knows?

Then some drunk fell into another drunk, starting a push and shove that turned a table upside down while a regular was holding a winning hand for a huge pot. He came out swinging a heavy cane he habitually carried for protection, especially in these parts.

The weighted cane bounced off the Neanderthal like skulls with a hollow resonance that only riled the recipients to greater heights of violence like a bee sting on a bear. The cane brandisher took no further part in proceedings as a winger and a fullback took an arm and a leg each hurling him bodily the length of the floor. The unfortunate man travelled down the building as though on ice and he was found later with his head jammed into the plaster lining board snoring like a lord.

A Welsh hooker (a front rower that is, not the other sort) used his long arms as scythes as he joined in the fray to cleave a path through the tangled melee on his way to the bar.

'A man has earned a drink or two after a bit of biffo.' He proclaimed loudly.

All of this happened in a flash and by the time Matthias' security men had caught on it was far too late, but they foolishly decided to put their own stamp on things and despite their best efforts, were thoroughly flogged for their devotion to duty.

For Matthias this was a shocking turn of events that resulted in his once well-ordered gambling den being turned into a ruin while the mahogany chairs and tables became matchwood under the crushing assault of rugby behemoths and his best security men were reduced to cringing quivering shells of their former fearless selves huddled together in corners or under what furniture remained intact.

The regular patrons of the more conventional anthropological variety had flattened themselves against the walls or fled via well maintained escape hatches built to avoid the remote possibility of a police raid. One poor soul had dived out of the window, forgetting they were on the first floor. Fortunately, he landed on a large overgrown hedge that cushioned his fall. He may have lost a bit on the cards, but he had a great win thanks to a long-forgotten attempt at horticulture.

Getting these thumping great hunks out of the place was going to be a very hazardous undertaking. Matthias decided to let nature take its course and as soon as the dust settled, he declared the bar open encouraging the boyos to drink themselves insensible. In the meantime, he put in a phone call for reinforcements and within an hour or two, a truckload of wharf labourers arrived having finished a night shift.

By then, the Welshmen were all sleeping like hibernating bears, arms around each other in fraternal contentment on every flat surface they could find. The wharfies filed in and scooped them up one by one and loaded them onto the truck for relocation somewhere far away. These boys from the coal mines of Wales who worked hard and slept hard did not stir so much as one gnarled finger in their semi-comatose state until the morning sun's rays shone upon the world-weary travellers. A strange sight greeted early morning walkers who came upon the slumbering sportsmen arranged in a neat row on the golden sands of St Kilda beach. It was a mysterious phenomenon that stunned the local citizenry and became a legend that could not be explained by anyone, particularly by the rugby club, some of whom believed they had been transported there by fairies.

Back in South Melbourne, Matthias Vogel totalled his losses and wondered if he had been delivered a divine message.

CHAPTER 20

1922–1923

MELBOURNE'S THREE RELIGIONS. CATHOLICISM, ANGLICAN AND SPORT

As a largely Christian society, Melbourne's dominant religious sects were the Church of England and the Catholic Church. The Catholic Church in Melbourne was led by the dour and controversial Archbishop Daniel Mannix ardently opposed to military conscription and a powerful advocate for a free Ireland. Strangely, he held a close relationship with John Wren a notorious proprietor of an illegal tote. Wren resided in a mansion 'Studley Hall' diagonally opposite Mannix home 'Raheen'.

Both men habitually walked to their offices and would often walk along together, the six-foot-tall and slender Mannix in a silk top hat overshadowing the diminutive five-foot four-inch Wren a man shunned by the establishment with good reason but still able to manipulate politicians.

John Wren was a self-made millionaire and illegal bookmaker who supported the working class VFL Collingwood Football Club. His relationship with Mannix was further complicated by his being a steadfast advocate of conscription and the war. However he was often an anonymous and generous donor for church charities and projects in the poverty stricken suburb from which he had made his escape.

Mannix was fiery and outspoken on several key cultural matters. Violent anti-British sentiment voiced loudly and endorsed by Mannix at the 1918 St Patricks Day march caused the event to be cancelled by the Melbourne mayor councillor Aikmen in 1919. Mannix was having none of that and on 20th March 1920 he organised his answer.

Approximately ten thousand first World War veterans marched with hordes of Catholic schoolboys, led by fourteen mounted Victoria Cross recipients who headed up the parade. They were followed directly by Archbishop Mannix in his carriage along Bourke Street.

No better example of his standing with British Intelligence could be offered than in 1920. While traveling from America to Ireland, his vessel was intercepted by a British warship. Mannix was arrested and taken to Britain where he was given his freedom under licence.

He was forbidden from making any public speeches, but was sure to have strengthened ties with the Irish Republican Army in their struggle for self-government. He was rumoured to have met with Michael Collins Chairman of the Provisional Government of the Irish Free State. The struggle for self-determination was often vicious, fuelling hatreds that were never forgiven and antipathies that screamed for revenge. It was also an era when assassins honed their skills.

Big Joe McArthur MP came from an Irish catholic family but was an outspoken opponent of the Provisional Government of the Irish Free State often creating outrage among the representatives of the Irish Free State in Australia. He had received several death threats that had to be taken seriously and at one stage, had a policeman guarding his house around the clock. But that didn't stop him from declaring in the House that any Victorian citizen identifying themselves as an Irish Republican supporter should be declared a security risk and deported back to Ireland. Old Joe was racking up enemies on a grand scale and on many fronts and one of his political colleagues advised him to 'pull yer big head in afore it gets knocked orf.'

At the Caulfield races, he had his elbow tugged by a nondescript little ruffian. Big Joe thought he was one of those racetrack urgers, attempting to persuade him to bet on a particular horse in order to take a commission out of the winnings.

'What do want yer little grub?' Big Joe was not happy to be interrupted when he was in full flow, expounding the values of one of his many projects to an audience that in all honesty couldn't give a fig.

The little man pressed a piece of note paper into Big Joe's hands and scuttled off through the crowd before he had a chance to open it. Which was just as well as the paper contained some threatening words from a group that called themselves Colonial Sinn Féin Warriors.

McArthur, you are a traitor to your heritage and your poisonous words will spill the blood of your kin. The threat was simply expressed and chilling in its intent, an effective example of the hatreds running hot through the populace.

In 1923, Melbourne was shaken to its core by an unthinkable social eruption. Victorian Police went on strike and with the benefit of hindsight, with good reason. The timing of this unprecedented industrial action by the upholders of the law was perfect in creating an impact. Timing is everything in comedy and is also a useful tactic in industrial strikes.

It started with 24 police officers walking off the job on the night of the 31st October, 1923 at Russell Street Police Headquarters. This was right on the eve of the spring racing carnival's major events threatening disruption to the famous horse racing season and all the festivities and tourist spending that came with it. Such was the importance of the carnival that over time many groups followed the police example and used it to apply pressure by withholding their labour at this critical time.

Where the police were concerned in 1923, their action resulted in them losing their positions altogether replaced by several thousand sworn volunteers, not all of whom were idealistic in the application of their temporary police powers. Media critics were unanimous in their opinion that the coppers had done themselves irreparable harm. Critics might say that the unarmed Victoria police force with the right timing had sadly managed to shoot themselves in the foot!

Now with the spring carnival looming again, the police commissioner himself, an avid horse racing fan, was determined that the 1924 season would proceed without 'let or hindrance.'

The message was crystal clear. A zero-tolerance policy was the order of the day and Leading Senior Constable Jim Foley was put in charge of a special task force to weed out trouble before it could take root in the racing industry. He was one of several overlapping forces given the responsibility of maintaining law and order in specific areas of the spring carnival.

One squad was set to patrol transport hotspots while another focussed on sporting and cultural events aside from horse racing.

Greater Melbourne was a vast sprawling city growing along the radial lines branching out from the centre of the train network.

'Did the rail lines follow the road systems or vice versa?' asked one of the sworn volunteers who had transited to full membership of the Victoria Police Force as he studied a huge wall map of the city and its far-flung suburbs. The maps were a mandatory item in every police station across the city. 66`Special Constable Sampson came from Sydney and was finding his way in his new hometown.

'A good question, Sampson. If you look south, the Mornington

Peninsula has developed as a holiday playground and tourist attraction. Now industry has followed providing employment, which of course leads into a need for housing and shops.' Here he stopped, scratching his full beard and studied the map. In fact, his nose was almost touching the glass of the framed chart. 'Were you aware that they opened a movie theatre in Frankston recently?'

'No, I wasn't, but it wouldn't be much good for you senior if you're 'alf blind.' Sampson was taking a big risk teasing his senior constable, but he had a lively sense of humour and a sense of slapstick self-deprecation that often had his colleagues in fits of laughter sadly at inappropriate times.

'Constable, were you kicked in the 'ead by the milkman's 'orse you flamin' galah? How dare you talk to me like that!' Senior constable McKenna retorted, only half joking. 'Come on lads, the wagon's here so mount up and we head off to bring peace to the land.'

'Blimey cobber 'ave you been readin' those penny dreadful's of yours again?'

This was the first day of the commissioners' spring crackdown and police across the city were being activated to detect and arrest any of the usual miscreants that crawled out of the back-street slums to prey on the unsuspecting citizens attempting to enjoy their free time.

A list of well-known fraudsters and petty criminals that usually showed up at this time of year was circulated among the constabulary, who were warned to be doubly alert.

'Con artists with their pea and thimble tricks, card sharps drawing in the gullible, purveyors of stolen or imitation jewellery and other genuine but stolen valuables.' The Deputy Commissioner was fiery in his briefing, extolling every constable, every officer 'to do his and, ahem, her best.'

'It's as if someone had opened a Pandora's Box to release all these blood-sucking parasites to feast on the general public.' The Deputy Commissioner liked to finish with a colourful analogy, often roping in the classics. He once made an impassioned speech leaning heavily on the Myth of Sisyphus to illustrate the tough, repetitive nature of police work. Most of his audience thought he was talking about syphilis and left the briefing very confused.

This time fired with enthusiasm after the Deputy's Commissioners rousing speech, Jim Foley's team were already aboard a Tait train on their way to Flemington. Recently, there had been a major scandal concerning an Irish trainer who arrived in the city last year from a dynastic Irish horse training family. He had displayed great talent and was granted immediate acceptance into his chosen trade, the horse racing industry.

In fact, he was the trainer of the fabulous stayer Tidal Wave favoured to win the Melbourne Cup. Sadly, all hope of glory was snatched from his grasp when he was exposed as a drug cheat when a vial of a prohibited substance was found in his stable at the track and instructions on its application had been found in his possession. None of the horses in his stable were found to have anything untoward in their systems but nevertheless the Victorian Racing Club deemed it serious enough to suspend Blaine O'Farrell's licence and subsequently cause Tidal Wave and all the horses in O'Farrell's stable to be suspended from racing for a period of thirteen weeks which took them outside the carnival period before the stable could resume racing.

A full investigation would take place immediately following the final event of the carnival, at which time O'Farrell's legal representatives would have a chance to present their case. O'Farrell had lodged a protest, which was dismissed on the basis of the prima facie evidence.

It was a massive shock to the industry and created headlines across the world, bringing embarrassment to the O'Farrell racing dynasty back in County Kildare. Blaine O'Farrell protested his innocence to anyone who would listen, but his pleas fell on deaf ears. All he could do was to sit on his hands until the protest committee sat in what would be the New Year.

Plowright's scheme had the desired effect avoiding possible bankruptcy with Windbag the 7/4 ultimate winner of the Cup ahead of a well-fancied pair of Manfred and Pilliwinkie.

CHAPTER 21

THE CURTAIN IS PULLED ASIDE

Captain Jenkins, aka Reggie Watford, aka Francis Willoughby Fifth Baron Middleton was enjoying a wonderful spring time in his recently adopted city of Melbourne. His several nefarious schemes were bringing in money from the gullible and the foolhardy in bucket loads. His recently hatched plan to entice investors in his elaborate fairy tale about a massive treasure to be found in the ancient cave system near Lahore in India was to be his tour de force.

So far, he had captivated two such dupes and wanted as many more as he could seduce before taking off for fresh pastures ahead of the fraud squad.

Right now, he was salivating over a wonderful lobster Mornay that was being served to him and his new best friend, Eugene Bradfield, the slightly eccentric and always amusing thespian. They had been discussing the affairs of the day and, of course, the sport of kings. They were each bragging about their winnings over the course of the preceding weeks on the track and across the tables at Matthias Vogel's establishment.

As they talked, they became aware of a discussion between two of the staff of Indian extraction who were incautiously and against all the rules of hospitality but with unbridled excitement discussing the pending arrival of a significant person. But since the conversation was conducted in Hindi, it was incomprehensible to both gentlemen.

Captain Jenkins was expected to have a working knowledge of India's most prolific language, but confessed that his hearing wasn't up to it. Jenkins determined he would find out what the excitement was about immediately after they finished their meal that previously had taken about three hours with eight courses, hors d'oeuvre, soup, appetizer, salad, main course, palate cleanser, dessert and petit fours. And then naturally gentlemen of their standing would be expected to finish with port and cigars in the hotel's bar.

The two staff members that Jenkins sought had finished for the day and were on their way to their accommodation, unavailable for Jenkins' enquiry, so he followed up from another direction. The waiting staff and the kitchen staff was made up of several nationalities. The chef was French, but he was supported by a specialist in Indian cuisine and they each had a team beneath them who performed the mundane tasks of the kitchen.

From the sous chef down to the 'swampy's' cleaning dishes, they were a highly efficient team that performed like a well drilled army troop. There was a strong vein of the sub-continental among staff forming a tight group who lived together and worked together, sending money home to poorer members of their families. Most of them had very little contact with the hotel's guests, with the exception of two waiters in training for higher things.

'Sanjeev, have you observed the one who calls himself Captain Jenkins?'

'I have Viraj, what do you make of this person?'

'I think he is as the whites say, 'full of it.' Viraj shakes his head in disgust. 'We can only pray that the Lord Krishna will see him and bring karma on his head.'

'Perhaps with the arrival of our senior ambassador for a cultural exchange, he will be revealed as a fraud and a thief?'

'We can only hope Viraj.'

While this conversation is taking place downstairs, upstairs in the dining room, the glamorous Captain Richard Fairlie Jenkins chatted amiably over port and coffee with Quentin Upjohn, the replacement gossip columnist for the deceased Johnny Kovacs, and like Johnny always on the prowl for something spicy to fill his weekly column. He had shamelessly stolen Kovac's contact diary from his desk when he was gaoled and had diligently followed up every single contact, dismissing many and ingratiating himself in best Kovacs tradition on the best. He was also gay, which some suggested as a perquisite for the job.

The Windsor Hotel had always been a happy hunting ground for Kovacs and Quentin Upjohn thought he might be onto something salacious to amuse his readers as Jenkins regaled him with lurid tales of sexual conquests in Melbourne and abroad, much of it produced in the fertile imagination of the gallant captain.

Jenkins can't help himself. If it's separating a thousand pounds from some sucker or a martini paid for by this little mud slinger, he would play along for it. Right now, he was having fun with Quentin Upjohn describing an imaginary orgy he had attended in the home of one of Melbourne's best-known socialites (name withheld).

He could see Upjohn's eyes almost popping out of his pointy little head with excitement as he signalled the waiter for another vodka martini on Upjohn's expense account, of course. Sanjeev loses no time in fetching the cocktail. Mr Upjohn is one his favourite visitors who always tips generously. Sanjeev often has some interesting titbits to relay to him regarding the secret life of the hotel's guests. In view of the symbiotic relationship between waiter and journo, these rumours are always couched in fairly vague language to protect and conserve the source.

Who was the leading property developer and manufacturer with the blonde bombshell on his arm enjoying lunch at the Windsor?

How embarrassing? Visiting wealthy grazier discovered sans pants in a lift on his way back to his third-floor room.

Too many 'ports' in a storm? State MP nods off and lucky not to drown in his soup while entertaining and we do mean entertaining visiting UK officials.

This was the type of 'village pump' gossip that readers of the *Truth* thrived on. Workers in workshops and factories around Melbourne would sit down at smoko time and try to work out who the sordid creatures were that were denounced, however abstractedly by Quentin Upjohn.

All good things must come to an end and the colourful pair bade each other good night, each feeling replete in their own ways. Jenkins wobbled off on alcohol impaired legs to his apartment within the lush hotel while Quentin Upjohn immediately started to scribble notes in his small pocket memo pad before alcohol does its thing and erases all memory of the salacious gossip he's just heard. He is just finishing when a polite cough attracts his attention. It's his number one informant, Sanjeev who in the process of clearing the table surreptitiously passes him a handwritten note and continues clearing the table.

Quentin Upjohn is no simpleton and realises as this is a break from normality, it must be something significant. He secrets the paper in his side pocket, removed his wallet and paid the bar bill and as usual left a more than generous tip on the tray for his collaborator. When he finally got around to reading the note the next day, he realised he should have made the tip substantially larger.

In fact, after he had done some research on the subject of the note he was holding in his hands, young Sanjeev will be in the money. Several days later and after many international telephone calls, he was stunned by what his initial searching revealed. Surely it can't be true? And if it was and he can provide incontrovertible proof, it would be one of Melbourne's if not Australia's greatest social scandals of the twentieth century.

Having withstood the doubtful comments of his editor, and endured shouting matches over the cost of his long-distance telephony he presented a synopsis of what surely would be an award-winning scoop to his ever-doubtful editor who was left utterly speechless. He was given carte blanche to pursue it to its end. This time, he has a chance to write a story that is not based on smut and innuendo. It would be seen as a public service and bring acclaim to his newspaper that normally resides at the bottom of the cockie's cage.

Truth, the voice of the working class, was left leaning, sensational, melodramatic and based on scandal generally around proceedings in the divorce courts. Quentin Upjohn's story would be a massive departure from his usual squalid reporting, but nonetheless still scandalous.

Chapter 22

Pampering A Beauty Queen

During the winter, the elegant paddle steamer Hygeia received a much-needed sprucing up called a re-fit after her long and busy summer transporting Melbourne's trades' people on their annual picnics plus the tourists seeking respite from the heat in the city.

Captain Fergus Galbraith took a deep breath as he boarded his charge, revelling in the smell of coal smoke and fresh paint. He had been a constant presence on board during her refit, overseeing everything the various trades were undertaking, from freshening the bilges to loading coal into her prodigious bunkers. He and the ship's engineer had inspected every moving part of her two mighty engines that each developed four hundred and eighty horsepower.

The excursions, as they were known, most often took a circular route around the bay. Named after the Greek goddess 'Hygeia' who was the goddess and personification of health, cleanliness and hygiene giving her Master, Captain Fergus Galbraith incentive to ensure his vessel would live up to the standards of the Goddess.

The ship and crew had a busy schedule over the summer, the direction of their journey around the bay dictated by the winds that varied according to the weather systems. By avoiding headwinds or high seas, Hygeia strove to give her passengers a comfortable and time efficient trip. Melbourne's winter winds on the Bay were generally steady and reliable, but of course only a few fancied a seagoing outing in winter. Those few that did venture out would enjoy the delightful restaurants aboard or snug and warm in the cafes or bars. A good day would be had by all despite the ambient temperature.

In the summer, the winds were much more variable, with strong northerlies that blew over the city having picked up heat and energy from the country's interior. A northerly tended to be strong at the city end of the bay, petering out towards the southern parts. Combined with a westerly, however, they could build damaging power and blast their way across the thirty-five miles of open waters to pound the Peninsula and its fragile Mornington Harbour. Winds from the south coming in from Bass Straight tended to push the northerly back and bring a cooling breeze to the city. These breezes, being cooler with a high moisture content, were therefore heavier and more powerful than the hot dry northerly.

Occasionally, a southerly buster will come in from the south-west appearing as a massive granite like dark cloud pressing down on the sea compressing the air beneath it, bringing all manner of meteorological hell that includes extreme winds and rain, hail and very dangerous seas. Then there were the strange persistent easterly's that would push in sometimes blowing across the Peninsula against the northerly. Blowing over greater Frankston into the bay this offshore breeze could be quite strong and last for days at a time. This would often occur after a sustained period of hot still conditions that caused the ambient inland air to rise leaving a low-pressure area that the easterly endeavoured to fill.

A wise captain took note of the portents of his weather and prepared accordingly. When the weather was nice, as it most often was, despite criticisms of Melbourne's weather, there was nothing better than to be on the waters of Port Phillip Bay with a sound vessel under your feet.

Hygeia had 'forced draught' for the boilers that acted in a sense like superchargers on an internal combustion engine requiring six firemen who shovelled about three tonnes of coal an hour into her eternally hungry maw giving her a top speed of twenty-two knots although it was claimed she had reached twenty-five knots on one run. The firemen or ships stokers never came on deck during a cruise and were very likely to come from a coal mining background in North and South Wales, Northumberland and Durham, Yorkshire, Lancashire all the mining districts of the mother country. They spoke with the variety of accents peculiar to their birthplace and kept mostly to themselves. The Lancashire lads could be heard to use words like: *Barm* (bread roll) *mitherin'* (pestering) *proper reet good* (that is very good) *scran* (food).

Each of them from their home counties had their own peculiar patois, but managed to understand each other and their superiors. Their singular distinguishing feature was their ability to work hard in hot torrid conditions without complaint.

The lightweight design of Hygeia's engines with their navy type boilers delivered tremendous power, allowing her to be constructed of fine light metal plates to a slim design that delivered excellent power to weight ratio enhancing her performance through the water.

While there was no doubt that the powerful engines were an important factor in the Hygeia's performance, she had also been built to provide luxury accommodation in her fit-out, none of which was overlooked by Captain Galbraith's inspection. Every corner of the vessel from stem to stern was examined, cleaned, painted or repaired where necessary with especial attention to her comfortable saloons, bars and dining rooms where her passengers sat down to quality meals. His inspection included the galley and ship's stores to the barbershop that provided hairdressing service to trim the hair and beards of the gentlemen excursioners who might also wish to purchase toiletries or seasickness cures.

Captain Galbraith welcomed his officers back aboard and they were busy with the crew that was largely the same each year. One or two drop off for various reasons and have to be replaced each year, generally transients who were always looking for something over the horizon.

The captain had the core of a good crew who repeatedly demonstrated good seaman like qualities, but even the best got a bit rusty during a layoff. A couple had contacts at the southern end of the bay among the couta boat fleet and could rely on enough work to keep body and soul together through the winter months down there fishing for barracouta in Bass Straight, the staple fish of Melbourne's fish 'n chip shops.

Others might work as labourers or warehouse workers. Now they were all aboard Hygeia again and working hard in their individual areas of expertise. One benefit was the benign weather they were experiencing as they slapped the company's colour scheme on her upper works wherever it was needed. Safety gear was checked and flags and even bunting replaced or cleaned.

With his inspection complete and all things ship shape, Captain Galbraith called his crew to the main promenade deck. Backed by his three officers he stood proudly in naval fashion feet placed wide and firmly on the deck with both hands thrust into the pockets on either side of his uniform jacket the gold braided design on the sleeves denoting his rank, his cap square upon his handsome head, his beard neatly trimmed looking altogether splendid.

His speech welcomes them all aboard again and congratulates them all for being the crew of the finest excursion ship in Victorian waters. He advised them that the company had them scheduled for a busy summer, the highlight of which promised a voyage none will forget.

In conjunction with Melbourne's most famous hotel The Windsor, Hygeia will be conducting a very special cruise. He then goes on to relate that it will be a cruise celebrating Melbourne's exciting summer and the approach of the Christmas holidays. An invited guest list of Melbourne's social elite, celebrity's, theatre stars and sporting people will join the Hygeia. A special theatrical performance would be performed and the guests would dine on a special menu prepared by the Windsor kitchen staff led by their French Chef Franco de La Vere.

A part of the main saloon will be converted into a casino with a one-off permit just for the event. Everyone who is anyone will be breaking their necks to be on board and for that reason there will be a strong police presence to ensure that any miscreants will be dealt with swiftly and discreetly. It will be an occasion on which everyone from stokers to deck crew, cabin crew to ships officers will need to be at their very best.

Two of Hygeia's deck crew, Daisy O'Connell and Sparra Dempsey, long serving and steadfast were taking all of this in with the usual scepticism of foredeck crews everywhere.

'Fair dinkum Sparra, I reckon the ol' man's gunna try and break all records again this summer which means one thing.'

'What's that cobber?'

'Bloody hard yakka mate, that's what, we're gunna be flat out like the proverbial lizard drinkin'.' Daisy shook his head ruefully, 'and don't get me started on that flamin' silver tails knees up the ol' man is talkin' about. Are we gunna be wearin' dinner suits and cotton gloves, huh?'

Both of the lads had filled in the winter, crewing on the coastal freighters running up and down Victoria's coast. Daisy O'Connell crewed aboard SS Casino a very busy little steamship of four hundred- and twenty-five-tons servicing ports such as Portland and Warrnambool and back to Melbourne.

Sparra Dempsey obtained a berth on the SS Casino alongside his best mate Daisy as they clocked up plenty of sea miles in the truly treacherous Bass Strait waters.

They both quietly looked forward to their time on the Hygeia as a relief from the parlous weather outside of Port Phillip Heads but true to form for working men all over they still had a bit of a grouse about the duties and hardships their 'oppressive' masters would put them through.

'Now let me guess, yooz two blokes are planning a mutiny, if I'm any judge.' The booming voice of third mate Bully Masterson a man working hard on obtaining a master's certificate and like the two lads he was addressing, had taken a berth on a coastal freighter during winter. The third mate of the SS Loongana had suffered a broken leg giving Bully a providential berth.

Back aboard Hygeia, Bully led his team through their duties, making sure that all the kinks were out of their systems. But he came away to report to Captain Galbraith that he was pleased with their progress and declared them ready for sea.

Captain Galbraith sent a telegram to his company head office of Bay Steamers Ltd, reporting his charge fully refitted, seaworthy and ready for the season ahead that included all the usual perils of the sea plus they would have the big Christmas knees up to contend with.

CHAPTER 23

JUNE 1924

HELL, IT'S ONLY A FEW BLOODY TREES AND A PATCH OF MUD.

Bloody developers ruin everything that's decent. Just look at this mess.'

Darcy Densworth Trucking, represented by Darcy himself, was at the wheel of their newly acquired 1924 Morris tray truck. She was a beautiful but expensive machine and Darcy would make sure his driver would spend more of his time behind the wheel of this new asset to recover its purchase price and make a profit. It was the latest addition to his large fleet that would grow to dominate the transport trade in Australia. There was plenty of work for him in Melbourne's rapidly developing economy.

One of the downsides of all this prosperity was the sacrifice of some beautiful forests and rich farmlands on the city's fringes. For decades, productive market gardens thrived on the black soil of the Yarra River's ancient alluvial plains providing fresh vegetables for the population. For millions of years the flood waters of the Yarra had laid down a rich black plain that welcomed the farmers plough. This delta fanned out around the head of the bay in a southerly direction from the mountains, then spread out east and west around the area of Greater Melbourne. It was this land that was becoming increasingly contentious. As the city's population grew, housing became a priority and would be for decades. Where there was need, there would always be opportunists.

'Yeah, I guess you're right boss, but Phillip Croker is doin' alright though ain't 'e?'

Phillip James Croker was an overambitious real estate agent who was taking advantage of a contact in the Lands Department who fed him information on people or organisations that owned large land banks. Croker was extremely talented at negotiating deals with such people to purchase outright or partner them in developing their acreage. Development meant bringing in the bulldozers.

Croker was largely despised as a price gouger and manipulator of public assets and funds. With a thick hide all and probing investigations failed to penetrate the armour of his ego.. In a love hate relationship with the public, he grew in stature to the point of legend with a local bush band who wrote a song about him. *'Don't play poker with that Shifty Phil Croker.'*

As Phil often said to his sycophantic underlings, 'you can't count yer chickens without breaking some eggs,' leaving them scratching their heads trying to work that one out. But the message was simple; you don't let sentiment get in the way a dollar. He once famously said that if his grandmother's house stood in the way of one of his developments, it would be goodbye Granny and show her to the rest home. Incidentally, PJ Croker owned a number of rest homes that provided shelter for older folks.

Apart from his property interests, Phillip J Croker ran a small chain of Pawn Shops in competition with Matthias Vogel to a certain extent that were manned by a ruthless bunch of hard-hearted Shylocks who would steal the pennies from a dead man's eyes. Observers would note customers entering the stores with a hopeful smile and exiting in tears, clutching the pittance they had received for their precious goods. The property appraisers were all on an incentive program to ensure that not one skerrick of profit left the store, regardless of the sob stories presented. And there were plenty of those.

As one wit described it, there were stories to, 'bring a tear to a glass eye' but the usurers of PJC Harmony Money Lending remained stoically dry eyed.

After a solid week of exhausting foreclosures and repossessions, Phillip James Croker was relaxing with a snifter of brandy at his favourite club when his eyes fell upon an unfamiliar gentleman ensconced in the corner in close conference with two other chaps who seemed to be hanging on every word that came out of his mouth. Phillip summoned the steward.

'Alfred, who is that gentleman in the corner over there? He appears to be doing some sort of business on club premises? If he was, it was a clear violation of club etiquette and he should be shown the door.' Phillip Croker defending club etiquettes; who would believe it?

'That is Captain Richard Fairlie Jenkins sir, late of the Indian fourth cavalry division. Quite the hero, I believe. We have checked his bona fides and find he resides at the Windsor. I could introduce you if you like, he's a fascinating character.'

'Hmm yes yes. When he's finished his business take him a cognac with my compliments. Not that nasty one you have for interlopers, but that French one... what's it called Alfred?'

'I think you mean the Baron G Legrand 1910 Bas Armagnac sir.'

'Yes, that'll do nicely.'

And so began the relationship between one unprincipled scoundrel and an outright rotter.

CHAPTER 24

1924

PRIDE COMETH BEFORE A FALL

Joseph Esmond McArthur MP; Nationalist for Warrnambool in Victoria's west was a long-time gladiator in the cut and thrust of state politics. He was a prime example of the tough, well-connected mover and shaker of the day. Nicknamed 'Gunna' McArthur as he was generally referred to by the cynical public and his enemies because he was always 'gunna do something.' He stood an above average six foot two inches tall and was built like a timber cutter. Broad shoulders, powerful arms and huge hands that could probably hold a dozen eggs at a time. His outward appearance was that of a big bear inside his tailored suits, when in fact, he was as smart as he was big. His intellect would have him in the upper ten percent of any population sample. His knowledge of law and parliamentary regulation was unsurpassed and with his thirty years of experience in politics, he could easily have co-authored Machiavelli's 'The Prince.' Here was a man who knew where the bodies were buried and who put them there. Any aspiring politician, either state or federal, would do well to have Big Joe on their side.

Big Joe had a lunch date with some important business people who supported his election campaigns, in turn receiving a sympathetic ear to their proposals. Today, in return for their loyal support, they would be made privy to a Big Joe deal. They would be discussing an interesting proposition brought to Joe by a man who crept out of the back door of the Parliamentary offices and sidled up to the big man whispering a piece of top-secret information into his ear. The public servant Stewart Monteith had been on the public payroll now for thirty-five years and had repeatedly been passed over for a more senior role. Stewart had tastes that exceeded his income and entered into this arrangement with Big Joe so that he could indulge himself in his passion for antique ceramics.

Joe employed a chauffeur who drove Joe about town in his 1924 Daimler limousine, a stately vehicle that drew the eye of the pedestrian public and envious motoring enthusiasts alike. It worked like a mobile billboard, advertising his presence wherever he went. His chauffer was an ex-footballer who had played with the Melbourne Demons. Bernard (Bull) Finlay gained a reputation as a hard man on the football field and retired after one hundred and twenty-three games. It should have been many more but for repeated suspensions.

Joe had received more than one death threat in his long and controversial career, and he wisely had Bernard provided with a certain set of skills and a licensed firearm. The Mark VI Webley Revolver resided in a specially crafted holster that was attached to the sidewall of Finlay's seating position within comfortable reach. He had only once reached down for the weapon. It occurred during an election campaign when Big Joe was touring his constituency and was confronted by an angry man who proved to be a crazed anarchist. The man charged Big Joe's vehicle waving a large knife. Bull Finlay stepped out of the front seat with the big pistol in his hand and fired a single booming shot over the man's head, who wisely reviewed his assassination plans and fled.

Big Joe always claimed that he came from a relatively humble family from the western district. 'I'm just a humble farmer, a man of the land.' His version of humble meant that they only grazed five thousand acres.

The McArthur family had originated in England and immigrated to Australia in the 1840s their obvious wealth immediately establishing them as upper class. The patriarch made the first move to establish his family in their new home by taking up five thousand acres of prime grazing land on the volcanic plains to the north of Warrnambool.

As the population exploded during the gold rush era, the patriarch Edward J McArthur farmed land on which he raised a quality beef herd to feed the burgeoning city population. The discovery of gold in the 1850s created a lucrative market for his beef and sheep meat in the goldfields where he charged premium prices to the protein starved miners at the same time quickly building up a flock of prime Merino sheep for their fine wool. It was a maxim that money made money and the old McArthur patriarch was doing his darndest to prove that proverb true.

A home in the city became a necessity after time and, of course, a stately mansion was duly constructed in the highly respectable suburb to the east of Melbourne named after a mansion, 'Toorak House' built by a merchant James Jackson.

Young Joseph had the best that his family's station in life could provide, a fine education at Scotch College with a degree in Law gained with honours at Melbourne University. He was a member of The Melbourne Club and the Melbourne Cricket Club and every other prestigious organisation in the city.

Despite being clearly recognisable as a member of Melbourne's elite, his charisma allowed him to represent a rural electorate of hard-nosed farmers and country people whose lives revolved around farming.

He was a strange fellow who at times preferred the company of the 'lower orders' as his father sneeringly referred to the middle class, particularly those attending sporting events. A keen fan of the VFL team Melbourne Demons, he attended every match his schedule allowed him. The 'Ashes', a cricketing competition between Australia and England, were a special treat and interspersed with boxing matches at various venues around town, his personal diary was generally full. When spring arrived Big Joe was a feature at all the tracks for the whole carnival. Over the years, he owned and raced a number of thoroughbreds.

He was enrolled as a member of the Victorian Racing Club when he reached his majority and had made good use of his membership since.

Big Joe could be described as a bit of a lad except where it came to official duties and parliamentary business, which were thoroughly intertwined and taken quite seriously. But he was great company and a man that everyone wanted as a friend.

Big Joe's lunch date was at Scott's Hotel in Collins Street. Known as the city home of country people, it was where Big Joe conducted quite a bit of business. These fabled premises drew together many strands of his life and interests.

The hotel had played host to such luminaries as the famous cricketer W.G Grace, while Dame Nellie Melba named it her favourite hotel. Joe held casual meetings here with other horse breeders and pastoralists. Auctions for pastoral properties were frequently conducted on the premises. On this occasion, Joe's guests were waiting impatiently for him in the dining room of the beautiful old hotel.

'Ah, here he is.' Announced Phillip Crocker, who stood to greet the big man, 'good to see you in such obvious good health, sir.'

'Thank you and good afternoon to you, gentlemen.'

Assembled around the table was an odd miscellany of business people of whom Crocker's crooked morality was deemed acceptable if not admirable. Arthur Fetchwell, Merchant Banker. Charlie Spriggs of Spriggs and Sons Property Valuers. Hugo Montrose, MH Builders and Developers. The last to rise and greet Big Joe was the money man Francesco (Frankie) De Luca. Frankie was a local businessman with interests in a number of areas. Market gardening, restaurants and nightclubs. He was reputed to have access to an investment fund that could supply loans at unbelievably cheap rates to invest in secure long-term projects. He had long well-established contacts in Calabria, his old country where it was thought he obtained the funds. There was a lot of speculation around Frankie, but it didn't pay to enquire too much. He had the dark-complexioned looks of his people with eyes as black as coal that seemed to miss nothing.

Canny Big Joe suspected his money was not entirely legitimate and was the proceeds of crime, looking for safe refuge after a little wash and rinse. Current interest rates were not unfriendly, but it would be preferable for the funding for this project to be from an unscrutinised source, hence Francesco de Luca's involvement.

Well, so be it. Big Joe would welcome assistance from Francesco for a slice off the top. Big Joe suggested they move their meeting to a more secure room. Management was pleased to oblige and a suitable room was provided where their lunch was served and the sanctity of their secret business was preserved.

⚜

CHAPTER 25

1925

THE DARKER SIDE OF THE GOLDEN CITY

Melbourne was a big sophisticated city with a largely law-abiding population in the 1920s, but like all big cities, she had her sleazy underside. Victoria's population had grown to almost 1,700,000 with females outnumbering males by 11,000, possibly due to wartime losses which were unimaginable. Poverty was rampant and public welfare was almost non-existent acting as the incentive for law breaking which was the only way some people were able to survive. A man could steal without fearing the long arm of the law because the law enforcers were generally few and far between while hunger and cold was a constant. So petty crimes were not only rampant but justifiable while the risk of arrest quite low.

Knowledge and use of drugs were limited to a few but growing exponentially. Sly grogging was still the most popular fundraiser among the desperate characters around town with small shopkeepers the main offenders.

The reliable cash flow provided by sly grogging gave young toughs an opportunity to start trading in narcotics. The gangs needn't go to Mexico or Afghanistan looking for supplies. Opiates could be procured from your local pharmacist. Opium smoking was still rife among the Chinese community. In 1923 the newspapers expressed shock that cocaine had reached Melbourne's slums with an epicentre in the notorious Little Lonsdale Street.

Dealers moved through the poorer areas of Melbourne, including Little Lonsdale Street, selling packets of cocaine. This type of criminal was called a 'snow seller.' One man, Henry McEwart, admitted selling cocaine to women in back street brothels at two shillings a packet after having made money sly grogging. Another gentleman in this profession, Lewis McNeil, was known to carry a firearm to ward off standover men. All in all, it was a burgeoning and pretty nasty business to be involved in.

The criminal class soon found one of the profitable uses for cocaine in the racing world. In 1923, a trainer and stable hands connected to a horse named Valdoid were arrested for doping at Moonee Valley.

As a leading rails bookmaker, Gordon Plowright had used drugs to have a competitors horse disqualified. Had it won he may have faced bankruptcy as he was holding several huge bets on it at generous odds. Now, following the raid on another training establishment, Gordon Plowright bookmaker and destroyer of another man's racing dreams was feeling a little nervous.

Since he engineered the banning of Blaine O'Farrell the Irish horse trainer, he had become more aware, more educated as it were about the owner of the champion stayer Tidal Wave Matthias Vogel and the very real danger he represented. If Vogel discovered the truth behind the suspension of his Cup contender, it would go very badly for Plowright.

Chapter 26
MARCH 1925
Putting the Hurt On

Matthias Vogel had organised a huge free BBQ and picnic on land he owned on Melbourne's outskirts to celebrate the arrival of summer. Anyone and everyone were invited to come and fill their shrunken bellies with meat, bread, and beer. A number of trucks and buses were provided to ferry the needy out to the Vogel's farm to enjoy the delights that waited for them there. Along with the food, a band and several singers would belt out the current favourites and during the breaks, a popular stage comedian would crack ribald jokes and sling mud at unpopular politicians.

Vogel had thrown his hat in the ring for the state elections due in June 1926.

He was hoping for a Labour Party endorsement to contest the seat of Melbourne South held by the Nationalist Thomas Payne and was wisely beginning a long campaign to win popularity with the constituents. The planned picnic was his first step in building his constituency.

Another notable Melbourne character, Roger the Razor was drinking in a shanty bar in a back street of South Melbourne with his motley crew around him.

'Lads our ol' cobber the German is puttin' on a bit of a nosh up at 'is spread this weekend,' he wipes beer dribbles from his chin with his sleeve, 'an' I reckon we oughta accept 'is invite.'

'E's a fair dinkum saint ain't 'e. We can enjoy a good feed an' maybe do a bit of the usual while we're at it. Could be a good day mates, whaddya reckon?'

If they were possessed of prescience, they would have stayed hungry and in one piece in their usual patch.

Came the great day which dawned as a sunny Sunday in early summer. Vogel's invitation had been gleefully accepted by a ravenous horde that crowded onto the transport provided, which then set off down the road as the crowd sang popular songs of the day. A merrier scene was hard to imagine. In amongst the crowd were experienced union organisers whose duty it was to ensure the working class knew who had their interests at heart.

Nestled in amongst the crowd in one of the buses were the street gang of Razor, Showbag, Tweeky and Plover, all with tummies rumbling in anticipation of beautiful roasted meats and bread fresh from the bakers' oven.

The destination was a grassy, well treed five acre block Vogel had purchased on impulse, inspired by his bucolic upbringing in the semi-rural area of his homeland. Something about the smell of the eucalypts and grass ignited long buried desires and before he knew what he was doing, his cheque book was out and the deal was done.

He had never put any cattle on the block to keep the grass down as he could never have time to look after them. Instead, a large smelly old billy goat was employed to perform that task.

The billy goat had been secured to a stake at the very back of the block out of harm's way for the day, as the cranky damn animal charged at everything that moved, his wicked horns employed like battering rams and the sharp points capable of inflicting terrible damage.

The convoy of potential voters arrived after a bumpy ride thirsty and eager for fun and games. The vehicles discharged their passengers who swarmed across the block, hurrying to secure a first-rate picnic spot out of the heat of the sun.

One such hunger driven denizen of the swampy under-caste was a malnourished, painfully thin bloke of about twenty or twenty-five years of age. His emaciated features scrunched up in a permanent scowl made it difficult to judge his age or even his genetic origins. In truth, he might have been a thirty-five year old descendant of the original owners if anyone gave a toss. Not that anyone did. Ronnie the Rat was a much-despised character who in old England may have been called a lickspittle. Defined as a contemptible, fawning person. But perhaps his worst characteristic was his total lack of loyalty to anyone or any cause, especially if he could gain something from his treachery. He once collected a reward for reporting a small-time sly grog shop and stood by watching as the cops hauled off his *mate's* aged grandmother, proprietor of said sly grog. Needless to say, that mateship ended very unhappily.

Ronnie the Rat was almost accustomed to being beaten like the cur dog he saw himself as, under everyone's feet and being no good to anyone he made his own way in life. He had spotted the street gang as they descended from the bus that brought them there. This would be a perfect opportunity in the Rat's devious mind. He had been hoping that he might bring the street gang directly to the attention of the German but could hardly round them up and send an invite.

'Hoo, hoo, hoo, Ronnie Boy how flamin' good is this.' Ronnie sing-songed to himself as he wandered into what he thought of as a free piss-up. 'The lambs are walkin' right up to the butcher's block.'

As soon as his smelly feet, clad in a pair of discarded and worn-out brogues two sizes too big for him, hit the ground he went searching for Vogel. He repeated his information to himself over and over, in case in his nervousness he forgot some of the detail. He knew the value of his intel and today would be payday. Just how did a lowlife like Ronnie the Rat come into possession of such valuable information?

Ronnie the Rat had found a number of sly grog shops around his neighbourhood that were frequented by the darker side of society who often drank more of the home brewed whisky or brandy than was wise. While taking a small libation one day in a favourite grog shop, he noticed an interesting phenomenon. While in their drunken state the drinker's fingers tended to fumble for coins that fell to the crude floor and then through the cracks to the bare earth beneath. The tiny silver threepenny pieces and sixpences were the most common but occasionally the shillings and florins as well. He had found a new revenue stream and it was a legal one at that, although it did involve the expenditure of a certain amount of energy that could be described as work, Ronnie would never admit to working, that was strictly counter to his code of behaviour.

Ronnie had pegged out several such places that provided enough underfloor space to crawl in and recover this booty. On one glorious occasion, Ronnie had found a gold sovereign shining up at him through the muck. Oh, happy day!

It was while he was beneath the floor of a particular sly grog at the back of Smith Street Collingwood that he overheard a conversation taking place directly above him. All sorts of detritus rained down on him every time someone scraped their boots or walked across the floor to top up drinks; that was just a minor inconvenience in his current vocation.

'...is a bastard but bastards allus seems to come out on top, don't they Razor,' said one voice, hushed to avoid being overheard.

Ronnie's ears pricked up when he heard that name and instantly realised the drinkers were their adversaries, the members of the Burke Street Gang.

'Yooz don't get ta be the biggest bookie in the bloody land by bein' a dunce Tweeky.'

'Well, we know he ain't a dunce after the way he took care of that Pommy trainer before the cup 'eh?' Chimed in another voice, probably Showbag.

'Yeah, that was a nice little earner for bugger all effort. Slippin' a note inta that galahs pocket was the hardest part. I wonder what was in that little bottle we dropped in the stable couldn't have been anyfink nice.

Razor added, 'how about ya shut yer gobs an 'get another drink in, ya tight arses.'

'Any 'ow 'e wasn't a Pommy he was a bloody Irish that codger, saw it in the paper.'

'I 'eard they've put more of them amatcha copper blokes on to patrol the stables. Do ya reckon they might ave been onta Plowright knockin' orf his opposition?' a worried Tweeky chimed in.

'Theyz called watchman. No idea, geez wouldn't that upset the apple cart, eh? I was 'opin' we could get a bit more work like that. That big bastard 'arry the 'atchet said we would.'

Suddenly, the penny dropped. Ronnie the Rat couldn't believe his ears. This bunch of galahs had been at the very centre of one of the country's biggest racing upsets in Australia's short history. Now he knew what had happened to the equal favourite in the world's richest handicap horse race. Ronnie stayed put until the conversation drifted off, finally descending into a symphony of snoring and farting.

Almost wetting his filthy pants with excitement and the search for stray coins forgotten, Ronnie the Rat wiggled and squirmed his way as silently as possible from under the floorboards of the grog shop and escaped into the alleyway, hoping to remain unseen.

Ronnie did his homework, checking back in the newspapers recovered from waste bins around town and reading (as much as a semi-literate could) every word connected to the big scandal. It had been reported in sensational terms by the racing scribes as an example of one mans greed for fame and money. There was barely a single word in defence of the Irish trainer who, up until this time, had an impeccable record and came from a legendary Irish training family. Blaine O'Farrell said to be heartbroken, was last seen boarding a ship to return to Ireland in shame. However, not one word of sympathy in the papers for the owner of Tidal Wave, Mr Matthias Vogel.

Ronnie, who had never wasted a single drop of sympathy on anyone but himself, could see the dreadful injustice in this and felt a strange unaccustomed emotion stirring in his chest. Sympathy for another!

Sitting in his dreadful squat the night of his eaves dropping adventure, Ronnie was chewing disconsolately on a wedge of cheese and a stale loaf he had stolen from an unwary shopkeeper the week before when a thought bubbled up in the murk of his brain. Here was a chance to dob those larrikins in and get a reward while they got theirs. Knowing Vogel's reputation Ronnie could count on their reward involving a lot of pain and that would serve 'em right. As a bonus, his information might be enough to clear the young Irishman's name and earn himself another reward.

'I would be a bigger public 'ero than that bloke that was flyin' air planes around the joint. What was 'is name? Charlie King Smiff? They made him a knight an' all.' So, with dreams of fame of sorts and riches yet to be, he washed down his stale bread with another mouthful of cold tea and slept like a lord while his ever-present housemates the bedbugs and lice enjoyed a supper of their own on his grubby carcase.

At Vogel's picnic, Ronnie the Rat slithered from the back of the truck he had hitched a ride on and came face to face with his enemies.

'Hey look what just crawled out of the sewer?' Razor had spotted Ronnie the Rat instantly and wanted to alert the whole world to his loathsome presence akin to the noisy miner birds alerting the bush when a predator was about. In a flash, the whole gang had gathered around him chanting nasty slogans mostly concerning obscene smells and dirty rats.

Ronnie endured it with a sly smirk, knowing that they would all be singing a different sort of tune before too long and he'd see if they sang that one in harmony with a, 'red 'ot poker up their arses?'

Matthias Vogel was having a fine old time ingratiating himself to his potential constituents. No matter how distasteful it was, it would pay in the long term when hopefully the buggers might be grateful enough to cast a vote in his favour.

'Some of dese people are little more than foul smelling morons tryin' to swallow as much of my free grog as possible. Zere's already one or two passed out in ze bushes.' Matthias muttered to a special guest on the day, the notorious gangster Squizzy Taylor who had become a frequent visitor to Vogel's illegal casino extracting 'protection' money. It was, in fact, paid insurance to guarantee that the little shit Squizzy wouldn't come in brandishing a gun and rob the place.

'Just look at zat bloody bunch will ya?' Vogel called to one of the goons he'd brought with him from the casino to deal with any unruly behaviour. 'Boof, fer Chris' sake go an' sort that lot out, will ya? Hurry up man, rattle the dags.'

Matthias was amused by some of the local patois and used it like a dinky-di Aussie. This was an expression favoured by sheep farmers when urging their flocks along.

Vogel and Squizzy continue the conversation they had been having about yesterday's races at the Valley when Boof interrupts them.

'Sorry Boss, sorry Mr Taylor, this bloke said he's got sumfink important to tell ya.' He had Ronnie the Rat by the scruff of neck and shoved him forward.

Matthias looked Ronnie up and down and saw something that looks like a body dragged from the bottom of a lake. 'Take za smelly bloody object over zere and give 'im a beer. I'll deal with 'im in a minute.' Vogel farewelled Squizzy who obviously had business elsewhere and needed to be gone. 'Right, vat's all zis about Boof?'

"E said 'es got somefink to tell yer Mr Vogel, an' he wants to talk to yer in private.'

'Okay vell, he better not be vaisting my time, danker Boof, get back to verk.' Vogel's English was failing him again as the day's pressures mounted.

Ronnie the Rat was dancing with excitement, spilling the beer that Boof has given him.

'Mr Vogel sir, I...I ahh it's about the Cup sir. I know what 'appened an' why.'

'What do you mean, you grub? How in God's name vould you know anysing about the sport of kings?'

Ronnie started his story again and not being a natural raconteur had Vogel interrupting him repeatedly for explanation. Eventually Ronnie got his story across and Vogel understood that he had been betrayed and how it came about by the hands of Gordon Plowright. Ronnie reached the end of his tale, sitting nervously, watching the explosive Vogel pacing up and down clenching and unclenching his fists muttering about being stabbed in the back by that damned bookmaker. It's painful enough losing money to him on slow horses, but this? This is war.

Ronnie feared for his life but he was on a quest and sucked in a big breath and asked the question. 'Do I get a reward, Mr Vogel?'

'Boof, get some help and round up zat bunch of thieving scumbags and put zem on za green bus. Tell zem I have some more special work for zem. They should come along quietly. Zen take zem out to the old barn and make sure they can't leave. Okay? You unnerstan' me?' he growls, 'Just don't let 'em outta ya sight. I've got plans fer dose gutter rats.'

Vogel turns to Ronnie. 'Now my little stool pigeon, I vill look after you don't worry but you better make sure you stay outta za vay of dose boys.' Matthias' English tended to fail him in moments of high excitement.

Vogel's brain was spinning like a top. He knew someone had set up his trainer, Blaine O'Farrell. He had a pretty good idea it may have been Plowright, but it would have been very dangerous to move against him as he certainly had protection. Either that thug Harry the Hatchet or some simple hard headed cops who would do his bidding for a bit of extra income now and then. He could not afford to mix it up with cops on a vendetta. Not to worry, he would take care of this gross breach of trust and sporting sabotage.

CHAPTER 27
OCTOBER 1924
AN AMUSING DAY AT THE RACES RECALLED

An unfortunate meeting between Eugene Bradfield and the man he had cuckolded, Sir Rupert Yarborough, husband and protector of the alluring Lady Lucille Yarborough, took place in the Flemington Racing Club members stand. Sir Rupert, a large and unforgiving man, had not forgotten his grievance with the sly dog and deliberately jostled Eugene, causing him to spill his glass of champagne in his lap, leaving an embarrassing stain. The result of the awkward encounter upset Eugene and when he instructed Skinny Jackson, his runner, to place a large bet for him he wrote out incorrect numbers. When Skinny returned with the ticket, Eugene berated him until he produced his boss' handwritten instructions. Instead of his fifty pounds going on a short-priced favourite, Skinny following the handwritten note, put the bet on a mostly untried mare in double figures.

'You blasted incompetent, why do I keep you on a retainer you idiot?' Eugene delivered an undeserved verbal slap on the unfortunate Skinny Jackson. 'Have you ever known me to bet on a twenty-five to one shot? Have you?' Eugene handed Skinny another fifty pounds and fresh instructions. 'Go back to the bookie and place the bet correctly before you miss the start and be quick about it before I strangle you.'

A thoroughly chastened but blameless Skinny Jackson returns shortly with a ticket for the amended bet just as the field of thirteen runners jumped away from the start. Eugene now has one hundred pounds in the race.

The field of horses cover the mile to the finish line in less than two minutes with the winner creating a colossal upset. Eugene's four to one selection is beaten over the line by half of the field with his rejected twenty-five to one shot coming second. Skinny Jackson went to ground as Eugene exploded about his rotten luck.

'It is obviously far too late now, Eugene old boy, but I make it a firm rule never to exchange an incorrect bet like that.' One of Eugene's party offered a bit of common racetrack wisdom that falls on unappreciative ears. It would be a long day for our unlucky thespian. Standing at the bar waiting to be served, he fell into conversation with a fellow punter who is lamenting the result of the same race.

Eugene places his drinks order and downs it in one gulp just as the words of a public announcement penetrate his irate ears.

'Protest race six, second against first, punters hold on to your tickets. Protest second against first race six.'

'Oh no, oh my God!' Eugene shrieked, barging through the crowd to the trash can where he threw his "losing" ticket to find the rubbish container sparkling clean and as empty as a politician's promise. A frantic search for the responsible cleaning staff resulted in a cleaner pointing him toward a tractor towing a trailer loaded with at least fifty trash cans, most of them filled with filth from the bars around the track.

'There ya go cobber, that's all the bins we got, so 'elp yourself.'

'What do you mean, help myself?' an indignant Eugene splutters.

'Do you expect me to dig through all that crap for you do ya? Well, you can just get stuffed mate.'

'How dare you, you blasted Neanderthal, be damned to you.' Eugene stalked off in a state of high dudgeon to hunt down Skinny Jackson to do the job.

The garbage supervisor called his mate. 'Hey Swooper, which of these bins came from the members bar?' Bluey indicated three bins and they got to work. In ten minutes, the winning ticket was recovered and the hard-working garbage men celebrated a two hundred pound pay day each and in record time emptied the bins into a hopper that was towed to the back of the course.

Eugene returned with a cowed Skinny Jackson in tow to find the bin recovery area devoid of staff and all the bins now emptied and stacked in rows.

Distraught Eugene with an equally downcast Skinny Jackson trailing sulkily behind, returned to the members bar and the company of his drinking companions. Everyone was keen to hear if his mission was successful and commiserate when he reveals the awful truth. The helpful gentleman who offered advice to his host earlier in the day unwisely chose the wrong moment to offer some more unnecessary advice.

'I say Eugene, old chap, there's a lesson there. One should not throw away one's ticket until you hear the 'all clear.'

Eugene responded to this unctuous advice by punching the wise one on the nose and in the ensuing melee, was escorted from the track. Three days later, a hand-delivered letter from the Flemington Racing Club disciplinary committee advised him that they have found him, *guilty of unseemly behaviour in that he struck a fellow member breaking his nose. It is the decision of the committee, therefore, to suspend your membership for a period of not less than three weeks or three race meetings effective immediately.*

'Damn and blast them!' Expostulated the frustrated thespian raising a few eyebrows in the Windsor's dining room. He often opened his mail with an early morning cup of orange pekoe his favourite blend. Adit and Damodar came at the run fearing the worst. This was not how he preferred to start his day.

It had been sometime since Sir Rupert Yarborough had graced Flemington Racecourse due to the blow to his self-esteem by his wife's infidelity and who should he literally bump into first up but that bloody sleazy stage actor Bradfield. He derived great pleasure from watching the fool engaged in fisticuffs across the bar. It was obvious the ponce had never thrown a serious punch in his life, the way he floundered around like a girl in a powder room punch up.

'God,' he blasphemed, 'when I literally ran into him it was all I could do to prevent my hands from closing over his throat and snuffing the life out of the little fornicator.'

'For God's sake, don't even think about it.' His companion Albert Graeme advises sincerely, 'I would hate to think of you sitting in a cell twenty years from now for murdering that worthless tow rag.'

'You're right, of course, but there must be a way to square up without being directly involved. I'd like to have him taken somewhere quiet and flay the hide from him.'

'That might not be beyond the bounds of possibility. Now over there is a chap who knows a chap.' Rupert's friend Albert pointed to a hard-looking man at the bar talking to an older, well-dressed gentleman wearing a homburg and an expensive tailored overcoat.

'The man in the hat is the infamous John Wren and the other chap is his hard man Curly Barker.' They both shift their gaze to avoid being noticed staring. 'I guarantee that man has broken more arms than your entire rugby team and if anybody knows anybody who could fulfil your daydreams, it would be that chap.'

'Hmm, well, let's not discuss it any more in case someone thinks I'm serious.'

I think someone already thinks you're serious about it, Rupert old son. I'll be keeping an eye on you. Albert Graeme was a highly regarded solicitor specialising in corporate law and was on a permanent retainer to his friend Sir Rupert's company providing support, obviously in company law, but also to guide him through the sometimes-baffling ways of this and other colonial outposts where he had business interests.

It was a pleasant afternoon of horse racing for the vast majority of the fans, with three out of five favourites getting home. There were always one or two exceptions to prove the rule as could be expected. One was unhappy bookmaker Mr Gordon Plowright, who had been under the uncomfortable gaze of Matthias Vogel all afternoon. Vogel had never left the betting ring except to relieve himself or grab a drink and something to eat before returning to his observation spot to glare balefully at Plowright, who shifted about nervously on his stand.

Plowright toyed with the idea of confronting him, but Vogel's reputation for violence was too daunting and he was fearful of being at the centre of an embarrassing set to. Eventually his nerves cracked, so he handed over the responsibility for his business to his penciller after race seven. Charlie the penciller and Plowright had had a long working relationship after Gordon discovered his skills with arithmetic and asked him if he would like a job.

Charlie the penciller already had his hands full under a bit of pressure and wasn't happy to have his concentration interrupted. It took a special skill to accurately handle odd bets when the punters were crowding the bag, yelling and thrusting their bets forward. For example, a punter might be going all in and want seven pounds each way on a horse at 13-2. Charlie mentally calculates that as 7 pounds x 6.5 = 45 pounds ten shillings for the win plus 11 pounds three and sixpence for the place. A total of 56 pounds 13 shillings and sixpence. Charlie would make that calculation and write out the ticket in the time it took the bagman to count the punter's money. God help him if he made a mistake and he had never made a mistake in the fifteen years he worked for Plowright.

It was obvious that somehow, to Plowright that Vogel had learned the truth about Cup Day and was using this non-too subtle form of harassment to let Plowright know he knew.

'You alright boss?'

'Nah, I've got a tummy upset; I'm headin' home. You can take it from here Charlie, there's not gunna be much action on the last.' After a quick look at the field, he added. 'Lay Crazy Hazy at five to one to see if you can shift some of the money that's going onto the favourite Gentle Raider. We're holding too much on that chaff bandit.'

'Righto Mr Plowright sir, no worries. I'll call ya later with the results after I tally up the bag. And I'll have the settling sheets done for ya by Monday as usual, take it easy boss.'

'Alright thanks a lot Charlie, I'll see you later.'

Gordon Plowright departed feeling the eyes of Matthias Vogel burning into the back of his head. *If Vogel did know how did he find out*? It must have been those little gutter rats he employed to do the handiwork. He should have known better. He'd call Harry the Hatchet to go sort them out and find out if they've talked. God help them if they have opened their grubby mouths because it will take more than a little clever back chat to get them off the hook. Vogel looked on disdainfully but pleased he had at least sent a message loud and clear to the crooked bookmaker.

⚜

CHAPTER 28

NOVEMBER 1924

DEEP IN THE CITY'S BACKWATERS A PLAN COMES TOGETHER.

November in Melbourne had flown by in a whirl of social activity for the idle rich and hardworking men and women alike. The heat and humidity were increasing to stifling levels, sapping the energy of man and beast alike. Weather watchers predicted a lot of storms this year and the Bureau of Meteorology put up no arguments. With the extreme humidity, the populace began to lose sleep and tempers began to fray and domestic violence escalated; there was unease in the air and in some specific circles the unsettling sensation that something dark was coming.

With the spring racing carnival out of the way, the social elite were searching for the next big attraction. Men had little to occupy their overactive minds with the football season over and the spring racing done and dusted until the serious cricket season began. The talk around the bars tended to be a rehash of the year's highlights.

While the majority of football followers were delighted to see the despised Collingwood Football Club beaten by ten points by the out-of-town Geelong Cats they would have preferred it to have been Melbourne or Carlton putting the sword to the unpopular working-class bunch known as the Magpies. The match was historic; it was the first Grand Final to be broadcast on the new technology radio, or the wireless, as it was fondly called. Further discussion was focussed on three new teams North Melbourne, Hawthorn and Footscray, vying to join the VFL from the competing VFA.

There was hope for continued prosperity with the conservatives, The Nationalist Party of Australia winning the November 14th election taking 37 of the 75 seats despite losing the popular vote.

Another historic note for this auspicious month was compulsory voting for the first time, causing a ground swell of grumbling that quickly subsided in the warm late spring weather favouring the city after a long and cold winter.

Melbourne continued to benefit from relatively low crime rates, or so it seemed. Looking closer, there was a strengthening sub-culture that would provide plenty of subject matter for the crime writers of the daily newspapers. Crime among the lower orders was a constant. The poor would always prey on each other rather than trying their luck on the more prosperous and better protected sections of society.

There would always be several significant plots either in play or being planned by the greedy and the needy as the rest of society rolled on, unaware of the dark forces at play.

Movies were becoming a popular form of entertainment and women were swooning over the latest Rudolph Valentino movie 'The Eagle.'

The Australian cricket team had sailed for Mother England to contest The Ashes series with the despised England XI. On the way, they stopped off to play Ceylon (Sri Lanka) beating the home side by 37 runs. It was a lacklustre team with not a lot of stars. Regardless of the standard cricket is a subject that can keep a gathering of aficionados chatting amiably for hours regardless of results.

There was plenty of amiable chatting at a number of colourful soirées around town as the summer social season began to pick up pace. Plans had been finalised for the round of seasonal parties and invitations had been sent, received and RSVP'd.

Captain Jenkins, among the first on any invitation list had always relied on his native cunning. His instincts that were now telling him that the time had come to gather his ill-gotten spoils and hit the road again. He thought South Africa could be a rich prospecting ground and was sufficiently removed from Australia as to have him disappear into the Dark Continent leaving pursuers behind. A Swiss Private Bank, Lombard Odier (Paris branch) was the guardian of his swelling accounts his greed had no end. He would like to top off those accounts before finally retiring to the villa he now owned on the Cote d'Azure at Saint Tropez and readied for him to live a life of comfort and security.

Arrogant and overconfident as a master fraudster he was sure there were still some low hanging fruit to be plucked from the Melbourne 'aristocracy' and there was no reason why he couldn't take a little icing and a cherry or two to cap off a successful raid on the gullible citizens of the Antipodes before departing for Cape Town. Particularly the woolly headed sheep farmers who came to town after the 'clip' to invest their wool cheques and tend to their banking. Some of these chumps were parted from their money with greater ease than their sheep were parted from their fleece. The hotels would be bursting with wealthy graziers in the lead up to Christmas, when they would be shopping for gifts for family and loved ones.

The word Christmas suddenly struck Reggie Watford aka Captain Richard Fairlie Jenkins like a physical blow. Despite his braggadocio and conceit, there was something missing in his life. Reggie Watford was beset with depressing loneliness. His was a singular type of loneliness with no one to confide in or share his successes. He had plenty of women of course mostly empty-headed socialites who shared his bed for a week or two before moving on. Reggie looked forward to bursting free from the chrysalis that was his carefully sculpted guise to find a genuine companion, the one thing that money could not buy.

Henry McWhirter and Lewis McNeil 'snow sellers' were busily recruiting new addicts for their deadly product as they dreamed of an entirely different 'White Christmas.' Both were using the same old tactic of offering the first taste for free and where cocaine was concerned, there was no such thing as free. They had expanded their teams of dealers who would stand on a corner or occupy a slum dwelling from which the 'product' would be moved. Competition was fierce and violence flared over encroachments on territory.

It wasn't hard to recruit a team to pursue anti-social activities from the desperate and undernourished inhabitants of the slums that many unfortunates called home.

One such desperate was a cunning, unwashed and underfed abnormal youth born and raised in the worst of the slums. Ralph Slater (self-titled the Wolf.) The midwife who had attended his birth commented to his mother that Wolf was the ancient interpretation of the name Ralph his mother had chosen to give him. His mother was illiterate and had taken the name from a racehorse (Run on Ralph 10-1) that had got home two weeks before his birth earning her ten pounds from which she paid the mid-wife and her priest their respective fees. Ralph's father had not been seen after he impregnated his mother.

As an imaginative child, Ralph learnt the ancient Norse meaning of his moniker and immediately adopted it. He had limited reading skills due to the failed efforts of his mother to keep him in school never the less he learnt from a school library book what a wolf was and his puny chest swelled with pride to be associated with such a fierce and powerful animal.

From the age of twelve, he began a long and merciless campaign of terror on the weak and defenceless. Always armed with a cut-throat razor (he called it his Wolf's fang) he used to intimidate his victims becoming a first-class menace and well known to the police force.

Jim Foley had arrested him on a number of occasions for fairly serious offences.

Ralph the Wolf, in his short life learnt the value of cultivating an angelic smile as he stood before the Beak. His charismatic smile had weak magistrates refusing to believe that this appealing youth should be burdened with a criminal record and repeatedly set him free when he promised to change his ways, but once parole was granted, he would immediately break it much to Jim's disgust.

The Wolf took to drug dealing like a fledgling duck to water and was shifting large amounts of the drug called snow on the street. At the age of fifteen, he had grown tall and was surprisingly strong given his poor diet. His physical superiority enabled him to intimidate smaller compliant children into becoming a gang of skilled thieves and dealers Fagan like under his direction.

❧ CHAPTER 29

Happily re-supplied by Henry McWhirter, who protected his best dealer like gold, Henry had almost come to the point of shooting his chief rival Lewis, who had persisted in trying to lure Wolf away from him. Such was the impact of Wolf's team on the streets that locally the incidence of theft and burglary had spiked as addicts were forced to find ways to feed the fires of their craving.

Senior Constable Jim Foley knew his foe and his habits well, and was determined to bring this mini crime wave to an end. But first he needed to trap him cold with a significant amount of cocaine in his possession so that he could prove to a sympathetic magistrate that this charismatic youth standing before the court was a dangerous criminal who had inflicted pain on his community and addicted many of its citizens to the deadly powder known by the benign street name of 'snow.'

Jim was maturing into a very shrewd copper who had recruited by fair means or foul a number of informants that could provide reliable information that had in the past assisted in putting away a number of criminals. He now called in two of these characters and briefed them on what he wanted. Find out when Wolf was due to be re-supplied by McWhirter and there would be a big reward in it for the one who brings him the accurate information. There were no more cunning snitches in the country than these two, and competition plus the offer of a large reward had their noses to the ground like a pair of terriers after a rat.

A tactical meeting was arranged by Jim Foley after he had decided on a targeting operation against Henry McWhirter and his number one drug pusher. The two snitches had been very diligent in their quest to nail down a re-supply date and time for the Wolf. Simply put Wolf would rock up every Tuesday for his re-supply that would be waiting for him.

In the meantime, as new recruits, the Wolf agreed to supply the snitches with a small quantity of the powder. A tiny amount but an expensive one. Wolf wasn't taking any chances and insisted on cash up front from the snitches that ultimately came out of Foley's operational budget. That is, his own pocket.

Anyway, in Jim's mind, it was only a couple of quid and worth it if he could nail these bastards.

McWhirter's headquarters were well known to Jim and half the force as he had been suspected of supplying sly grog and running an illegal gambling den on the premises, attracting more than one raid over time. McWhirter proved resilient and would soon be back in business almost before the ink dried on the charge sheets.

Jim Foley knew he was putting his career on the line by not submitting his operation without receiving approval from headquarters. He took the risk because he was sure it wouldn't get off the drawing board if he did, especially since McWhirter had a protector within the ranks. The colleagues Jim took along on the operation were all loyal conscientious coppers who understood the risk they were taking but were also dedicated to bring these criminals and peddlers of the deadly powder to face a court for their crimes.

Meanwhile, after being convinced by the two smart young grafters employed by Jim Foley that he could expand his operation, Wolf was excited as he believed he had made the big time now with a mob of his own and now the opportunity to run a second mob under his control on the other side of town.

Henry McWhirter invited Wolf to the security of his grog shop to discuss this development. McWhirter had been around a long time and contended with many competitors and imitators attempting to usurp him, plus the cops flushed with a religious fervour trying to wipe him and his trade off the map. He wanted to be assured this was not another attempt.

'Righto cobber, tell me wots yer lurk then, tell me orl about it. An' remember if these blokes are snitches and bring the Johns down on us it'll be you wot gets it in the neck.'

Wolf relates his tale to Henry and how the two hopefuls had turned a ten-pound packet of snow into thirty quid and did it in three days.

'Okay, just don't forget who yer dealin' with an' wot'll 'appen if ya stiff me.' Growled McWhirter.

Things were going well for the young entrepreneur and he left the grog shop in a great frame of mind, unaware that he had been followed and his conversation observed.

Jim Foley had his team organised and was ready to strike when he heard from his comrade-in-arms. Tuesday morning the team were in place ready to pounce, including Dorothy Green dressed in civvies who has been tagging the Wolf. If he was street smart, he would be carefully watching for 'Johns' and would not suspect a 'skirt' as being the law.

Business was brisk at Henry McWhirter's grog shop, where people were coming and going on various missions. There was a card game running for the last twelve hours in the back room for high stakes and a team of young blokes running refreshing ales and snacks to the players. There was also number of dinkum young coves used to 'run the rabbit' as it was known, delivering grog to customers around the near neighbourhood.

The weather was warm and the sky clear and bright, which lifted the spirits of the raiding party who were splashing through the ever-present mud holes and slosh filled wheel ruts of the unpaved streets. Jim felt as though he would grow webbed feet at times, as so much of his time was spent patrolling the poorly drained back streets of the western suburbs of Melbourne and the poorer working-class areas in the north. His feet would be wet from dawn to dusk. He was fortunate enough to be able to afford several pairs of serviceable boots. His boots today were already darkened by moisture to just above his ankles.

The muddy water was not the only thing the police had to contend with, it was the overpowering stench of the gutters that clung to the back of their throats and impregnated their clothing so badly at times that they would need to remove them before they entered their homes.

Dottie Green had her baton in her copious handbag to defend herself if she was sprung, plus she had a police whistle that she would use to send a shrill signal to the squad to close in when the exchange occurred.

The rest of the squad was made up of Constables Roger 'Bluey' Farnsworth, Nobby Clark and Butch Mills. The latter two were very strong and capable coppers. Nobby Clark had a regular spot in a VFA football team and was fleet of foot and match fit, Butch Mills was an amateur light heavyweight boxer and a hopeful competitor for an Australian title. He was not a huge man, but at one hundred and seventy-five pounds near the light heavyweight limit he was a fearsome opponent. Today he would rely on his police issue baton like his male comrades, and he knew how to use it.

The squad took up their positions and waited for Constable Green's police whistle to sound the charge.

Jim planned to lead the way by casually walking up to the door like one of McWhirter's customers coming out of the bright sun, counting on it to blind his quarry as he looked up to see who was entering the gloomy interior of the shop.

The store was too busy with four or five customers buying grog, drugs or waiting to trade stolen goods to notice a large figure blocking the doorway. No one said a thing until a little kid of about five years called out in a whiney voice. 'Hey look Ma, a bloody rozzer.'

What happened next could have been straight out of a Keystone Kops movie as the cry went up. 'Cops!'

The back room exploded with a panicked urgency as card players attempted to scoop up their stakes and as much of their oppositions coin as they could, resulting in a wild brawl breaking out. One combatant was hurled bodily against the wall that was never built to withstand that sort of impact. On the outside of that wall, three loafers sat about smoking and taking a tipple. Suddenly, they were buried in masonry and the semi-conscious body of a card player.

Men yelled warnings to run, women screamed and the only one to show a bit of mettle was the five-year-old boy who ran straight at Jim shouting 'Piss off copper bastard,' punching Jim in the groin doubling him over in pain. As Jim struggled to regain normal breathing, he cursed his rotten luck. 'Please don't tell me I'm being put down by a bloody five-year-old?' Jim could already hear the chorus of jibes that would greet him back at the station.

That's what we call putting yer nuts on the line, Jimbo. Ha ha.

Ya gotta have balls fer this job, Jimmy Boy.

One bloke went out of the window even though it was closed finishing on the ground looking like he'd been through a cheese grater with cuts everywhere except the soles of his feet.

Another gentleman who was supposed to be acting as a lookout had tilted his chair back against the wall of an adjacent structure and dozed off in the warm morning sunshine. A jug empty of the ale he had quaffed sat in his lap and a hand rolled fag hung from his bottom lip. Bluey Farnsworth kicked the chair out from under him and he sprang up, swinging punches. Still foggy from his nap, his pugilistic skills were way off and Bluey simply rapped him on the head with his baton and he sat down again with a thump on his upturned chair smashing it to kindling. Jim, meanwhile, was issuing orders as he bent over in pain, cursing the little rat of a kid.

The exercise was generally carried out swiftly with skill, a 'minimum' of violence and great enthusiasm. Butch's baton cracked a couple of skulls and Nobby Clark ran down one fleeing collaborator, belting him across the back of his knees with his truncheon putting him on the ground. Dottie Green had her hands full with the screaming mother of the five-year-old who had now turned his attention to her screaming louder than his mother and using language usually heard only on the wharves.

The Wolf fell to the ground whining like a recently weaned pup when confronted by Jim Foley, who used his baton to break the fearless street warrior's arm when he stupidly pulled out his razor.

Henry McWhirter failed to put up a fight as a severe case of diarrhoea had him ensconced on the toilet from where, undaunted, he completed the transaction with the Wolf five minutes before. He remained there during the entirety of the melee, like a native Chieftain waiting for obeisance.

The nett result of the operation was three hard core miscreants arrested on a variety of charges from trafficking drugs of dependence, conducting an illegal gambling venue, selling alcohol without a license, assault police, resisting arrest, indecent language and contributing to the delinquency of a minor. Among items seized was a box containing 37 neatly packaged individual shots of cocaine ready for marketing, pipes and assorted drug paraphernalia, one .38 calibre five shot Colt Long Shot revolver and two packets of ammunition, one Lee Enfield .303 rifle and ammunition, one illegally modified shotgun, one set of knuckle dusters, and various dangerous knives and clubs.

The story was leaked in advance to a Herald crime reporter, Lex Mortimer, in order to make the evening's front pages, which it did in large font with photographic coverage and statements from the senior officer and raid organiser Senior Constable James Foley. A profile of the main miscreant detailing his less than salubrious record had made a connection between McWhirter and several criminal elements in the city. The paper's editorial warmly congratulated the police force on the success of the job and the removal of a serious, thriving gang feeding on the addictions of vulnerable people. The real shock to the papers proprietors was the large number of deadly weapons captured by the heroic unarmed police. 'A sizable cache of weapons providing the capability of large-scale terrorism or at best the committing of major crime.'

And last but not least Ralph the Wolf was reduced to a mewling pup after receiving a sentence of three years hard labour in Ararat Prison and after serving twelve months he was transferred to Langi Kalkal Prison Farm where he spent a further eighteen months working in the fields before being paroled.

Jim Foley was not mentioned in the editorial, but he was mentioned in heavy black ink in a thunderous internal police report charging him with ignoring departmental protocol, glory hunting, endangering the public 'and spitting on the sidewalk.' Said Bluey Farnsworth sarcastically.

In a fairer world, Jim should have received an award for courage and meritorious leadership. But this was not a fairer world and rather than recognition of his policing skills, he was reprimanded and stood down for two weeks with loss of pay. Again!

Over a special meal to cheer him up prepared by Maureen, his wife, Jim spoke quietly answering one or two questions from his uncle Deputy Commissioner Francis Foley never once complaining about his treatment by the force that employed him. His aunt and uncle were invited to the dinner and now his uncle sat at Jim's table, critical of his nephew's action.

'Uncle, I know I violated force protocol but can't we look at the results? We removed a large number of weapons and shut down a drug dealer and grog shop. He had been operating openly for years and gotten pretty brazen…'

'James, there is no place for individual actions like this.'

Francis Foley was losing his patience with his nephew, 'Think of the dangers not only to yourself and your squad but to the public as well.'

James had inherited his uncle's short fuse and fired up. 'Well, what about the danger to the public from illegal guns and drugs? I see that as a greater priority.'

'That's true my boy, but here is what you failed to consider. Perhaps the drug squad was in the process of conducting a larger operation and maybe you put one of their people in danger.'

Isabelle Foley tapped her husband's arm and shushed him quietly, suggesting he might want to be more encouraging and less critical, particularly when seated at his son-in-law's table.

Jim's twin sons George and Harry played happily on the floor of the dining room, taking no notice of the adult's conversations. At the age of four, their toy soldiers were of greater importance than anything the old people were saying. The ladies had tired of the never-ending work-related talk and despite several attempts were unable to divert them.

Isabelle Foley and Maureen had retired to the sitting room with coffee and cake, leaving the men to their debate.

'Uncle, I did what I did, and I'd do it again if I thought I could get the same result. Plus, and this is a big plus, this guy was able to continue operating because someone in head office is tipping off the crooks while having his palm greased. Good police work deserves to be supported, not impeded by someone selling us out.' Now he looks sideways at his uncle, 'I don't mean to be disrespectful sir, but let's not forget why you're known as 'First through the door Foley.''

The answer was a painful truth for Deputy Commissioner Francis Foley. This epithet was earned as a bold young copper who always led the charge and was frequently accused of recklessness. But he had a mentor who had argued strongly in his favour and instead of reprimands, Francis Foley was celebrated within the force. Commendations came and promotions followed. 'First Through the Door Foley' had a stellar career, rising swiftly through the ranks, and now he had been caught out hypocritically criticising his nephew for using the same tactics that had launched him on his own career path.

Uncle and nephew reached an impasse and agreed to drop the subject, joining their wives in the sitting room. For the next few weeks of his suspension Jim intended to spend as much time as he could with Maureen and the twins.

Lex Mortimer had called on Jim at his home and asked for an interview which he included in a longer investigative piece in the weekends paper. The essay was supportive of Jim's actions and critical of the Police chastisement of their conscientious Senior Constable.

Jim read the article and groaned. This was an inflammatory article that would be sure to cause him further grief. Rule number one; never, ever talk to the press! There was a school of thought that bad publicity was better than no publicity. That was all very well in the civilian world, but Victoria Police was a giant bureaucracy where this type of exposure was to be avoided and the subject of the article (Jim) would be castigated by his seniors. This is not what Jim Foley needed at this point in his roller coaster career.

The city continued to roll on with all its intrigues, scandals, robberies, and murders. Major crimes being planned or committed unseen. Yet Jim foley found himself on the mat once again for attempting to thwart the plans of one dark individual.

CHAPTER 30

FEBRUARY 1924

A Failure to Plan is a Plan To Fail

A more immoral bunch of brigands, it would be hard to assemble under the one roof. At least not in Melbourne. The only difference between this mob and a gang of bushrangers was their clothing and their modus operandi. The expensive suits, manicured nails, clean hands and neat haircuts set them aside in appearance; their morals however, came straight out of the same slush pit. Arthur Fetchwell, Merchant Banker, Charlie Spriggs of Spriggs and Sons Property Valuers, Hugo Montrose MH Builders and Developers, and not to forget Phillip Croker, Francesco (Frankie) De Luca Business man and market gardener. This was the same gang that had met several times prior. Now a partnership satisfactory to all had been hammered out with finance sourced and guaranteed by Frankie de Luca.

Joseph Esmond McArthur, MP Nationalist for Warrnambool and 'fair dinkum sly dog', in the opinion of his detractors, had called a meeting of similarly inclined business men in Scott's Hotel to discuss a secret financial matter that could conceivably make a fortune for the participants in the scheme.

It was not for the first time, nor would it be for the last time, that the scheme involved real estate and corrupt public servants.

Big Joe had received a tip off from his man inside the state's bureaucracies of the government's intention to rezone and release a parcel of public land in a proposed corridor that would open up an industrial area close to the waterfront. It was a large parcel estimated to be at least twenty acres. If the first rule of real estate was 'position' then this was a winner. The potential profit from capital growth alone was huge and would be all the better if it was purchased with low-interest loans. This was where Frankie de Luca came in. Frankie had access to enormous amounts of cash from some mysterious source that would be loaned to the group at stupidly cheap interest rates.

Big Joe suspected Calabrian money laundering, and he wasn't too far off the mark. The Melbourne syndicate would need to be perfectly clear that they were dealing with the devil, and such arrangements came with strings. This was one aspect of the deal that truly concerned Big Joe. On his trips to the USA in recent years, he had learned a little about the mafia and quite frankly, it terrified him. Okay the interest rates were very low, but the loan would need to be repaid sooner rather than later and if it was late, what were the ramifications? If they weren't careful, they could find that the mafia wound up owning them lock stock and barrel. Big Joe was nobody's fool and recognising these risks was already three steps ahead of his colleagues.

Now speed was of the essence before the government decided to gazette the property and it became public knowledge.

There were no minutes taken at this meeting, in fact there would be no record of the group's membership, meetings or planning. Joe was very specific about this and for the reasons he outlined, they were in full agreement. A silently amused Big Joe thought it would be an interesting exercise to throw a ten-pound note into the middle of this group and see what happened. He suspected blood would be spilt.

Having achieved what they came for, the meeting broke up as the participants scurried away to meet their private demands and commitments. Big Joe strode away up Collins Street to return to his Spring Street Parliament office, where a gentleman was waiting patiently to meet him.

Joe had organised this meeting some time ago after laying down the details of the land grab his syndicate was plotting to pull off. The gentleman he was about to meet represented very powerful European connections interested in the opportunities the great south land could provide.

In Joe, they believed they had found a compliant two-way conduit and their judgement had been proven infallible as usual.

Joe trusted in the Swiss more so than he did the Calabrian's, believing that with the Swiss he had things under his masterful control. However, he had no idea of the true power of these Calabrian's, people who not only controlled vast wealth across the world but their influence was felt in such places as the Vatican and the governments of Europe and the United States.

'Ah, good afternoon Mr Brunner, welcome to my office. Have they been looking after you? Would you like a coffee before we take our trip?' The dapper Karl Brunner politely declined Joe's offer and complimented him on the décor and outlook of his office. They spent a few minutes examining various awards, gifts and souvenirs decorating what would otherwise be a fairly austere wood panelled box. Karl Brunner had an interest in a soccer team in his homeland and had been a talented athlete in his youth. He was curious about the VFL football mounted on a small pedestal on the bookcase. After explaining what it was, Joe promised to provide a tour of the MCG and maybe even a visit to his beloved Demons club rooms.

Joe's phone on his desk rang, and a disjointed voice advised him that his car was ready and waiting for him.

Joe and his guest left the office and made their way to where Joe's stately 1924 Daimler limousine usually sat. Instead, with its engine running quietly, was a 1920 Rolls Royce Phantom limousine. His chauffer Bull Finlay stood patiently by the rear door which

He deftly swung open and saluted the two gentlemen as they took their place on the comfortable back seat. The Rolls Royce was an eye catcher, but would not be linked to Big Joe. As they leaned back, Joe offered cigars and a silver flask of fine brandy. Both politely declined.

The gleaming black incognito sedan wound through Melbourne's streets down through the dock and industrial areas, giving Monsieur Karl Brunner a thorough introduction to the great city and all of its important components. Brunner's mind was like a steel trap, missing nothing and asking many pertinent questions. Joe had laid a large-scale map out across their knees with which he identified the places they were visiting, marking them off with his fountain pen while emphasising their strategic importance.

Joe had already explained to his guest that his vehicle was very well known and would surely be remarked upon if they were to take it to inspect the land he wanted to discreetly show his guest.

The land sits between the Maribyrnong River and the docklands on the lower reaches of The Yarra River. The land in question was currently owned by the taxpayer after Federation.

Under instruction from Big Joe, the driver toured the area Joe traced on his map with a large manicured index finger. Then he produces something that was still a rarity, a large aerial photograph of the location taking in its surrounds. The area was almost totally covered by ramshackle buildings housing one enterprise or another some legitimate others not so. No one owned the land they stood on, some was actually leased from the government for a 'peppercorn.'

Joe pointed out the road and rail systems, driving home to his guest the strategic importance of the land and its relationship to the city centre. Having seen enough, Joe directs Bull Finlay to return them to The Melbourne Club for drinks and lunch.

Monsieur Karl Brunner was pleased with what he had seen and impressed by the rough sophistication of his host, who he believed was presenting a golden opportunity for his bank to stake an important place in this 'semi-civilised' city. After a couple of scotch's Brunner claims weariness and declines lunch with a desire to retire to his hotel, which is only a short walk. He is staying at the Windsor so he declines the use of Joe's limousine. Bull drives his boss home to his domicile and retires to the comfortable apartment provided for he and his family above the garage that was the original stable in the old mansion.

Monsieur Brunner arrived at his hotel feeling that the time taken to travel to this backward country could prove to be well worthwhile. The land that he been shown by the politician certainly had promise and his phone call back to his bank would reflect that opinion. But right now his focus was on writing a letter to his beautiful wife Elena, who waited at home with their two small children, two lively boys six and four. He had proudly displayed the family photograph to the Australian at lunch, who seemed to be genuinely delighted.

Later, he would spend the afternoon composing a comprehensive report that would be carried back to his superiors by the new airmail system and it should be in the hands of the bank within two weeks. Amazing to think that you could span half the world in less than fourteen days.

After a refreshing shower and a change of clothes, Karl made his way down to the dining room for his supper. A very particular man, his dietary needs were almost exclusively vegetarian except for the very fine beef he was used to in his homeland. He was mulling over the menu with a martini (very dry) when he was approached by a gentleman who had been sitting at another table.

'Excuse me sir, I hope you don't think me to be rude and intrusive,' said Captain Jenkins, 'but I couldn't help but notice your accent and I was wondering if you needed assistance with your menu?'

'Ah well no I don't believe so although it is kind of you to offer.' Karl summed up the man quickly and saw an intelligent youngish man with an air of well to do and an athletic bearing and his curiosity was aroused. 'Please, would you care to join me for an aperitif?'

Introductions were completed and Captain Jenkins, as a familiar resident at the hotel, called for his favourite waiter and ordered a bottle of fine French Champagne. He has summed up this well-dressed gent and correctly guessed his nationality as either French or German, but he won't say anything, rather he will let it become part of the "getting to know you" routine.

'Monsieur Brunner, if I may be so bold, I take it that you have only recently arrived in the city. May I ask, where do you call home?'

Karl Brunner hadn't just fallen from the clouds. He had become convinced this man had an agenda and was not what he seemed.

'My hometown is Lucerne, a lovely area south of our capital, Zurich.'

'So, yes, I am aware of it but far from familiar. I think it's on a lake of the same name, am I correct?'

'Yes, you are sir, quite correct.'

They raised their glasses and toasted each other. 'To Lucerne.'

The attentive waiters were at Jenkins beck and call, always recognizing the opportunity to make a decent tip when he was in the room and were buzzing about refreshing glasses. What they were really doing was eaves-dropping. They both knew that Captain Jenkins was a fraudster and were fascinated to watch him at work. There was no doubt that the distinguished 'French' gentleman would soon be pulling out his cheque book, keen to be an investor in one of Jenkins fraudulent schemes. But they were doomed to disappointment.

This gentleman was neither French, nor foolish. He was in the country on a very special mission. He had met his host, Mr Joseph McArthur, at an international conference in Zurich and they had become friendly. Big Joe recognised his dinner companion as a valuable connection into European business and Karl Brunner thought that the sheep farmer from Australia was an extraordinarily intelligent man with a highly developed understanding of economics. The fact that he was also a senior sitting member of parliament with enormous influence in his states affairs was a further attraction.

Monsieur Brunner was in the country at the invitation of Big Joe to investigate the proposed purchase of a critical parcel of land described in detail to him by McArthur that would provide the owner with unhindered access to both the city and the docks. He would not even consider travelling such a vast distance for one thing only. As the Swiss proverb goes,

'*Every man is the maker of his own fortune.*' His company would be following up with further investments to take advantage of Australia's lower wages and relatively high unemployment rates to source that labour and various investment opportunities opening up in this new land. Acreage this close to this city, any city, was becoming increasingly scarce and almost non-existent. Heavy industry would need to move further and further out to the city's west to be viable here. Brunner hadn't come this far on a whim; he had done his homework.

This timing of this particular deal was critical due to secret draft legislation going before the lower house at the opening of Parliament in the New Year. The proposed legislation would make it illegal for a foreign government or corporation to own or maintain a controlling interest in large commercial land holdings. It was secret at this stage because the Nationals feared if the opposition got wind of it, they would scream about preventing investment. To the Nationals though, the whole thing was a way of drawing attention away from another scandal brewing over a wild late-night party held in chambers by younger members of the party.

After a late-night session debating the proposed bill in their party room, the Nats saw that the legislation if passed was a great opportunity to dish out real estate licences to curry financial and political support and decided to see if they had the numbers to push it through.

This top-secret information had come from a senior politician and sheep farmer who was now working hard with the Swiss to lock the land up before the legislation was approved. To achieve this advantage had been very simple as the big Australian had offered Karl's company the information for free and guaranteed the front running for a success fee. That fee negotiated in a Swiss Chalet overlooking Lake Lucerne would sit very nicely in Joe's offshore bank account, gathering a solid interest rate well away from prying eyes. From the Swiss point of view, it would be worth following up and if it proved to be a dud, then they would have a pair of eyes to look for other investments in the country. Big Joe and Karl Brunner toasted each other with a glass of fine French wine from Sauternes.

'Do you like the wine, Joe?'

'Yeah, not a bad drop.' Was the laconic response, leaving the Swiss crestfallen having selected wine from possibly the best winery in the world for the occasion.

Back in Australia, at his palatial home in Melbourne's Toorak, the Honourable Joseph Esmond McArthur MP was savouring a delightful meal prepared by the family cook. Almost every component on the table came from the McArthur land. From the choice spring lamb to most of the vegetables and preserves. But no Sauternes from France or anywhere else.

Sumptuous desserts were enhanced by the inclusion of eggs and dairy products from Stamford Downs named for the region the McArthur family had farmed in England.

As he tucked into a magnificent apple pie with thickened cream, he pondered the day's proceedings. His Swiss guest was sitting in the palm of his huge hand, and would soon wrap up the purchase of the industrial land with him to receive a very desirable capital gains. His reasoning for introducing a foreign partner was multi-faceted. Greed being the driving force.

His arrangement with the local business group was a smoke screen providing cover for his real intentions.

Should that local arrangement (conspiracy actually) proceed, and there was every chance it would succeed with his assistance, he would at best have a roughly sixteen percent share in the property. That was nowhere near enough for him. That would be better than a 'poke in the eye' as the saying goes but why settle for a small slice of the pie he chuckled to himself as he eyed the huge slab of apple pie in front of him when you can just like this apple pie have a big slice.

His arrangement with the Swiss had already delivered an envious potential benefit, a huge 'success fee.' Plus, he would have a thirty percent share in the property through a shelf company set up in Switzerland for that purpose in his name.

Once more away from prying eyes, a nice day's work by any standards.

Chapter 31
December 1925
Eugene Musters his Support Group and Dispenses Blessings and Champagne.

Rhoda Day, leading Australian theatrical agent, Elvira Rochester movie casting director, and Madame Rosetta Gloria Parmentier Age Newspaper's senior theatre critic, were enjoying high tea in the Windsor's elegant lounge. Each of the ladies had extravagantly printed visiting cards printed with the legend of their names and roles embossed in gold lettering. They never failed to dispense these at every occasion in case someone mistook them for common members of the herd.

Having been welcomed on arrival with a glass of sparkling champagne, they had been shown to a table set with crisp starched linen with fine china, silver and crystalware that reflected the late morning sun shining through the tall windows into every corner of the elegant room. The ladies were clad in the latest exquisite styles. Rhoda day chose an Ivory sheath style with ethereal lace embroidery and exquisite sheer details. Madam Rosetta wore a gorgeous aristocratic style with raised waistline to an empire fit and layered skirts featuring rich embroidery. Elvira looked as if she had paid a visit to the wardrobe department of her movie studio. Utterly divine in more rich lace and layering's of fine materials. All three wore a dazzling array of enough jewellery to stun the public but remain within the bounds of the elites dubious good taste.

A triple tiered silver cake-stand crowded with savoury appetizers, patisserie, ribbon sandwiches and fresh baked scones with house made Windsor jam and double cream awaits their delectation. They could also select from eleven teas served in elegant silver teapots.

'Oh my, I don't know where to start, it all looks so lovely and I am famished.'

'I can recommend the ribbon sandwiches Elvira; they are always so fresh and tasty.'

'Oh, to heck with diets and table manners, I am going to stuff my face with those beautiful scones with jam and cream.' Rhoda laughed.

Around them every table was taken up by groups of finely dressed citizens, male and female, all chattering away filling the vast lounge with the sound of people enjoying life in excellent company. A string quartet was playing classical selections in the far corner, adding another layer of elegant civility to the room.

The ladies had been meeting at the request of Eugene Bradfield to help him plan the social event of the decade. Eugene would present a one act play aboard the famous and popular paddle steamer Hygeia as part of this year's Christmas celebrations. It promised to be a fantastic event and the highlight of the season if not the year. Melbourne's finest would be on the guest list to enjoy the sea air, fine food and a cultural event all while traversing the beautiful waters of Port Phillip Bay.

The cunning thespian Eugene had brought these women together to take advantage of their business connections and vast knowledge of show business. Together, there would be few people of influence in the Australian entertainment industry that the trio would not know on a first name basis or someone who could provide a useful introduction.

They spent the morning debating which of several plays would be suitable considering the limited space and time they would have to present a laudable and entertaining version of the work they select. Neither these ladies nor Eugene wanted to be associated with a production that would attract derision.

It was a tough decision to make. Should they select a Shakespearean play? Or something contemporary, a comedy or drama? Could they possibly present a musical, say something from Gilbert and Sullivan? It was decided that the offering should reflect the whole joyful occasion, something light and humorous, and in one act. They finally settled on a recent play by an American writer Arthur Goodrich, first staged in 1922. It was a comedic piece titled *This is London*. The 'selection panel' decided that it was an excellent fit for their purposes, light-hearted and pertinent. It depicted an Anglo-American clash between a wealthy Anglophobic American shoe manufacturer who arrives in London to find his son is marrying the daughter of English aristocrats.

Now all that needed to be done was just about everything. Including the production of props that could easily be broken down and taken aboard the paddle steamer and quickly assembled ready for curtain up.

They would recruit the carpenters and painters from His Majesty's Theatre to handle that task while Eugene and Rhoda conducted auditions for the support roles. Eugene would, of course, play one of the leads and they would find the son and the young sweetheart. Rehearsals would need to begin as soon as possible. Musical backing would be provided by the ship's excellent orchestra, saving a big hit to their production budget.

When they reported back to Eugene and announced the name of the play, he was delighted with the selection and congratulated the ladies on their choice. Overall, he was very pleased with the progress they had made. Unfortunately, he had other matters on his mind at this stage. And those matters revolved around money, as usual. Since being readmitted to the racetrack after his dust up with his fellow club member earning him a three-week hiatus, he was now betting overtime to make up for lost opportunity. A smart gambler knows when to stop, but Eugene wasn't that smart. He had picked up right where he had left off. A good win would soon be flushed away with a series of poor decisions. He was still a regular at Matthias Vogel's gambling den where his luck was always more reliable, due to his skill at cards and reading body language. As an actor, it was an ingrained proficiency to read the moods and emotions of other people. Poker players are alert for 'tells' those little involuntary nuances displayed according the hand in front of them. Yes, he could read the other players like a book and all he needed then were the cards. He had found over the years he had developed another important skill, counting cards remembering them as they fell. Employing these skills carefully and betting moderately, it was a rare occasion these days when he lost, most often going home with his pockets swollen only to be deflated on the horses.

'The bloody horses! Why do they do it to me, Captain? Dear God, it is so maddening.' Eugene complained to Captain Jenkins in the bar at the Windsor while they waited for the dinner service. 'If I back the blasted creatures to win, they run a place. If I back them to run a place, they finish out of the money fourth.'

'As a cavalry man, I would be expected to have an intimate knowledge of horse flesh, but I must confess I have no more luck than the next man.' Jenkins sympathised, 'Cheer up old chap you still have your cards.'

CHAPTER 33

OCTOBER 1925: CAPTAIN JENKINS. CAVALRYMAN

EXPERTS ONLY NEED APPLY

Captain Jenkins faux cavalry man was no expert horseman, in fact, he had never been on a horse. The bloody things terrified him. As far as he was concerned, they were just a thousand pounds of bad-tempered cattle.

A recent embarrassing moment had occurred when Jenkins' skills in the saddle were to be put to the test in a couple of chukkers of polo at the insistence of Lady Constance, who had unwittingly become an investor in one of Captain Jenkins' mad schemes. Naturally, she credited an Indian cavalryman with the skills to play polo and bolster her team's chances in a forthcoming annual event. Almost choking on the words, he feebly replied that he could think of nothing he would rather do and then with a rush of blood his self-assurance soared back.

'Why Lady Constance, you know it's been such a long time since I played a chukker or two I might need to get a bit of practice in before I could find my seat again and be considered a threat to the opposition.'

'Well, we have plenty of ponies out at our Mount Macedon property, so please pop out there any old weekend and we'll set you up.' Sir Harry offered helpfully, 'In fact, why don't we make a date of it this weekend? I'm sure you can teach us a thing or two about how the game is played in India. Whaddya say old boy, are we on?'

'Oh, er, ah, yes of course delightful, thank you Sir Harry I look forward to it.' If anybody noticed the hesitancy in his voice, they were far too polite to mention it.

Captain Jenkins was forced to fake a debilitating injury to avoid the awful consequences of trying to feign the riding skills of an accomplished polo player.

A cavalry officer should know a thing or two about horses, thoroughbred or otherwise, but this particular horseman was absolutely no help whatever to Eugene in equine matters. Every time he had gone near a horse in the past, he had suffered for it. On one meeting he had with a huge placid draught horse that somehow and without malice-aforethought immediately stood on his foot breaking several small bones. Another occasion saw him suffering a painful bite to his shoulder from an ungrateful beast when he turned away after feeding it an apple and reluctantly patting the damn thing. But he was not alone in being tormented by horses.

'I can't explain it,' Eugene whined to Matthias Vogel. 'The damned animals are an irresistible attraction for me. Just look at that creature, and look at the sheen of its gorgeous coat, its powerful musculature, just the way it tosses its head. They are magnificent animals and I sometimes feel they're almost trying to seduce me.'

Matthias Vogel turned and gave Bradfield a long, hard look. He'd heard all sorts of rumours about English actors and their peculiar habits, but surely not that.

Vogel and Eugene are leaning on the rail of the mounting yard at Flemington watching the field parade for the next race, an unusual thing for Eugene, as he generally preferred to haunt the members' bar and bet on the horses unseen.

'If only they could talk and tell me if they were likely to win a blasted race now and then.'

'Here comes my horse number seven,' he lowers his voice conspiratorially. 'I have engaged a top jockey and ve bin lucky wis za barrier draw.' Vogel's perfect English had gone out the window again indicating his level of nervous excitement. 'She's a powerful mare mit excellent heritage undt a powerful finish. Her trainer tells me she iz in peak condition tuned to za minute for zis race. I'm not a racetrack coat tugger Eugene, but at za odds it might be a good sing.'

'Well, that's as close to the horse's mouth as I expect to get. What are her odds?'

'She vas five to one when I last looked.'

'Right, where's that runner of mine? Here Jackson, make haste you sloth.' Melvin Jackson had been enjoying a hand rolled smoke as he lazed in the sun staring at the horses and daydreaming about a little filly he had met in the bar two nights ago when his bosses' voice broke into his reverie.

'Mr Jackson, if you please. Here, take two hundred pounds to Plowright and put it on Valley Girl to win and bring the ticket back to me, got it? That's two hundred to win on horse seven. Please don't stuff it up.'

'Why do you bet wiz zat bastard you can get better odds anywhere?'

'He and I are engaged in a small betting war. Nothing huge you understand but a bit of a grudge match. I want to take back some of the money he has taken from me and more.'

The field has paraded; the jockeys legged up into their saddles and the horses filed out onto the track. The field trotted away to arrive behind the one-mile starting gate where they circled around, waiting to be called forward by the stewards in a multi-hued swirl of jockey's silks above the shimmering coats of the thoroughbreds. In an odd reflection, the ladies' frocks swirl about in a colourful riot of shimmering of colour as they jostle subtly along the rails for the best view.

In the last minutes before the horses jumped away, a great clamour arose from the betting ring as bookies shouted alluring odds, creating a sense of urgency to draw a few more bets from the punting crowd. The punters themselves waved fistfuls of cash, desperate to get their bets on at the best odds offered so far by the bookies.

After what seems an age and a cacophony of shouting, the field was settled down behind the five-strand spring powered wire starting barrier. The official starter is shouting at the jockeys to bring their mounts up until he's satisfied with the line then he releases the lever and the wires spring upward. In a massive explosion of energy, the horses leapt forward, discharging pent-up power as their jockeys gave them a clip with the whip and shouted in their ears to urge them on. The crowd erupted with a deafening cheer audible to the jockeys from the other side of the track.

Eugene had his glasses on Vogel's jockey in his personal colours of the red and white horizontal stripes of the Austrian flag and loses them in the first seconds as the field leaps out and immediately falls into an extended line two or three horses deep from the rails. Eugene picks up the red and white stripes of Valley Girl as the colourful field travels up the back straight. The field had finished jostling for position after the first few furlongs leading up to the continuous, long left-hand turn. The bulk of the rail obscured much of the horses, apart from bobbing heads, while the jockeys appeared above the obstruction, heads down skinny rear ends in the air, whips held ready for action. One or two challenged for better positions in the field, creating hazardous shifting and adjusting. Valley Girl sat one out from the rail about four or five places from the leader who brought the field around the sweeping bend coming closer to the long straight. Eugene, who seldom watched a race from start to finish, is an intense observer on this occasion.

'She's in a good spot and looking strong Matthias.'

There was a little more shuffling about, with jockeys trying to get their mounts into the best position according to their riding instructions. They wanted to be able to forge a path through the pack once they entered the straight, providing their mount had the stamina. The jostling of the field was mirrored by the crowd jostling forward to be as close to the track as possible. Valley Girl was obscured momentarily and for a heart stopping second, Eugene thought she had lost her rider but no, there he is, perched perilously on her back as they bunched up for the run down the long straight. Valley Girl has moved out from the rail and was in fourth position coming to the clock tower. Eugene's heart was in his mouth, his ears deaf to the loud roar of the crowd around him.

Experienced jockeys hold their mount back until this famous point now spurring their them on with cracking whips and shouted urging. The field had bunched up impossibly close to each other as the commentator observed that 'you could throw a blanket over them.' Now the sound of hooves on turf comes clearly like muted drums, the shouts of the jockeys and the sharp slap of the whips reaching a crescendo of hope for supporting punters, their anticipation of monetary gain crushed seconds later when the field opens up and stretched out by the leaders down the straight. The course commentators' frenetic voice has ascended to high C and is totally over whelmed by the crowd noise becoming an unintelligible gabble.

Valley Girl is swept up in the surge, holding her position until the one-furlong mark when her jockey shouts in her ear simultaneously giving her several sharp cracks with the whip to which she answers with an amazing burst of speed quickly scooping up the three leading horses to get her nose in front. She looks to have the race in her grasp when out of the pack behind her explodes the favourite known for its withering finishing stride in the run home. At this point, it sounded like the course commentator is about to fall out of his box or burst a blood vessel. The two horses stretch out, heads bobbing in unison absolutely locked together like Siamese twins leaving the rest of the field to also ran status. The riders of the leaders are straining forward, as if trying to lift their mounts across the line. The crowd were on their feet, screaming encouragement to their selection. Every horse in every race will be carrying the money of some hopeful but judging by the volume of cheering it seems everyone is on one of these two.

Eugene lost all sense of decorum, screaming for Valley Girl to, 'get up, get up,' repeatedly and thumping Matthias on the back.

The horses came to the finish line locked together, heads bobbing with their jockeys laying along their necks using the whip freely, urging their mount across the line with a blistering burst of shouted obscenities to be shared by horse and challenger.

Over the PA system the course announcer calls it a photo finish in a voice at breaking point but he quickly recovers to call the rest of the field over the line for the benefit of other place getters as the excitement bleeds out of his voice like a deflating tyre.

Eugene was dancing about like a young boy in need of a toilet. 'Oh my God, she's won, I'm sure of it. Can't these fellows make a decision? The waiting is soul destroying.'

'Gene, Gene be patient. It takes time to examine za film but I have a strong feeling Village Girl has held on.'

The judges had a high-speed motion picture of the finish to consult and after an interminable wait, the announcement was made. 'The winner of race six by the shortest possible margin is number seven Village Girl.'

A cry of despair goes up from the supporters of the favourite as Matthias and Eugene cheer madly, slapping each other on the back.

'Oh dear God, what a race, oh the rush. That's why I bet on horses Matthias; no drug could get me that high.'

❦

Chapter 34

JULY 1925

Vice Regal Visitation, 'Ead Covers n Fevvers'

If Eugene had lifted his binoculars slightly and pointed them in a south-easterly direction to the right of the city skyline, he might have been able to make out the distinctive outline of a large ocean liner manoeuvring into position alongside Station Pier at Port Melbourne. It carried a passenger list that included immigrants from Europe in steerage and one or two wealthy business people in first class cabins.

Of singular note was one passenger who brought with him a large entourage. He was Maharaja Hari Singh, the last ruling Maharaja of the princely state of Jammu and Kashmir in India. He had arrived at the invitation of Victoria's Governor Col. the Right Honourable George Edward John Mowbray, Earl of Stradbroke, KCMG, CB, CVO, CBE AD who was at the dock to greet him in full regalia. In the welcoming party was a wealthy western district sheep breeder who produced pure bred Merinos. When one travels, it's always nice to bring along a few little comforts from home. In the Maharajas case, his comforts were a retinue including ten of his favourite gaily dressed dancing girls, and twenty servants, all wearing colourful turbans. The rich raiment's and glittering jewellery bedazzled the onlookers, giving them an exotic experience that they would otherwise never see in a lifetime. All of this colour overshadowed his soberly dressed animal husbandry team brought along to supervise the selection and purchase of a breeding flock of merino sheep.

The welcome was observed closely by a couple of idle wharf labourers.

'Gaw lumme look at all that fruit salad on 'is chest, if he falls in the drink 'e'll go straight to the bottom,' commented a worker known to his mates as 'The Judge' because he was always sitting on a case.

'Wots the strength of all this, do ya reckon Judge? An' 'ooze the swells wif all them 'ead covers?' queried a second wharfie, releasing a huge blast of flatulence. The second bloke is known as 'Brown Sugar' because he's coarse and unrefined, not surprisingly.

Their foreman arrived just in time to walk into the fug of Brown Sugar's postern blast and reels back. 'Fair dinkum Sugar, do you ever wonder why the Guvnor don't invite you to tea?'

The foreman took a position leaning against a column. 'They're called turbums or sumfink, like a crown any 'ow.'

The foreman, like everyone else on the docks, has his own nickname. Behind his back he is referred to as 'Singlet' because he's always on yer back. If nothing else, the wharfies have a sense of humour.

Presently a fleet of gleaming limousines spirits away the semi-regal party to Government House, sitting grandly between Kings Domain and the Royal Botanic Gardens where another more populous greeting party awaits the arrival of the Maharajah and his party.

While this visitation was *exciting* news for Melbourne's glitterati it was exiting news for the man known to all as Captain Jenkins, who departed without farewell for parts unknown.

Melbourne society was made up of the same layers as cities the world over. The upper echelons were all within six degrees of separation. They all went to similar schools separated along religious lines. Protestants had their halls of learning and the Catholics had theirs. There was little differential when it came to the mixing of the two, but neither really fancied dropping down the ladder to mix with the hoi polloi. Clubs were another familiar intermingling point. Some were sporting organisations, like the Melbourne Cricket Club or Victoria Racing Club. Many purely social, such as The Kelvin Club, The Melbourne Club, The Melbourne Savage Club, The Athenaeum Club. The most exclusive of them all was The Australia Club. Many business men were also members of that semi-secret organization, The Masons.

Their women folk could enjoy the exclusive surrounds of the Alexandra Club (previously The Wattle Club) or The Lyceum Club. It was enormously important to have been to the 'right' school and hold membership in one or more of the 'right' clubs.

Some Australian elites still followed the British tradition of sending their daughters to a European finishing school, followed by a tour of the continent and home, as England had always been thought of.

Basically, Melbourne's upper class moved in a sort of swirl of familiarity or social circularity. This week at the tennis club, the next week at the snowfields or any of the private clubs or sporting events. They were all brought into contact by the demands of the calendar.

The thin veneer of gentility would drop away when it came to the possibility of hosting the English aristocracy or indeed the nobility' from just about anywhere. The pending arrival of even some minor potentate or second-string royal would have the social set involved in heated competition to see one's name and beaming photograph in the social pages alongside the celebrity as host and new best friend.

One of the largest and most ostentatious properties in Toorak had been leased months before in anticipation of the arrival of the magnificent entourage of Maharaja Hari Singh of the princely state of Jammu and Kashmir. Following their rural visitation to view the flock they intended to purchase, the party would retire to the mansion to settle down for the night in the style His Highness was accustomed to. A lavish dinner prepared by his kitchen staff with entertainment provided by his musicians and dancing troupe. Several key business and political figures were on the guest list, along with their gushing and barely constrained wives who would have their social circle green with envy.

The primary reason the Maharajah's visit was to make the purchase of a small flock of precious merino sheep he wished to eventually build into a more substantial flock on his home pastures. With unlimited funds and labour available to assist him, his dream was to create an industry based on fine wool. In hindsight, this didn't seem to be a great idea given that Australia held the Merino breed very dear. Somewhere in the backrooms of Parliament, some fool was trying it on.

With him were his animal husbandry team who along with His Highness, would visit the property where his flock had been bred to learn as much as they could about the breeding requirements of the animals. Australia held the variety exclusively and releasing these precious animals to a foreigner had created much debate in both Federal and state parliaments fuelled by outraged citizens in the papers.

The citizenry imbued with an attitude of inferiority that demanded obeisance to the Mother Country, Australians in general, refrain from tugging their forelock to any minor aristocrat visiting from the 'auld sod'. So it came to be an embarrassing contrast that the Melbourne elite clamoured to throw themselves at the feet of the Maharajah.

There was a notable absentee from the sycophantic hordes clamouring to touch the robes of the blessed Royal. The usually ebullient Captain Richard Fairlie Jenkins Officer of the 4TH Royal

Indian Cavalry DSM Veteran of France and Flanders.

Questions were being asked. One would have thought that here was a chance for the gallant cavalryman to pay his compliments to His Princely eminence. Strangely, he was nowhere to be seen and rumours abounded.

Before disappearing, he had 'accidentally' let it slip to one of the attentive Indian waiters that he was actually flying up north to attend an auction of thoroughbred racehorses at a breeding establishment there. Of course, no one condescended to ask the waiting staff if they knew where he might be and they weren't volunteering the information out of some twisted sense of loyalty to their most generous provider of gratuities. In fact, he was holed up in a country hotel in Victoria's high country, a hideaway favoured by several rapscallions on the run before him.

After the official welcoming dinner at Government House, the agenda of the Maharajah was very crowded. First item to be ticked off was the drive to Moorcroft Downs the breeding establishment of the magnificent Merino rams that would make the long sea journey to their new home in the Kashmir where they would be expected to cover as many of the Prince's sheep as possible. It was a long and exhausting drive over some pretty rough roads that were not an unfamiliar experience, given similar conditions in most of India.

Somehow, the Maharajah maintained a measure of dignity while exercising the 'Great Australian wave' to chase away the maddening flies while asking many pertinent questions relevant to the breeding and animal husbandry of the precious creatures. His entourage were busy taking notes and even taking photographs armed with several modern 35mm Leica model A cameras. The flock consisted of six rams and thirty ewes that had been penned up for the Prince's inspection and the next day they would be on their way to the ship waiting at Port Melbourne to begin their transportation to the Kashmir.

After a tour of the property, a shearing exhibition had been arranged, to be followed by a BBQ lunch. Spare the steaks on religious grounds for the Prince and his party.

The luxurious interior of the Governor's Rolls Royce allowed the Maharajah to catch up on some sleep once the rough country roads were behind them. If he thought the Aussie bush flies were a persistent pest, he hadn't reckoned with the Aussie socialites that likewise were waiting in significant numbers for him to reappear.

Once refreshed, their attention turned to briefly celebrating the acquisition of their prize. Then it's off on an exhausting round of

Diplomatic receptions with politicians and industry.

At every reception the Maharajah or his party were queried about the dashing and decorated Captain Richard Fairlie Jenkins, receiving puzzled expressions in reply. Eventually the pressure forcing the Maharajah to make a statement to the effect that no one in his party were aware of a cavalry officer by that name and description which sent a small tsunami of alarm through the community.

Finally, the glamorous visitation was at an end and the weary party loaded up the first-class accommodation on a passenger liner and departed from Station pier, following in the wake of the ship carrying the precious flock of sheep to their ultimate destination Calcutta.

On the dock waving them off was the Vice regal delegation and a significant representation from various government departments surrounded by a number of members of the press including Australasian Gazette shooting film of the event for their silent black and white news presented as a series shown at movie theatres around the country, patrons would be treated to the vision of significant events such as bushfires and floods and other dramas.

Along the dock, looking on with great interest, was another distinguished party conducting their own valedictory. Singlet and Brown Sugar were looking on while The Judge was holding court on a packing case and passed commentary as the departure progressed.

'There 'eh goes, the kingpin, the 'ead Serang. 'es the one with the fancy 'ead gear. Where ya reckon they get all them fevers, Sugar?'

'Dunno, but I reckon a few birds are feelin' the cold right now.'

They were passing comment on the Regal party sporting exotic plumes from any number of species in their turbans.

'Geez, look at 'em, what a buncha nobs.' Singlet bought in, 'I reckon those blokes 'as got more dough than sense. Wonder what it's like to be that filthy rich. Bet 'e never 'as to lift a bloody finger. Probably got a little tart to wipe 'is arse for 'im an' all.'

'Is that the Guvnor the bloke in the topper with all the flamin' medals? Crikey, 'e musta been in a few scraps to win all them.'

'Ha ha I 'ope 'e doesn't bow down too low he might struggle to get up again.' Singlet is referred to the weight of the medals on the small man's chest. His remark brought an appreciative round of guffaws from the crew. Finally, everyone had boarded as the ship gave a long blast on its steam whistle and with the aid of a smoke billowing tugboat she pulled away from the pier on the beginning of its long journey home. First stop will be Perth, where the Maharaja has another interest. This time an experiment in frozen or chilled lamb production.

Chapter 35
ANY CHRISTMAS
Cultural Oddities: Snow in Summer

December in Melbourne can bring radical variations in the weather, but generally it becomes hot and humid with at least one or two days above forty degrees centigrade. As the weather builds, so do the moods of the populace who fall into two broad groups. Those that become over excited and fantasize about Christmas and the other group who fall into deep despondency.

December is summer in the southern hemisphere, which fails to bring a dose of reality to the fantasisers who decorate their homes and shop windows with fake snow, snow men, sleighs and all the winter paraphernalia of Mother England. The shops are flooded by excited Christmas shoppers buying gifts, food and alcohol, decorations and smart new clothing for the occasion.

At the other end of the scale, suicide rates begin to climb as the despondent sink into the condition known as 'The Black Dog.' Loneliness, poverty, alcohol and substance abuse are huge contributors to this sad social blight.

On the positive side of life, one notable thespian was almost hyperventilating with excitement as the date for the spectacular Christmas cruise aboard the marvellous paddle steamer Hygeia drew closer. Flats had been designed and constructed after elaborate measurements of the designated area of the ship's promenade had been recorded. Construction took place at the building that housed Her Majesties' props and costumes. Fiery discussions had been held between designers, script writers, directors and senior stage hands as to the placement and operation of the stage production over colours, textures and decorative items on the set.

Thankfully, it would be a one act play that would simplify things somewhat. However, theatre people being of a certain nature, felt it beholden on them to be as fussy and pedantic as humanely possible with frequent emotional outbursts punctuating proceedings. This was all very familiar to Eugene Bradfield, but nonetheless bloody annoying. A full-dress rehearsal of *This is London* was planned aboard the vessel on a weekday when she was not traversing the bay. This would be the week immediately before the great day.

Eugene's committee ladies Rhoda Day, Elvira Rochester, Madame Rosetta Gloria Parmentier, had been working tirelessly. They had decided that an A-list should be established and given first rights to the premium tickets. When all First-Class tickets were sold, a flyer would be sent to what amounted to a B list, advertising the event and advising them when tickets would be on sale. They expected there would be a mad flurry of sales from this group of nouveau riche and social climbers who would trample each other to be there.

There was another sub-group, unaware of each-others' intentions to join the cruise, all of whom would know each other, and all armed with similar dark intent.

The organising committees order of printing materials in addition to the all-important tickets would be souvenir programmes printed on rich high-quality linen stock to be sold as part of the First-Class packages. A cheaper but still high-quality version would be made available to purchase on board. These would be a sought-after souvenir and bring another revenue stream to off-set costs.

Next item on their busy agenda was the menu to be served in the plush section of the restaurant. Again, this meal would be inclusive in the First-Class packages.

The ship had various stations aboard where simpler meals could be obtained from the bar in the form of sandwiches, the ever popular meat pies, fish and chips. Including the drunks all-time favourite pickled onions and boiled eggs free from the bar. The bars would be open and staff briefed to strictly control dispensing of beverages to avoid drunkenness and unacceptable behaviour. So the ship was all set up to cater for the blue-collar passengers, while first class had higher expectations.

First-Class attendees would be expected to adhere to the strict dress code of cocktail wear while the hoi polloi would be advised to adopt business wear or smart casual. There would be no slovenly dress or behaviour tolerated.

Finally, the busy little trio settled into the selection of casual music to be played across the day to background the whole voyage. This ignited a rapid exchange of personal preferences and unleashed a barrage of vitriol on some of the day's popular music.

Rhoda Day ventured her selections 'Vivaldi perhaps or Puccini and wrap it in the silken arms of song.'

Elvira plumps for some more current favourites 'Oh you must have that delightful music from George Gershwin's musical Lady Be Good.'

Madame Rosetta Gloria Parmentier pushes her preferences for some current jazz. 'The Charleston, that wonderful sound that has people's feet tapping and drawing them out onto the dance floor. It's a joyous occasion, let's have joyous music. You don't want that funereal stuff, Good Lord!'

Madame Rosetta Gloria Parmentier's argument carries the day, so jazz and the Charleston it will be.

Another less than joyous group, Arthur Fetchwell, Charlie Spriggs, Phillip Croker, Hugo Montrose, the money man Frankie De Luca had gathered in the library of Fetchwell's large luxuriously appointed home. Notably, Joseph McArthur was absent.

They were three quarters of their way through a large decanter of Scottish Highland whisky that was fuelling their rage.

News had come through to them from a source within the state Parliament that a deal had been done to sell the dockside land to a foreign investment company and at the centre of the deal was none other than the man supposed to be their partner the man who stage managed this whole fiasco, none other than the absent Joseph McArthur MP.

Arthur, Charlie and Hugo were incandescent with rage. Charlie Spriggs was actually foaming at the mouth, almost choking in his fury. Arthur placed a hand on his shoulder in an attempt to placate him before he has a heart attack and has his arm swept away in an angry slap by Never mind that shit, Arthur.' Spriggs fire would not be doused by an arm around the shoulders, 'If the bastard were in this room right now he would feel my knife in his ribs just as he put it into our backs.'

The dreadful news disrupted months of planning. The creation of shelf companies and offshore bank accounts and shifting of finances all under third party names had all been for nothing as a result of the Frankie de Luca revelations. He had contacted them earlier in the day and arranged this emergency meeting that they had thought was called to update them on progress in their scheme that would be guaranteed to deliver the significant near city parcel of very valuable land into their greedy clutches. Instead, they found they had been betrayed by political viper, Joseph Esmond 'Gunna' McArthur MP. The swine had been using them to create a sense of urgency in his offshore partners, a tactic that cost them far more than their pride. Their blood pressure rose to explosive levels. They all felt the same sense of immense loss and humiliation and a desire to string the conspirator up from the nearest light pole.

While the group of Arthur, Phillip, Hugo and Charlie ranted, Frankie de Luca had sat quietly in a large Chesterfield wing back chair in the corner sipping his whiskey, watching them from under his dark bushy eyebrows and taking an occasional puff on his cigar waiting for the eruption to subside. Finally, they ran out of breath and expletives, collapsing exhausted back into their seats.

Arthur looked across the room at him. 'Mr de Luca you haven't said a word. What are your thoughts on this treacherous swine?'

'My very good friends, the milk is spilt and crying over it will achieve nothing. We have no grounds on which to sue for recovery of our losses because we were in fact operating on an unethical level.' He took a big puff on his cigar and sat forward, pointing it at each of his frustrated business partners. 'Allow me to quote from my ancient countryman Niccolò Machiavelli, who said, "Politics has no relation to morals." Our former partner is an example of what he meant.'

'We are now faced with a dilemma. We can attack Big Joe publicly and in doing so expose our part in this fiasco which would be a pyrrhic victory.' Now he sat back to emphasise his next comment. 'Or we wait patiently for the right moment to savour our revenge.'

'What are you saying, Sir?' Hugo leapt to his feet once more, outraged, 'Do we just forget it and walk away with the seat out of our trousers? Are you bloody mad?'

'No, I'm not. I am saying if someone does something rash we may find ourselves at odds with the law and become guests of Her Majesty, remember the maxim, "Revenge is a dish best served cold."'

'Crickey, do ya have any more bloody helpful quotes? What the hell then, what do we do?'

The curses and threats continued in a subdued manner until they realise the wisdom of de Luca's words. After a final round of drinks, they shake hands swearing allegiance and leave in their individual transports all united in the one unshakeable ambition; find a way to destroy Joseph McArthur, MP. They all arrived at their businesses the next morning tired and far from placated. God help the first humble employee who steps out of line that day.

CHAPTER 36

JULY 1924
THE WAGES OF SIN

Buster Yarrow, former head of the Robbery Squad was now known universally as 'Pants Down Yarrow.' The shameful handle had followed him to where he was now stationed. Recently, his time had been taken up in investigating a gang of livestock thieves. Professional cattle thieves were known as 'cattle duffers' in the bush. It was a very serious and dangerous criminal activity that could be financially crippling to the grazier and was usually conducted by hardened criminals. Sometimes it was a one off conducted by some poor bloke trying to prevent his family starving or a small-time gang travelling interstate with an eye out for a quality flock of sheep or herd of cattle that they could snatch in one district and flog off further up the road to an unscrupulous farmer. Cattle duffing was another thing altogether. Cattle normally were branded with the 'logo' of the farmer and were placed in a highly visible spot on the beast. Stealing the cattle therefore required altering the brand. These blokes that Yarrow targeted were more professional stealing the cattle and altering their brands. The current mob Yarrow was pursuing seemed to be well informed and equipped, taking as many as ten or twelve heifers at a time. The heifers were worth a hundred pound per head making this a substantial crime. This had been going on for some time.

The local police and this meant Yarrow was under siege from the graziers and the local Chamber of Commerce to do something about it. The bulk of the complaints fell on Buster's rounded shoulders. Everyone, including the commissioner, wanted results and they wanted them now by God.

There was a big German Lutheran presence in the district, hardworking God-fearing people who practised strict discipline in their lives and prayed to God to forgive the unholy, for they never would.

Word of Buster's shocking indiscretion had gradually made its way up the Western Highway to shock the puritanical ladies of German descent who would prefer their men greet him at the gate with a shotgun rather than recover their stolen herds.

Poor old Buster, sure he was a crooked cop who still had his grubby mits in a few enterprises back in the Big Smoke, while working on a few little partnerships here and there to idle away the hours. He was the only cop they had, so one or two were forced to swallow their straitlaced attitudes. In Busters own words he 'couldn't give a monkeys about some bloody cows unless one was on his plate well done with some roasted spuds.

Buster kept an eye on things back home and was seething with a manic desire to square up with the bloody little upstart copper that sprang him coming out Doreen McKillop's bar and bawdy house destroying his career and what had been a very pleasant evening entertaining one of her new girls. She was a sixteen-year-old distant cousin of Doreen's who had come to the city to get into show business. Dear old Aunty Doreen was most obliging and promised her the world, but of course she would have to start off at the bottom, right? You couldn't get any closer to the bottom than to be putting it out for a scumbag copper like Buster. Especially as a freebie! Buster being Buster, spared no tenderness or consideration for either house madame or young would be "actress" taking abusively and never giving, he could not expect his downtrodden women to leap to his defence. They were eager to see the nasty bastard put away.

The young victim of Buster's brutality would appear in court at the forthcoming enquiry in the New Year into the matter and her evidence as a sixteen-year-old virgin at the time who was subjected to Buster's rough and depraved treatment might well send him to prison. Doreen McKillop was sure to be called as well and provide the 'belt an' braces' to the prosecution's case. It had already cost him his wife and a house as well as his career. Buster should have been stood down but the full circumstances of the case were unknown at the time and rather than throw him off a bridge the Commissioner had him sent into exile in the bush to get him away from the press who had already smelt blood and were howling for details.

So the once powerful Detective Inspector had been downgraded to Detective Sergeant in charge of rounding up some lost cows. He would make someone pay for this humiliating come down and the first one in line would be that bloody Deputy Commissioner's nephew the snobbish Jim Foley who was rising up in the ranks on his uncle's coattails.

His phone begins to ring insistently, breaking into his vengeful mood.

'Sarg, there's a mister Gruber on the phone claims his prize Boar has been stolen, can you take it?'

'You will address me as Detective Sergeant, Constable, do you hear?' Buster was still a touch niggly about his loss of rank, 'Now put the call through.' The hurt young copper red faced followed the harsh instruction.

Buster Yarrow slammed his phone down in annoyance and it bounced out of the cradle and lay on the desk, failing to disconnect.

Buster continues in a private rant as he waits for the call to come through. He is totally unaware that the call is connected to his phone and the caller, Herr Gruber of Hamilton Pork and Smallgoods Pty Ltd, an influential member of the Shire Council and Chamber of Commerce, picked up on every word Buster growled loudly into the empty room.

'Christ, that's the last bloody straw. Some flamin' Kraut sausage eater has lost a bloody pig and I've got lumbered with the silly bugger. It probably fell down a well or something. Bugger me.'

Rapid footsteps echoed down the corridor as the constable from the front desk rushed in waving his hands around desperately, trying to communicate that the caller was still on the open line.

'Well, what do you want you sorry arsed excuse for a copper? Where the hell is that phone call from that Herr Hinkleberger or whatever his bloody Kraut name is?'

The young constable who was not without a sense of wit smiled disarmingly and pointed to the phone, 'He's right there, *Detective Sergeant Yarrow,* listening to your every word.'

Young Constable Brereton returned to his desk hurriedly, mirth lighting up his handsome young face straining his self-control until he bolts out of the front door out of hearing to the sanctity of the station's front garden and bursts into fits of uncontrollable laughter. 'Take that *Serg.*' He rejoiced.

CHAPTER 37

A Rising Star

A couple of hundred miles to the south-west, completely unaware of the retribution being imagined by Detective Sergeant Buster Yarrow if the two should ever meet, Jim Foley was doing some planning with his direct superior old Leather Lungs, Senior Sergeant George Manifold. At the age of thirty-three, Jim Foley had been sailing through his courses on his way to improving his standing in the force and was now a proud Sergeant. After eleven years in the force, he was growing impatient to move up. His next move was to join the crime squad, hence the need to pass additional courses.

Right now, their focus was on the Christmas cruise being planned to take place aboard the fabulous Hygeia. This would be an exceptional event in the social calendar but most significantly it will mean that a great number of Melbourne's who's who will be aboard including the Police Commissioner and Jim Foleys uncle, Deputy Commissioner Francis Arthur Foley (First in the door Foley) who will be a valuable addition to the police presence on board. Anyway, he would have his favourite truncheon under his service coat, keen to demonstrate its lethal force to the other dignitaries should the opportunity arise.

One or two state politicians, notably Big Joe McArthur, of course, and Melbourne's Lord Mayor Sir William Brunton. Also expected to be aboard was the great lady of opera herself, Dame Nellie Melba escorted by some of the lesser but just the same important members of theatre and song, all a bit twittery with excitement and nervousness in equal measures.

The ABC radio station had applied to have several of their journalists aboard to record interviews and report on the voyage. In view of the popularity and scarcity of tickets, their request was denied, instead Madame Rosetta Gloria Parmentier Age Newspaper's senior theatre critic appointed an Age staff photographer to accompany her to provide coverage for the readers of the Age. This was her turf and she would not give it up to a couple of nobody wannabe's.

Because of the nature of the event, it could be expected that the ladies would be showing off their finest haute couture set off by half a hundred-weight of gold and diamonds presenting a juicy target for thieves and pickpockets.

Jim's previous experience aboard the vessel with his female companion Constable Irene McCarthy when pursuing the Bourke Street Rats lent him a valuable insight into the layout and running of the ship. Given the importance of this event, Jim would head up a team consisting of the two constables, Dottie Green and Therese McCarthy, along with Bluey Farnsworth and Whispers Richardson.

Buster Yarrow had been advised to take a couple of days of his annual leave and he intended to use them to pay a flying visit to Melbourne and meet secretly with his old cronies. In fact, Buster planned to keep things tightly under his control and take care of Foley in a way that provided him with plausible deniability. But while back in Melbourne, he needed to persuade the witnesses to have a change of heart when it came to providing evidence against him in his trial.

While he had been out of town, he missed his daily read of the mainstream press. Now one story caught his eye and set his mind to wondering. The Melbourne newspapers were alight with a mystery that had transfixed the community. A group of known thieves were rescued from a barn on a remote property where they had been held against their will, apparently. It appeared a neighbour had entered the property searching for a runaway pony and heard some strange noises coming from the barn. He went to investigate and was confronted with a shocking sight. Four youths, naked, cold and terrified were chained to the walls of the horse stalls. It was evident that they had been tortured and beaten.

The farmer who found them reported they were sleeping on straw mattresses thrown on the floor when he discovered them, at first thinking they were dead. They had been denied any food or water and were in a dehydrated state.

As the story unfolded, it was revealed that the youths had last been seen together at a picnic held by the notorious Matthias Vogel known as The German on his property south of the city. When questioned none of Vogel's staff could, or would, provide any information on the mystery and Vogel when questioned simply gave a non-committal shrug of his shoulders and pointed out, a little indignantly that there had been several hundred at the picnic that he had paid for out of his own pocket for the benefit of the poor and he could not possibly entertain his supporters and keep track of everyone.

The youths spent a week in the Alfred Hospital recovering where they were besieged by the media trying desperately to meet the demands of their readers for details of the mysterious event.

Rumours abounded as usual, highly imaginative tales about white slavers, witchcraft cults, and sexual sadism.

They had indeed been tortured horrendously, mentally and physically, to reveal their part or parts in the nobbling of Tidal Wave as per the information provided by Ronnie the Rat and the disqualification of its trainer Blaine O'Farrell. Their ordeal yielded the information sought fairly quickly, as these were no hardened types. It went on much further as they were being punished for being part of the conspiracy. It was made clear to them what would happen if they ever spoke about it. In fact, it might be a very good idea to leave town on the first bus.

Matthias Vogel had been very careful to stay well away from the 'interrogation' and make sure he was surrounded by credible witnesses to confirm his whereabouts. Information extracted from these low-level crooks by his hard men had proved once and for all that his trainer Blaine O'Farrell had been set up, depriving the man of his Victorian licence to train and bumping Tidal Wave out of the Melbourne Cup field.

Sadly, the information thus extracted couldn't be used to redeem Blaine O'Farrell's good name or his career in Australia nor award the race to Tidal Wave. However, Tidal Wave went on to win several important Graded Races and was retired after he bled badly at the end of a staying race in Sydney. Blaine O'Farrell returned to Ireland and continued training in his family stable and it was later reported that he had happily married his fiancé.

Vogel now had confirmation of what he had suspected and was determined to find a way to even up on Gordon Plowright. He had the resources to have him knocked off by anyone of three or four thugs starting with the posse that worked the truth out of the street gang. One way or another, he would have his revenge but not by putting his own liberty and life at risk.

CHAPTER 38

JULY/AUGUST 1924

A Cowardly Plan

Buster Yarrow had wrapped up the case of the disappearing pig that unlike Yarrow's career, had not fallen down a well and on advice from his superiors he had taken a couple of days of annual leave that he used for a flying visit to Melbourne and a clandestine meeting with two of his old cronies. After a catch-up on some of their nefarious deals and a split of cash extracted by one means or another from grog shops, brothel operators and shopkeepers they got down to the important business (as far as Yarrow was concerned) of how and what to do to cripple the hopes of the upstart copper Jim Foley. Yarrow's dodgy mates were not too pleased about conducting a full-on hit on a fellow member of the force, particularly one so well connected as to be totally unthinkable.

'Jesus Buster, do you know what you're suggesting? Deliberate murder of a policeman by other police would have the whole force up in arms.' Senior Constable Clarence Thurgood was terrified at the prospect. 'Nah, no way, look what happened to Ned Kelly, strung him up in Pentridge jail.' Thurgood was referring to the notorious bushranger who killed two of the police sent to arrest him.

'Listen yooz blokes, if it waddnt fer me yez'd ave the arse out of yer strides. I set yez up to make a nice little earn and yez owe me. I've got a plan that'll make the bastard disappear without a trace. No body, no proof of a crime, right?'

'Yeah, but Jesus Buster, another copper?' Detective Sergeant Weatherby whined. 'Can't we set him up to take the fall on a dodgy charge? You could persuade that bloody old McKillop cow to, you know, drop 'im in it for coppin' freebies or somethin'?'

Buster stood abruptly, almost upsetting the table they were drinking at in the back bar at The Builders Arms Hotel in Gertrude Street Fitzroy, sending their beers splashing across the table filling the ashtray and running off to stain the ancient carpet.

'Look 'ere Weatherby you got stuck with your hand in the till and were gone for all money an' who got you out of that shit storm, an' you Peterson ya got more priors for assault on yer prisoners than any thick-headed jailer an' it's only been me that's kept you in the job an' on the money trail so don't either one of ya whine to me.' His face is blotched red with anger and indignation as he jabs the air with an angry digit to emphasise the words he's thrown at the two.

'Open yer bloody ears. I said I've got a plan to make 'im disappear, gone, missin'. 'An all I want from you two thick 'eads is to run interference for me.'

The barman comes in with a fresh jug of beer and cleans their table top while exchanging a few words.

'Are you blokes in for a meal, we've got a ripper roast on tonight with all the trimmings you'd be crazy to miss out?'

'May as well, then I'm paying' a little visit to me favourite old whore Doreen McKillop and get a few things straight on 'er witness statement.'

The grim trio decides to take advantage of the barman's offer of a 'ripper roast with all the trimmings' then they spilt up. Buster heading off to Doreen McKillops for a tasty little dish from a different menu. Meanwhile, Senior Constables Weatherby and Petersen headed into the city centre to amuse themselves hassling the youth and vulnerable in the city's streets.

Doreen McKillop was in her mind a hard-working and caring madam running her establishment with an eye trained by years of experience for any shenanigans on her premises. Her girls were well cared for and were all receiving their rightful share of their earnings. They all had dreams of leaving the world's oldest profession and graduating to something more socially acceptable. But such was Madam Doreen McKillop's skill in managing her stable that it became more and more difficult to part ways. Now and again some silly cow will fall for a cove outside of work or be stricken with syphilis or get pregnant and would be given her marching orders.

Doreen had a couple of low life blokes who hung around for freebies and a pot of beer who took care of anyone stupid enough to rough up the girls. Quickly and effectively rendered unconscious, their lifeless forms would be taken out to the back alley where they would be found among the foul detritus of the alleyway stripped of their trousers. They could appeal to God for forgiveness, but they would never find any at Madame McKillip's.

It was a Wednesday night and as usual at this time of the week things were fairly quiet with a couple of tradesmen downing their grog in the bar after a session with one or two of the girls that were available. Doreen McKillop dozed quietly by the fire with her favourite tipple, a large gin with a slice of lemon and ginger ale. It was an odd drink, but one she enjoyed at the end of the working day. The tranquillity was shattered by a sudden sharp bang as the door flew back at the behest Buster Yarrows big right boot which hammered it off its hinges.

'Oh shit, oh gawd, what is it, what's happening?' Screeched Doreen as she leapt out of her comfy chair with alarm spilling her drink. 'Oh, bloody hell it's you Buster you bastard. What do fink yer doin' smashin' down my bloody door like that?' Her voice was loud and strident with a mix of fear and outrage. 'Brickhead, Chump (her bouncers) get yer lazy arses in 'ere now.'

The two drinkers at the bar abandoned their drinks and took off at high speed through the now shattered entrance, shouldering the remains of the door still swinging on one hinge out of their way.

'They're too bloody gutless, you sleazy bitch.'

Buster had the front of Doreen's dress in his left hand and drives his large, gnarly right fist into her face again and again reducing her features to a bloodied pulp. She slumped down unconscious, still held in his powerful left hand like a rag doll, which he swings around to face the two thugs who rush into the bar to defend their employer.

Buster's blood was up now in an uncontrollable rage. He hurled Doreen's limp body straight at the goon called Chump, knocking him down and followed up with a savage kick to the goon's head. Goon number two chooses discretion over valour and takes off like the devil was in pursuit. Doreen is showing signs of revival, prompting Buster to snatch a jug of beer from off the bar and hurl the contents into her face. Doreen splutters and moans in agony, spitting teeth and blood.

Buster leaned right into her messed up face and growled at her to wake up and listen. 'Remember this you slut, before you show up at court you should think back on this and if you're still stupid enough to talk, then I'm gunna turn you into mince-meat and feed ya to the neighbourhood dogs. Do you hear me you bloody crone?' Yarrow gave her a parting kick in the ribs then searched the premises for the niece at the centre of his issues with this bordello to apply the same disincentives to her. It appeared she heard the ruckus and put two and two together, got out of a back window and took off.

The fruitless search instead of enraging the crooked cop further has the reverse affect and suddenly he is overcome by exhaustion and slumps down on a stool by the bar. He finds himself staring at the moaning form of Doreen feeling no pity, just a dull sense of impending doom. He won't find that little tart now, but he's sure she got the message. The prosecution would find their star witness, the alleged victim, was nowhere to be found. He reached over the countertop and grabbed a bottle of rum, lifted it to his lips and gulped down several mouthfuls of the potent brew, belched, then casually emptied Doreen's money belt. Now for that bastard Foley.

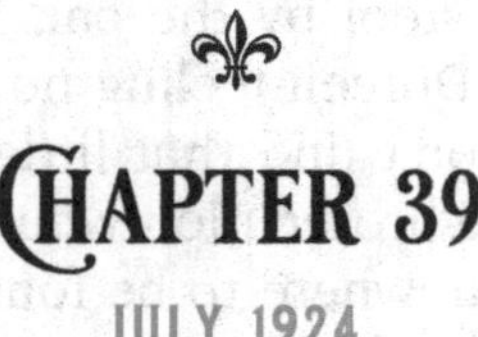

CHAPTER 39

JULY 1924

BAD MOON

The winter months had dragged by, wet, cold, and depressing. Compared to some of the worst weather around the world, though it wasn't half that bad but people still complained that there was something about Melbourne weather. The fact that the wonderful city was one degree of latitude above the roaring forties was lost on most people who preferred to attribute bad weather as a singular characteristic of Melbourne.

Bluey Farnsworth and Bob Barrows were taking time out of the biting cold and rain for a hot cup of tea and a sweet bun in a little café in Lygon Street.

'This bloody Melbourne weather, Christ I'm cold,' said Barrows

'This aint cold, mate. I read the other day that in Chicago the temperature drops below minus ten degrees Fahrenheit. Plus six feet of flamin' snow. Now that's bloody cold.'

Bluey and Bob managed to survive the winter months along with the rest of Melbourne's citizenry and now spring with all its glories had come and gone too.

Christmas was approaching with the usual rapid stealth that seems to catch people unprepared every year. Melbourne weather at this time of year varies from very hot to very hot and muggy, broken up occasionally by a cooling thunderstorm with hailstones that damage property and rain that flushes out the gutters, leaving the city glittering clean again. The resulting cool air flows through windows and doors left open to take advantage of the change that lifts the mood of the populace to cheerful once more.

The more buoyant mood is reflected in the smiling faces of the shoppers and office workers as they vie for shade from the sun or shelter from the rain as they bustle about on their Christmas shopping expeditions.

'No one would complain if it was one or two degrees warmer would they? I'm getting chilled to the bone.' said Barrows.

'Do ya want a bit of hot weather mate? I read the other day that in Marble Bar in the north west the temperature reaches one hundred-and ten-degrees Fahrenheit before lunch. Plus, it hasn't rained there in six years. Now that's a nice warm environment.'

Only a few weeks later the mood of the general population was cheerful with the notable exception of several disgruntled groups currently plotting and planning to avenge their sorely damaged ego's and personal fortunes. A change in the weather had restored the populations faith that spring had actually arrived and summer was just on the horizon.

On the cheerful side however, preparations for the social event of the year were progressing with almost military precision. The venue Hygeia was looking spotless having been cleaned and spot painted from stem to stern, removing every trace of the wear and tear inflicted by the early excursions she had undertaken at the opening of the summer cruising season.

Captain Galbraith would brook no excuses for sloppy seamanship and was very rigorous in his inspection of his vessel. He had met with Eugene Bradfield to discuss his full-dress rehearsal of his one act play that his company, Huddart Parker & Co, had agreed would bring wonderful publicity to the company's fleet of steamers. But from the captain's point of view, it was something of a nuisance interfering with the smooth running of his ship. He wanted to ensure that there would be no impedance to the safe operation of the vessel in his charge, nor interference with his crew. He was also concerned the theatre stage hands might inflict irreparable damage to Hygeia's decks. Eugene Bradfield was hard at work assuring the captain of the skills and professionalism of all the theatre staff and in the unlikely event that damage was incurred, he would ensure reparations would be made in full.

'I do understand why you are so particular captain,' Eugene and Galbraith stood on the lower promenade deck in the middle of Hygeia in the area where the play would be presented. 'She is a truly magnificent ship and we feel privileged to have this wonderful opportunity to showcase our theatrical talents on board.'

'Thank you, sir. My responsibilities in this matter are twofold. The safety of the ship and its passengers are foremost and secondly; I have to try to provide a stable platform for your performers. The former I can influence to a large degree; the latter will be weather dependant and we rely on God's benevolence for that.'

As the days of December passed by, the weather remained predictably unpredictable, no two days the same. One predictable at this time was the social temperature that continued to climb and the pressures begin to show as all the participants of the Christmas Cruise refine their preparations, some for pleasure and some for war.

In the familiar surrounds of The Hotel Windsor's restaurant, another meeting was is taking place between the stalwarts of the Melbourne theatre industry Rhoda Day, Elvira Rochester and Madame Rosetta Gloria Parmentier.

The Triumphant Trio, as Eugene has begun to call them, are in a celebratory mood as every single ticket has been sold and indications are that twice that number could have been taken up. In the circumstances and for a job well done, Eugene has treated them to a champagne lunch with all the trimmings. The ladies have been interviewed by every newspaper in the land and several prominent radio stations. And doing their very best to service the flow of the country's champagne supplies. Dizzy with their success and several more celebratory flutes of chilled champagne totally ignoring the intoxicating effect of the bubbles. They were having a fine old time, their voices rising higher and higher their hearing dulled by alcohol. They were now cock a hoop but as with many things in life, their happiness proved to be short lived.

Up at the other end of town at Russell Street Police Headquarters, yet another meeting was underway, this time conducted by old First Through the Door Foley aka the -Deputy Police Commissioner Francis Foley. In attendance were his chosen team that would provide security aboard the Hygeia during the Christmas excursion.

Acting Senior Sergeant Jim Foley, Senior Constables Roger 'Bluey' Farnsworth, Martin Richardson, Constables Dottie Green and Irene McCarthy and two surprise reinforcements from the Robbery Squad who had strangely 'volunteered' for the assignment, Senior Constable Walter Weatherby and Senior Constable Clarence Thurgood. Without doubt, some strings had been pulled by someone with a bit of clout. The two were collaborators with Buster Yarrow and came with their own quiet agenda, sitting at the back of the room staring malevolently at Jim Foley's back.

Jim Foley's predicted meteoric rise through the ranks was becoming a reality but it wasn't as the envious and less talented suggested. He had worked hard to achieve outstanding results at every qualification level. The force was desperate for talented and devoted members after the tumult and annihilation of the force after the strike. Any young copper willing to put in a bit of extra effort was rewarded. As Jim advanced, he became more confident and seemed to have largely left the 'Fumbles Foley' tag behind him.

Deputy Police Commissioner Francis Foley asks Jim Foley to deliver a description of the successful arrest of the professional pickpockets aboard the Hygeia. He was asked to describe the ship's layout and identify any potential blind spots on board.

Jim, who by now had developed a keen interest in teamwork and the value of sharing successes, pointed out that Constable McCarthy as an important part of the team, had been on that assignment with him and as a result had intimate knowledge of the ship's layout. If anyone had any questions in that regard either Jim or Irene were there to assist.

Jim was pleased to see Constable McCarthy had blushed with pride. The team had asked for and received a copy of Hygeia's floor plan of all decks and the proposed program for the cruise and they spent some time going over the plans identifying where the play would be enacted. The likely distribution of crew members and passengers. Time was spent most importantly discussing possible tactics that could be employed by members of the criminal element. That was main reason for the police presence on board.

At this juncture, they were planning for incidents of light-fingered robbery given the amount of flash jewellery that would be aboard. On another level and more likely were drunkenness and fist fights among the blue-collar guests for whom an exposure to strong sunshine, alcohol and subsequent mal de mare would be a cocktail for disaster.

As the afternoon wore on, most of the team had contributed enthusiastically coming up with some great ideas, strangely though Senior Constable Weatherby and Senior Constable Clarence Thurgood had remained mute. After an hour and a half Francis Foley called for a tea break and they all stood and stretched gratefully, then headed for the table bearing a just delivered urn of hot water for tea or coffee and a large platter of pastries.

Francis Foley took advantage of the break to collar the two Robbery Squad constables.

'So boys, you've arrived with no stationary. You must be relying on memory, are you?'

'Not exactly sir, we wuz on a job before we arrived and it took our focus away sir, sorry sir.' The standard response when a copper gets caught out late to a meeting or failing to produce paperwork or any of a hundred other minor indiscretions.

'You two haven't had much to say? What advice can you give us from your experience in Robbery Division?' Francis Foley had been watching the two since they arrived without notebooks or pens. The two haven't really prepared for this situation and 'um and ah' and mumble some nonsensical gibberish before being cut off by their senior.

'Listen, just try to find a way to be helpful, and if that is beyond you then just stay the hell out of the way of my people.'

'Yeah righto boss, we'll be in there wif ya so yez can count on us.'

The Deputy Commissioner was not convinced nor happy to have these two dead weights along. He had received notice from the Robbery Squad that they were sending two officers along to gain experience and lend their authority. Having these two notorious shirkers turning up was an unexpected let down.

Jim Foley relayed information to his uncle that an informant had sought him out with a story that a murder was planned to take place aboard the ship during the cruise. The informant could only say that the intended victim was someone with a high profile, more than that he could not add. The informant seemed to be well placed to provide such information and was well known to police.

The guest list on the cruise was peppered with people who were capable of raising the hackles on any number of enemies in business or politics, misfits from all quarters might be planning mischief as Jim and his team are sent out onto the streets to shake up their informants to see if they can pick up any whispers. On a higher-level Francis Foley was trawling through his black book for ideas. They later agreed that there were evident threats from a number of different warring factions, but were they serious enough to commit murder during a well-publicised event?

Everyone they spoke to remarked on the apparent tension in the air in circles connected to the cruise and the usual snitches were very nervous and saying nothing.

The big man Sir Rupert Yarborough had Eugene in his sights, following a late-night drunken argument with his wife Lady Lucille. Someone carrying a grudge had whispered in his ear that Eugene had been seen in her company again at a champagne supper at Lady Louise's. The enraged man had had enough and confronted her violently, demanding a divorce. Lucille, in defending herself, had sworn it was not true. Yes, she had been at the gathering, but she knew Bradfield was on stage at Her Majesties at the time and unwisely challenged Rupert to use his stupid thick head for once and to check before accusing her. It was all he needed to charge at his terrified wife like a crazed bull elephant. Lucille picked up the nearest heavy item she could lay hands on which happened to be a large cut-crystal vase and hurled it with all the strength she could muster, striking him right between the eyes with the accuracy of a big game hunter, dropping him unconscious and bleeding to the carpet.

When he recovered, it was morning and Lucille had packed a bag and departed. Despite everything, he was deeply in love with her and now in the harsh dawn light with his head thumping like it might explode, he regretted the things he had said and done the night before. He would find her and make amends, but not without finding that two-timing rat Bradfield and settle him once and for all and the perfect occasion was coming up. First, he needed to clean up and see a doctor to stitch the gash in his forehead courtesy of Lucille's accuracy with interior décor items.

Francesco de Luca was known to be a wealthy man whose wealth came to him from years of hard 'honest' work. A well-respected businessman who owned or had control over a number of different enterprises and was suspected of having some very dark connections back in his hometown in Calabria. While usually maintaining a facade of pleasant civility and Latin charm but when provoked, he would display an entirely different persona.

Frankie's eyes would darken to an obsidian blackness in which the observer would swear he could see hell. Frankie, as he was commonly known, was among the tallest men in his village and was about average height in Australia at five foot seven inches. Years of hard farm work had filled out his frame into a powerful physique. Frankie still appeared in the market gardens where he grew vegetables that were sold in the Footscray market. During long hours in the fields his upper body became taut and deeply tanned, he revelled in hard work driving himself and taking pride in his exertions, knowing his physical strength might be called on one day.

Francesco de Luca came from a Calabrian village that was at the heart of *Ndrangheta,* the Calabrian mafia.

He had grown up with the hard men and quickly adapted to their way of life, being accepted into its ranks as a birthright. As a boy of eighteen, he was sent on an errand to take part in the assassination of a neighbour known to be conspiring against his capo and who had ignored an important decree. Charged with an unauthorised revenge killing against *ndrine* protocol. A capital sin in their society.

After one or two similar tasks and proving his loyalty in many ways, he received his reward. He would be sent to Australia to establish their clan in the southern hemisphere. He would pave the way and provide sanctuary for any ndrine on the run from the Carabinieri. In doing so he would be richly rewarded.

Coming to Australia had worked out brilliantly for the clan who had benefitted from de Luca's astute business acumen. So much respect had he won that when he travelled back to his village after years away, he was presented with a virginal girl of sixteen as his bride. Always pleasantly polite with a friendly smile for all he met, De Luca though, was not a man to cross as one or two potential rivals had found out to their horror.

Now he had a big score to settle. That *grosso bastardo* Big Joe McArthur had betrayed Frankie and his partners over a land deal. He should have known better than to trust that *politico bugiardo*.. Worse than that in Frankie's mind, was that they had been used basically as bait to lure in a bigger fish from Europe. This was a shameful loss of face and one that could only be redressed by the spilling of blood. Fortunately for Frankie, the Capo back home were forgiving of Frankie but Frankie was merciless.

Big Joe was popular and very well connected as a state politician. In de Luca's way of thinking, this guy would have been taken out back in his home in Calabria. Nevertheless, political assassination was almost unknown in Australia and would generate a massive outcry. Frankie was not alone in this. Perhaps there was another way.

Francesco de Luca wasn't in Calabria anymore, and he was aware that he would need to tread very carefully. He had the innate characteristics of the Calabrian badger, fearless, resourceful, unwavering and when necessary, ferocious. He would make this fat greedy politician pay for his duplicity.

Three constables who had completed their overnight shifts were enjoying a cup of tea in the canteen at Russell Street HQ.

Constable Charlie Stokes was reading an article in the Age newspaper about the violence in Germany since the war. Germany's Weimar Republic was a deadly place to be for politicians and government officials. By 1922, as many as 354 politicians and government members had been murdered.

'By crikey, they're knockin' orf a few in Germany right now. Who'd be a pollie there?'

'You're pretty safe in good old Oz, mate,' chimed in Constable Bert Entwhistle, 'We don't get too many murders for starters and I think there's only been one assassination, a pollie in Queensland knocked last year, remember? I was up there then, Albert Whitford, MP.'

'Of course, the Great War was kicked orf by an assassination remember, they potted the old Archduke Franz Ferdinand an' that was that.'

'Aah they're all bloody mad as cut snakes over there. Would never 'appen 'ere,' having made his opinion on the matter known, he attended to more relevant business, 'anyone want another brew?'

CHAPTER 40

1924 LATE NOVEMBER

INQUISITION

There had not been a more felonious assembly of men in the short history of the colony than that drawn together by their mutual disrespect in the bar of the Victorian Club.

Gordon Plowright accompanied by his muscle Harry the Hatchet Sidell who sat opposite Mattias Vogel and his man on loan from John Wren, the notorious Curly Barker. The subject under discussion was the last Melbourne Cup and the explosive claims that saw Vogel's horse Tidal Wave withdrawn accused of doping. The horse's trainer returned home to Ireland in disgrace and his Australian stable broken up. The conversation thus far had been relatively convivial as all the aspects of the race were broken down and evaluated. At no point did Vogel directly accuse Plowright of any wrong doing however it was obvious that the dead weight of guilt hung over him like the sword of Damocles

Vogel had been informed that the man responsible for the whole sordid affair was none other than the man sitting opposite him now. Plowright was as guilty as hell and hoping like hell that Vogel didn't know the full story but to be on the safe side had brought along his heavy. Vogel knew for certain that Plowright had set up his trainer and was now intent on playing a cunning hand. He also knew Plowright would bring along some muscle so he brought along some of his own. The bookmaker was hoping desperately to assuage Vogel's very apparent outrage by pleading ignorance and the shared love of thoroughbred horse racing.

Both men felt that this schism between two former friends was an impediment to the growth of their individual businesses and something needed to happen to diffuse it. Plowright knew Vogel was more than capable of snuffing the life out of him but would he be so rash as to openly attack him. Vogel on the other hand, knew that if Plowright were convinced that he knew that he was responsible he would be going out of his mind waiting for him to strike. This was the real punishment that Vogel could dish out, psychological uncertainty that would eat at him until he would be almost suicidal. It would play with his imagination and have him jumping at shadows and all the while he, Vogel, would be smiling, friendly? All the while testing the wind for a time to figuratively put him in the ground.

Plowright had invited him to lunch in an effort to reconcile him somehow or bring things to a head, but Vogel was all affability and gave nothing away. The two heavies ate nothing, drank nothing, and just sat glaring at each other, daring the other to try something on. They were both used to seeing people, their victims, quivering with fear and unable to look into their eyes. This was like two prize-fighters at a weigh in trying to force the other guy to blink.

Plowright went away from the lunch with nothing to show for it but a colossal case of heartburn. He had enjoyed a lucrative racing season and was looking forward to taking some time for himself and his wife. As a Christmas surprise for his wife Helene, he had purchased two first-class tickets for the forthcoming cruise on the bay ferry Hygeia. When he presented her with the tickets, he thought she was going to explode with excitement. His generous gift cost him more than the price for admission, as his dear one called up her best friend and the two fashionistas headed out looking for the haute couture of the fashion houses.

In racing parlance, it was odds on that they would be bumping into one or two other very fortunate guests as they bounced around the leading couturiers in the city. The women were having the time of their lives. The first to meet was Maurine McArthur, Big Joe's mother, and her daughter-in-law, Irene McArthur. Helene Plowright knew Irene also as they were members together at the swanky South Yarra Tennis Club.

Who should they bump into when they took a break for coffee but a handsome new arrival to Melbourne who had a few hearts astir? A minor aristocrat from a wealthy banking and insurance family associated with Lloyds escorting a glamourous companion Lucille Yarborough as she shopped for her cruising outfit? That's a pairing that will set the village gossips tongues wagging. A comment is made that the young man should be warned off for his own safety.

They were with Dianna Beckman wife of property tycoon Godfrey Beckman whom Captain Jenkins had targeted with one of his dubious schemes before disappearing mysteriously.

Melbourne boasted it was the Australian centre of high fashion, and the designers, dressmakers and milliners were reaping a rich reward from the much-vaunted Christmas cruise. Coming so close to the end of the spring racing carnival when the fashion business usually went into hibernation for a period, it was proving to be the cherry on top of the cake as their bank accounts swelled delightfully.

For the ladies about town, this was going to be one of those tremendously important events that would be the cause of great regret if it were to be missed for any reason.

For a number of factions, it was an event not to be missed for very different reasons. Those intrigues, conspiracies and deadly machinations were beginning to take shape as plans were laid to even scores and collect dues.

Melbourne's stultifying summer heat and humidity were hotting up and so was the collective atmosphere among the passengers gathering for a pleasant pre-Christmas cruise aboard a luxurious steam powered paddle boat. Many ladies in the elite levels of the social set were outwardly calm with a stirring anxiety inside as they were determined not to be outshone in the glamour stakes by any would-be social climbers. There were many challengers at this level creating enmities that only the contenders could fully understand, and they were as bitter as any rivalry anywhere. To make their lives more difficult, the changeable weather made the selection of a suitable outfit almost impossible. Oh, the trauma, tempers frayed and hissy fits thrown, all over one day on a paddle steamer. Unfortunate husbands bore the brunt of their wives' ill temper.

The days passed by slowly twenty-four long hours at a time made harder to endure as the humidity soared past 70% while the thermometer never dropped below seventy degrees Fahrenheit during the night and touching high nineties during the day. Sleep was difficult and made almost impossible in some areas where poor drainage had assisted a population explosion of blood-sucking mosquitoes.

The result combined with the usual pre-Christmas stresses presented a population ready to explode. The joyous greetings and well wishes of Christmas were buried under a surly cloud of barely constrained antagonism. This was the type of weather spoken of by white missionaries in the tropics. All that was needed to complete that picture was a background of native drums. This was the heat and humidity that elevated drunkenness and general violence, driving men mad. Now it blanketed Melbourne in a suffocating pall, tying the police force up in a never-ending stream of complaints about domestic violence and public exhibitions of drunkenness and vandalism.

Jim Foley and his squad were run off their feet, following up one domestic after another, very often intercepting another incident on the way to the reported one. The Weather Bureau could offer no sign of relief in the forecast period.

Captain Galbraith watched the barometer closely, knowing that these high humidity periods usually broke with a drenching thunderstorm. They were still six days out from the proposed Christmas cruise and an unsporting storm at the wrong time would be a heartbreak for the hard-working teams on board and ashore.

Galbraith had put through a telephone call to Eugene Bradfield to advise him to create a plan B, just to be on the safe side.

'The one thing we cannot guarantee, sir, is the weather.'

Bradfield hadn't taken that well, in fact he responded that the cruise would go ahead in any event and slammed the phone down forcefully.

Monsieur Karl Brunner had been enjoying the company and hospitality of the rather unpolished cattle farmer politician when travelling to view Big Joe's cattle herd in the countryside. He had been treated to the BBQing of an artery clogging mountain of meat with baked potatoes and corn. The Swiss love their meat, but this was astonishing.

Monsieur Brunner was impressed by the rich volcanic landscape surrounding the McArthur estate and was already considering how his bank could invest in this prosperous landscape and the cattle farming it supported in apparent plenty.

Big Joe was happy to drive him about and introduce him to the neighbours, including the local Elders Real Estate representative Mr Jock Hadley, who would be delighted to help him find some acreage that would suit the requirements of his bank.

Big Joe was already planning how he would announce the Swiss investment in Victoria and claim credit for it and all the more kudos to him if it led to further investment. While Big Joe was imagining great things to come, he had ignored his former business partners whom he had shamelessly dumped. He had given them, nor the outrage they must be experiencing, no thought at all, either through ignorance or cold-heartedness. It may have paid him to remember his Bible studies in particular Galatians VI.

'As ye sow, so shall ye reap.' Big Joe's blissful dreams could yet turn to nightmares.

CHAPTER 41
DECEMBER 1925
THE FABULOUS CRUISE

There are few things on earth that occur without forewarning. There is always some indication or presaging, sadly most often recognised in hindsight. The most destructive volcano in history, Krakatoa, which was also reputedly the loudest noise ever heard, gave a few hints of its impending explosion as early as several months before the major eruption.

An astute observer of social interaction in Melbourne might also have picked up a few early warning vibrations of social eruptions yet to come, but the observer would need to be very sharp.

The Christmas cruise was seen as the perfect venue for several sets of antagonists to bring about their reprehensible schemes. It was going to be a very interesting excursion and calm seas would not prevent the storm developing aboard the beautiful vessel.

As a prelude to the excursion, the organising ladies always referred to as *The Committee* had invited select holders of the premium tickets to a special lunch at their favoured venue, The Windsor. It's another opportunity for participants to mix with their equals and make the acquaintance of some new faces. The invitation was taken up with enthusiasm almost unanimously. For *The Committee* however, there were some surprise absences and some shock acceptances.

The dining room was full again thanks in large part to the idea of Eugene Bradfield and his committee. If there were a gauge capable of measuring the level of passionate energy in the room, that gauge would be redlining. Below the deafening high-pitched chattering of dozens of excited females all nattering at once another layer of intense emotions swirled and eddied around certain cliques, creating a whispered sibilance audible only to wild animals.

Mr and Mrs Gordon Plowright had been having a wonderful time. Helene, from a humble yet comfortable family had never dined in the Windsor before, so it was quite a thrill just to be here and with some of Melbourne's finest was doubly so. Looking about, she recognised many faces she had only seen in the society news. It was everything she imagined it would be. The food was divine and the service was amazing. The four-piece band in the corner was playing some beautiful classical music she didn't recognise, nonetheless she enjoyed it. Gordon was very happy for her. Life as the wife of a bookmaker was far from ideal, however she had never failed to support him even when he had almost bottomed out after a terrible run.

Just then, Gordon's eyes fell on his arch nemesis on the other side of the restaurant with his wife Helene. As his eyes met with Vogel's, the gambler raised up his champagne flute in salute and mouthed the words 'good luck my friend.'

Plowright felt no friendship coming his way from the dangerous casino proprietor. In fact, the only thing he felt was fear. He knew Vogel or one of his agents might strike at any time and waiting for the threat to materialise was psychologically damaging. Consequently, his judgement in the betting ring was a little off centre, resulting in a couple of punters getting under his guard grabbing bigger odds than they were perhaps entitled to. He was sleep deprived as well, with every night noise sounding like an intruder. He had taken his shotgun into the bedroom with him every night to his wife's consternation, propping it up against his bedside table loaded with the safety catch off. It was an old weapon that up until now, had resided in the stables to dissuade intruders and rats.

'Gordon, I have no idea what's got into you. That bloody thing only needs to fall over and it will blow your legs off.'

Every night with the lethal shotgun he patrolled around his home, testing the locks on doors and windows peering out into the darkened garden for shadows that never revealed a threat, all the while fingering the hammers on the ancient weapon. He had sent his teenage children away to live with his brother on the other side of town and purchased a guard dog that so far hadn't even barked at the bloody possum raiding his fruit trees but managed to eat its weight in dog food every week.

Mrs Plowright was less than happy with her children away and a blasted great hound ruining her lawn with its massive turds that she refused point blank to pick up.

Add to that the huge beast terrified her, denying use of her own garden to her, where she used to exercise her tiny miniature poodle. She feared the hound would eat her precious little Giselle in one gulp.

'Gordy, is that the terrible gangster you're so worried about?' her question was met with a grunt that she interpreted as a yes. 'Why he looks perfectly charming in that foreign way they have,' she breathed with a dreamy look on her face.

'He'd smile like that as he stripped the skin off your back, make no mistake.'

'But why is he threatening you? What have you done, you silly man?'

'It's best that you remain ignorant, my love. Are you enjoying the petit fours?'

Quentin Upjohn was in raptures sitting at the same table as Eugene Bradfield, Elvira Rochester, Madame Rosetta Gloria Parmentier. Rhoda Day was conducting a last-minute interview with Quentin Upjohn while his newspapers camera man fussed about taking snaps. Madame Rosetta was presenting a sour face as the fidgety pint-sized gay was taking far too much time after having jumped in ahead of the Age reporter and camera man. In fact, she had no idea how the little sneak had got passed security as she had personally scanned the guest list to weed out opposition media. Besides which, he was asking the most frivolous questions.

'Mr Upjohn, I must declare your questions are, ahem, a tad basic and more than a little wearisome. Have you got enough?'

Eugene looks at her across the table and raises an eyebrow. 'Now, now Rosetta, let the young man practice his profession. Remember, there is no such thing as too much publicity. Now what was your question again, Mr Upjohn?'

Madame Rosetta Gloria Parmentier was completely affronted by Eugene's remarks vowing to mark his performances down in future. After all, he was reduced to basically, 'singing for his supper' quite literally lately and had lost a lot of respect in theatrical circles as a result.

How much of this inverse snobbery was due to their unspoken disapproval of Eugene's innovative idea, of combining dining and theatre in a small acoustically doubtful space, such as the Windsor's dining room and very soon aboard a day excursion boat, was yet to be assessed fully.

Two tables away, Joseph Esmond McArthur and Monsieur Karl Brunner were lunching with a special guest who had been introduced to them by Frankie de Luca earlier. He was a charming multi-lingual Italian who claimed to be a financier, a little embarrassed that his introduction had interrupted a conversation between Big Joe and his Swiss collaborator.

Joe had excused the interruption and after a brief 'get to know you' conversation, he was intrigued to find out more about this urbane individual and invited him to join them at their lunch table.

Watching this small interplay across the room was the familiar figure of Frankie de Luca nodding in approval as he watched his man charm his way into the confidence of the crooked politician and now there, he was sitting down for lunch with the politico swine.

Alessandro Accardi Barone was a paid assassin. A cultured individual who had used his consummate charm to get close to his targets. His weapon of choice was the very Italian and deadly stiletto. One expert strike between the ribs under the left armpit targeted to penetrate the heart would create horrendous internal bleeding, resulting in death within seconds. Done with Alessandro's skill, any witnesses would be convinced the victim had suffered a heart attack. There was generally very little external blood to prove otherwise.

Alessandro Accardi Barone's skills had been in high demand in Europe, where he was at the beck and call of a small number of well-placed people within his city, Reggio Calabria, but he often had duties further afield. His work was so discreet and dispensed with such deadly efficiency that he had once answered a call from within Vatican City.

At the table, the talk centred on international finance and the current state of the stock market. As a fresh bottle of wine was ordered, various Australian wines were discussed and dismissed as being hopelessly outclassed by Italian and French offerings from the Bordeaux region. The legendary Chateau's were mentioned, including Chateau d'Yquem, Chateau Lafitte Rothschild and Chateau Mouton Rothschild. Big Joe was well out of his depth on this subject and sat fascinated as his two guests reeled off one outstanding wine after another and the grand meals they had enjoyed all over Europe, leaving their host feeling like a backwoods clodhopper. There were some things Big Joe was yet to experience and should he survive the day, he may yet get to sample them.

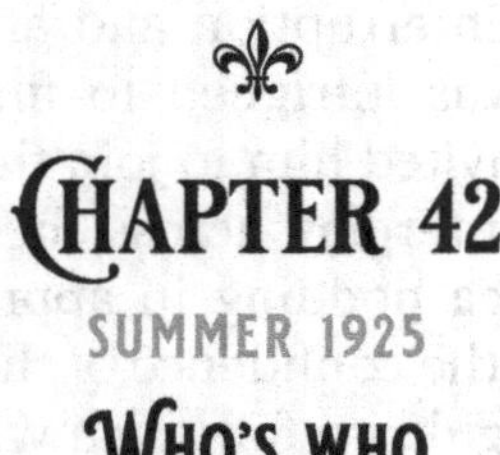

CHAPTER 42

SUMMER 1925

WHO'S WHO

The much-anticipated day had dawned with the sun rising with the promise of hot summer weather as it climbed above the Dandenong Mountain range to the north east of the city. Captain Galbraith received the forecast which predicted a clear day with a top temperature expected between eighty-two and ninety-five degrees, with wind from the north at five to ten miles per hour. There was a slight chance of a thunderstorm in the evening. Seas on the bay were currently calm to moderate. Galbraith was pleased with the report knowing that the further south they went the less influence the northerly would have as it ran into the fresh southerlies coming in off Bass Straight. A fairly typical summer's day on Port Phillip Bay.

The pleasant meteorological conditions forecast allowed the ladies to select just the right apparel as they primped and preened themselves for the wonderful day ahead.

The male guests had also gone to some extremes to ensure their attire matched the quality of their partners and most were immaculately groomed, bathed, shaved and dressed in their finest Italian wool and silk suits, finishing with handmade leather shoes

Now the first of the passengers began arriving at Station Pier Port Melbourne in a huge fleet of cabs and private vehicles, bringing with them a festive mood. Some were arriving in elegant horse-drawn carriages and others in glittering chauffeur driven motor vehicles. The variety and number of passenger vehicles threatened to cause an impossible traffic jam at the foot of the pier until a squad of constables assigned for the purpose took control. Thereafter, an orderly line of vehicles was able to swing in and discharge their passengers at the foot of the boarding ramp before looping around and departing the area.

At a safe distance, a familiar little group of wharfies were gathered unnoticed in the morning shadows, bestowing on every worthy passenger with their droll critiques.

The excited colourful crowd were as noisy as children, calling excitedly to each other, men whistling loudly to attract attention, car horns tooting over and above the clatter of horses' hooves and guttural exhausts of the internal combustion engines and the perpetually hungry seagulls squawking and squabbling in the hope of finding something to eat.

In its design, Station Pier resembled nothing more than a huge bus stop, which in effect it was. Two stories in height to allow boarding onto the newer, larger liners on two levels. The area at ground level was vast and wide open, echoing with the joyous sounds of the excursioners. Passengers already aboard called to their friends still arriving on the dock. The ship's crew were shouting instructions to the boarding passengers, urging them to move away into the further reaches of the ship to enable a smooth take up of the rest of the guests.

'Cripes, what a lot o' yammerin." As usual, The Judge opens the batting. 'Strike me, what a difference to them Rajahs an' wot not we saw off?'

'Cop an eyeful of all them jools an' stuff, a man could retire on wot theys wirf.' Typically, Hydraulic Jack focuses on the valuables in the tradition of wharfies the world over, hence his nickname Hydraulic Jack who would lift (steal) anything.

'Cobber, you would be banged up by the rozzers for just lookin' at 'em.' A warning from Brown Sugar. 'This is that Christmas cruise thing the Hygeia's crew was talkin' about. Ya got every silver tail knob in town aboard that ship today. Crikey 'magine the bloody mess if she should sink?'

'Geez yer the cheerful one today, Sugar.' Singlet begins to chuckle loudly, 'oh heck ave a decko at this bloke. 'E must reckon theys on the way round the 'orn.' They all gawked at the odd site of a timid senior public servant from the states Treasury Department who was nagged into the trip by his social-climbing wife. The poor chap obviously led a sheltered life and suffered a morbid fear of the sea and was festooned with all manner of buoyancy equipment. He looked quite absurd, causing consternation among the crew who battled to restrain their laughter.

Sugar redeems himself with the final comment. 'Any 'ow if she did sink, none of 'em would drown 'cos their noses is so ígh in the air.' General laughter rewards the humourist.

Eventually, all passengers were safely aboard. *Daisy* O'Connell and *Sparra* Dempsey, overseen by the first mate Bully Masterson, were checking numbers as they usually did for any regular excursion but on this occasion there was an additional security layer for very good reason. The competition for tickets on this very special cruise had been intense and the organisers were expecting some ticketless desperates would attempt to get aboard by fair means or foul.

To assist at the boarding ramp, Jim Foley had stationed two of his most able-bodied senior Constables Roger 'Bluey' Farnsworth and Martin Richardson, to provide support for the committees ticketing personnel who checked each ticket and matched the passenger by name. True to form, one or two tried it on and were escorted ashore looking embarrassed and chagrined. Finally, all was well, all paying passengers accounted for and aboard, the boarding ramp was sent off and the crew gone to their stations for the first leg of the journey.

With the band striking up *'Waltzing Matilda'* and an enthusiastic cheer from the excited passengers that echoed under the large roof span of the pier Captain Galbraith orders three long blasts of the ships fog horn while First Mate Gunner Patrick uses the bridge Engine Order Telegraph to ring down to the engine room for 'slow astern'. The fog horn alerts other shipping in the area to be aware that his vessel was reversing away from its berth into a wide semi-circular course towards St Kilda. The helmsman holds the wheel down until Hygeia's prow pointed south-west, the heading for the Western Channel and Queenscliff at which point Captain Galbraith rings down to the engine room for 'slow ahead'. The massive paddle wheels come to a complete stop before churning the sea to foam as they fight to overcome the reverse momentum. Huge dense plumes of dark smoke belch from the twin funnels as an indication of the power spent in the manoeuvre. Once she gains forward momentum, Galbraith orders his first mate to ring down again, this time for 'full ahead.'

Once underway, the majestic vessel threads its way south between the channel markers keeping the red to starboard as required when exiting port in Australian waters.

Some of the passengers were taking an interest in the sights, but most were intent on having a good time. The café and the bars were open and doing a roaring trade. The café barely keeping up with orders for tea and scones with whipped cream and jam. The bars were already pouring beers at a rate that put them in competition with the ship's bilge pumps.

The stressed bar manager expressed some concern that they might need to refuse service to some patrons who had already exhibited signs of over-indulgence.

Jim Foley had instructed his crew not to fall into a sense of complacency. They had their orders and were expected to begin regular patrols around the main decks of the vessel, maintaining a visible presence to reassure any nervous passengers worried by the unsociable behaviour of others.

'I guess some people just don't have any sea legs at all Bluey, look at that poor miserable bugger.' Martin Richardson pointed to a toff already hanging over the side, seeing his breakfast off, 'it's gunna be a bloody long journey for him I reckon.'

Jim Foley joined his uncle, Francis Foley on the bridge with the captain. They were giving the captain a brief to ensure that he was aware of the police methods.

The captain recalled that Jim Foley had carried out his previous assignment professionally and was satisfied that he would do his duty again without fuss.

Around the ship, the passengers moved and shifted as their attention was drawn to various aspects of the vessel and points of interest outside the ship as she progressed. Fishing vessels coming in to market followed by swarms of ravenous seabirds feeding as the catch was cleaned and the offal thrown overboard with the unfortunate by-catch. Occasionally a dolphin yet to fill its belly with its own catch was seen to join in for a top-up meal competing with the gulls, to the delight of the ladies who all confessed to a strange attraction to the creatures.

The band was playing sentimental old favourites and some contemporary tunes which drew couples out onto the dance floor. The band was a truly professional outfit and could render excellent versions of the current hits by any artists. *'Ain't Misbehavin'-Fats Waller, 'Makin' Whoopee' -Bing Crosby, 'Swanee'-Al Jolson, 'West End Blues'- Louis Armstrong, 'Down Hearted Blues', Bessie Smith, 'Sweet Georgia Brown'* and *'Yes Sir That's My Baby.'* Appropriately *'Paddlin' Madeline Home'* and of course *'The Charleston'* which had some talented young glamour queens with their partners dazzling the older guests on the dance floor. Some of the oldies tried to compete to the detriment of their ankles and hamstrings.

Big Joe had his Swiss guest under his wing and was standing on the starboard side forward of the huge paddlewheel, appearing to be pointing out features on the shoreline. Not that there were many. The country on this side of the bay was flat and featureless, being comprised of miles of wetlands, flat paddocks and little else. In the distance was a small mountain range known as the You Yangs standing over some fertile farmlands. In fact, neither one cared a fig for the view the subject of their conversation was the business that brought them together.

Lurking about in the shadows was Buster Yarrow, who had business of his own to discuss just as soon as he could find his two cobbers. He couldn't believe his luck when his two crooked mates, Senior Constables Weatherby and Senior Constable Clarence Thurgood, with a little push from above, managed to get themselves assigned to duty on the Hygeia. It could not have been better if he'd organised it himself.

He finally met up with them in the midships café where he pressed them insistently, hoping to bring them to his cause without having much luck. Just because they were here didn't mean they were in lockstep with his murderous plans.

'Look here you blokes, I don't expect yez to git yer 'ands dirty but I do expect ya to back me up.'

Buster was leaning across the table in earnest appeal, his rough features tortured by his hatred for Jim Foley into ugly, unshaven contortions. 'I'm gunna gut that bastard and nail 'is hide to the shed, mark my words.'

Buster's hatred of Jim Foley was undimmed after several years and not entirely down to the fact that he had been arrested by the then 'wet behind the ears' no-account cop. He was also fired by an emotion he would never admit to; jealousy, a red-hot burning jealousy that consumed him. He had always lied about his background, which explained his anger at his current rural posting. He had been raised in a small country town in a family that was always on the brink, living in a ramshackle hut down on the flats. His father held the contract as the town's night soil carter and was nicknamed Turdy Tom, which meant Buster had to fight his way through school spurred by constant insults which, thank God, hadn't followed him into the force.

Here he was fifteen years in the job and he had been made to scrabble and claw his way through the ranks, always copping the rough end of things. Then along came this pampered brat pushed up the ladder by his uncle and given every chance. The bastard lived in a house Buster could never dream of visiting, let alone owning.

The two Senior Constables had no idea what their boss is on about. He was just ranting and swearing revenge, which made no sense at all. He couldn't possibly think of taking the life of a fellow policeman in this situation, or anywhere else for that matter. Victoria still had capital punishment and the killer of a policeman would almost certainly hang.

Buster Yarrow had an infallible plan. He would make it work and restore his pride. He believed he had shut down the prosecution's case against him coming from matters occurring at Madam Doreen McKillop's bawdy house and to wipe the slate clean he wanted to give that smart-arse young copper some grief. He had thought it through, using all his policing experience. He would be the executioner and the platform for his performance would offer the means to carry it off undetected.

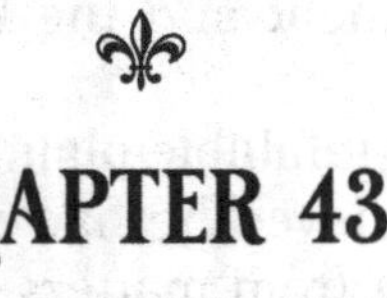

CHAPTER 43

MID DECEMBER 1925

VOYAGE OF THE DAMNED?

Allowing for time spent in shoving off and manoeuvring away from Station Pier, Hygeia could expect to be abeam Queenscliff Pier in just on two hours in good weather. After cruising at eighteen miles per hour (just over fifteen and a half knots) on a flat sea the graceful vessel now sat motionless in a stretch of water known as Victory Bight to allow her passengers to take in the scenery and admire the skilful work of a pilot boat motoring out through the heads to meet an incoming cargo ship. These were truly treacherous waters with several hidden reefs positioned just perfectly to rip the bottom out of the unwary. The pilot service was legendary for providing their expertise in extremely hazardous conditions experienced year-round in the treacherous Rip. Their seamanship was something to behold. Although Galbraith's seamanship and his confidence in it was in every way comparable, like most sensible skippers, he would stay well clear of this challenging area.

Normally, Hygeia would pull into the Queenscliff Pier to allow her passengers time ashore. The pier ran out to sea in a south-easterly direction, making it subject to the enormous tidal forces at this point. Great care was required to bring the ship in on the Northerly side with a flood tide and the opposite side during an ebbtide, thus avoiding the vessel being pinned against the jetty by the rush of the tidal streams.

Today, the defence installations of HMAS Point Lonsdale and across the Rip, the gun emplacements of Fort Nepean could be clearly seen. The historic hotels and novelty shops would only be seen from a distance.

Today the decision had been made to by-pass Queenscliff due to the unusually busy on-board agenda. Instead, they would proceed from here to Sorrento tying up to a far safer, more sheltered pier to discharge those passengers. Those who wish to participate in a light morning tea served on the grassy foreshore area sheltered from the sun by a stand of huge cypress trees planted along the roadway behind the park. Passengers could also take the opportunity to paddle in the sea at the narrow sandy beach on the eastern side of the ferry landing.

The passage from Queenscliff was always the favourite with passengers, as there were many fascinating sights to see and the thirty- or forty-minute trip would seem to be over in the blink of an eye.

But not for Senior Sergeant Jim Foley working his team under the scrutiny of his uncle, old 'First Through the Door' Foley. It was the most exhilarating and trying time in his career. Things started to develop before the majestic vessel reached the waters of the Western Channel between Swan Island to the north of Queenscliff and Popes Eye, a rock structure intended to be a fort but never completed.

Never before in the history of the colony or its police force would so many separate skirmishes occur at the same time and in the same impossibly constrained area as the decks of a moving ship. Jim Foley and his team would be headline news across the nation before this excursion was over. The question was, would they all be there to applaud their success (or failure) together?

Jim's first tour of the vessel discovered a group of determined gamblers who had already been asked to leave the main bar, having reached their limit in the opinion of the bar manager. They had become too boisterous and after being shown the door, had gathered in a sheltered area toward the rear of the vessel and were involved in a spirited game of two up. This had become violent as a toss was disputed due to the slight movement of the ship. The loser had just lost a big stake and was using any excuse to call for another toss, and it had come down to fisticuffs to settle the question.

Jim Foley and two of his team rounded the players up, reminding them that gambling was forbidden on board and should they continue to flout the law, then the game's organisers would spend the rest of the voyage in the ship's cell.

Constable Irene McCarthy took Jim aside and quietly informed him that the ships lock-up was currently occupied by a female drunk on champagne and over-exposure to the sun who had caused her husband to be badly beaten when he discovered her in the arms of another much larger and more able man. The poor husband was now residing in the sick bay and his assailant was in chains below. All this in the first few hours of the cruise.

'Good Lord Constable McCarthy, that didn't take long, did it?' Jim shakes his head in wonder at the human race. 'Not three hours into the voyage and two in custody and one in medical care?'

The gamblers were moving on as another group occupied the vacated space, not to fight or gamble, thank heavens. Jim Foley moved towards the front of the ship, trying to locate the man who swore he was going to do him harm. Senior Sergeant Foley was fuming when he had initially discovered that Buster Yarrow's partisans were to be assigned to his team and had argued as hard as he might, but they remained in his team with no explanation or apology. Then compounding his anger and fears, he saw Yarrow coming aboard as a paying passenger. *`What kind of foolery is this*?' He was desperate to keep an eye on the man trying to anticipate any attack that might come from that direction because there could be no other reason for him to be aboard. He was hardly a fan of picnic cruising.

Jim Foley was not alone in maintaining his vigilance. After their coffee and cake, Gordon and Helene Plowright decided to walk off the cake by taking a stroll around the promenade deck, but before they could move, a familiar contemptuous figure approached.

Good God what is this swaggering bastard up to now? In his anxiety Gordon failed to realise that he had a crushing grip on Helene's hand causing her to yelp with pain.

Matthias Vogel was enjoying his psychological games with Plowright and decided it was time to step it up a bit. Wearing the sincerest smile of a fox approaching the hen house, he had a steward place an ice-bucket and champagne on Plowright's table then presented himself with a gorgeous woman on his arm.

'Guten morgan beautiful people, I have taken za liberty of bringing an excellent French champagne zat I hope you vill join with me to celebrate this beautiful day.'

Plowright was stunned and his wife perplexed. Was this the monster that had her husband jumping at shadows?

'What the hell are you playing at Vogel? Take your bloody wine and jump overboard with it.' Plowright leapt to his feet, fists clenched voice raised in anger. 'I'm sick of the little games you're playing. If you have a score to settle with me, then let's get it on you Kraut bastard. We kicked your arse in the war and I'll kick your arse again right here, right now.'

Vogel laughed and spoke in a patronising tone, suggesting Plowright calm down before he had a heart attack.

The row attracted the attention of Constable Bluey Farnsworth, who stepped in between the two men calling for calm. Helene Plowright joined her husband and in standing, hastily knocked over her chair. If they needed to attract more attention, then Gordon's next move would do it. Picking up the champagne bucket, he slammed it into Vogel's chest telling him to go stuff his head up dead bear's bum. He is rewarded with laughter from the onlookers.

Vogel's was slightly puzzled by Plowright's instruction, when he thought he was going to make Plowright cower humiliatingly one more time in front of the showgirl he had brought along. Instead, he had been embarrassed by Plowright's spirited response and forced to walk away with the champagne bucket in one hand and as the saying goes 'his arse in a sling.' Inside, he was in a cold fury and quietly vowed to have Plowright's head in the bucket before he was much older. His showgirl with the IQ level of a cumquat was giggling and asked him why should he put his head anywhere near a dead animal.

'Veronique, do yourself a very big favour and shut za fuck up.' Vogel hurled the bucket and its bottle of expensive champagne over the rail in anger and disgust.

'*Das ist es. Ich werde diesen bastard toten bevor der Tag voruber ist.*'

Vogel had reverted to his native tongue to express his anger, threatening to kill Plowright before the day is out.u His furious outburst catches the showgirl by surprise. Thinking she has done something wrong she totters off in tears on her high heels looking for a place to hide.

Jim Foleys team is working rotation around the decks with increased vigilance since shutting down the two-up school. Word came to him of the confrontation between the dangerous Vogel and some bloke who was supposed to be a big-time bookmaker named Plowright. He would need to keep an eye on developments there. There had been spot fires breaking out all over the ship and they were yet to reach the midway point of the voyage. To say Jim was a little nervous was to understate the case. He had been patrolling with Constable Dottie Green who stopped to console the show girl who had become distressed thinking the German was going to do her harm.

They had been patrolling the lower decks where the restaurant and bars were. Jim made his way to the stern alone. There was an open area at the extreme end of the vessel with large windows that opened out and folded back on themselves, allowing passengers to relieve the stuffy atmosphere that tended to develop in this space. Despite the light through the windows at the stern, the space immediately ahead of it was still dim as a result of the deep shadows under the upper promenade deck. Right at that point, the air was thick with tobacco smoke spiced with the fumes from the ship's massive steam engines and food smells emanating from the galley. The set-up was familiar to Jim from his previous experience aboard, so he thought to do the community thing and swing the windows wide, allowing more air to flood through and more natural light into the space.

Jim shot the bolts that held the windows tightly in their frames and leaning out securing the left one and turned to repeat the operation on the right-hand side when from the corner of his eye he detected a dark figure charging out of the gloom coming straight at him.

Intinctively, Jim hunched down as the figure hit him with a stunning force, throwing him back against the bulkhead with a violence that knocked him into a world of darkness.

Big Joe and his Swiss business colleague Monsieur Karl Brunner had been enjoying every aspect of the trip. Karl Brunner was explaining to Big Joe that he and his family regularly travelled aboard the wonderful paddle steamers on Lake Lucerne. A whole fleet of steam powered paddle boats operated on the lake. They were very beautiful and similar in design to Hygeia, but quite a bit smaller.

'Mind you, zey are required to move in tight waterways and be nimble in za harbours.' Big Joe hadn't noticed Karl's accent before and was wondering if it's an affectation or he's simply forgotten where he was.

They found their way to the upper promenade deck and were drawn to the stern. A wind change and alteration of the ships heading had earlier seen a cloud of smoke descend on the decks, making things mildly unpleasant. Oddly, having moved away to avoid the fumes from the ship, Big Joe, craving a different kind of smoke, withdrew a cigar holder from his inside jacket holding four quality cigars and offered one to Brunner. Karl declines and produces a beautifully carved Briar pipe and loads it with an aromatic tobacco. They stand there shoulder to shoulder, savouring their choice of smoking material. Leant against the rail above the stern of the ship their eyes were drawn to the flocks of Australasian Gannets working a school of tiny bait fish. They made quite a show with their bright yellow heads and large black-tipped wings folded back against their bodies as they dove, several at a time onto the huge school of bait fish, almost like a well-controlled production line, surfacing to take flight again juggling their prey in their beaks before swallowing the white-bait whole as they adhered to a strict flight plan ascending to come around again like aircraft in the landing zone without risking a mid-air collision. Their catch would be disgorged to feed their young later when they returned to their nesting sites on Popes Eye.

The Hygeia was now crossing the area known locally as 'the heads' where a rolling swell came through from Bass Straight in the south-west lifting the big vessel gently up and down causing one or two dancing passengers to miss their footing raising a ripple of laughter throughout the ship as drinkers desperately grabbed for glasses and bottles that threatened to topple.

Both Joe and Karl were smoking and enjoying a glass of imported 1920 Chateau Latour that Karl had arranged to bring aboard, being no fan of the local vintages despite Big Joe's enthusiastic endorsements. A steward at Brunner's request had brought the extravagant tipple up from the bar where the Swiss had placed it earlier. It had seemed like a good idea at the time but the ships movement made it difficult to balance the salver on the rail. Never the less two glasses were successfully poured and the remainder taken back.

Big Joe was enjoying the rich complexity of the wine complemented by his cigar thinking of the grapes ripening in a Northern summer many miles away at the other end of the earth as he watched the cigar smoke disappear on the strong breeze. He was brought back to the present by his charming Italian lunch companion from the Windsor.

'Buongiorno Senors, *come stai.*' A beaming Alessandro Accardi Barone was striding across the rising and falling deck like a seasoned sailor.

'*Buongiorno senor Barone*' responded Karl using Italian.

'*Comme c'est bien de te voiri*' in this time in French. 'And good to see you, gentlemen.'

Big Joe felt obliged to join the greetings, 'Ah g'day Al, how the hell are ya?' And laughs.

Unknown by Karl Brunner and Big Joe, Alessandro had breakfasted with Francesco de Luca early this morning before boarding. De Luca had declined an invitation on the cruise and now waited at home to hear Alessandro's report after completion of his contract. Alessandro was compelled now to see it through when the right set of circumstances aligned. He was not a man to hasten when charged with an assignment like this.

As the three gentlemen chatted about the joys of the voyage so far, Big Joe was called away by Phillip Croker, who seemed to be very agitated. Big Joe walked him away to seek some privacy and find out just what has got Croker so stirred up. Would he stupidly choose this time and place to attack Joe over the land deal? If so, best to keep him away and out of earshot of Karl. It's just as well, as Croker appears to have enjoyed a tipple or two himself, face flushed, eyes red and tongue furry, Mr Croker is steamed up ready for a fight. Big Joe is more than willing to leave Karl Brunner and Alessandro admiring the scenery as he leads Croker away, as though he might be identified by the Swiss as one of his failed rivals. If Karl recognised the insignificant real estate developer, he showed no sign of it and continued his conversion with the charming Italian comparing touchpoints in their homelands where they may have crossed paths. Ten minutes later, when Big Joe returned neither of his erstwhile friends are anywhere to be seen.

'That's curious, I wasn't gone for that long. Perhaps they've gone in search of coffee. Bloody Europeans can't seem to live without it.'

A slightly disgruntled Big Joe wandered off but didn't get too far when he is waylaid by several of his constituents again and within minutes is engaged in a complicated debate about some recently tabled legislative matters.

⚜

Chapter 44

A Dark Cloud on a Sunny Day

Eugen Bradfield planned to present a performance as good as any in a major theatre. He would not be satisfied with anything less than rave revues for his one act play presented after a light luncheon served to guests on route to Mornington. He planned to bring all of his cast together when Hygeia tied up at Sorrento with passengers going ashore for their 'Brunch on The Beach' as it was being promoted. He was hoping the majority of passengers would leave the vessel, giving his team the chance to conduct a last-minute rehearsal unhindered. Precision timing was the key to their success.

Passengers and crew, with some notable exceptions, were enjoying a wonderful cruise. The sky remained a beautiful cobalt blue with pure white fluffy clouds sailing serenely in from the south, highlighting the vivid azure sky. The temperature had climbed steadily throughout the morning but was brought to heel by the alleviating sea breeze promised by the early morning forecast.

The band had proved immensely popular, even lifting the spirits of the few passengers who had earlier complained of a touch of motion sickness. The deck space allocated as a dance floor was never empty, with a lively crowd of mostly younger patrons burning up energy at about the same rate as the mighty steam engines propelling their ship across the water.

Jim Foley's team had finished yet another tour around the ship covering every level of the ships decks, bars, the café and restaurants. Constable Irene McCarthy even stuck her head in the barbershop once or twice and got a big hurrah from the hairdresser and his clients.

Jim Foley hadn't been seen for a while and his uncle was concerned that he may have been neglecting his duties. Sitting in the café deep in conversation with a number of Melbourne's leading lights, he spied Constable Dottie Green and called her over.

'Constable, can you find Senior Sergeant Foley and ask him to report to me here please?'

A large table in the centre of the ship's restaurant was reserved for Sir Rupert Yarborough and his guests. His temporarily reconciled wife Lucille sat to his left and the Australian CEO of his company sat to his right with his young, attractive wife. On the opposite side of the table sat Albert Graeme, a very influential financier and power broker in Federal Politics. His wife was not present as they were in the process of divorcing. In her place was a gorgeous young blond who had a few heads turning and people whispering as they had been watching her. On the dance floor, her revealing outfit left little to the imagination.

'Is there a single group on the planet,' wondered Sir Rupert, 'so easily stirred to emotion as the ageing female demographic. When they spy someone so full of life, so vivacious and lovely as this girl, they just burn with a merciless envy?'

The truth was that any female on board over the age of thirty-five who had been exposed to her beauty and joie de vivre would gladly have thrown her to the sharks. The men, however, were experiencing an entirely different emotion that would have them diving overboard to rescue the ravishing creature.

Sir Rupert had an eye for the ladies like any red-blooded male watching and appreciating this young lady's assets. His eyes, however, were employed elsewhere, scanning the decks for the man who ruined his marriage and shamed him as a cuckold. Sir Rupert was a man who could not keep the fox out of the henhouse.

He'd heard all the sniggering and the jokes that for a man who had represented his country as an elite athlete, one who regularly put his body in the way of harm to defend his team mates, felt the verbal sniping like bullets through his chest. His honour would not be restored until he had dealt with that sleazy actor. On a table well away from the dance floor, was a serious group of men who not only had a mission to restore their honour but to explore methods to restore their fortunes as well. This six-man posse represented the core of investors in Captain Richard Jenkins far-fetched scheme to find the lost treasures of the Maghul Emperor Shah Jahan that Jenkins had convinced them would almost rival Ali Baba's cave of the Forty

Thieves or King Solomon's Mines. They were convinced by Jenkins' silver tongue that they could have a share simply by investing in his trust fund that would finance the recovery expedition.

The truth had come to them earlier, after the visit of the Maharaja. While lunching at the Windsor, one of the investors Mr Godfrey Beckmann was speculating as to why Jenkins had not appeared to greet this important visitor who was one of the Indian Armies Supreme Commanders and a Royal Personage. The staff waiting on Beckmann's table were the inscrutable pair of hard-working Hindi waiters, Adit and Damodar, who had never been in any doubt about the veracity of the Englishman who called himself Captain Jenkins. They of course, would never reveal his duplicity but were almost choking with suppressed laughter when they were serving his table and overheard the sheer *bakavaas* (Hindi for garbage) that flowed so easily from his lying mouth like the wine they poured into his glass.

Beckmann had reached that happy level of intoxication that was neither drunk nor sober while his inhibitions were melting like the ice in his whiskey glass. He was at that happy level where young men stupidly lost control of their emotions and launched marriage proposals or physical challenges and dares that could not be wound back. On an impulse he tugged Adit's sleeve and asked him politely if he, as an Indian, could explain the mystery of Jenkins absence from the Regal visit. Adit was shocked to be addressed personally and directly by a patron and was embarrassed and frightened.

Adit began to shake, almost dropping the wine bottle from which he was serving.

Dianna Beckmann was alarmed, thinking Adit was having some kind of fit and leapt up, putting her hand reassuringly on his shoulder, doubling his embarrassment.

Adit had dropped his head respectfully when spoken to by Godfrey and now swivelled his head to look at the madame sideways. As soon as their eyes met, she saw his face appear to darken with anger and she stepped back alarmed, letting out gasp.

'Dianna, are you alright? Has he said something?'

'No, I think he's a little too upset to be questioned.'

'Oh Sir, I am so sorry sir, but my friend here Damodar and myself have heard Captain Jenkins talking about our homeland.' Poor terrified Adit's head swivelled back and forth in some sort of involuntary reaction. 'Sir I mean no disrespect as it is not our place to speak ill of the hotel's guests.' Adit's face was creased with concern now, 'But this man is a fool, clearly he has never been in our country and we don't believe he could have ever served in the Royal Indian Cavalry.' Adit was gaining confidence now but still very concerned that his outspokenness might cost him his job.

'Now look here young man, you need to be careful choosing your words. Captain Jenkins is a gentleman and an officer.' Godfreys words, although sincere, sounded a little uncertain.

'Please let him speak darling, the poor boy's terrified.' Diana pleads.

'We are humble servants in this esteemed establishment and we must know our place.' Adit stands hands clasped in front of him, head bowed looking the very definition of contrition.

His next words though, were angry, forced through gritted teeth. 'We must never comment on guests and their behaviour or appearance, but this man sir is an evil blasphemer.'

Adit's words hit Godfrey Beckmann like blows. He has committed ten thousand pounds, already transferred to the account of Captain Richard Fairlie Jenkins, Cavalry Officer DSM Veteran of France and Flanders.

Could he really be a fake and an unscrupulous conman? Godfrey would decide to pay a visit to the Indian Consulate in Melbourne to see if they can shine any light on the man. He would be told that nothing was known about Jenkins. At the time of the Maharaja's visit, his representatives having heard of him from several of their Australian hosts had made enquiries about him and concluded that he was just another glory seeker of no account.

Godfrey Beckmann knew other investors in Jenkins' scheme which he now viewed with perfect twenty-twenty hindsight, as crazy. With no time to lose, he rounded up his co-investors and delivered the dreadful news. Six very angry men left that meeting vowing to pursue Jenkins to the ends of the earth and deal with him. They had no idea where their money had gone, so to pursue the miscreant with injunctions was a useless tactic, as would be a letter of demand or any other legal instrument.

The fraud squad was been notified, and their advice was to sit tight while they investigated the man's bona fides. Sit tight bedamned!

The vigilante group now clustered conspiratorially in Hygeia's restaurant knew that the recovery of their 'investments' was impossible, however they could ensure that Jenkins could receive no joy from the profits of his criminality. But how? Perhaps enough pressure could be brought to bear to have his passport cancelled, preventing him leaving the country. This was perhaps the first sensible measure to be raised after all the bluff and bluster of the previous hours' meeting. Make the truth public, humiliate him in the newspapers. In short order, he would become a social pariah, finding doors slamming shut in his face. Hopefully one of those doors would be the one on his prison cell. These were basically good law-abiding men and the thought of violence never really came up until a conversation was had with Gordon Plowright's enforcer, Harry (The Hatchet) Sidell.

The advice that The Hatchet imparted was shocking, but when seen against the magnitude of Jenkins crimes, which included hoodwinking old ladies from their savings, it seemed almost appropriate. It was however a level of violence that none of them were prepared for. If the vigilantes followed Harry the Hatchets prescription, Jenkins would spend the rest of his miserable life in a world of never-ending agony. Harry the Hatchet showed genuine and almost petulant disappointment when his plan was rejected.

CHAPTER 45

DECEMBER 1925

A Lost Lamb

Constables Dottie Green and Martin Richardson were worried. They had been searching for their leader Senior Sergeant Jim Foley. The team had broken up into pairs and from the bow of the ship and upper promenade deck to the full extent of the main deck, including the bars, café and restaurant. The anchor chain locker and lifeboats had been searched thoroughly to exclude all possibility's.

The decks of the Hygeia had become almost deserted with the mass exodus of passengers going ashore for the Brunch on the Beach when a cry went up from the stern. Jim Foley's unconscious form was discovered laying hard up against the concave bulwark. Seen from astern, this area was served by vertical windows that in rough weather would be closed to avoid being swamped by a high following sea that might 'poop' the ship. With the windows closed, the lighting was quite dim and the air damp and foul. It was this situation that Jim had been trying to relieve when he was assaulted. The dark shade of his uniform and the deep shadows had served to make him almost invisible despite the sunshine of the day. Bright blood runs from a wound to the back of his head and he appears he may have suffered a broken or bruised collar bone.

'What the bloody hell's happened?' Bluey Farnsworth kneels beside his colleague. 'Cripes, tell me he's not dead, Dottie?'

'Not dead, thank God, but pretty bashed up.' Dottie, like Bluey, is very fond of their bright young Senior Sergeant. 'There must have been someone else involved, the ships not tossing about enough to cause this.' Instinctively she scans the deck looking for some indication of violence but sees nothing. 'Bluey, treat this as a crime scene until Jim, that is, until Senior Sergeant Foley, regains awareness and can throw some light on this.'

Jim was carried away supported by Bluey Farnsworth to the ship's sick bay with a concerned Dottie green by his side, where the doctor examined him as he slowly regained his senses. The diagnosis was concussion and a heavily bruised shoulder with no breaks, fortunately. The doctor inserted three or four stitches into the scalp wound and he was done. Jim was advised to stay where he was and get as much rest as he could.

'To hell with that,' Jim was struggling to his feet against medical advice, wincing with pain.

The smallest copper on the force Dottie Green exerted her womanly authority to insist he at least stay there while she fetched a cup of tea to wash down the pain killers the doctor had prescribed.

Dottie was soon back with a soothing cuppa and some biscuits and after checking the dressing on her Sergeant's scalp she sat down satisfied that everything was under control.

'What happened Serg, can you tell me?'

'All I can remember is reaching out for that window to close it, then all of a sudden a figure rushed me from my right crashing me into the frame and knocking me out.' Jim sat up, his head in both hands rubbing his temples finally shaking his head he goes on, 'one thing I did notice was my assailant was using a standard issue police truncheon.' Jim rotates his injured shoulder gingerly, 'by God Dottie, I think that was that bloody lunatic copper Yarrow.' His voice rising with excitement. 'He's on the bloody boat, I saw him boarding at Port Melbourne.' Jim sits up with a sudden rush of excitement and is almost put down again by an attack of vertigo for his trouble. 'C'mon Dottie, we have to find the swine before he gets ashore at Sorrento and bolts.'

Jim struggled to his feet, Dottie couldn't resist putting a hand under his elbow to steady him.

'Thanks Dottie, just give me a second and we'll get going.'

Bluey meanwhile, was following Dottie's suggestion while Constables Martin and McCarthy kept people away from the lower deck while assisting in the search for clues.

The poop deck, where Jim had been standing was a little damp due to the sea spray drawn through the window that Jim had opened. There were a couple of scuff marks on the deck and Jim's cap laying in the bilges. A little further away, he discovered another item adding to the mystery. It was a beautifully carved tobacco pipe that still contained a half load of tobacco partially smoked. Did this belong to the assailant? Unlikely, as you don't attack someone while smoking a pipe? Bluey was a pretty competent copper, but he was no Sherlock Holmes and he couldn't imagine how this object was connected to Jim's assault, so he attributed no importance to it. He dropped it into his coat pocket and continued combing the area and quickly forgot about it.

Hygeia was within a boat length of her destination as her captain guided the vessel gently and expertly into position against the Sorrento Jetty. As she nudged up, Daisy O'Connell and Sparra Dempsey scurried to handle the mooring lines while dodging around onlookers some of whom eagerly tried to lend a hand. The crew warn them off sternly. The forces that can be generated on these lines by the ship's movements against wind and tide can be lethal and spare no pity for stray limbs.

Meanwhile, first mate Bully Masterson harassed his crew to get the boarding ramp up off the jetty and into place for the convenience of the disembarking passengers.

A cheerful flood of happy voyagers were soon streaming off the ship in such numbers that they have covered the tee shaped jetty from side to side with gaily coloured parasols and summer dresses of every colour under the sun looking like a Claude Monet flower garden. Many of the younger women were wearing fashions of the day influenced by the Jazz era's flappers. Below-knee length drop-waist dresses with a loose straight fit. Cloche hats and bobbed haircuts and lots of beads. The men's fashions were not quite as bright, but just as cheerful. White or cream was the dominant choice. All white, slacks over shoes with contrasting jacket in red and white checks crowned with a white Panama. A boldly striped jacket over a white cotton shirt and bow tie with a variety of headwear from straw boaters, trilby's, to bowlers. Several brave souls had discarded their jackets altogether and were dressed in light cotton long-sleeved shirts, their trousers held up by colourful braces. One or two men were prepared for the meridian sun with practical garb, including the popular Panama hats, but always rigidly correct, no slovenly attire here.

The current temperature is a comfortable seventy-five degrees Fahrenheit. The colourful parade made its way off the jetty and across to the grassy area where long trestle tables and serving staff were set up patiently waiting for their arrival all part of the 'committee's' wonderful organisation.

Back aboard Hygeia, Eugene had rounded up his team. The stage hands have already begun assembling the set and electricians are laying cables for the lighting. The cast are in a quiet corner by themselves, practicing their lines. Eugene is encouraging them with some flattery and helpful tips.

'Now remember,' he stops and laughs, 'this is a comedy and I would hope that you recalled that little detail.' He goes on. 'Comedy is perhaps the hardest genre of our profession. The key... to-to-to comedy... is timing.' His deliberate stumble receives laughter. 'Let's have no one coming in over someone else's punch line... please.'

While they had the time, Eugene kept them at it until the lead stage hand attracted his attention to let him know that the set was finished.

'Right, let's go and have a look and become familiar with our places before the herd comes back.' He claps his hands for attention. 'Johnson!' (his lead stage hand) 'I want the curtain up with set covered before our audience returns. Can you oblige please?'

A welcoming party of locals is keeping the picnickers busy on shore; the ever-present bush flies and greedy seagulls. Despite the flies and seagulls attacking the food and the picnickers alike, they still manage to enjoy a unique experience. For some among them, Sorrento and Portsea are very familiar landscapes where their families have owned summer holiday homes for years scattered along the cliff tops and beachfronts. This however is more about the event happening aboard the beautiful Hygeia. To be celebrated with their own kind, the rich and privileged citizens of Melbourne many of whom would soon be returning to spend the summer in their beautiful clifftop homes. Driving down the Point Nepean Road a mostly rough single lane strip that wound its way painfully around the coast. A typical trip from Melbourne to Sorrento could be a slow and tiring three to four hours during peak travel times in summer.

CHAPTER 46
MID VOYAGE – DECEMBER 1925
REVENGE? SMILE AND MOVE ON

Jim, still nursing a cracking headache, had his team break up and search the ship for that corrupt and dangerous Buster Yarrow who Jim was now certain was the coward that staged the attack on him.

They would be disappointed searching for Yarrow and his two kowtowing offsiders aboard the ship. They had been among the first down the gangplank, scuttling away toward the Koonya Hotel directly opposite the staging area for the jetty where they settled into a quiet corner of the bar to discuss their next moves. More correctly, the moves to be discussed were strictly down to Yarrow. The other two specimens were reluctant recruits from the very beginning when he announced his intentions and now were urgently looking for a way to separate themselves from the crazed detective.

'I nearly had the bastard, got him good wif me baton an' 'e went down like a sack of spuds.' Yarrow related his assault on Jim Foley to his wide-eyed compatriots. 'I was just about to hoist 'im up an' give 'im the old heave-ho over board when I 'ears 'is cobbers or someone comin' and I had to scarper.'

Senior Constable Weatherby and Senior Constable Clarence Thurgood are appalled and plead with Yarrow to call off his personal battle with Jim Foley, reminding him that when Foley discovered him running from Mrs McKillops it was pure chance. As a result, he had been lightly dealt with in that regard. The other matter of the underage girl was his own fault and he needed to answer for it. In trying to get Yarrow to see reason, Constable Thurgood had probably gone a step too far and he now found a pint glass smashed over his head for his troubles.

'Bloody hell Serg, have you gone completely troppo? Ya might 'ave killed 'im.' Weatherby grabbed his mate by the arm to stop him falling from the chair to the floor. A bloodied Thurgood is propped precariously on his chair, blood dripping down his face from a serious scalp laceration. Weatherby offered his kerchief to press against the wound, hopefully to stem the flow.

The sudden burst of violence has not gone unnoticed by the pub's bar manager who threw his cleaning cloth down and hurdled the bar, fully intent on bouncing these city bred thugs out of his pub. Yarrow was a natural born street fighter and was on his feet in a flash, shaping up to the young local barman Will Sanders who realised he was one out against three.

Even so, he demanded that the group finish their drinks and get the hell out of his pub. By now he had a reinforcement, the cellarman with a wooden mallet in his hand. A useful instrument for hammering bungs into barrels or hammering sense into heads. Tubby Nichols is a man who stands by his mates and now stands by Will Sander's right shoulder, glaring at the three drinkers.

'You heard 'im, git yer arses out the door right now.' Tubby stood six foot three and played fullback for Sorrento Football Club as a formidable foe. His team nickname is Steam Train.

In the face of this threatening duo, it seemed the crooked coppers had no choice but to backdown and go back aboard ship and maybe take their chances with Foley when they get there. The disgruntled trio decide to visit the picnic on the foreshore before and at least find something free to eat. Thurgood would be little use in any further conflicts suffering a large gash in his scalp, concussion and general confusion.

Deputy Police Commissioner Francis Foley had joined the picnickers on the foreshore, sitting on a canvas camping stool holding a plate of delicate mixed sandwiches in his large right hand as he quaffed a pint of beer from his left. He had been enjoying himself despite being on duty. That is until he heard the news about his nephew's assault and his suspicion that it was that disgraced Buster Yarrow. The thought caused him to belch loudly suddenly suffering heartburn.

'God damn that blasted man.' He cursed under his breath, his left hand fondling the smooth grip of his truncheon.

The list of alleged charges to be answered by Yarrow was long and varied, from taking bribes to running a stand-over racket.

First Through the Door Foley's gaze wanders over the crowd of happy people and who should he see pushing his way toward the food tables but top-of-mind crook Buster Yarrow.

'Why you foul dog, what are you up to here?' He muttered under his breath. 'I'll keep an eye on you until we're back aboard and then with young Jim's help we can take you in hand.'

The Honourable Joseph Esmond McArthur MP was concerned for his guest Karl Brunner, who was last seen chatting amicably with the charming Italian Alessandro Barone at the ship's stern. Big Joe had been drawn away by that bloody pest Phillip Croker, a frustrated partner in the land purchase, and was quite rightly feeling screwed over it. He had lost a lot of money gearing up to handle his share of the acquisition. Croker was pretty well liquored up and determined to tell Big Joe what he thought of him. Big Joe advised him politely to go somewhere quiet and sober up.

Somewhere at the back of Joe's brain his neurotransmitters were signalling that all was not well here. Croker was part of the group that Big Joe had outflanked in the purchase of a critical piece of real estate, and he had been waiting for backlash in one form or another from these blokes. They were a tough, obstinate and unforgiving bunch and would not be expected to simply walk away without pushing hard for compensation in one form or another. Joe had briefed his driver bodyguard Bull Finlay to be on his toes and keep his pistol loaded and close to hand. Bull had joined the cruise on Big Joe's ticket and had stood a respectful distance from him during the journey so far with the big Mark VI Webley Revolver tucked into a shoulder holster under his left arm. Very few people from either side of the tracks carried side arms, so Bull would prefer to depend on his exceptional strength and the lead weighted cosh in his right pocket.

'So,' mused Joe, 'how come this little weed, this small-time crooked developer, is suddenly shirt fronting me? Does he think I'll break down and confess all?'

Joe's well -developed survival instincts are still sending warning signals barely eased by Bull Finlay's bulky presence. The big MP began his search for the Swiss from the stern along the upper promenade deck descending to the lower deck, making his way as best he could along both sides of the ship. One of the hazards of being a recognisable politician in a situation like this was not being able to move about freely. Every few yards someone would call his name and he would have to be prepared to stop and politely enquire after the voter's health and perhaps answer a question or two about current business in the House. The result was the ship had virtually emptied out of all of its passengers ashore before he completed one circuit. Still, he decided to check the bar and café to be sure before joining the masses ashore in search of his guest.

Exiting the bar, he ran smack bang into a policeman almost knocking him over. 'Oh, sorry old boy. Say it's Foley, isn't it? You look a little frayed sir, are you ill?' Big Joe spots the blood on Jim's collar and expresses alarm.

'No, I'm fine, thanks for caring but you must excuse me, I'm in rather a hurry. I'm looking for someone.'

'Coincidentally, so am I' said Big Joe. 'I think my man must have gone ashore so I will follow suit. Care to walk along with me?'

Jim still felt groggy as a result of his concussion and decides it's probably not a bad idea to have some company until he catches up with one or more of his team, who seemed to have scattered to the winds.

As the odd pair approach the shore along the lengthy jetty, they notice quite a few ships guests being shepherded back to the ship by the crew.

'Ah, here's a chance Sergeant. We can take a stand right here and watch the crowd filter past us. Surely we'll spot our man then, watcha think?'

The two searchers stand behind a bollard, using its bulk to deflect the dense returning crowd around them. Presently Jim Foley was pleased to see his uncle the deputy commissioner scurrying along with Bluey Farnsworth, apparently hot on the heels of Buster Yarrow, who has his cap pulled down to his eyebrows, head down dodging among the crowd hoping not to be seen.

'Ha! Here's my man Minister, stand by.' Senior Sergeant Jim Foley crouched slightly and withdrew his baton timing his attack to perfection, allowing Yarrow to be just adjacent to his position on the opposite side of the jetty. He threaded his way through the crowd stealthily coming up behind the dangerous criminal copper and without hesitation landed a stunning blow behind Yarrow's right ear, rendering him temporarily senseless. As Yarrow sank to his knees, Jim was onto him in a flash handcuffing the felon's hands behind his back.

As Yarrow's awareness began to return, Jim bent down and whispered hoarsely in his ear.

'Gotcha ya cowardly bastard, how does my baton feel on *your* thick skull?'

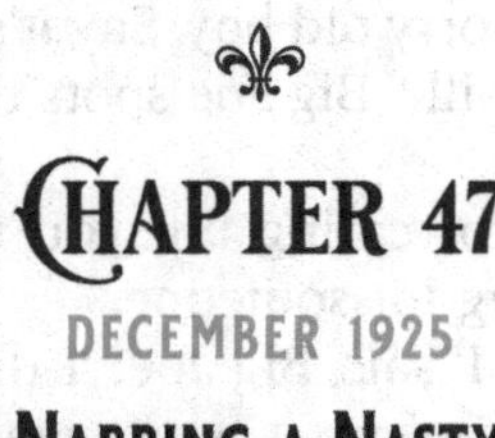

CHAPTER 47

DECEMBER 1925

NABBING A NASTY

Jim Foley was swiftly joined by his uncle and Bluey Farnsworth, who dragged Buster to his feet. The criminal is still pretty groggy and staggered slightly, almost threatening to plunge off the jetty.

'Great work Senior. I saw this corrupt individual ashore and alerted Constable Farnsworth. We saw him come out of the Koonya Hotel with his cronies.' Foley senior was very concerned for his nephew, whom he held in high regard despite having been critical of him on several occasions. 'We thought they might be headed for the bus terminal so we grabbed this dangerous cove before he could do anymore damage.'

'Farnsworth told me you had received threats from the man and believed it was he that attacked you. Can you confirm that?'

'I can't be one hundred percent certain as I only got a glimpse of the attackers weapon. As it appeared to be a standard issue police baton and given his recent threats, I would bet on Yarrow being the cowardly mugger that he is.'

The Deputy Commissioner is in control of Yarrow now, 'Constable Farnsworth will assist you to get this man under lock and key aboard the ship, where he will stay until we get back to Port Melbourne.'

The Deputy Commissioner is all business now. 'We still have those other two running around somewhere; we need to bring them to heel too.'

'That will have to wait sir, I'm sure I saw them running for the bus back to Mornington. They'll be on the train to Melbourne in a couple hours. We can phone ahead and have 'em picked up when they arrive.'

The stunned Buster Yarrow doesn't let out a squeak as he is led off to the tiny cell in which an over refreshed Toorak belle is still recovering. Arrangements were hastily made to accommodate her elsewhere while Yarrow fills the space.

Captain Galbraith appeared on the scene to be advised of the current situation and asked for a quiet word with Deputy Commissioner Foley. They retired to the captain's tiny cabin and after making themselves comfortable, the captain gets right down to it, dispensing with any small talk.

'Deputy Commissioner Foley, I've asked you here to impart some disturbing news I have received by telegraph from Melbourne. My radio operator has written the transmission down verbatim and I will give you a copy. The matter is so urgent however, that I felt I should bring it to your attention as soon as possible. Captain Galbraith looked deeply concerned as he leant forward and lowered his voice.

'In essence, Deputy Commissioner, our head office has been advised by the Federal Police that there is a very high probability that an IRA assassin may be aboard this vessel.'

'Good God. Yes, we were warned about the likelihood of a threat of violence aboard today. Have they given you a name or description or anything we can use to find him?'

'Very little. The man might be Irish, of course, we can speculate on that as we can speculate on his target if indeed his target is aboard the ship as well. It's all very much a guess work from our end.'

'I am having a lot of trouble coming to terms with this Captain. I have a pretty good idea of our passengers and their standing in the community, and I can't think of one who would warrant a professional assassin. Perhaps we can scan the passenger list starting at the top and see if we can identify a potential target.'

'Good idea. When one thinks of that profoundly sad situation in Ireland, a chap starts to have problems getting past one Archbishop Daniel Mannix and the problems that he stirred up in years gone by. Perhaps that's another clue as to who we're talking about and why.'

Within a short period, the passenger list had been scanned without finding anyone who would justify such attention. Apart from one, Mr Joseph McArthur, state MP who had recently made an incendiary attack on the opponents of a unified Ireland under British rule. But being at the other end of the world, would his words be enough to warrant an attack several years later? That's seemed unlikely.

No, there had to be a better reason unless the intelligence was wrong and there was another target or another motivation altogether.

But the intelligence was pretty strong that a professional killer was on the prowl so be warned and alert.

The Deputy Commissioner called his meagre police force together and briefed them on the conversation he had with the captain. He is sceptical about the information but strongly urges his team to be alert for any sign of 'shenanigans.'

Timing, as Eugene put it when coaching his cast earlier in the day, is everything and with perfect timing Big Joe interrupts the police briefing to report that his guest Karl Brunner is missing.

Joe informed the police that he had searched the ship from stem to stern and had also gone ashore to look for him there. He had seen nothing of him and it appeared that neither had anyone else. He had just disappeared. As he spoke several things happened at once. The passengers had all returned back aboard under the direction of the ship's crew with Eugene's stage hands assisting. The excitement levels were still high and one or two passengers are showing signs of over-indulgence. Regardless of individual condition, they are all anticipating the presentation of the one act play which has been promoted as the theatre presentation of the year. Which might be going a bit large, but anyway it was a spectacular venue.

The second thing to occur was a deep rumbling under the feet of all passengers and crew as the ship's powerful engines were engaged to manoeuvre the vessel away from the Sorrento Pier and point her bows north to Mornington. The massive paddle wheels start to thresh the sea on which Hygeia had sat serenely until now above all earthly cares, indifferent to the dramas playing out on her decks.

By now Big Joe had told the police everything he could about his missing man Monsieur Karl Brunner: Swiss bank director. After an intense interrogation, Big Joe firstly dealt with the question of an IRA hitman and revealed that he had never received any threats or experienced any intimidation from the direction of the Irish Independent State.

The conversation turned to Brunner and his mysterious disappearance.

Big Joe had to explain his relationship to the Swiss banker, a person who was as likely to be met on a Melbourne street as an Eskimo.

Several of the police volunteered that they had seen him with Minister McArthur but admitted that they would have a problem recognising him again. Big Joe was asked if Brunner had any distinctive features or habits. Big Joe could only describe him as an urbane gentleman, fashionably dressed, well-groomed, and clean shaven.

'His clothing and accent are quite distinctly European.'

'What about jewellery or any other personal decoration such as tattoos?' asked Jim. 'Does he use snuff or smoke cigars? Sorry sir, but all of this will help us build a picture of the gentleman.'

'I could not confirm the tattoos, but he is married and wears a wedding band. When I last saw him he was smoking a distinctive carved briar pipe.'

Bluey Farnsworth had been trying to pay attention, but his concentration has been waning as the interrogation went on and on. At the mention of the briar pipe, he snapped back. He had found such a pipe at the scene of Jim's assault. Now, where was it?

'Sir, I found a pipe that may match that description at the back of the ship in the area the sailors call the scuppers.'

'What the hell are the scuppers?' The Deputy Commissioner was showing signs of his famous short temper, 'and why, in God's name, did you not mention this before?'

'The scuppers are like a drain in the gutter around the edge of the deck sir.' Poor old Bluey was wishing he'd abandoned ship when he had the chance. 'That's the extreme outer edge of the deck, sir. It was laying there in the shadows and when I picked it up, it was still warm. I know that Senior Sergeant Foley don't smoke no pipe so I didn't think it was relevant to his assault. I'm really sorry sir.'

'Constable, *all* material taken from a crime scene is *relevant* and *evidentiary*.' The Deputy Commissioner emphasises each word angrily. He is about to explode, his voice rising to the level of a mid-roar just short of bursting neighbouring eardrums.

'That is why we stop people trampling all over the place and taking things from the scene constable,' Bluey is shrinking into his service jacket under the Deputy Commissioner's tirade. 'Do you not understand this one fundamental of crime scene management?'

'Wait a minute then.' Big Joe interrupted the Deputy's rant. 'Where's that pipe constable? May I see it?'

'Of course sir, I have it right here.' With that Bluey Farnsworth, wishing he was a hundred miles away, reached into the side pocket of his jacket and with a bit of a flourish, held the object up so the whole room could see it.

'That's it, that's Karl Brunner's pipe.' Big Joe exclaimed, snatching it from the mortified constable's hand. 'Where exactly did you find it constable? Come now, show us the exact spot.'

The Deputy issued orders for the non-involved police to continue their patrols paying particular attention to the bars and taking heed that the stage play is being conducted as they speak and caution should be practised to avoid any disturbance of the cast or audience. The rest of the group, The Captain, Deputy Commissioner Foley, Constable Farnsworth and Big Joe, leave the cramped cabin and descend to the upper promenade and then made their way down to the stern. Constable Farnsworth is called upon to point out exactly where the distinctive pipe was laying.

'Right there, sir.'

'That's to the right of where you were found Sergeant Foley laying. Was Brunner here at the time of your assault?'

'Sir if I may.' Bluey Farnsworth interrupts, 'that would have been impossible. When we discovered the Sergeant, there was no sign of anyone else in the area and we had Constables Dottie Green and Martin Richardson set up a crime scene preventing anyone coming or going.' Cautiously, in view of the Deputy Commissioners current mood, added, 'and of course sir most of the passengers were forward preparin' to go ashore in Sorrento, sir.'

'Besides which, gentlemen, Karl Brunner and I were standing directly above this area on the promenade deck. As I have already stated, he was there with Alessandro Barone when I last saw them and Brunner was smoking his pipe then.'

Senior Sergeant Foley walked over to the window at the dead centre of the expansive rear deck and put his head out looking upward to the promenade deck.

'You know, it's just possible that if Brunner was leaning on the rail up there. He could have dropped his pipe. If he did, there is plenty of opportunity for it to have fallen straight through the window onto this deck.'

There are puzzled looks all around as they take this in.

'Okay, so your friend Brunner drops this valuable pipe and doesn't pursue it. Why would that be Minister?' Deputy Commissioner Foley demands of Big Joe. 'Then both he and Barone disappear together? Very odd, I think there's more to this than meets the eye.'

Foley senior realises he has a first-class mystery on his hands. 'There are many more questions than answers at present. I think we can dismiss any connection between the assault on my nephew Senior Sergeant Foley and the disappearance of two gentlemen from the promenade deck directly above?' After a moment's pause, he added, 'apart from timing.'

Looking genuinely puzzled, he concluded, 'Both matters appear to have occurred simultaneously and yet there is absolutely no connection between the three men involved here.' He scans the faces around him and asks the inevitable question. 'Does anyone have a theory about what happened here?'

While Big Joe was concerned about the assault on the policeman, he was more concerned with the mysterious absence of his International guest and business partner Karl Brunner. This could well lead to an international scandal. He can't afford too much scrutiny around his relationship with Brunner. With perfect hindsight he now realises they should have ceased any socialising until Brunner had left Australian shores or at least Melbourne's boundaries. Now, it was essential for his political and social survival that he expunge any and all connection he has had to the land purchase by the Swiss company. He must double check to find and erase any paper trail that would lead to his connection to a certain Fijian company that was registered in the name of his sister-in-law. A company that he wittily and now regretfully in retrospect named Berge de Riviere (French; River Bank) in reference to the riverside location of the parcel of land purchased by a Swiss consortium of which he was a thirty percent shareholder. For the first time in his long and shady career, he experienced an unusual emotion. Fear.

CHAPTER 48

ANOTHER VILLAIN DEPARTS STAGE LEFT

Eugene had lost himself in the character he had played so adeptly delivering an amazing performance enthralling the audience.

'My dear Eugene, how do you do it? You are simply brilliant!' Elvira Rochester gushes, perhaps just a smidgeon too enthusiastically.

'Elvira, my darling, thank you.' Eugene took the question seriously, although tempted to come up with some fantasy about selling his soul to the devil.

'It is,' he stated pontifically, 'by using a method bordering on black magic and practised over my entire career a skill that I have perfected over many years. I have learnt to transmute; becoming the subject I play, feeling their character 'from the inside' as it were.'

Suitably impressed, Elvira sighed deeply and took another sip of the champagne that she had been constantly infusing all day. She had reached a level now, causing a slight loss of inhibition and the onset of debilitating hiccups.

Coming off stage, it takes Eugene several minutes to regain his self-possession, but he never loses his natural rat cunning. Eugene is still very hopeful about a new career in movies and Elvira Rochester has the keys to the big door of opportunity after teasing him several times with a possible script. He would play along with her flattery unashamedly, so long as it led in the right direction.

The general audience had been entranced by his performance and demonstrated their appreciation with generous laughter and applause.

But there was one member of his audience whose laughter was more mocking than amused. Sir Rupert Yarborough had been nursing his hatred for the star of the play for a long time. In his initial rage on finding his wife in bed with this sleaze, he had vented his rage by beating him so severely Eugene Bradfield had been hospitalised, his famous handsome features altered permanently.

Fortunately, police were not involved but all the same Yarborough had taken the opportunity to depart the scene, returning home to visit family and recover his nerve.

While he had time on his hands, he had managed to rearrange some of his financial affairs selling off some non-productive shares and looking for other opportunities. That's when his eyes fell on a perfect investment. The owners of Her Majesties' Theatre in Melbourne were seeking investors for the coming season. There was a list of productions they proposed to present and a whole slab of financial stuff about the company and its owners' successes.

Sir Rupert didn't waste any time reading the fine print, instead he called his broker, ordering him to offer his core company as a major sponsor. The result was Sir Rupert, through his company RY Southern Pacific, found himself to be in a very influential position for the season ahead.

Now as he sat and watched Eugene bouncing about on the tiny stage, he was mentally massaging various scenarios in which he, as a major sponsor, would deliver the lines the deceitful little prat would never want to hear. 'You sir are sacked and are no longer welcome in this theatre.'

Enjoy yourself for now, you lecherous rat, but your day has come. Rupert tells himself, *Oh I could have repeated the beating I gave you, that would be too easy and could land me in gaol. Whereas I have other plans for you, my man.*

Hygeia had now steamed up the coast to Mornington through slightly lumpy seas that presented no impediment to the powerful paddle steamer where she now swung at anchor half a mile off the coast under cobalt skies. The distance by sea from Sorrento is just over seventeen miles and allowing time for Eugene Bradfield's production Captain Galbraith has had his vessel throttled back to deliver about fifteen knots. Along the coast his ship has had to avoid the fleets of several sailing clubs and being a gentleman Galbraith ensures that no competitor is disadvantaged by his passing. Fortunately, his course was largely well to seaward and rarely came in contact with small dinghy sailors.

Finally, the play concluded to rapturous applause with several curtain calls. The cast and crew celebrated 'behind the scenes' with champagne before joining the rest of the guests for the lunch prepared by French Chef Franco de La Vere, seconded from The Windsor's kitchen for the occasion. In addition, Chef Franco has recruited several of his most reliable waiting staff to serve the meals which will need to be tabled with all haste. Among those he has brought with him are the matchless pair of Adit and Damodar working the tables with their usual skilful aplomb. The meal itself was a superb combination with a heavy concentration on local produce by Chef Franco and his kitchen staff. Each course from entrée to dessert specifically designed to suit the occasion.

Chef Franco was working in a climate of sub-tropical heat and humidity at a frenetic pace, occasionally losing self-control by hurling abuse at any of the kitchen hands he thought may be slacking off. He reminded them that his and the hotel's reputations are on the line.

He is cautious not to abuse his sous chef, who had a reputation for knife work, not always confined to the kitchen. After all the hysteria and unwarranted panicking and temper tantrums, Chef Franco and his maître d' agree that it is time and the plates start going out like a true production line to the delight and surprise of the guests.

The passengers are offered a set menu or table d'hôte consisting of the following: Entrée of mixed salad or soup, a terrine, main course choice of two local spring lamb, or locally caught baked snapper with potatoes rice or pasta, a local selection of breads and pate's ending with a dessert. Plus a matched wine list.

There are one or two who have lost their appetite for one reason or another. Possibly due to overindulgence at 'Breakfast on the Beach' or dealing with queasy stomachs having over-indulged in free pickled onions and boiled eggs at the bar.

Chef Franco needn't have worried. The fresh sea air had worked its miracle on appetites as most plates cleared from the tables by Adit and Damodar are bare.

The coastal village of Mornington provided a pretty backdrop sitting in a slight depression between Mt Eliza and Mt Martha. As the sun begins its mid-afternoon journey toward the western horizon, it highlights the golden blonde sand of the beaches and the colourful red rock cliff formations of Snapper Point and Red Bluff that embrace the harbour. Beyond the foreshore, the Mornington citizens were going about their daily routines with barely a glance at the familiar ferry at anchor off their shoreline. On the sand, family groups continued to frolic in the sun and sea, the beaches sprinkled with colourful sun brollies and beach towels. Excited children squeal and laugh, their cheerful voices skipping off the water clearly heard aboard Hygeia. A far different scenario than that experienced by Lieutenant Matthew Flinders, who landed nearby during his exploratory voyage in 1802.

For the large part, the passengers were delighted with every aspect of the excursion so far and the level of chatter and joyful laughter during the meal reached new heights. Background music from members of the orchestra helped to maintain the ebullient mood.

Captain Galbraith had been required to resume his role as host and leave the investigation into missing passengers to the police. He is at the head of his table and despite that background issue, he was appreciative with the performance of his vessel and her crew.

As he sipped his mineral water and looked about at all the beautiful, happy people filling the dining area he had to remind himself that the majority have had an enjoyable experience they will never forget. Thank God the anxiety he felt had not spread to the passengers.

At the back of his mind is a concern for matters over which he has no control but none the less has him speculating on how the police investigation will end and will there be any lasting collateral damage to Hygeia's reputation.

The trip has thus far been deemed a success by the organisers, but there had been something dark, something sinister aboard, threatening the sanctity of his ship. He was less than sure that the malevolence had decreased with the incarceration of the crooked copper. There was still the matter of the missing international business man.

❖

CHAPTER 49

A Single Room with a Sea View Please Sir.

Deputy Commissioner Foley requested the assistance of a crewman and a ships boat to take him and his prisoner Detective Sergeant Buster Yarrow ashore to have him placed in the security of the cells at Mornington Police Station in Main Street where he lodges a report of his prisoners assault on Senior Sergeant Jim Foley. He also files a report on the missing man Monsieur Karl Brunner, and his suspicion that he may have been a victim of foul play. He requests that a similar report be sent to Queenscliff and any information forthcoming be forwarded to him aboard Hygeia or failing that to Police HQ Russell Street.

The Deputy Commissioner's arrival at the police station creates quite a stir as matters such as this were few and far between at a quiet country town and coming as it did on a lazy summer's day provided a badly needed distraction for the bored rural coppers.

Yarrow is banged up in the old cell block and will surely suffer a cool night, an even cooler bowl of soup and a slice of bread that was so hard it failed to soften even after soaking it in his soup. For company, he will have a thousand mosquitos and one or two dozen voracious bedbugs.

The officer in charge is Senior Sergeant Kirby Tonkin, who conducted the Deputy Commissioner to his office where he listens with interest to the Deputy's report and they discuss the various possibilities. The Senior Sergeant was a veteran of fifteen years in the force and carries his authority like a battle standard. His face is etched by his years in a rural station attending to community matters at all hours and in all weather. Dark bushy eyebrows shade stern dark eyes that put the fear of God into the local miscreants. The main feature of this notable face is a thick handlebar moustache that protruded an inch on either side of his cheeks, curling up into twin waxed points. The Senior Sergeant's fingers involuntarily caress it as he listens intently to the description of the dramatic events aboard the Hygeia.

The afternoon bus from Sorrento came in earlier and two blokes had disembarked and left aboard the railway train. They would link up with the mainline to Melbourne at Frankston. From their descriptions, they were most likely Weatherby and Thurgood, who had made themselves scarce since Hygeia docked at Sorrento. Never mind, a phone call to Frankston police and they would deal with them when they arrived.

The Deputy Commissioner signalled that he wished to wrap things up by standing. Senior Sergeant Tonkin invited him to stay and take a glass of whisky from his collection but the Deputy politely declined with thanks and calls Thurgood in from the station kitchen where he has been making the acquaintance of a couple of the local Constables over a cup of tea.

They walk down to the jetty where Daisy O'Connell waited with the ship's boat to take them back aboard the Hygeia.

When the Deputy Commissioner arrived back aboard, things have changed. Eugene's stage hands have finished packing up the simple set and the space has been turned over to the band and the eager dancers are already expending enough energy to power the ship.

He is greeted by Big Joe as he climbs the boarding ladder anxious for news from ashore about his guest, of whom there has been no sign.

Francis Foley takes the big man aside and tells him that Brunner had not been sighted at Mornington. Had he taken the only transport available from Sorrento, he would have to have passed through Mornington. Unless, of course, he had somehow managed to find a ride with a motorist.

Joe was upset by the lack of news but was intrigued by the thought that the suave Italian Barone could be at the centre of the mystery.

He disappeared at almost the same time as Brunner. Was this just a coincidence or part of some conspiracy? Did Brunner bring enemies with him when he travelled to Australia? Could Alessandro Barone have something to do with his disappearance? If so, how? There were many questions to be answered before this cruise was over.

CHAPTER 50

POST MERIDIEM OR POST MORTEM?

Captain Galbraith checked his pocket watch and determined that it was time to hoist the anchor and begin the final leg of the excursion. Froggy Dempsey hoists two flags; 'D' requesting any traffic to keep clear and 'P' flag, vessel is about to sail.

'Thank God this nightmare is nearly over' he says to his first mate Gunner Patrick.

'Yes sir, ya can say that again captain, in all my years at sea I've never seen a man lost overboard in such conditions. Now the word is that there's two blokes missin.' Blimey what a turn up.

Unfortunately for Captain Galbraith and all aboard Hygeia, they would soon discover that the nightmare was actually far from over.

Ships Engineer Gabby McInerny has been anticipating each order before receiving them. He has been attending both of his two big charges with loving care, ensuring that nothing is overlooked. In the boiler-room six coal dust encrusted stokers are toiling hard, feeding the ravenous steam engines the three tons of coal per hour that provide the steam that will drive the big vessel forward to her destination.

The foredeck crew hoisted the anchor and when the Engine Order Telegraph rang down to the engine room for slow ahead, the power was there waiting like an obedient servant. The massive steam engines build traction as Galbraith calls for a long blast on the ship's foghorn that reverberates through the Mornington township and for a brief second, silences the children on the beach. As the paddle wheels gain ascendancy over the reluctance of the seas to part for her. Once underway, he rang down a request for full ahead and the huge paddle wheels begin biting into the briny with purpose as Hygeia moves slowly forward eventually reaching her optimum cruising speed. At eighteen knots she will finish the final twenty-two nautical mile leg in just over an hour.

Captain Galbraith was a good man who has served honestly and with pride in his chosen profession, having little contact with the type of evil that stalked his decks. If he was aware, he would surely have taken some pre-emptive action to curb the violence that was hanging in the air.

With several individuals yet to conclude their score settling, the cruise was about to finish with a bang rather than a whimper.

Quentin Upjohn, replacement gossip columnist for Johnny Kovacs, had been almost overwhelmed by the wonders he saw about him on the ship. *My God*, he thought, *it hasn't even been a full day and I've filled my notebook with enough gossip for my column for the next six months.*

No, not gossip, this was joyful off the leash mischief by Melbourne's elite who must have thought they were inviolable while aboard Hygeia. Like naughty boys and girls away from mum and dad on school camp. The cavorting and drunkenness were amazing, but that was just the froth and bubble on the excursion cake. The real story was a mystery, a real enigma that seemed to have the significant police presence on board completely befuddled. He had approached the senior policeman several times for a comment and had been brushed off. One of the crew, a man they called Daisy, had told him that an important passenger was missing and it was thought that he had met with foul play. He was apparently still aboard as the ship approached Sorrento and was last seen just before they docked.

Quentin realised early in the cruise that there was basically a feast of tomfoolery to be had aboard when the wine and sunshine did what it always reliably does in loosening the morals of young women and the libidos of young men. There was a corresponding increase in the lecherousness that seems to strike middle-aged men in circumstances such as this, men who should know better but seldom did.

He was acting as a real journalist for a change instead of a… well whatever he was when he was sniffing about for scandal. He knew he had plenty of the usual sordid stuff that he would feed into the system while his focus would be elsewhere. Quentin was choosing to concentrate on the main game that had begun to reveal itself. Instead of the short snappy clips full of innuendo that were his bread and butter, Quentin could see a feature piece in this. Real journalism as he began to sketch his draft that would be fleshed out later as more facts came to the surface.

He had the field and therefore the story to himself if only he can put together enough of the social sensation to convince his cynical editor.

The sooner he started on it, the better and right now his energy levels were high. Taking his Underwood portable typewriter from where he had stored it when he came aboard, he sat down at an isolated table in the café and started writing. After four strong coffees he had produced one page of the outline per coffee for the story he would present for the delectation of his readers.

There were some fascinating characters aboard that were probably worth a book apiece, one day. Powerful business men and politicians and really dangerous men who attracted women like flies and knew their way around when it came to violence. Quentin chose to avoid actual names ever alert to the risk of slander cannily choosing synonyms that gave a slight hint to the well-connected who might have an educated guess at the real identities.

One of these prominent identities was Matthias Vogel who had Gordon Plowright firmly in his sights while currently dreaming up a ploy to avenge the outrageous stunt that had his horse and trainer barred from the Melbourne Cup. That foul deed almost certainly costing Vogel a strong chance of winning the Cup. It had also been heartbreaking to see the young Blaine O'Farrell's Australian career ruined and his plans crumble about him. He had returned to Ireland in disgrace, and despite his pleas of innocence his family and the Irish racing public had treated him with great suspicion. He was shunned and abused by old school friends. At his home track, he had been insulted several times by disgruntled punters who blamed him for the lack of success for any horse he trained, regardless.

On a positive note, his fiancé had welcomed her man home and they had been married in a simple service in the pretty Saint Brigid's Catholic Church, The Curragh, County Kildare which was Blaine's parish church

Blaine wanted to return to Australia to clear his name and take on the career he had planned when he first arrived in the Great South Land. Matthias had promised to back him if he did, simply because he knew the secret of the scandal that had ruined their promising stable. That seemed an unlikely mission at the moment, mainly because the witnesses who could clear them in a minute were a nondescript bunch of street thugs who would be given no credibility in a court of law or anywhere else for that matter. Besides, after the cruel grilling they received at the hands of Vogel's hard men, it was considered out of the question for them to appear in court. Sadly, one of the pack had taken his own life by jumping in front of a train. It was probable that rest of the gang had broken up and gone to ground deep within their own society.

Vogel was tossing around a number of possible tactics to destroy his arch enemy when it occurred to him that it would be impossible to achieve anything through the racing industry. He would have to think outside of the box and for a man like him, with his life experiences that was no chore at all.

Finally, he decided to utilise a ruse well known around the world as a 'honey trap.' He had the contacts and resources to pull it off. That's the route he decided to take and immediately went about setting it up. His first call would be to Curly Barker, who he knew had used a honey trap as means of blackmailing a citizen or two with an otherwise spotless reputation. All that was needed was an opportunity to bring four components together. A gullible sucker e.g. Gordon Plowright who thinks he's God's gift to women, an alluring and willing young woman, a talented photographer to capture the moment, and of course, a suitable venue where it all comes together, a *chambre d'amour*. If the target is stupid enough to pay up, he is bled dry. If he doesn't, well, the consequences can be far more costly and will be on his own head. In this instance, Vogel wanted Plowright humiliated before his wife and his fellow parishioners.

Meanwhile, his target, Gordon Plowright was feeling no pain thanks to the effects of the champagne and sunshine and was well settled into a fascinating discussion with Eugene Bradfield that encompassed horse racing, poker and vintage wines. If a spiritualist were present, she might see some evil spirits circling over the heads of these two gentlemen who were totally unaware of the fates being planned for them by some people with very cruel intentions.

There was another scoundrel who was unaware that his life of luxury and easy money was about to come to a crashing end. Captain Richard Jenkins, hero of the Great War in France and His Majesty's 4th Indian Cavalry, was about to receive an interesting visitation. Waiting for him on Station Pier was a delegation from the Indian Consulate in Melbourne and a reporter from two newspapers, the Age and The Sun. They have one basic question.

'We know you aren't who you say you are, so who are you?'

Some collateral embarrassment was coming the way of Madame Rosetta Gloria Parmentier, who had been taken in by the conman Reggie Watford aka Captain Jenkins or The Honourable Francis Willoughby Baron Middleton of Walloton. When her newspaper exposes him as a fraud, poor Rosetta would be mortified. In her office, she proudly displays a wall of photographs taken alongside him at theatre premiers, cocktail parties and the racetrack. She would feel she had become a laughingstock by her association with him. She would suffer further chagrin when that little semi-literate twirp from the Truth has his story of the excursion published as a three-parter and carries off several journalism awards. Unless she can turn adversity into advantage by writing up her own experience with the master imposter? Yes that would do it, deception from the inside; illustrated.

CHAPTER 51

A STEALTHY DEPARTURE

Jim Foley was resting on one of the comfortable seats in a quiet part of Hygeia's saloon bar after the arrest of Buster Yarrow. He felt a great encumbrance has been removed allowing him to once again breathe deeply and freely to concentrate on the enigma of the missing passengers. Despite his head wound and pounding headache, he had been trying to solve the riddle of the missing passengers because in reality there were two who had disappeared at the same time. The Swiss businessman and the sophisticated Italian Alessandro Barone seemed to have vanished from the ship together? Surely they couldn't have had a row and in their struggle, fallen overboard? In doing so, Brunner's pipe may have fallen down to the lower deck. No, hardly possible for two such urbane gentlemen meeting for the first time and then engaging in a fight to the death within minutes. This was an international banker and a gentleman of impeccable manners, not a couple of ruffians punching up over a football game. But all the same, how and why the pipe finished where it was found could be part of the explanation. Unless there was some underlying motive that did not immediately become obvious. The Swiss gentleman's credentials were sworn by the MP Joseph McArthur and were impeccable. Who then was the Italian who came late into the picture? Who provided a reference for him? Did he have a previous relationship with Brunner? Jim Foley decided he needed to speak with Big Joe again and asked Constable Irene McCarthy to find him and bring the man to him.

After an extensive and concentrated interrogation, Big Joe could add nothing new. As for the Italian gentleman all he could say was the man was introduced to he and Brunner by Francesco de Luca while they lunched at the Windsor. Barone impressed as a sophisticated, urbane gentleman who could talk about art, wine and finance in several languages Other than a number of short but enjoyable conversations with the Italian he could add nothing except to say that Brunner and Barone had seemed to hit it off from the beginning.

Big Joe had thought that they had commenced what could be a lifetime friendship, given the number of shared touchpoints in their lives. But all their talk since then had been about the horses or the Christmas cruise. Francesco de Luca was not on board so unavailable for questioning, he would have to wait until they returned from the cruise.

Jim Foley was no more enlightened by his questioning of the State Minister although he had no doubt that the deeply concerned McArthur had been frank in answering his questions. Jim studied the sparse notes he took during his interrogation as he sat in the ship's saloon. One thing he has concluded is that there is a fatal connection between the three men, but his notes reveal nothing. He shared his suspicions with his uncle who was far more politically aware than his nephew, and after looking at Jim's notes and pondering the situation, recalls rumours of a scandal over a land purchase on the river front. And who was at the centre of that? None other than Big Joe and the new land owner, who was Karl Brunner or, more correctly, Brunner's Swiss Bank.

The rumour heard around was that there was another party that had been led to believe that through a connection within the lower house they would grab first rights on the large parcel of industrial land before it went through the usual gazetting processes.

'If these rumours are correct, and I have no reason to doubt them, then people would have many reasons to be upset.' The Deputy Commissioner displayed his business acumen with his forensic like examination of the situation from an insider's point of view. 'You see Jim, if you were to be involved in a scandalous piece of work like this you would need to be well organised and that organisation would cost you plenty.'

Jim is impressed with his uncle's assessment and sits listening intently as he goes on.

'Having been ambushed by the foreign bank, the syndicate has not only missed on a potentially huge capital gain but also lost a fair amount of seed money that was used to grease palms and set up offshore bank accounts.'

'There is nothing like money to break up friendships.' Laughed

Francis Foley 'especially if it's your friends knockin' it off. Ha ha ha.'

Jim was thinking, *seriously could this be the connection he was looking for? Could it be the motive for kidnapping or murder?*

One man who could shed a lot of light on this mystery was at that time travelling up the highway from Queenscliff to Melbourne in a motor car provided by Francesco de Luca heading for Melbourne's principal airport at Essendon. The plan was to fly him out of Melbourne as soon as possible to Sydney, where he would board a ship under an assumed name and eventually arrive back in Europe in a few weeks' time.

Alessandro had carefully disguised himself before slipping away from the crowd that disembarked at Sorrento for the picnic on the foreshore. Instead of following the crowd to the shore, he had ducked around the large shed on the jetty to find a private fishing boat waiting for him with its motor running unseen from Hygeia. On board was a young Italian born employee of de Luca.

Carlos was a young man on his way up and could be relied on for his discretion. He assisted Alessandra to step aboard and showed him where he could conceal himself under the foredeck. Once comfortable, Carlos handed him a tarpaulin to further conceal himself. Alessandro would now make his escape unseen and leaving in a boat that was, for intents and purposes, a rather tired looking fishing boat going about its business.

The young man was an expert boat handler and had not bothered with mooring lines in the interests of expediency, simply keeping his boat balanced snugly against the pylons of the jetty, using the tide and engine power to keep it in place. When they were well away at sea and out of sight, Alessandro came out for air remaining below the gunnels to be out of sight to passing fishing boats and the shore. It would never occur to Alessandro of the dramatic irony of the assassin literally crossing paths with his victim as he fled across the water to Queenscliff by boat while his victim's body rode the tide in roughly the same direction toward the heads.

As they closed in on the Queenscliff Harbour in deep water, the youth noticed his passenger withdraw a thin shiny object from his jacket deftly flicking it overboard into the deep. Carlos judiciously ignored the actions of his passenger, who then ducked out of sight again. Once inside The Queenscliff Cut, the youth expertly steered his vessel with the tide racing through the moorings to the broad shallow Swan Bay beyond. He nudged the craft roughly into its allocated pen where several dark looking men have been waiting patiently for his arrival. Wordlessly, Alessandro was spirited away to a waiting car.

CHAPTER 52

AND THE BAND PLAYED ON

Deputy Commissioner Francis and Senior Sergeant Jim Foley were still aboard Hygeia, trying to understand what had happened. They have almost exhausted the ship's supply of note paper as they considered one scenario after another without finding any conclusive factors. The most likely was the consequence outlined by the Deputy Commissioner. The only one of the syndicate that might have had the contacts to organise an assassin at short notice was de Luca through his Calabrian connections. It now became urgent to find de Luca and interview him.

The ship and its cargo of citizens most of whom were still in a carnival state of mind and various levels of sobriety, others whose lives had changed irreparably for better or worse was steadily approaching Port Melbourne. Both policemen, uncle and nephew are keen to contain all the relevant parties and take a statement from them all. No one should be allowed to leave the ship until all such statements are taken and contact details filed.

In the meantime, a very worried State Minister, the Honourable Joseph McArthur sat at the bar in the ship's saloon with a double shot of scotch in his hand as he contemplates the possible scenarios before him. There is no doubt that the disappearance of Karl Brunner, an important international visitor, will create enormous interest in the State and Federal Parliaments and consequently in the press. Questions will be asked, tough questions that he will not be able to answer. The scandal will spill over into the Federal sphere almost certainly. Monsieur Brenner's disappearance is an international scandal and his Swiss bank employers will press Australian foreign affairs for answers.

There are several possibilities for him personally. He could be disbarred from the House, face criminal charges based on the abuse of his parliamentary privileges, and then God help him if the Australian Tax Office came sniffing around. Whichever way he turns he knows his professional life as an honourable servant of the people is over. If he manages to stay out of gaol, he will be exiled back to the bush from whence he came stripped of his power and influence gone forever.

He decides to take action and strides purposefully to the ship's bridge to find Captain Galbraith.

'Captain sir, a moment of your time, sir.' In an urgent tone.

'Minister, as you can clearly see, we are about to come onto the dock. I need full concentration, as do all my crew to avoid any incidents, so the answer to your request is no. But if you allow us to complete our work, I'll be more than happy to speak with you then.'

Hot on Big Joe's heels comes the Deputy Police Commissioner Foley with an urgent request.

'Captain, I would ask you to delay disembarking passengers until we are in a position to separate out those of interest in the matter of the missing men.'

The annoyed captain now rings down 'stand by' to the engine room. With no attempt to hide his annoyance, he rounded on the policeman, hands on hips. 'Very good sir, if we must, how do you propose to handle it?'

'Captain, I will have my people at the boarding ramp to reverse check the passengers ashore. Anyone we have failed to interview or with known criminal connections will be stood aside for questioning. Are you okay with that, sir?'

'That's fine sir,' he said pointing to the crowded dock, 'but you should be aware that the delay will cause some very disgruntled people ashore as well as on board.'

'That cannot be helped Captain, we have two men, two fit healthy important men who have gone missing in very mysterious circumstances. While I sympathise with people having their evening meal delayed that is nothing by comparison to what we are facing here.'

Deputy Commissioner Foley was affronted by having this obvious delay pointed out to him as if it may not have occurred to him while attempting to drive home the seriousness of his investigation, which was yet to be acknowledged by the good Captain.

'There is one other thing of equal importance.' He squared his shoulders to ensure his posture properly reflects his authority, 'I would like you to immediately telegraph Point Lonsdale at Queenscliff, Mornington, and Sorrento police to hurry them up with their missing persons responses. I need to know if they have anything at all.'

'Aah Commissioner, I'm feel negligent. I sent that request over an hour ago,' turning away from Foley to the chart table beside him, he lifts a sheet of paper. 'This arrived only minutes ago.' intending to hand it to the policeman as he turned, 'and Point Lonsdale advised us that they have... may have...'

He realised he is talking to thin air as Francis Foley has departed as quickly as he arrived to brief his team and set up a security system to ensure order and the control of any elements stood aside for later interrogation. It will be essential to create accurate records of all those interrogated before they are allowed to disembark.

The captain was left holding the typed and folded sheet of paper that he had offered to the Deputy Commissioner. It is a response to his enquiry to Queenscliff Police. Frustrated, he called a deckhand, Daisy O'Connell and ordered him to chase the policeman and make sure he received this report.

Daisy O'Connell is quick on his feet and finds Francis Foley in seconds, thrusting the sheet of paper into his hands.

'With the Captain's compliments sir.'

The Deputy Commissioner has been anticipating a response to his request for information but hadn't thought it would turn up so quickly. In the mayhem of over-excited passengers, many of whom are now well refreshed, he looked for a bit of privacy where he can concentrate on the report. When he opened it and began to read, he was at first shocked, and then in a strange way relieved by its contents.

CHAPTER 53

A MOURNFUL MISSIVE

The report that was sent by telegraph from Queenscliff Police and typed by the heavy hand of Third Mate *Bully* Masterson on the official letterhead of Messrs Huddart, Parker and Co. presents as follows: -

Senior Sergeant Colin Matthews, Officer in Charge.

Victoria Police Queenscliff

19/12/25

Interim Report as requested by Deputy Commissioner Francis Foley aboard the PS Hygeia

Sir,

It is my solemn duty to inform you that earlier today, a professional fisherman returning from the fishing grounds came upon the body of a male person being carried through the heads on the outgoing tide. The fisherman was able to recover the body and brought it into the Queenscliff Cut, where he has a permanent mooring.

Recognising the urgency of the matter in view of your request, I took the liberty of summoning our coroner supported by a local GP to examine the remains. I am therefore able to report the following. The body was that of a mature male, very well dressed and carrying several items in the pockets of his well-cut jacket that included a fine leather wallet, fob watch and a silver item used by gentlemen to clean and tamp down their pipes. The wallet contained personal ID that revealed the deceased to be Monsieur Karl Brunner, a foreign traveller from Switzerland. A cursory examination failed to reveal any obvious injuries or cause of death save drowning. As the deceased attire did not lend itself to a day spent fishing, it was assumed that the man had perhaps fallen overboard from the excursion vessel Hygeia that had passed through the area earlier. The weight of his clothing and the sea state meant he had quickly drowned. A later more detailed examination once the victim's clothing was removed revealed a tiny but deep wound under the left armpit. The coroner on examination believed it may have been expertly inflicted by an extremely sharp implement, possibly a stiletto. The coroner has had experience of such wounds during service in Europe. He respectfully suggests that you will be seeking a professional killer possibly of European origin.

Arrangements have been made to transport the body to the Melbourne morgue to be attended by the Victorian Coroner to conduct a final autopsy to determine the exact cause of death. The writer is available should you have any questions and hopes that this assists in a speedy resolution to your current investigations.

Respectfully
  Senior Constable Colin Matthews.

'This is it Jim, here's where he went, over the side of Hygeia, mortally wounded and Queenscliff is suggesting he may have been attacked by a professional killer,' said the Deputy Commissioner, and handed Jim the report.

'How the hell have they concluded it was a professional?' he takes the report from his uncle's hand and re-reads it for himself.

'A stiletto! A bloody stiletto!' An outraged Jim cried, 'that bloody dago must've had that on him the whole way down the bay waiting for the right time to literally stab that man in the back. The bloody cowardly bastard. We've got to get him, Uncle.'

Jim was shocked and furious, shaking the report in his right hand. To the average Australian, using a knife as a weapon is an abomination and its user is considered the lowest of the low.

'Are we thinking the same way Uncle? That shifty politician it is involved in this somehow.' Having vented, Jim was now more reflective. 'It may be outside of our remit, but it opens up a line of enquiry on Mr Joseph McArthur MP.'

'You are quite correct, I'm afraid Jim, the Honourable Joseph McArthur MP will have a few questions to answer before he's much older. And not only from the police but his constituents,' said Francis Foley, who could envisage a huge barrage of bureaucratic obfuscation looming before even the first of those questions are put to Big Joe.

'Speaking of skill sets, any guesses for who might have the connections to find someone with the skill set to pull this off? And could those connections be used to aid the Italian assassin's disappearance at Sorrento?'

The two men are in fierce agreement taking it on as a personal challenge determined to get as far into this as they can, hopefully to snare the Italian before he can leave the country and before Victoria Police protocol will dictate that the case will be taken from them by city homicide.

Believing that the only escape path would be back to Melbourne along Point Nepean Road a hurried phone call is put through to Senior Sergeant Kirby Tonkin at Mornington Police from the watchman's office on the wharf to search buses and the Frankston bound train if it's not too late. Also to conduct roadblocks on the main roads to search for the Italian killer. Extreme caution was to be taken, as he was believed armed and dangerous.

The Deputy Commissioner is now cursing himself for falling into the old trap of making an assumption about Barone that he would still be aboard the Hygeia. He must have fled using the picnickers for cover at Sorrento. And why would he choose the obvious escape route?

Heading back to Hygeia Francis Foley experiences a cold, horrible thought. Would he go to ground in Sorrento until the dust settled? What if he had some collaborator waiting to transport him by boat across to Queenscliff? Surely this was something unexpected to throw the police off his trail as an international killer would plan to do. They were dealing with a skilled experienced killer who would have his every move well planned in advance.

Back to the stuffy office of the watchman, who was beginning to think Francis had become a little rattled. Very probably it's too late, but he calls Senior Constable Colin Matthews at Queenscliff and offers his thanks.

'I appreciate your taking time out from your regular duties Senior Constable, thank you for your support it's been invaluable.'

Francis puts down the receiver and turns to his nephew. 'Oh God, what a mess! There's nothing more we can do. Well it seems quite clear Jim that we have been outsmarted by a professional who can adapt to his circumstances. But I cannot stop thinking that he must have had some local support. We need to work on that.

Well, if there's one thing to come out of this voyage, it appears my uncle is softening up to me, Jim consoled himself as he walked away from the little storage space that his uncle had chosen as a secure place to read the report and digest its contents.

He would not feel so comfortable if he knew what was gnawing away at his uncle's thoughts.

❧

ℭHAPTER 54

₮HE ₭ONG ₩AY ⫴OME

The drama aboard the elegant vessel was still a long way from its cruel finish. There were scores yet to be settled and Jim had come upon one. Earlier, while the shipboard search was being conducted, the sharp eye of Jim Foley had noticed a group that appeared angry and threatening forming up on Captain Jenkins' the suave self-styled Royal Cavalry Officer. Jim can identify a small sample of Melbourne's' wealthiest business people in close consultation with non-other than Harry the Hatchet in attendance.

'Now what the hell is that all about?'

The centre of their mutual attention seemed to be none other than sometime Captain Jenkins. Jim had been under the impression that Jenkins had left town in a great hurry after being unmasked. Now he looked like he wished had taken that option. When last seen, the group had Jenkins wedged into one of the padded booths in the saloon bar. Jim was pretty certain they weren't shouting him drinks in good fellowship.

Godfrey Beckman, Laurence Brown and Darcy Dankworth, all men of considerable means had been sucked into Captain Jenkins aka Reggie Watford's tall tale of a fabulous lost treasure and stupidly handed over large chunks of cash to be partners in its recovery. By now they had realised that they were victims of their own gullibility and greed. Nevertheless, still boiling with anger and indignation, this confrontation helps to soothe their battered egos but does nothing to restore their money.

Their guide to those dazzling riches was nothing less than a smooth talking little weasel who they held wholly responsible for their losses. Unable to recover their funds, they intended to take it out of his hide. Now the man who had scammed them was sitting here shivering with fear.

The man was, of course, the erstwhile Captain Jenkins who seemed terrified, far from the war hero he portrayed himself to be, especially with Harry the Hatchet's huge right arm around his shoulders in anything but a warm embrace. Harsh words were spoken, accusing fingers pointed at his pale, drawn face. Godfrey Beckmann appeared to be the most vociferous and passionate, his colleagues and the alarming Harry repeatedly hurled insults at Jenkins in high-pitched voices while insisting he keep his voice down stop whining, but not before Jim heard snatches of their words. 'Low life, lying huckster… Lying thieving conman… Flogging is too good for you…' And so on. This was not going to end well for Captain Jenkins.

Jim decided to intervene, fearing for Jenkins' safety and assigns Constables Martin Richardson and Dottie Green to keep an eye on things and step in if it becomes physical as they perform their main task of crowd control.

On the docks, a huge crowd of casual onlookers, friends, relatives, employees and taxis are gathered waiting for their people to disembark. There are food sellers and music and even dancing. Unfortunately, they'll be waiting a little longer today as police complete their investigations into the mystery of the missing passenger.

Back in the saloon, Constables Martin Richardson and Dottie Green try to make sense of the scene playing out before them with the benefit of snatches of audible dialogue. Predictably, in their experience, the problem involves money; money that has been rightly or wrongly obtained by Jenkins.

It seemed that Harry the Hatchet is taking control of a terrified Captain Jenkins. Whatever he whispered in his ear had certainly grabbed his attention as he nodded, whining and whimpering and begging for a chance to make things right. The group, however, don't appear to be satisfied with just the return of their money. They have been humiliated and they want blood and Harry is the man to deliver it.

The constables meanwhile remain at a distance alert for any indication of violence without which they have no cause for intervention. There is a definite air of impending bloodshed, making it imperative for Constables Richardson and Green to remain vigilant.

Not that far distant, the committee ladies Rhoda Day, Elvira

Rochester and Madame Rosetta Gloria Parmentier, by contrast, are still sitting around the ice-bucket draining yet another bottle of champagne. Their concerned drink's waiter is astounded at the capacity of the three ladies before him and experience tells him they will surely feel their excessive intake when the time comes to stand.

The pleasantly inebriated trio had been made aware that there might be some unavoidable and irritating delays in disembarking. Their suggestion was to persuade the band to continue playing. Perhaps offer a prize for the dance pair that present the best version of the Charleston.

Currently residing at the opposite end of the emotional spectrum to the unfortunate Captain Jenkins, the trio couldn't be happier sitting in the luxurious surrounds of the restaurant swilling fine champagne and congratulating themselves on a job well done. Giggling at the smallest bon mot and an ever so slight sway as they sat on their comfortable chairs.

Elvira in making some animated comment knocked her champagne flute over as she reached for it.

'Oh dear these glasses don't like the rolling of the ship girls. Steward, steward another glass if you don't mind dearie. And may I have one that won't fall over?'

'Oh Elvira what a shame to waste such lovely bubbly.' And to the steward, 'while you're at dear boy please bring another bubbly bottle er bottle of bubbly.'

The band members were not too happy to be called into action again but with no chance of disembarking and a promise of an open bar tab from the committee they pitched in anyway, ensuring that as Hygeia came into Port Melbourne she did so with a cheerful musical score and loud cheers for the dance competitors.

The meeting in the saloon was reaching a heated conclusion, totally confusing the terrified Captain Jenkins, who now wished he really was in Flanders Fields in World War One. He knew he was to be unmasked as a fraud and a lot of anger would be unleashed upon him. He always knew when he embarked on his perilous trade that this day could possibly come. The pity was he had decided the time had come to clear out his stashes and hit the road to his dream retirement to the villa he now owned on the Cote d'Azure at Saint Tropez, readied for him to live a life of comfort and security.

But he had become complacent and overconfident, always a fatal risk for the dancer who took to the stage only needing to 'put just one foot wrong and it's all undone.' The playboy hero that strutted the social stage known to all as Captain Jenkins was retreating back into the cringing shell that was Reggie Watford from the slums of Whitechapel, England.

Reggie Watford, just plain Reggie, felt a cold hand clamp around his vitals. The walls were closing in and he can see no way out. He watched carefully as the ship drew near to the dock, hoping he might have an opportunity to run and get away from this threat. He knew these men. He had socialised with them; he knew they weren't gangsters or killers. That is with the glaring exception of the frightening Harry the Hatchet.

He couldn't help wondering how on earth he earned that intimidating identity? At that very moment, imagining the very worst fate, the door of opportunity swings wide open.

The Hatchet excused himself and headed for the restrooms to relieve his overburdened bladder.

Meanwhile Darcy Dankworth, the trucking magnate, decided he could use a drink.

'I need a beer Goddo, do you reckon you and Laurence can sit on this bastard until I get back? Happy to get drinks in, if you'd like?'

Reggie judged from his limited view of the world outside the saloon bar that the vessel was closing on the dock, giving him his opportunity. If he could get free from his oppressors, he might be able to make a dash for the dock as the ship came alongside. He would need to take a terrible risk and leap across the space between ship and shore. If he made it in one piece to the wharf, he was sure he could lose this bunch of drunks in the crowd. Then it would be a matter of grabbing a cab.

There was still a bit of the Whitechapel street fighter in Reggie and when cornered, even the most craven coward can find some inner determination to survive. Godfrey Beckman had earned his living as a builder and developer, although now in mid-life he was still as tough as the thousands of nails he had driven home as he built his empire and would find Reggie a soft opponent. Whereas the third man, Laurence Brown, was an heir to a large retailing chain. He had never lifted anything heavier than the pen he used to sign off his own pay rises.

He would be Reggie's exit path. Taking a deep breath, Reggie swung his right elbow high and hard into Godfrey's nose, shattering the bone immediately putting him out of commission.

'Get outta me way ya little tosser.' The effeminate man who is definitely not there to supply muscle cringes back as Reggie regressed back to his hard-teenage years in the back alleys of East London, clambered over him and out of the booth. He looked rapidly about and saw the ship was now closing up to the dock. He would need to make his move now or never. The passengers waiting to disembark were pressed up to where they guessed the gangway would be. This worked for and against Reggie. The denser crowd provided cover in which he would be lost to eyesight and protection against gunfire. For Reggie, the next few moments would mean life or death.

He ducked down in hopes of concealing himself behind the crowds milling about, enjoying the last few minutes of the cruise. He threw all caution and courtesy to the wind, crashing through the cheerful passengers waiting patiently to disembark, desperately fighting his way to where he hoped the boarding ramp would be waiting.

Throwing a glance over his shoulder he was horrified to see the huge frame of Harry the Hatchet hot on his tracks. Coming after him were two of the cops that had been aboard since the tour started earlier in the day. In a flat panic, Reggie's eyes were blurred with sweat and tears, he was like a wild animal, a zebra with the lion's breath on its flanks. Nothing counted but to escape. The crowds shouted as he and his pursuers crashed their way through them. A gap opens, through which he glimpsed a clear stretch along the rail. Without hesitation he charges at it. He recalled that there was a large flat area ahead of the paddle wheel called a sponson. If he could make it there, the drop to the dock was only a few feet, surely he could jump clear and leave these clumsy oafs behind.

Still running flat out, he leapt onto the rail and launched himself toward the sponson. Too late and under the irresistible influence of his forward momentum, he saw he had made a deadly mistake.

Manning his duty position on the sponson is Sparra Dempsey. Jenkins' feet hit the sponson and slides on the damp surface colliding with Dempsey and rebounding into the sea with a loud shriek of terror.

The ship was still manoeuvring, not yet snug alongside and he has fallen perilously close to the churning starboard paddlewheel just as Captain Galbraith has ordered 'half ahead.' In the blink of an eye, the dapper Captain Richard Fairlie Jenkins Officer of His Majesty's 4th Indian Cavalry Division DSM Veteran of France and Flanders is dragged under the threshing paddlewheel to the horror of the crowd lining the dock. Most of them are there as sightseers or to meet friends on board the Hygeia with many more to witness the colourful ship coming alongside. Instead, they witnessed the ghastly demise of Reggie Watford.

❧ Chapter 55

The Big Wheel Keeps on Turning

Among the horrified spectators still onboard was Quentin Upjohn, almost fainting with the shock of such a ghastly accident at the end of a magnificent excursion that was all colour, light, and laughter. *What on earth could have prompted that poor man to leap into the sea like that? It was just too awful.* Then his scandal writing brain clicked in. What a 'full stop' to his story of love, lust and death on the high seas. Quentin was becoming a little florid in his thinking and would need a disciplined editor to pull him back into line, but he was energised and eager. He was hanging about where he thought the gangway would be swung down, clutching his precious notes and his battered Underwood portable typewriter. He was already name checked against the passenger list and prepared to dash down the ramp and grab a taxi into the dingy office he occupied at The Truth headquarters in La Trobe Street to begin writing his revealing story.

He had decided this final shocking incident would provide the title to his story, 'Death on the Ferry Hygeia.' There's a well-worn saying, 'don't count your chickens until they hatch.' Young Quentin might have been advised to remember that cliché for on the dock was a seasoned crime reporter Lex Mortimer. Mortimer came from a police family which gave him the jump on his competing reporters. Word had come to him through his sources (never to be revealed) that a major crime would occur on the Hygeia during this trip. Unfortunately, the tip-off had come too late for him to get on board for first-hand observation, but a copy of the passenger list when he got his hands on it (from another source) had made fascinating reading. He could almost predict what would happen.

Lex made his way through the large boisterous crowd, eyes habitually scanning faces. He reached the side of the dock just in time to see the form of Captain Jenkins take its plunge. He shared in the horror of watching the struggling man come to the surface and realise he was being drawn under the crushing starboard paddle wheel. His terrified screams were silenced by the massive paddle wheel but would forever echo in the nightmares of Lex Mortimore during the small hours of restless nights to come.

Looking up to where the victim came from, he was brought up short when he spotted the notorious Harry the Hatchet leaning over the rail looking down at the doomed man in the water. Harry's face is contorted as he mouthed profanity. Lex can't be sure it's because of the tragedy he had just witnessed or having exerted himself sprinting after the man. Lex was sure Harry the Hatchet would provide sufficient motive for anyone to prefer the perils of the darkening water to a one on one with Harry and his hatchet.

He sucked in air, as though he had just completed a hard run, shook his head turned and pushed back through the crowd.

So just what is going on here? Lex was determined to find out what level of horror would frighten a man enough that he would choose such a perilous escape route. Looking at the retreating back of Harry the Hatchet, he believed he may have answered his own question.

The crew had been alerted to the man's ordeal and brought the paddlewheel to a stop as several brave souls leapt into the water in a vain attempt to save him. The attempted rescue was gallant but far too late to save him from his horrible fate. The courageous swimmers instead turned their hands to recovering the shattered body as it bobbed up in the still swirling waters momentarily before threatening to sink out of sight. There were several flashes of news cameras trying to capture the drama and the general hubbub, with women fainting and men screaming unintelligible directions to each other. Lots of pointing and running back and forth, more shouting as ropes were brought into play to assist those in the water. After a long interval, the body was recovered and raised up onto the dock. Hygeia completes its docking procedure and the ramp is finally let down onto the dock.

Before the dreadful incident, the crew had begun checking off the passenger list as people presented themselves to disembark. Under the supervision of Third Mate Bully Masterson, Constables Dottie

Green, and Bluey Farnsworth a slow trickle of passengers shocked by what they have just witnessed make their way ashore, the women among the passengers are crying and comforting each other, men are shaking their heads in disbelief.

Lex Mortimore had a man on board, one of his team of investigators who fed him information and tips. Lex spotted him and waved frantically, receiving acknowledgement. Within fifteen minutes Lex got what he came for and with his informant he dashes for his waiting driver and is heading back to his paper the afternoon *Melbourne Herald*. The drive was slow on the poor roads, giving Lex the opportunity to dictate his story to his secretary who sits alongside of him with the informant on the other side. By the time they reach their office in Flinders street with the rough draft completed and a dramatic headline composed. 'Death on the Ferry Hygeia' stealing Quentin Upjohn's headline!

In the background, a learned little group had gathered to give commentary to the departure of the elite passengers as they disembark but this time getting more than they bargained for.

CHAPTER 56

JOSTLING JOURNO'S AND AN MP'S DILEMMA

'Bloody hell! That poor geezer fell in front of the paddle wheel.' Brown Sugar cries.

'Oh my Good Gawd, that's a bloke plum outta luck!' decrees the Judge. 'Should we help?'

'Nah! Against Union rules, we'd be in all sorts if we did,' responded Singlet.

'Not as much as that poor bastards in I'd reckon.' The rest of the observers silently nod in solemn agreement.

The Station Pier jury deliver their verdict. Accidental and deliberate violence is not an unknown on the docks. Many is the score that has been settled by a timely nudge at an open cargo hatch.

Lex's Mortimore's report for the Herald is pretty accurate considering that the police onboard and at the scene are still puzzling over certain details. But the main plot out of the several possibilities had got past him. He was still unaware of the police report from Queenscliff that revealed the identity of the man pulled from the sea and his probable cause of death. Quentin Upjohn will table those trump cards in his featured report winning all the plaudits in the hare and tortoise race between he, and Lex Mortimore.

Big Joe McArthur was a hugely worried man as he departed the ship, totally ignoring the drama behind him that has shocked the passengers loitering aboard and sightseers on the dock. When the news breaks, it will cause horror and outrage across the city.

Joe heads off, determined to find some peace and solace before the coming storm. He realises there will be a huge uproar in the House when the Opposition get wind of the disappearance of Karl Brunner and start asking questions about his obviously close relationship with the Honourable Member for Melbourne North. At this point, Big Joe was unaware of the police report confirming the identity of the male body hauled from the sea and the cause of death.

He knew he would be called to give an account to the Swiss Consul and explain how their citizen ostensibly on a peaceful business mission came to disappear while in the company of a senior Minister of State in the ruling party. He prayed fervently that Brunner may yet be found alive somewhere with a perfect explanation, wiping away any call for intense interrogation. He recalls an event at his son's school when a boy went missing on an excursion. Police, teachers and parents joined in a frantic search for the lad, fearing some horrible fate had befallen the lad causing him to miss the return bus. He was discovered sound asleep in a toilet cubicle having been trapped by a faulty lock.

After the Ambassador has had his confrontation with Big Joe, he will need to provide the same explanation to his Premier. And then there's the press. Tough and ruthless as a flock of vultures ready to rip the flesh from his bones. It is patently obvious even at this early stage that Big Joe McArthur's political career was well and truly cooked. And that would be okay if he were able to simply walk away, but the media wouldn't allow that to happen.

There would be an Inquiry or, Heaven forbid, a Royal Commission. In any event, he would have to face no end of press interviews and what might be the most chilling prospect by any measure would be a Police investigation. Right at that moment, they were busy gathering evidence and taking witness statements. The end result would almost certainly be criminal charges for the inappropriate use of his parliamentary powers, leading to the very real possibility of a lengthy prison sentence.

Looking back on his life from this point in time, Joseph McArthur could recall as a young idealistic man winning his first election being suffused with a desire to improve the life of his fellow citizens. Lift the people out of poverty by providing education, subsidised housing and medical aid. He was soon put straight by older grizzled members who dealt him costly lessons in the art of compromise. Before too long, he couldn't tell where he started or what his final destination was to be. He became befuddled through the haze of deal making and broken promises. At first compromising only that which he could with a clear conscience use to sway the opinion of others. One election followed another, and the bright young MP soon became a hardened horse trader in the arena of state politics. Confidently striding across a minefield of deals, betrayals, handshake and unshakeable agreements and duplicities, never once doubting his judgement.

CHAPTER 57
EARLY AUTUMN 1926
THE NET CLOSES

Joseph McArthur, in a state of deep depression, took his stately Daimler from the garage without speaking to his wife or his chauffeur, Bull Finlay, all of whom were preparing to sit down to their midday meal in different parts of the large home. He headed down the highway to the Warrnambool district and his family homestead. Now things had changed dramatically, leaving him only one or two paths to follow. Resign and take up cattle breeding again or put himself into exile somewhere overseas out of the spotlight. He could not bring himself to face his party leader Sir Alexander Peacock or his dear trusting wife Irene Rose or his father, who had done so much to advance his career.

The State Labour Party would offer a third alternative that would have him well and truly out of the spotlight. The conniving bastard had a cell waiting for him in HM Prison Pentridge and come Hell or highwater they would put him there. Though they would yet be disappointed.

Lex Mortimore's story had driven his management and readers into a frenzy for more, and while Lex sat back, smoking the cigar of triumph, the story moved ahead.

While Mortimore was creating headlines, Francis Foley and the rest of the police aboard Hygeia were trying to piece together all the events, both tragic and puzzling that occurred in such a short time aboard the cruise boat. They had created a timeline against which they plotted the individual events.

Hygeia had been tied up on the jetty, finally bare of passengers as the exhaustive roll-call had ground to an end. Then with no paying passengers left aboard, the police conducted a search for clues or evidence from stem to stern and back again examining every space and locker right down to the bilges and into the forepeak, even looking behind the heaped chain and massive anchors.

When the search was complete, they sat down to compare notes and share ideas.

The most intriguing and highest priority was the disappearance of two distinguished passengers, Monsieur Karl Brunner, and the Italian Alessandro Accardi Barone.

It was now apparent that no struggle had ensued between the Swiss and the Italian at the after-end of the upper promenade deck, shortly after Joseph McArthur had left their company. Rather, the Italian was the assassin who was rumoured to be aboard somehow confused as an IRA killer. The fatal wound was delivered with surgical precision and the victim's body conveniently tumbled over the side. The Swiss lost his pipe as he fell into the sea, which miraculously dropped through the window onto the lower deck where it was found by Bluey Farnsworth. The body of the unfortunate Swiss had tumbled over the upper rail following a similar path to his pipe but ending in the sea where the outgoing tide presented it to the alert fisherman returning from the fishing grounds outside of the heads. Had he not intercepted it, the body would have headed out into Bass Strait, where no doubt sharks and other sea creatures would have fed on it and it would never be seen again.

The politically aware and wise Francis Foley proffers a paradox for his team to consider.

'Let me ask you a question. Why? *Why*,' he emphasised, 'would an Italian assassin come all the way to Australia to kill a Swiss merchant banker?'

Nobody had the answer, so he offered an explanation he deemed worthy of consideration. 'Always remember the lust for money is the root of all evil. Follow the money, always.' This was a good point and one that he has always preached in his police work.

'Recently we had a large expensive parcel of industrial land on the city's fringe pass into foreign hands. A Swiss bank, in fact. Our recently deceased gentleman was part of a very clever land grab that involved the Honourable Joseph McArthur who had double crossed a group he put together just to create a sense of urgency to draw the Swiss bankers in. The trouble for Big Joe was the group he initially put together were not too pleased at having lost a small fortune each. Now to rub salt into their wounds they discover they have been used as motivation for the Swiss bank giving McArthur a bigger share of the deal.'

'So, they hired the Italian. Who, by a happy circumstance was in Melbourne to provide his services to kill Big Joe, and the bastard got the wrong man?' said Bluey.

'No! He got the right man.' pronounces Francis Foley, nodding solemnly.

One hundred and ninety-five kilometres to the west, Stamford Downs sprawls across the volcanic plains away from the shores of Lake Corangamite towards the setting sun. Long shadows of trees and structures stretch across the flat landscape, painting a surreal image. Big Joe's shadow follows him across the stockyard to the large barn. The big man swings the barn door wide on its creaking hinges and steps inside. To his right, a work station sits amongst farm machinery framed by a shadow board heavy with tools. To his left, the space is taken up by hay bales and assorted stock feeds in sacks. His nostrils fill with the familiar and comforting smell of the hay and his eyesight is blurred by a million dust motes that dance on the sunbeams that leak through the old warped planks on the western wall.

Big Joe takes a seat on a hay bale and makes himself comfortable while behind him he can hear the skittering of the resident field mice among the hay alarmed by this intrusion. His mind is still heavy with an overwhelming sense of guilt and shame. He had decided to spend some time with his local priest and seek solace, but in the end, he knew no prayers or time in the confessional would ease his tortured soul. People who had been trusting friends had put their faith in him and he had betrayed them. One or two may not survive the financial loss that his deception had cost them. And then there was Monsieur Karl Brunner, Swiss bank director. Without doubt, one of the finest men Big Joe had ever met.

A consummate intellectual gentleman, cultured and charming. He had lost his life due entirely to Joe's greed. Joe recalled the lunch he had with the Swiss, who proudly produced a photograph of a beautiful young woman that was his wife and two smiling little boys who would now grow up without a father.

The sun had now reached the horizon and descended rapidly as night reclaimed the sky, scattering a million stars across its domain. A large flock of noisy corellas that had settled in the gnarly old gum tree at the rear of the barn took flight in raucous alarm at the sudden sharp bark of a shotgun from within the barn. Big Joe was gone.

CHAPTER 58
LATE JANUARY
A CAPTAIN'S RIGID DISCIPLINE

Captain Fergus Galbraith was a rigidly self-disciplined and proud man who believed the command of his ship depended on his ability gained over decades to protect passengers and crew while ensuring his vessel was always in first class mechanical condition ready to sail at a moment's notice. He brooked no nonsense from crew or passengers alike. Anybody upsetting the status quo of his vessel would be dealt with sternly, and only a mutinous fool would step out of line a second time. He was a devout Christian and read his bible each night.

He was sitting in his tiny cabin, trying to come to terms with the events that had unfolded on his vessel on one fateful day. A passenger missing, possibly overboard and drowned, the dreadful inexplicable death of a man who was apparently so terrified by something or someone on board that he took that impossible leap and paid with his life. A policeman on duty, severely beaten and found unconscious in the scuppers. Each one terrible in its own right, but to have this catalogue of crime occurring on the one day and on his vessel was shocking beyond belief.

This event had started out as a grand plan to provide an unforgettable excursion for the elite of the city, raising badly needed funds for the children's hospital. A marvellous theatrical performance had been successfully staged on board to a standing ovation. The luncheon was a triumph of the Chef's culinary art and he too received a standing ovation by the appreciative patrons on behalf of their sophisticated palates. And the one thing that not even Captain Galbraith had control over, the weather had remained sublime for the whole cruise. With all those wonderful elements working for them, his ship had now become a crime scene. Outside on every deck, police were crawling over the ship in what seemed to be an endless pursuit of the infinite.

It had been explained to the captain that in fact two investigations are being conducted simultaneously.

One had sought the whereabouts of the missing passenger who had now been discovered in the sea off Queenscliff and on how the deceased came to fall from the ship was yet to be officially resolved. The report from the Queenscliff Police revealed that a limited initial examination of the body had revealed what could possibly be a knife wound under the left arm. They would have to wait for the official post mortem by the state coroner for confirmation. The second concerned the tragic death of the passenger known as Captain Jenkins, a permanent resident of the Windsor Hotel and reputedly a decorated hero of the war in France. This was no accident. The death of the individual was caused solely by the passenger's own lack of self-possession. Witnesses had so far been in total agreement that the man appeared to be driven by fear, but fear of what. What horror could cause a man reputed to be a war hero, a man believed to stand fast in the face of almost certain death; to flee panic-stricken and by such a parlous route. Unthinkable!.

Meanwhile, Hygeia sat idle at her mooring on Station Pier, her crew sent ashore, her massive, powerful steam engines sitting cold and forlorn in the interim. Despite every effort by Hygeia's operators Huddart, Parker, and Co, she had been ordered to remain at her berth while valuable bookings were cancelled and the revenue went elsewhere.

The worst of it was to see her living heart, the massive engines cold and cobwebs in the coal bunker. The ships engineer had been prevented from running the engines despite warning the police that a forced shutdown could be damaging to her power plants.

Captain Galbraith lit his pipe and wandered out onto the bridge deck puffing on his preferred tobacco mix, Players Navy Mixture not surprisingly, and watched the coppers apparently wandering about aimlessly.

'A lot of flat-footed fools leading each other in circles.' Just then, to his horror, he spotted a copper about to attack the door to a ticket booth with a sledgehammer. His stentorian voice booms out across the deck like cannon fire.

'You there! That man. That door has a blasted door handle. Has it occurred to your neanderthal brain to use it?'

Senior Sergeant Jim Foley witnesses the outrage and reddened with embarrassment and anger. It had been a continuous battle to prevent damage and petty theft by some of the constables brought in to assist who, with the run of the ship, had lost any sense of decorum.

CHAPTER 59

THE POST MORTEM BEGINS

'*My theory is this,*' Deputy Commissioner Foley had spent a lot of time working through the information he had at his fingertips and believed he had enough to put it all together, 'The syndicate of some of Melbourne's finest were conspiring with the Honourable Minister, who by virtue of his position of influence within the Government was tipped off to a large strategic parcel of land that was due to be gazetted. McArthur intended to get ahead of that process by purchasing the property from the state at a lower price than he could expect through a public auction.' Deputy Commissioner Francis Foley was enjoying his presentation and so far, had his audience listening in rapt silence.

'Not wishing to risk all of his cash into the venture, McArthur pulled together a syndicate of similar minded business people to join him to spread the risk and share the reward. However, Big Joe was playing a double game. He had met his Swiss partner on a recent European tour and made him aware of the investment possibilities available in his home that he may have described as the last frontier.'

Francis Foley took a sip of water and proceeded to further enlighten his attentive audience.

'Joe was aware that the Swiss are a conservative race by nature and he decided that if he could demonstrate that a powerful local investment group were hot to trot, it might help to provide the right level of incentive to have their interest.'

'Seems okay on the face of it, sir, but surely this is a long way to come to buy a block of land?' Volunteered Constable Irene McCarthy.

'Not just a block of land but a block of land that includes a senior government minister as a partner.' If anyone would know the advantages that could be had by 'owning' a senior public official, it was the Swiss who had been trading favours for centuries. Brenner was smart enough to know that this deal would lead in to many others.

'So if McArthur was the villain why was the Swiss killed and not McArthur?' queries Bluey Farnsworth.

'Well, someone wanted to even up after the betrayal. It could have been any one of the syndicate or a very cunning opportunist.' Francis stopped and scratched his chin. 'But you know what, Big Joe is a high-profile politician and political assassination is virtually unknown in Australia except for the case of a Queensland MP a few years back. It would create an absolute furore now and they couldn't hope to get away with it.'

'Well, I still don't get it sir, why kill the Swiss?' queried Irene McCarthy

'There are many ways to destroy a man without actually killing him.' A couple of heads are nodding, some brows are wrinkled in concentration until the penny finally drops.

'Bloody hell,' Bluey Farnsworth erupted, 'they destroy Big Joe and all he stands for without laying a hand on him. The cunning bastards.'

'The word for that is Machiavellian, a well thought out devious scheme,' said Francis Foley.

Helene Plowright and her sister Anthea are enjoying a delicious breakfast of fresh fruit, poached eggs, bacon and coffee on the large patio of the Plowright home shaded by luxuriant wisterias in full bloom their lavender blue, pink and purple blossoms glowing in the morning sunshine. Helene has been delighted by the attention paid to her by her husband Gordon, who lately has become very romantic.

She has confided in her sister that he has taken her back to her honeymoon days as though courting her again with flowers and restaurant dining. She has never been happier.

It's a lovely summer morning, already quite warm and promising to heat up later. Indeed, Gordon would feel a lot of heat later during this blissful morning.

Helene became aware that the front doorbell was ringing and she hastened through the house to take delivery of serious looking envelope from a courier bearing her name and stamped 'Personal' in red ink on both sides. She takes it back to the patio unopened and sits again before tackling the item.

'What have you there, darling? Is Gordon spoiling you again you lucky girl?'

Smiling with anticipation, she used a bread knife to slit one end open to reveal the contents. The note on top reads simply 'From a friend offended by your husband's behaviour.'

Next is a bundle of what proved to be a set of explicit photographs of her beloved husband in 'flagranti delicto' with a naked and very attractive young woman who appeared to be enjoying Gordon's attention as much as Helene had in recent times. In shock, she rapidly stuffed the offending items back into the envelope.

'Helene, what is it darling? You've gone white.'

Chapter 60
SOME TIME LATER: 1926
Unleash The Hounds

Eugene Bradfield had been celebrated since the wonderful success of his one act play aboard the paddle steamer Hygeia. Sadly, a series of murky events had overshadowed the virtuosity of the presentation, but while that was unfortunate, he had felt sure it had cemented his reputation as a consummate performer who could deliver a performance in any circumstances. Eugene had, in his fairly recent past, created a debt that could never be repaid. It was a debt of honour when his lustful urges had led him to dishonour the wife of a man who was physically robust, with almost unlimited financial clout and an equally powerful network of business, government and social connections. It all came together to mean almost nothing was beyond his influence. Coupled with those assets was Sir Rupert Yarborough's total pledge to 'execute terrible vengeance' upon the man that tarnished the sanctity of his connubial bliss.

Ignoring his first rush of blood that he would punish Eugene Bradfield in the extreme, he had decided on a more humiliating and drawn-out tactic. Sir Rupert had set his CFO to work tracking down anything of Eugene's that looked like an asset or revenue stream and shut them down.

'Pour poison all over his credit rating, begin whispers in the banking halls of town of gambling losses and failed investments. Sow the seeds of rejection and distrust and then we can step back and watch the painful disintegration of the pompous little thespian.'

Sir Rupert's hatred was pouring forth almost uncontrollably, mystifying his financial team who would never know why, but loyalty was their watchword and they stepped up their efforts.

'Thespian? For God's sake, he's a monkey trained to amuse a bored population encouraged to throw peanuts as reward for his antics on the stage.'

Sir Rupert's team worked efficiently and tirelessly tracking anything like income and either diverted them or shut them down. Eugene had long since burnt his connections to his home and family. Things were looking decidedly grim for the fabulous thespian.

Rhoda Day Leading Melbourne Theatrical agent, Madame Rosetta Gloria Parmentier, Age Newspaper's Senior Theatre Critic and Elvira Rochester Movie Casting Director and Accredited Talent Agent were the core of Melbourne's entertainment industry. At least in their own estimation. The success or failure of any entertainment or actor was held firmly in the hands of these three woman.

It was well into the first week of 1926 and after a stupendous celebration seeing the New Year in and allowing for the blistering heat of mid-summer, things had settled down to some form of normality. They were taking tea at their favourite venue, The Windsor of course, faultlessly attended by Adit and Damodar. They had moved past Ceylon's finest product now and were currently lowering the level of their second bottle of Great Western Champagne, the very same sparkling beverage that Dame Nellie Melba was reputed to have bathed in.

They were curious that there had been no sign of their favourite stage performer, Eugene Bradfield, since the events of the nineteenth of December aboard the Hygeia. He had strangely kept out of sight since then, which was quite odd. His play aboard the ship had been a triumph such that he could be expected, as he normally would after such success to have been the light of any number of New Year's Eve soirées around town.

'Excuse me waiter,' Damodar, who was trying to be unobtrusive as possible, was removing some soiled crockery from the ladies table without intruding flinched as if suffering a mild electrical shock at being addressed.

'Yes madame,' bowing from the waist, 'how may I help the lady?'

'Tell me waiter, has Mr Bradfield gone away? Only, we haven't seen him in some time.'

Damodar was not being entirely truthful, being simply too embarrassed to relate the awful incident he had witnessed in the dining room several days previously.

Eugene had presented himself at table, and after studying the menu in his usual fastidious manner called Adit over to place his lunch order.

'Adit dear chap, may I have my usual aperitif please and then today I think, the trout?' Eugene smiling cheerfully in anticipation of the delicious poached trout.

There would be no satisfying pre-lunch thirst quencher today, instead the restaurant manager accompanied by the hotel's accountant carrying what looked like an accounts book arrived at Eugene's table looking decidedly grim. Eugene was asked to follow them into the tiny office of the maître d' where the manager turned to him with the expression of a man enduring intense heartburn to him with the expression of a man enduring intense heartburn.

'Despite our repeated pleas, sir, you have chosen to ignore your commitments. At this point, your indebtedness to this establishment is totally unreasonable and repayment from you extremely unlikely...'

Eugene cuts him off with yet another plea. 'Oh, ah look here I established a large amount of credit here with management after the performance I produced in your restaurant last year. Are you telling me that I have no standing now?'

'Please Mr Bradfield you have entertained a great many of your guests here since then and I'm afraid you have run that credit down some time ago. Your bank sir has informed us that you are bankrupt. You have nothing in your accounts, your cheques have all been dishonoured.'

The manager hands Eugene a formal letter informing him in writing of his current situation.

The letter reads that he will no longer be granted credit in this house until all and any outstanding bills are paid in full, including the last two month's outstanding rent of his apartment. Furthermore, unless he can provide immediate proof that he has the where-withal to meet these considerable commitments, he will be required to vacate said apartment with immediate effect.

(Eugene faints centre stage, curtain down.)

CHAPTER 61

JANUARY 1926

LOVE, LUST AND TYPEWRITERS.

Quentin Upjohn had been bashing the life out of his travel weary old Underwood portable typewriter night and day since coming ashore from the eventful cruise, trying desperately to make the deadline for his first instalment of 'Death Stalks the Hygeia.' Sub-titled 'Life and Death with Champagne and Canapés'.' That had become the revised title of his proposed three-part expose on the cruise. His original title having already been used by Lex Mortimer, Herald newspaper crime reporter who lodged the story on the ghastly death of Captain Richard Jenkins.

He hadn't had to try too hard in pitching the story to his editor, who had been pacing up and down waiting for his gossip columnist to arrive. If written in the usual salacious style of *The Truth* it was guaranteed to create a storm of interest and push circulation figures through the roof. Advertising within the paper around the story would be at a premium. The editor, Ezra Norton, was a very experienced newspaperman who knew a hot story when he saw one and this was one of the hottest he had seen in some time.

Celebrities, socialites, gangsters, gamblers, politicians, actors and leading business people. This was a mixture you wouldn't dare invent. Toss in a violent death and the murder of a Swiss banker and you have everything.

The timing for the release of the story was financially critical, coming right on Christmas. The cruise had taken place on Saturday 19th December. Ezra Norton wanted the first instalment in the final issue of the year hitting the streets Wednesday 23rd a mere three days to write the first tranche of his three-page expose. The second instalment would need to be on the street Wednesday 30th just before New Year's Eve. The third instalment would then boost circulation numbers from Wednesday 6th of January. Holiday reading at its finest. Ezra Norton was absolutely possessed with the story and the timeline to cap out his circulation figures for 1925 and give 1926 an accelerated start. He was already on the phone, selling it to his major advertisers. Quentin had better come good with the piece.

Quite a challenge for a gossip columnist. Young Quentin was nobody's fool, however, he knew if he brought this story in he was a possibility for a journalism award, and a move to the main news desk with the prestige and the pay rise that would come with it. But his long game was to win an appointment on one of the major daily's to become in his words, 'a real journo.' There was little or no loyalty in the newspaper industry adequately demonstrated to Quentin on more than one occasion, so he would lose no sleep over ditching *The Truth*. His only regret being that his story wouldn't reach the widest readership of the majors as he was tied to the scandal rag. He hoped Ezra Norton might syndicate the story to the Sydney edition of *The Truth* where they were always looking for a bit of dirt on Melbourne. He was smart enough to ensure by negotiation through his lawyer (he felt he needed one now) that he retained copyright on the story that would result in the book.

Guided by the four pages of notes he had recorded aboard PS Hygeia as things delightful, baffling and unbelievable were unfolding before his eyes, he was nearing the end of instalment one. He was very grateful for his temporary and rare burst of professional common sense, for if he hadn't kept the notes as he had, then he may have suffered champagne induced amnesia.

All the juicy quotes and conversations, the beautiful socialites in their finest, the fantasy of Eugene Bradfield's stage play against the grim reality of the police work. The truly tragic loss of Captain Jenkins and the mystery of the missing passengers. All could have been well and truly washed away without any coherent recollection of the events and conversations he was privy to. Who said what to whom, who was in and who was out and who was doing what to whom and who knew about it?

That was what he was striving to produce, that rich colourful social tapestry woven from the intricate relationships of blood and wealth seasoned by envy, lust, and greed.

Melbourne society, rather than be shamed by this revealing

narrative, revelled in it. A copy of *Truth* was secreted out of sight amongst the regular shopping by prim and proper women who would never admit to reading it. Spirited home to be savoured with cup of tea or snifter of brandy within the sanctity of the home. Every word of Quentin's chronicle was scanned thoroughly from one end of Melbourne to the other, bringing faux cries of disgust and genuine loud guffaws over a neighbour's exposure. There was also great disappointment in more than one or two high society households not to have gained a mention at all.

Quentin's work was read and deciphered in every coffeehouse, pub, hair salon, club and gathering place the length and breadth of the Metropolis and was quite literally the talk of the town for most of the summer that year. That was, until a massive thunderstorm struck the city midway through February, causing serious structural damage, flash flooding and loss of life. Elizabeth Street in the CBD had been built over the route of an ancient creek bed and swiftly reverted to its original form washing away cars, flooding shops and cafés. Several pedestrians were forced to cling to tramway structures to prevent being swept away and potentially drowned. Now the public focus swung away from the Hygeia onto more practical and mundane matters, such as drainage and roads.

Quentin was soon back at his typewriter churning out the sort of vomitus that was the grist of *The Truth*, soon sinking out of sight to be found dead in a gay bathhouse in two years almost to the day of his last award winning instalments release.

CHAPTER 62

1926

A Little Tidying Up

South of the great city, the Hygeia was an hour or so into yet another excursion on the bay's bright, shining waters. The oppressive heat was left behind on the dock as the passengers delighted in the sights and sounds aboard the wonderful vessel.

Captain Galbraith had pondered an approaching storm front and considered his options. He could continue on his current course and ride it out or heave-to bows to weather and let the wind and rain flow over his decks while the passengers sheltered inside the commodious bars, cafés and restaurants. Having been battered several times in his career by these southerly busters, he elected to adopt the latter strategy and swiftly issued orders to have his ship battened down in good order to meet the brute massing to the south-west.

He wasn't nervous about potential damage to his charge or the delay to the voyage. He was a supreme professional and totally confidant of his and his crew's abilities to handle another bump in the road.

He puffed contentedly on his pipe, enjoying the rich aroma of his old favourite tobacco, Players Navy Mixture and not for the first time prayed that there might be sufficient rain across his decks to wash away all memory and the stain from the ships timbers of the Christmas cruise and that would live with him as sure as any shipwreck or mutiny might curse a ship's captain to sleepless nights.

Senior sergeant Jim Foley, once considered to be a derisible target for those knockers within the force envious of his family's prosperity and his connection to the senior ranks that generated accusations of nepotism, was now seen as he should always have been seen. A very capable and brave young copper who led by example and got the job done. Both he and his uncle had received commendations in their files for their actions aboard the Hygeia.

He stood on the steps of the magistrate's court with the afternoon sun warming his handsome features.

The court had just concluded the sentencing of Detective Sergeant Clarence (Buster) Yarrow, once proud leader of the feared Robbery Squad, now dismissed from the force in shame and facing three to five years gaol for the litany of crimes brought against him by the Crown. It should have been a lot worse for him, but any day a copper spends behind bars among the general gaol population was like time spent in hell. With good behaviour Buster could leave prison in 1930, which Jim thought would be a dark day for society.

Jim squared his shoulders and walks away from the court, well satisfied with his part in the incarceration of his nemesis and his two crooked mates, all of whom could no longer use their police authority to harass the population. Senior Sergeant Jim Foley headed back to Police Headquarters in Russell Street where he had a meeting with his uncle. They're planning a non-police matter, a surprise birthday party for Jim's wife, Maureen. She had been an invaluable support to her oft times accident prone husband and without doubt her encouragement had enabled him to focus on his studies while still conducting his day-to-day duties. At the end of the day, she was always there for him as the perfect copper's wife a fact he pointed out to her at every opportunity that and how much he loved her for it.

Jim was a proud and accomplished policeman with a beautiful wife and two lively twins. He had finally earned the respect of his colleagues and his uncle. Looking back over the last two years, they had been enormously eventful. Never dull and always exhausting. His life experience had gone from practically zero to a man possessed of hard-earned wisdom. He was now almost the complete policeman, well on his way to a stellar career.

Jim Foley was pondering his future as he strolled along, the hot summer sun still beating down late in the day still had enough bite to trigger a river of sweat down his spine as he steers a course through the shady sections of the pavement.

Despite a nation-wide search, there had been no sighting of the mysterious Italian who was believed to have been employed to kill the Swiss banker in order to shame and reveal Big Joe McArthur as a thief in retaliation for his duplicity. Francesco de Luca had been interviewed (read: interrogated) answering monosyllabically and failing to provide any information at all.

The city had been rocked by the news of the tragic suicide of one of its leading citizens, the Honourable Joseph McArthur. While it came as a shock to Jim and his uncle, they had no doubt the weight of public scorn and the humiliation of being cast down from his previously exalted position would drive his despondency into the depths of depression leaving death as a resolution to his pain. Jim had begun to wonder if there was any more damage to come from what was supposed to be a carefree picnic cruise. There was no real way of knowing and his uncle had sagely reminded him they had done everything in their power to protect the lives of the passengers and crew. They could do no more than their duty, which they had performed well.

1929 would be Jim and Maureen's tenth wedding anniversary and he planned to make that a wonderful year of celebration. Life was looking pretty good. What could possibly go wrong?

IL FINALE:
SOMETIME IN EARLY JANUARY
A CALABRIAN TRADITION

There was another group that had wasted no time in tying up loose ends after the Christmas voyage aboard Hygeia. An old Calabrian tradition had been conducted in a secluded barn on the farm of Francesco de Luca just north-east of the small farming settlement of Little River midway between Geelong and Melbourne. The summer sun descended in the west in an eruption of glorious blood red and orange colours adding a strange hue to a Satanic scene taking place. An intense wood-fire contained in a large barrel threw eerie shadows over the walls. The fire's hungry flames were devouring the once beautifully tailored attire of Senor Alessandro Accardi Barone

Inside the rough building under dim lights, two men in blood spattered slaughtermen's overalls work diligently with an array of saws and knives processing the Italian assassin's earthly remains which are fed through a mincer and mixed with bran. Frankie's large ravenous pigs will dine well that night.

Francesco de Luca was tidying house.

END

CHARACTERS:

THEATRICAL PEOPLE AND OTHERS

- Rhoda Day Theatrical agent.
- Elvira Rochester Movie casting director.
- Madame Rosetta Gloria Parmentier Age Newspaper's senior theatre critic.
- Eugene (Lawrence) Wallace Bradfield. Actor, gambler, philanderer and cheat.
- Eugene's play to offset his hotel debts. William Shakespeare: The Comedy of Errors.
- One Act play aboard Hygeia: 'This is London.' by an American writer Arthur Goodrich first staged in New York 1922.
- Kristoffel (Chris) Bern Eugene's butler.
- Janos (Johnny) Kovacs gay gossip columnist.
- Quentin Upjohn. Replacement gossip newspaper crime reporter. Rhyming slang; The Current Bun.
- Hugo Marcovitz: Movie producer.
- Melvin (Skinny) Jackson stage hand gopher and part time pimp.
- The Windsor's Hindi waiters: Adit, Damodar and Sanjeev.
- Sir Rupert Yarborough the cuckolded husband. RY Southern Pacific.
- Lucille Yarborough. One of Bradfield's courtesans.
- Albert Graeme. Rupert Yarborough associate.

GAMBLERS

- Gordon Plowright. Leading Melbourne bookmaker.
- Helene Plowright.
- Matthias Vogel. *The German*. Casino owner, pawn broker, pimp and fence for stolen goods.
- Richard Bradfield Horse trainer of 1924 Melbourne Cup winner Windbag.
- Blaine O'Farrell. Irish horse trainer. Third generation trainer. County Kildare Ireland.

FOLEY FAMILY

- Superintendent/ Francis Arthur Darnley Foley (First in the door Foley).
- Isabelle Foley Wife of Francis.
- Frederick James Hartwell Foley. Police Sergeant Prefers to be called Jim.
- Lillian Jim's mother.
- Maureen his wife.
- George and Harry. Jim's infant twins.

POLICE

- Senior Sergeant George Manifold. (Old Leather Lungs) Jim's boss.
- Senior Sergeant Kirby Tonkin.
- Constable Irene Therese McCarthy Jim Foley's colleague.
- Martin *Whisper* Richardson never shouts a drink.
- Dorothy (Dottie) Green Female Police Constable.
- Roger 'Bluey' Farnsworth Fellow Police Academy graduate of Jim Foley.
- Bob Barrows.
- Butch Mills.
- Nobby Clark.

BIG JOE

- Edward J McArthur: Patriarch of the Australian MacArthurs.
- Maurine McArthur Big Joe's mother.
- Joseph Esmond McArthur MP Nationalist for Warrnambool. Big Joe. Edwards grandson.
- Irene McArthur Big Joe's wife.
- Big Joe's Chauffer (Bull) Finlay.

STREET THUGS

- Marlon *The Plover* Richardson teenage felon possibly part aboriginal skinny legs.
- Ferret Richardson.
- Jonathon *Showbag* Rutledge Pickpocket. Full of crap.
- Bert *Tweaky* Thompson.
- Ralph Slater aka The Wolf. Street punk.
- Ronnie the Rat. Stool pigeon and all-around rat.

REGGIE WATFORD AND HIS ALIASES BELOW

- Captain Richard Fairlie Jenkins. Officer of His Majesty's 4th Cavalry Division DSM Veteran of France and Flanders.
- Francis Willoughby Baron Middleton of Walloton in the County of Nottinghamshire.
- Pillai: Fictitious character in Jenkins Indian treasure scam.

CAPT. JENKINS VICTIMS

- Laurence Brown. Business man and poker player.
- Darcy Dankworth Trucking entrepreneur.
- Godfrey Beckmann a very successful property developer.
- Dianna Beckmann.

HYGEIA.

- Captain Fergus Galbraith.
- French Chef Franco de La Vere. Aboard Hygeia for the Christmas cruise.

HYGEIA'S CREW.

- *Daisy* O'Connell.
- *Sparra* Dempsey.
- Third Mate *Bully* Masterson.
- First Mate *Gunner* Patrick.
- *Froggy* Dempsey.
- Engineer *Gabby* McInerny.

PROPERTY SWINDLERS

- Phillip J Croker.
- Arthur Fetchwell Merchant Banker.
- Charlie Spriggs of Spriggs and Sons Property Valuers.
- Francesco (Frankie) De Luca Business man and market gardener.
- Hugo Montrose MH Builders and Developers.
- Stewart Monteith: Public servant Who leaked information to Big Joe McArthur.
- Monsieur Karl Brunner: Swiss bank director.

CROOKS

- Henry (Harry) Mc Ewart the snow seller.
- Harry The Hatchet Sidell. Gordon Plowright's enforcer.
- John Wren. Business man, SP bookmaker and suspect gangster.
- Curly Barker. John Wren's heavy.
- Joseph Squizzy Taylor Gangster and alleged murderer.

- Mrs McKillip Brothel keeper.
- Alessandro Accardi Barone. Italian assassin.

CROOKED COPS

- Detective Sergeant Buster (Clarence) Yarrow former head of the Robbery Squad.
- Senior Constables Weatherby.
- Senior Constable Clarence Thurgood.

BOURKE STREET RATS

- Jonathon *Showbag* Rutledge.
- Squizzy Taylor.
- Soapy Mullins.
- Roger *the Razor* Wood. Sharp as and fence for stolen goods.
- Martin *the Ferret*. The Plovers brother.

WHARFIES

- Brown Sugar.
- Singlet.
- The Judge.
- Hydraulic Jack.

KOONYA HOTEL STAFF

- Tubby Nichols. The Brick.
- Will Sanders.

GLOSSARY OF AUSTRALIAN SLANG:

- **Babe Ruth:** US baseball player. Rhyming slang for popular weekly gossip rag. The Truth.
- **Barney:** A brawl.
- **Biffo:** Fight, brawl.
- **Black Stump:** A mythical place that denotes a large area or a long way away.
- **Bloke(s):** Man. Men. Seldom used in reference to a female.
- **Bluey:** An Australian man with red hair.
- **Bluey:** Humping the, refer swagmen.
- **Bob:** One shilling equivalent to ten cents.
- **Coat Tugger:** someone who offers a punter a tip for a percentage of the winnings.
- **Cobber:** Older form of mate. He's a cobber of mine.
- **Coit:** Fundamental orifice
- **Coppers:** Police, wallopers, rozzers, narks, demons. Troopers early gold field days.
- **Cove:** Young man.
- **Dead bears bum:** Curse. As in 'stick yer head up a dead bears bum'. Australians sometimes call the wombat a 'bear.'
- **Dead cert:** Certainty, sure thing.
- **Decked:** Knocked out.
- **Decko:** Take a look at.
- **Deener:** One shilling.
- **Dob in:** Report a misdeed. Usually anonymously for reward or favours.

- **Drongo:** A fool
- **Drop kick:** A style of kicking a football favoured for its accuracy
- **Fair dinkum:** The truth. 'Is that fair dinkum?' 'He's a fair dinkum hard worker.'
- **Flat-out like the proverbial lizard drinkin':** Denotes a very busy period. A lizard drinks while laying on its belly hence flat out like a....
- **Furlong:** Old horse racing term. Imperial measure for 200 metres.
- **Galah:** A large pink and grey parrot known for its raucous behaviour in large noisy flocks.
- **Gaw lumme:** God love me.
- **I'll go he for tiggy:** Childs game involving a chase where one tags (tigs) the other. Signifies certainty.
- **Jumbuck:** male sheep.
- **Kingpin:** Leader of a push or gang
- **Knees-up:** Party, shin-dig.
- **Kookaburra:** Australian kingfisher with harsh laughter like cry
- **Larrikin:** A street rowdy, hoodlum.
- **London to a brick:** Gambling. Exaggerated odds, illustrates confidence in an outcome
- **Mad as a cut snake:** Two interpretations. 1. Insanely angry. 2. Wildly eccentric.
- **Penny dreadful's:** Cheap crime novels.
- **Porridge:** Prison. Main sustenance offered to prisoners.
- **Pull stumps:** A term taken from cricket. End of play. Quit, knock off.
- **Push:** Gang of young street toughs. More common in Sydney.
- **Quid:** One pound. Twenty shillings to a pound. 240 pence to a pound.
- **Rails bookmaker:** a bookmaker fielding in an area where he may be required to take bets from clients willing to risk losing higher amounts.

- **Rattle the dags:** Hurry up. Sheep. Faeces clings to the wool on a sheep's rear end in dags, when herding the animals hurrying them up has the dags rattling.
- **Red Rattler:** Tait train. Named after Commissioner Sir Thomas Tait. Early electric train
- **Ridgy-didge:** Similar to fair dinkum. Straight up reliable.
- **Run the rabbit:** A delivery system for alcohol utilising youths.
- **Sack of spuds:** A large bag of potatoes. Dropped like… used to illustrate a man falling unconscious.
- **Serang:** Head man, boss. Pronounced *sher*-ang
- **Sheila:** Female. Skirt. Sometimes Charlie Wheeler in rhyming slang.
- **Shout:** as in pay for a round of drinks
- **Silver tails:** Elites

Shawline Publishing Group Pty Ltd
www.shawlinepublishing.com.au